DAVID BALDACCI

Redemption

MACMILLAN

First published 2019 by Grand Central Publishing, USA

First published in the UK 2019 by Macmillan
an imprint of Pan Macmillan
20 New Wharf Road, London N1 9RR
Associated companies throughout the world
www.panmacmillan.com

ISBN 978-1-5098-7440-8

Printed and bound by CPI Group (UK) Ltd, Croydon, CR0 4YY

Visit **www.panmacmillan.com** to read more about all our books
and to buy them. You will also find features, author interviews and
news of any author events, and you can sign up for e-newsletters
so that you're always first to hear about our new releases.

To Lindsey Rose,
who made all the trains run on time
and handled so much with grace and efficiency.
Congrats on the new gig!

Redemption

CHAPTER

I

On a refreshingly brisk, beautifully clear fall evening, Amos Decker was surrounded by dead bodies. Yet he wasn't experiencing the electric blue light sensation that he usually did when confronted by the departed.

There was a perfectly good reason for this: None of these were *recent* deaths.

He was back in his hometown of Burlington, Ohio, an old factory city that had seen better days. He had recently been in another Rust Belt town, Baronville, Pennsylvania, where he had narrowly escaped death. If he had his druthers, he would have avoided such minefields for the foreseeable future, maybe the rest of his life.

Only right now he didn't have a choice.

Decker was in Burlington because today was his daughter Molly's fourteenth birthday. Under normal circumstances, this would have been a happy occasion, a cause for joy. But Molly had been murdered, along with his wife, Cassie, and his brother-in-law, Johnny Sacks. This devastating event had happened shortly before her tenth birthday, when Decker found them all dead in their home.

Gone forever. Taken from life in the most outrageous manner possible by a deranged mind hell-bent on violence. Their killer was no longer among the living, but that was of absolutely no solace to Decker, though he'd been instrumental in ending that life.

That was why his birthday visit was at a cemetery. No cake, and no presents. Just fresh flowers on a grave to replace ones long dead from a previous visit.

He figured he would be here for every one of Molly's birthdays until he joined his family six feet under. That was his long-term plan. He had never contemplated any other.

He shifted his weight on the wood and wrought-iron bench next to the twin graves, for daughter lay next to mother. The bench had been gifted by the Burlington Police Department where Decker had once toiled, first as a beat cop and later as a homicide detective. On it, tarnished by weather, was a brass plaque that read: *In memory of Cassie and Molly Decker.*

There was no one else in the small cemetery other than Decker's partner at the FBI, Alex Jamison. More than a dozen years younger than the mid-fortyish Decker, Jamison stood a respectful distance away, allowing her partner to visit his family in solitude.

Once a journalist, Jamison was now a fully fledged, duly sworn-in FBI special agent, having graduated from the Bureau's Training Academy in Quantico, Virginia. Under a prior arrangement, she had been sent immediately back to the task force where she and Decker were members, along with two other veteran agents, Ross Bogart and Todd Milligan.

Sitting next to the graves, Decker cursed his condition of hyperthymesia. The perfect recall had been initiated by a wicked blindside hit on an NFL playing field that triggered a traumatic brain injury. Decker awoke from a coma with the ability to re-member everything and the inability to forget anything. It seemed like a wonderful attribute, but there was a distinct downside to the condition.

For him, the passage of time would never deaden the details of painful memories. Like the one he was confronted with presently. For the overwhelmingly intense manner in which he recalled their deaths, Cassie and Molly might as well have been laid to rest today instead of four years ago.

He read the names and inscriptions on the tombstones, though he knew by heart what they said. He had come here with many things he wanted to say to his family, but now he inexplicably suffered from a complete failure to articulate any of them.

Well, maybe not so inexplicably. The brain injury that had given him perfect recall had also changed his personality. His social skills had gone from high to quite low. He had trouble voicing his emotions and difficulty dealing with people.

In his mind's eye he conjured first the image of his daughter. It was sharply in focus—the curly hair, the smile, the cheeks that rode so high. Then the image of his wife, Cassie, appeared—the anchor of their family, the one who had kept Decker from succumbing to his condition, forcing him to interact with others, compelling him to come as close as possible to the man he used to be.

He winced in pain because it actually physically hurt to be so close to them, because they were dead and he was not. There were many days, perhaps most, when he simply could not accept that state of affairs.

He glanced in the direction of Jamison, who was leaning against a broad oak about a hundred feet away. She was a good friend, an excellent colleague, but absolutely powerless to help him through what he was facing now.

He turned back to the graves, knelt, and placed the bundles of flowers he had brought on each of the sunken plots.

"Amos Decker?"

Decker looked up to see an older man walking slowly toward him. He had materialized out of the dusk of elongating shadows. As he drew closer, the man almost seemed a ghost himself, so very painfully thin, his features deeply jaundiced.

Jamison had seen the man coming before Decker did, and had started striding toward them. It could simply be someone from the town whom Decker knew. Or it might be something else. Jamison knew that crazy things tended to happen around Amos Decker. Her hand went to the butt of the pistol riding in a holster on her right hip. Just in case.

Decker eyed the man. Aside from his unhealthy appearance, the fellow was shuffling along in a way that Decker had seen before. It wasn't solely due to age or infirmity. It was the walk of someone accustomed to wearing shackles when moving from point A to point B.

He's a former prisoner, speculated Decker.

And there was another thing. As he sometimes did, Decker was seeing a color associated with the man. This was due to his also having synesthesia, which caused him to pair colors with unusual things, like death and numbers.

The color tag for this gent was burgundy. That was a new one for Decker.

What the hell does burgundy mean?

"Who are you?" he asked, rising to his feet and brushing the dirt from his knees.

"Not surprised you don't recognize me. Prison takes it outta you. Guess I have you to thank for that."

So he was incarcerated.

Jamison also heard this and picked up her pace. She actually half drew her pistol, afraid that the old man was there to exact some sort of revenge on Decker. Her partner had put many people behind bars in his career. And this fellow was apparently one of them.

Decker looked the man up and down as he came to a stop about five feet away. Decker was a mountain of a man, standing six-five and tipping the scale at just about three hundred pounds. With Jamison's encouragement and help in getting him to exercise and eat a healthier diet, he had lost over a hundred pounds in the last two years. This was about as "lean" as he was ever going to be.

The old man was about six feet tall, but Decker figured he barely weighed a hundred and forty pounds. His torso was about as wide as one of Decker's thighs. Up close, his skin looked brittle, like aged parchment about to disintegrate.

Hacking up some phlegm, the man turned to the side and spit it into the consecrated ground. "You sure you don't recognize me? Don't you got some kind of weird-ass memory thing?"

Decker said, "Who told you that?"

"Your old partner."

"Mary Lancaster?"

The man nodded. "She was the one who told me you might be here."

"Why would she do that?"

"My name's Meryl Hawkins," said the man, in a way that seemed also to carry an explanation as to why he was here.

Decker's jaw fell slightly.

Hawkins smiled at this reaction, but it didn't reach his eyes. They were pale and still, with perhaps just a bit of life left inside them.

"Now you remember me, right?"

"Why are you out of prison? You got life, no parole."

Jamison reached them and put herself between Decker and Hawkins.

Hawkins nodded at her. "You're his new partner, Alex Jamison. Lancaster told me about you too." He glanced back at Decker. "To answer your question, I'm no longer in prison 'cause I'm terminal with cancer. One of the worst. Pancreatic. Survival rate past five years is for shit, they tell me, and that's with chemo and radiation and all that crap, none of which I can afford." He touched his face. "Jaundice. You get this, it's way too late to kick it. And it's metastasized. Big word, means the cancer's eating me up everywhere. Brain too now. It's the last inning for me. No doubt about it, I'm done. Hell, maybe a week at best."

"Why is that a reason to release you?" asked Jamison.

Hawkins shrugged. "They call it *compassionate release*. Inmate usually has to file for it, but they came to my cell with the paperwork. I filled it out, they got doctors to okay it, and there you go. See, the state didn't want to foot the bill for my treatments. I was in one of those private prisons. They mark the bill up to the state, but it doesn't all get reimbursed. Gets expensive. Hurts their bottom line. They figure I'm harmless now. I went into prison when I was fifty-eight. Now I'm seventy. Look like I'm a hundred, I know. I'm all jacked up with drugs just to walk and talk. After I leave here, I'm going to be throwing up for a few hours and then take enough pills to sleep a bit."

Jamison said, "If you're on prescription painkillers, somebody's helping you."

"Didn't say they were *prescription*, did I? As a matter of fact, they're not. But it's what I need. Not like they're putting me back in prison because I'm buying street drugs. I cost too much." He chuckled. "If I'd known that, I woulda got sick years ago."

"Do you mean they don't provide any help for you on the outside?" asked Jamison incredulously.

"They said a hospice place would take me, but I got no way to get there. And I don't want to go there. I want to be here." Hawkins stared at Decker.

"What do you want from me?" asked Decker.

Hawkins pointed his finger at him. "You put me in prison. But you were wrong. I'm innocent."

"Don't they all say that?" noted Jamison skeptically.

Hawkins shrugged again. "I don't know about anybody else but me." He glanced back at Decker. "Lancaster thinks I'm innocent."

"I don't believe that," said Decker.

"Ask her. It's why she told me where you were." He paused and looked at the dark sky. "You got another chance to get it right. Maybe you can do it while I'm still alive and kicking. If not, that's okay, so long as you get there. It'll be my legacy," he added with a weak grin.

"He's with the FBI now," interjected Jamison. "Burlington and your case are no longer his jurisdiction."

Hawkins looked nonplussed. "Heard you cared about the truth, Decker. Did I hear wrong? Come a long way for nothing if that's so."

When Decker didn't answer, Hawkins pulled out a slip of paper. "I'll be in town the next couple of nights. Here's the address. Maybe I'll see you, maybe I won't. But if you don't come, well, fuck you from the hereafter."

Decker took the paper but still said nothing.

Hawkins glanced at the twin graves. "Lancaster told me about your family. Glad you found out who killed 'em. But I suppose you still felt guilt, though you were innocent. I can damn well relate."

Hawkins turned and walked slowly back between the graves until the darkness swallowed him whole.

Jamison turned to Decker. "Okay, I know nothing about this, but it's still nuts. He's just taunting you, making you feel guilty. And I can't believe the guy would come here and butt in while you're trying to…trying to spend time with your family."

Decker looked down at the slip of paper. It was clear from his features that something akin to doubt had just now crept into his mind.

Jamison watched him, resignation spreading over her features. "You're going to see him, aren't you?"

"Not until I see someone else first."

2

Decker stood alone on the porch. He had asked Jamison to not accompany him here. He preferred to conduct this visit alone, for a number of reasons.

He remembered every inch of the more than four-decades-old split-level ranch. This was not simply due to his perfect recall, but also because this house was nearly an exact copy of the one in which he and his family had once lived.

Mary Lancaster and her husband, Earl, and their daughter, Sandy, had resided here for as long as Lancaster had been on the Burlington police force, which matched Decker's tenure there as well. Earl was a general contractor who worked sporadically owing to the fact that Sandy was a special needs child who would always require a great deal of time and attention. Mary had been the family's primary breadwinner for a long time.

Decker stepped up to the door. He was about to knock when it opened.

Mary stood there dressed in faded jeans, a blood-red sweatshirt, and dark blue sneakers. Her hair had once been a pasty blonde. It was now full of gray and hung limply to her shoulders. A cigarette was perched in one hand, its coil of smoke drifting up her slender thigh. Her face was as lined as a thumbprint. Lancaster was the same age as Decker yet looked about ten years older.

"Thought I might see you tonight," she said in a smoker's gravelly voice. "Come on in."

He checked for the tremor that used to be in her left hand, her gun grip hand. He didn't see it.

Okay, that's a good thing.

She turned, and he followed the far shorter woman into the house, shutting the door behind him, a tugboat guiding a cargo ship safely into port. Or maybe onto the rocks, he didn't know which. Yet.

Decker also noted that Lancaster, always thin to begin with, was even more gaunt. Her bones seemed to jut out at odd angles within her loose clothing, as though she had left multiple hangers in them.

"Did the gum stop working?" he asked, glancing at her lit cigarette.

They sat in the living room, a small space littered with toys, stacks of newspapers, open cardboard boxes, and a layer of chaos that was palpable. Her home had always been like this, he knew. They'd started using a maid service before Decker left town, but that had come with its own set of problems. They'd probably decided terminally junky was preferable.

She took a drag on her Camel and let the smoke trail out her nostrils.

"I allow myself one a day, about this time, and only when Earl and Sandy are out. Then I Febreze the hell out of the place."

Decker took a whiff and coughed. "Then use more Febreze."

"Meryl Hawkins found you, I take it?"

Decker nodded. "He said you told him where I was."

"I did."

"That was taking a liberty. You knew why I was in town. I gave you a heads-up."

She sat back and scraped away at a spot on her skin with her fingernail. "Well, I sure as hell didn't do it lightly. But I thought you'd want to know."

"Hawkins also said you believed him."

"Then he went too far. I told him I could see his point."

"Which is what, exactly?"

"Why would he come back here, dying, to ask us to clear his name if he's not innocent?"

"I can think of one reason, benefiting him."

She took another puff and shook her head. "I don't see it that way. You get to the end of the line, you start to think differently. Not a moment to waste."

Decker looked at the open cardboard boxes. "You guys moving?"

"Maybe."

"Maybe? How can you not be sure?"

Lancaster shrugged. "What about life is guaranteed?"

"How're things in Burlington?"

"Town's hanging in there."

"Unemployment's down around the country."

"Yeah, we have lots of ten-dollar-an-hour jobs. If you can live on twenty grand a year, even in Burlington, more power to you."

"Where are Earl and Sandy?"

"School function. Earl handles those more than me. Work's been a bitch lately. Bad times make for bad crimes. Lots of drug-related stuff."

"Yeah, I've seen that. Why did Hawkins come to see you?"

"We worked that case together, Decker. It was our first homicide investigation."

"When did he get out? And is he really terminal? He definitely looks it."

"He wandered into the station two days ago. Shocked the hell out of me. At first I thought he'd escaped or something. I didn't accept his story but straight away checked with the prison. He's telling the truth about his cancer. And his release."

"So they can just kick out terminally ill prisoners to die on their own?"

"Apparently some see it as a good cost-cutting tactic."

"He told me he's staying in town a couple more days. He's at the Residence Inn."

"Where you used to live."

"He could use some fattening up with the buffet, but I doubt he has much appetite. He says he gets by on street drugs, basically."

"Sad state of affairs."

"He wants to meet with me again."

She took another puff. "I'm sure."

"He came to see me at the *cemetery*."

Lancaster took one more luxurious drag on her smoke and then crushed it out in an ashtray set on a table next to her chair. She eyed the remnants with longing.

"I'm sorry about that. I didn't tell him exactly *why* you were in town when he came back to the station earlier today and asked, though I did tell him about your family. And I didn't actually tell him to go to the cemetery." She studied Decker, her pale eyes finally focusing on his. "I presume you've gone over the case in immaculate detail in your head?"

"I have. And I don't see any issues with what we did. We went over the crime scene, collected evidence. That evidence pointed like a laser to Hawkins. He was arrested and put on trial. We testified. Hawkins's lawyer put on a defense and cross-examined the crap out of us both. And the jury convicted him. He got life without parole when he could have gotten the death penalty. It all made sense to me."

Lancaster sat back in her chair.

Decker ran his gaze over her. "You don't look so good, Mary."

"I haven't looked good for at least ten years, Amos. You above all should know that."

"But still."

"You've lost a lot of weight since you left here, Amos."

"Jamison's doing, mostly. She's got me working out and watching my diet. She cooks a lot of the meals. All salads and vegetables, and *tofu*. And she got her FBI badge and creds. Worked hard for them. Really proud of her."

"So you two are living together, then?" said Lancaster with hiked eyebrows.

"We are in the sense that we're residing in the same condo in D.C."

"Okay, then are you two more than work partners?"

"Mary, I'm a lot older than she is."

"You didn't answer my question. And, news flash, lots of older men date much younger women."

"No, we're *not* more than work partners."

"Okay." She sat forward. "So, Hawkins?"

"Why are you having doubts? It was a clear-cut case."

"Maybe too clear-cut."

"That doesn't make sense. And what's your evidence?"

"I don't have any. And I don't know if he's telling the truth or not. But I just think since the guy's dying and he came back here to clear his name, maybe it's worth a second look."

Decker did not look convinced but said, "Okay, how about now?"

"What?" she said, looking startled.

"Let's go over to where the murders took place. I'm sure no one's moved in there after all this time, not after what happened." He paused. "Just like my old home."

"Well, you're wrong there. Someone *did* move into your old place."

Decker's jaw slackened. "Who?"

"A young couple with a little girl. The Hendersons."

"You know them?"

"Not really. But I know they moved in about six months ago."

"And the other place? Is there someone there too?"

"Somebody moved in there about five years ago. But they left about a year ago when the plastics manufacturing facility closed down and went overseas to join all the other factories that used to be in the Midwest. It's been abandoned since then."

Decker rose. "Okay, you coming? It'll be like old times."

"I'm not sure I need any more 'old times.'" But Lancaster rose too and grabbed a coat that was hanging on a wall peg. "And what if it turns out Hawkins was telling the truth?" she asked as they headed to the door.

"Then we need to find out who really did it. But we're not there yet. In fact, we're not even close."

"You don't work here anymore, Decker. Finding a murderer here after all this time isn't your job."

"Finding killers is my *only* job. Wherever they might be."

CHAPTER

3

THE RICHARDSES' HOME. The scene of the crime thirteen years ago.

It was down a rutted crushed-gravel road. Two houses on the left and two on the right, with the Richardses' now-dilapidated dwelling smack at the end of the cul-de-sac on an acre lot of dead grass crammed with fat, overgrown bushes.

It had been lonely and creepy back then, and it was more so over a decade later.

They pulled to a stop in front of the house and climbed out of Decker's car. Lancaster shivered slightly, and it was not entirely due to the coolness of the night.

"Hasn't changed all that much," said Decker.

"Well, the family that was living here fixed it up some before they left. It needed it. Mostly on the interior. Paint and carpet, things like that. The place had been abandoned for a long time. Nobody wanted to live here after what happened."

"You'd think a banker would have lived in something nicer."

"He was a loan officer. They make squat, especially in a town like this. And this house is a lot bigger than mine, Decker, with a lot more land."

They walked up to the front porch of the home. Decker tried the door.

"Locked."

"Well, why don't you unlock it?" said Lancaster.

"Are you giving me permission to break and enter?"

"Wouldn't be the first time. And it's not like we're screwing up a crime scene."

Decker broke the side glass, reached through, and unlocked the door. He switched on his Maglite and led her inside.

"Do you remember?" said Lancaster. "That's a rhetorical question, of course."

Decker didn't appear to be listening. In his mind's eye, he was a recently minted homicide investigator after riding a beat for ten years and then working robbery, burglary, and drugs for several years as a detective. He and Lancaster had been called to the Richardses' house after the report of a disturbance and the discovery of bodies inside by the first responders. This being their maiden homicide investigation, neither wanted to screw it up.

As a rookie uniformed cop, Lancaster had worn no makeup, as though to make herself less conspicuously female. She was the only woman on the entire force who didn't sit behind a desk and type or go make coffee for the guys. The only one authorized to carry a gun, arrest people, and read them their rights. And to take their lives if it was absolutely necessary.

She hadn't taken up her smoking habit yet. That would come when she began working as a detective with Decker, and spent more and more of her time with dead bodies and trying to catch the killers who had violently snatched away those lives. She was also heavier back then. But it was a healthy weight. Lancaster had gained the rep of a calm, methodical cop who went into every situation with three or four different plans on how to manage it. Nothing rattled her. As a beat cop she'd earned numerous commendations for how she handled herself. And everyone had come out of those situations alive. She'd conducted herself the same way while working as a detective.

Decker, on the other hand, had a reputation as the quirkiest son of a bitch who'd ever worn the Burlington police uniform. Yet no one could deny his vast potential in law enforcement. And that potential had been fully realized when he became a detective and partnered with Mary Lancaster. They'd never failed to solve a case to which they'd been assigned. It was a record of which any other police department, large or small, would have been envious.

They had known each other previously, having come up in the

same rookie class, but hadn't had much interaction professionally until they exchanged their uniforms for the civilian clothes of a detective.

Now Decker went step by step in his memory from that night as Lancaster watched him from a corner of the living room.

"Cops were radioed in about a disturbance here. Call came in at nine-thirty-five. Two squad cars arrived in five minutes. They entered the house a minute later after checking the perimeter. The front door was unlocked."

He moved over to another part of the room.

"Vic number one, David Katz, was found here," he said, pointing to a spot at the doorway into the kitchen. "Age thirty-five. Two taps. First gunshot to the left temple. Second to the back of the head. Instant death with either shot." He pointed to another spot right next to the door. "Beer bottle found here. His prints on it. Didn't break, but the beer was all over the floor."

"Katz owned a local restaurant, the American Grill," added Lancaster. "He was over here visiting."

"And no evidence that he could have been the target," stated Decker.

"None," confirmed Lancaster. "Wrong place, wrong time. Like Ron Goldman in the O. J. Simpson case. Really shitty luck on his part."

They moved into the kitchen. It was all dirty linoleum, scarred cabinets, and a rust-stained sink.

"Victim number two, Donald Richards—everyone called him Don. Forty-four. Bank loan officer. Single GSW through the heart and fell here. Again, dead when he dropped."

Lancaster nodded. "He knew Katz because the bank had previously approved a loan to Katz for the American Grill project."

Decker walked back out into the living room and eyed the stairs leading up to the second floor.

"Now the last two vics."

They climbed the stairs until they reached the second-floor landing.

"These two bedrooms." He indicated two doors across from

each other. He pushed open the door on the left side and went in. Lancaster followed.

"Victim number three," said Decker. "Abigail 'Abby' Richards. Age twelve."

"She was strangled. Found on the bed. Ligature marks showed that some sort of rope was used. Killer took it with him."

"Her death wasn't instantaneous," Decker pointed out.

"No. But she fought hard."

"And got Meryl Hawkins's DNA under her fingernails," Decker said pointedly. "So, in a way, she beat him."

Decker moved past her out of the room, across the hall and into the bedroom there. Lancaster followed.

Decker paced over to a point against the wall and said, "Victim number four. Frankie Richards. Age fourteen. Just started at Burlington High School. Found on the floor right here. Single GSW to the heart."

"We found some drug paraphernalia and enough cash hidden in his room to suggest that he wasn't just a user but a dealer. But we could never tie any of that to the murders. We tracked down the man supplying him, it was Karl Stevens. He was a small fry. There was no way that was the motivation to kill four people. And Stevens had an ironclad alibi."

Decker nodded. "Okay, we were called in at ten-twenty-one. We came by car and arrived here fourteen minutes later."

He leaned against the wall and glanced out the window that overlooked the street. "Four neighboring homes. Two were occupied that night. No one in those houses saw or heard anything. Killer came and left unseen, unheard."

"But then you found something when we went through the house that changed all that."

Decker led her back down the stairs and into the living room. "A thumbprint on *that* wall switch plate along with a blood trace from Katz."

"And the perp's skin, blood, and resultant DNA under Abby's fingernails. In the struggle with her attacker."

"He's strangling her with a ligature and she grips his arms to make him stop and the material gets transferred. Anybody who's ever watched an episode of *CSI* knows that."

Lancaster's hand flicked to her pocket and she pulled out her pack of smokes.

Decker eyed this movement as she lit up. "You cashing in on tomorrow's allotment?"

"It's getting close enough to midnight. And I'm stressed. So excuse the hell out of me." She flicked ash on the floor. "Hawkins's prints were in the database because the company he had worked for previously did some defense contracting. They fingerprinted and ran a background check on everyone who worked there. When the print matched Hawkins in the database, we executed the search warrant on his house."

Decker took up the story. "Based on the print, he was arrested and brought to the station, where a cheek swab was taken. The DNA on it matched the DNA found under Abby's fingernails. And he had no alibi for that entire night. And during the search of his home they found a forty-five-caliber pistol hidden in a box behind a wall in his closet. The ballistics match was spot on, so it was without a doubt the murder weapon. He said it wasn't his and he didn't know how it got there. He said he didn't even know about that secret space. We traced the pistol. It had been stolen from a gun shop about two years before. Serial numbers filed off. Probably used in a string of crimes since that time. And then it ended up in Hawkins's closet." He glanced at his old partner. "Which raises the question of why you think we might have gotten it wrong. Looks rock solid to me."

Lancaster rolled the lit cigarette between her fingers. "I keep coming back to a dying guy taking the time to come here to clear his name. He has to know the odds are stacked against him. Why waste what little time he has left?"

"Well, what else does he have to do?" countered Decker. "I'm not saying he came to this house to murder four people. Hawkins probably picked this house to commit a lesser crime of burglary and it snowballed from there. You know that happens, Mary. Criminals lose it when they're under stress."

"But you know his motive for the crime," said Lancaster. "That came out in the trial. Without really admitting his guilt, the defense tried to score some sympathetic points on that. It might have been why he didn't get the death penalty."

Decker nodded. "His wife was terminal. He needed money for her pain meds. He'd been laid off from his job and lost his insurance. His grown daughter had a drug problem and he was trying to get her into rehab. Again. So he stole credit cards, jewelry, a laptop computer, a DVD player, a small TV, some watches, and other miscellaneous things from this house and the vics. It all fits. His motivation might have been pure, but how he went about it sure as hell wasn't."

"But none of those items ever turned up. Not at his house. Not in some pawnshop. So he never realized any money from it."

Decker said, "But he had money in his pocket when he was arrested. We could never prove it was from fencing the stolen goods, and he might well have been scared to try to move it after the murders. That's what the prosecutor postulated at trial, although, reading the jury, it seemed to me that they thought the money he had was from selling the stuff. It's just a cleaner conclusion."

"But none of the neighbors saw a car drive up or leave other than David Katz's," retorted Lancaster.

"You know it was storming like hell that night, Mary. Raining buckets. You could barely see anything. And if Hawkins didn't have his car lights on, maybe no one would have noticed it."

"But no one *heard* it?" said Lancaster.

"Again, the noise of the storm. But I see you really have doubts about the case now."

"I wouldn't go that far. I'm just saying that I believe it deserves a second look."

"I don't see it that way."

"Despite your words, I can tell that you're at least intrigued." She paused and took another puff of her smoke. "And then there's the matter of Susan Richards."

"The wife. Left around five that day, ran some errands, attended a PTA meeting, and then had drinks and dinner with a couple of friends. All verified. She got home at eleven. When she found us here and learned what had happened, she became hysterical."

"You had to hold her down or I think she would have tried to hurt herself."

"Not exactly the actions of a guilty person. And there was only a fifty-thousand-dollar life insurance policy on Don Richards, from his job at the bank."

"I've known people who have killed for a lot less. And so do you."

Decker said, "So let's go."

"Where?"

"Where else? To see Meryl Hawkins."

* * *

As they pulled to a stop in front of the Residence Inn, Decker had a moment of déjà vu. He had lived here for a while after being evicted from the home where he found his family murdered. The place hadn't changed much. It had been crappy to begin with. Now it was just crappier still. He was surprised it was still standing.

They walked inside, and Decker looked to his left, where the small dining area was located. He had used that as his unofficial office when meeting potential clients who wanted to hire him as a private detective. He had come a long way in a relatively short period of time. Yet it could have easily gone the other way. He could have eaten himself into a stroke and died inside a cardboard box in a Walmart parking lot, which had briefly been his home before he'd moved to the "fancier" Residence Inn.

When she stepped out into the lobby Decker didn't look surprised.

Jamison nodded at Lancaster and said to Decker after reading his features, "I guess you expected me to turn up here?"

"I didn't *not* expect it," he replied. "I showed you the paper with this address on it."

"I looked up the basic facts of the murder online," she said. "Seemed pretty ironclad."

"We were just discussing that," said Lancaster. "But maybe the iron is rusty." She eyed the badge riding on Jamison's hip. "Hear you're the real deal FBI agent now. Congratulations."

"Thanks. Seemed the logical next step, if only to manage Decker a little better."

"Good luck on that. I was never able to, despite *my* badge."

"He's in room fourteen," interjected Decker. "Up the stairs."

They trudged single file up to the second floor and halfway down the hall to the door. Decker knocked. And knocked again.

"Mr. Hawkins? It's Amos Decker."

No sound came from inside the room.

"Maybe he went out," said Jamison.

"Where would he go?" asked Decker.

"Let me check something," said Lancaster. She hurried back down the stairs. A minute later she was back.

"The front desk clerk said he came in about two hours ago and hasn't left."

Decker knocked harder. "Mr. Hawkins? You okay?" He looked at the other two. "Maybe he's in distress."

"Maybe he died," said Lancaster. "The guy's terminal."

"He might have just passed out," suggested Jamison. "Or overdosed. He told us he was taking street drugs for the pain. They can be unpredictable."

Decker tried the door. It was locked. He put his shoulder to the door and pushed once, then again. It bent under his considerable weight and then popped open.

They entered the room and looked around.

Sitting up in a chair across from the bed was Hawkins.

He was clearly dead.

But the cancer hadn't taken him.

The bullet wound in the center of the man's forehead had done the trick quite effectively.

4

So anyway, a dead guy gets murdered.

It sounded like the opening line of an abysmally poor joke. A man terminal with cancer, who would probably be dead within a few days or weeks, gets hurried along to the end by a bullet.

Decker thought this as he leaned against the wall of Meryl Hawkins's room while the two-person forensic team carried out its professional tasks.

The EMTs had already come and pronounced death. The medical examiner had then made his way over and told them the obvious: death by a single GSW to the brain. There was no exit wound. Small-caliber probably, but no less lethal than a big-ass Magnum with that relatively soft target lined up in its iron sights.

Death was instantaneous, the ME had said. And painless.

But how does anyone really know that? thought Decker. It wasn't like they could go back and debrief the victim.

Excuse me, did it hurt when someone blew your brains out?

What was significant were the burn marks around the forehead. The muzzle of the gun had to either have been in contact with or within inches of the skin to make that imprint. It was like touching a hot iron. It left a mark that would be impossible if the iron was six feet away. Here, the gun's released gases would have done the work when the trigger was pulled.

Decker eyed Lancaster, who was overseeing the forensic team. Two uniformed officers were posted outside the door looking bored and tired. Jamison, leaning against another wall, watched the proceedings with interest.

Lancaster finally came over to Decker, and Jamison quickly joined them.

"We've taken statements. No one heard anything, and no one saw anything."

"Just like when Hawkins went to the Richardses' home and murdered them," said Decker.

"The rooms on either side of this one are unoccupied. And if the perp used a suppressor can on the gun?"

"When I lived here there was a rear door that never properly locked," said Decker. "The killer could have come and gone that way and the front-desk person wouldn't have seen them."

"I'll have that checked out. Hawkins's door was locked until you popped it."

"Presumably he let in the person who killed him," said Jamison. "And these doors automatically lock on the way out. Time of death?"

"ME's prelim is between eleven and midnight."

Decker checked his watch. "Which means we didn't miss them by much. If we had come here first instead of the Richardses' place?"

"Hindsight is absolutely perfect," noted Lancaster.

"Decker?"

He turned to look down at the woman in blue scrubs and booties. She was one of the crime scene techs. She was in her midthirties, red-haired and lanky, with sprinkles of freckles over the bridge of her nose.

"Kelly Fairweather," he said.

She smiled. "Hey, you remembered me."

"That's pretty much a given," said Decker, without a trace of irony.

Fairweather looked over at the dead man. "Well, I remember *him*," she said.

Lancaster joined them. "That's right, you worked the Richards crime scene."

"My first year doing this. Four homicides and two of them kids. It was quite an introduction to the job. So, what are you doing here, Decker?"

"Just trying to figure things out."

"Good luck with that. But I always thought Hawkins should've gotten the needle for what he did. I know that doesn't excuse what happened here."

"No, it doesn't," said Lancaster firmly.

Fairweather took that as a not-so-subtle nudge to move on. "Well, good seeing you, Decker."

As she moved away, Decker walked over to stand directly in front of the dead man, who still sat there like a statue. Lancaster and Jamison joined him.

Decker said, "So the shooter walks up to Hawkins, who's sitting in this chair, presses the gun against his forehead, and pulls the trigger." He looked around. "And no sign of a struggle?"

"Maybe he was asleep," suggested Lancaster.

"After letting the person in, the guy sits down in a chair and dozes off?" said Jamison.

Decker said, "He told us he was taking drugs. Did you find any?"

Lancaster shook her head. "Nothing in here or the bathroom. No discarded wrappers or empty pill bottles. Just a small duffel of clothes, a few bucks in his wallet. The post will show if he had anything in his system."

Decker looked around the room again, taking in every detail and imprinting it on his memory. He had already done this, but decided to do it again. His memory had been having a few hiccups of late and he didn't want to take a chance that he had missed something. It was like printing out a second copy of a photo.

Hawkins's yellowing skin had given way to a translucent paleness. Death did that to you, what with the stoppage of blood flow. At least the cancer was no longer a factor for the man. With death it had immediately stopped eating away at Hawkins's innards. Decker figured a fast bullet was preferable to a slow, painful death. But it was still murder.

"So, motives and possible suspects?" said Lancaster.

"Not to state the obvious, but does Susan Richards still live in the area?" asked Decker.

"Yes, she does."

"That would be my starting point," said Decker.

Lancaster checked her watch. "I'll have her picked up and taken to the station. We can interview her there."

"So, you want us involved?" said a surprised Jamison.

"In for a dime," replied Lancaster.

"The thing is, we have a day job," said Jamison. "Which often extends into nights."

"I can call Bogart," said Decker. Ross Bogart was the veteran FBI agent who headed up the task force of which Decker and Jamison were members.

"So, you really want to stay and dive into this?" asked Jamison warily.

"Do I have a choice?" asked Decker.

"You always have a choice," said Lancaster, gazing knowingly at Decker. "But I think I know what that choice will be."

Jamison said, "Decker, have you really thought this through?"

He indicated the corpse and said forcefully, "*This* is significant. The guy comes to town saying he's innocent and approaches me and Lancaster to prove him right. Now somebody just killed him."

"Well, like you just suggested, it might be Susan Richards, the widow of the man Hawkins was convicted of murdering."

"It might, and it might not."

Decker turned and walked out.

Lancaster looked at Jamison. "Well, some things never change. Like him."

"Tell me about it," replied Jamison wearily.

5

Ross Bogart said, "This is unacceptable, Decker. And I mean totally unacceptable."

Decker was on his phone, heading to the Burlington police station.

"I understand how you could think that, Ross."

"There's no understanding anything. I let you go rogue once before with the Melvin Mars case. And then when you wanted to stay back in Baronville and work the case there because it was connected to Alex's family. But I can't let you go off willy-nilly whenever you feel like it."

"This is different," said Decker.

"You say that every time," barked Bogart. "You've not only blown up the exception to the rule, you've blown up the rule. The bottom line is you work for the FBI."

"I'm sorry, Ross. This is my hometown. I can't turn my back on it."

"You've made your choice, then?"

"Yes."

"Then you force me to make mine."

"This is all me. Alex has nothing to do with it."

"I'll deal with Special Agent Jamison separately."

The line went dead.

Decker slowly put the phone away. It seemed that his days at the FBI were numbered.

He looked over at Lancaster, who was in the car with him.

"Problems?" she said.

"There are always problems."

They drove on.

* * *

Susan Richards was not pleased. "You're shitting me, right? You think I killed that son of a bitch? I wish I had."

Decker and Lancaster had just walked into the interrogation room at police headquarters. Jamison had gone back to her hotel because Decker had not received authorization from Bogart to work on the case. And that permission obviously would not be forthcoming. Bogart had probably already contacted her.

They had had to wait for a few hours while the paperwork was drawn up to bring Richards in after she angrily refused to voluntarily comply with their request. And the fuming woman had apparently taken her time getting ready while the uniforms impatiently waited.

Thus it was now nearly five in the morning.

Lancaster looked ready to fall asleep.

Decker looked ready to question the woman for the next ten years.

The interrogation room's cinderblock walls were still painted mustard yellow. Decker had never known why, other than maybe that was the color of some old paint the custodians had found somewhere in the basement. Leaving the cinder blocks their original gray would have been nicer, he thought. But maybe no one wanted "nicer" in an interrogation room.

Richards had been forty-two when her family was wiped out. She was in her midfifties now. She had aged remarkably well, Decker thought. He remembered her as tall, but plump and mousy-looking, her light brown hair hanging limply around her face.

Now she was much thinner, and her hair was cut in a chic manner, with the tresses grazing her shoulder. She had colored her hair and blonde highlights predominated. Her mousy personality had been replaced by an assertive manner that had made itself known with her outburst the moment the two detectives walked into the room.

Richards looked from Lancaster to Decker as they sat down across from her. "Wait a minute, you're the two from that night. I recognize you now. You know what he did." She sat forward, her sharp elbows pressed against the tabletop. Her face full of fury, she snapped, "You *know* what that bastard did."

Lancaster said calmly, "Which is why, when he was found dead, we thought we needed to talk to you. So that you could tell us where you were between around eleven and midnight."

"Where in the hell do you think I was at that hour? I was in my bed asleep."

"Can anyone verify that?" asked Decker.

"I live alone. I never remarried. That's what having your family wiped out will do to you!" she added fiercely.

"What time did you get home last night?" asked Decker.

Richards took a moment to compose herself and sat back. "I got off work at six. Three days a week, I volunteer at the homeless shelter on Dawson Square. I was there until around eight last night. There are people who can vouch for me."

"And after that?" said Lancaster.

Richards sat back and spread her hands. "I drove home, cooked some dinner."

"What'd you have?" asked Lancaster.

"Oh, the usual. Smoked salmon on crusty bread with cream cheese and capers to warm up my appetite, then a Waldorf salad, some linguine with fresh clams, and a nice little tiramisu for dessert. And I paired that with a wonderful glass of my favorite chilled Prosecco."

"Seriously?" said Lancaster.

Richards made a face. "Of course not. I made a tuna sandwich with a pickle and some corn chips. And I skipped the Prosecco and had iced tea instead."

"Then what did you do?"

"I ordered something from Bed, Bath & Beyond online. You can probably check that. Then I watched some TV."

"What program?" asked Decker.

"I was streaming. *Outlander*. I'm really getting into it. Season two. Jamie and Claire in France."

"What was the episode about?"

"Lots of political skullduggery. And some pretty intense sex." She added sarcastically, "Want me to describe it in graphic detail for you?"

"And then?" said Decker.

"I finished watching that. Then I took a shower and called it a night. I woke up when the police knocked on my door. *Pounded*, more precisely," she added, frowning.

"You drive a dark green Honda Civic?" said Lancaster.

"Yes. It's the only car I have."

"And you live on Primrose, on the north side?"

"Yes. I have for about five years now."

"You have neighbors?"

"On both sides of me and across the street." She sat up. "One of them might be able to tell you that I was home last night. Or at least that I didn't leave once I got there."

"We'll check that out," said Lancaster. "Did you know Meryl Hawkins was back in town?"

"I had no idea. What, do you think he'd knock on my door and ask for a handout? I thought he was in prison for life. And I still don't know why he wasn't."

"He was terminal with cancer, so they cut him loose."

"Well, that seems shitty," said Richards. "Don't get me wrong, I hated the asshole. But they just kicked him to the curb because he was dying?"

"Apparently so. And he never tried to contact you?"

"Never. If he had, I *might* have tried to kill him. But he didn't and so I didn't."

Decker said, "You opened a florist shop, didn't you? With the proceeds from your husband's insurance policy? I remember seeing it. Over on Ash Place?"

She eyed him warily. "I buried my *family* with a chunk of the insurance money. And then I went on living. I'm not sure how."

"And the florist shop?" persisted Decker.

"There wasn't that much left after the funeral expenses. But, yes, I opened a florist shop. I've always loved gardening and flowers. It did okay. Provided a decent living. Even did some holiday events for the police department. I sold it a few years back. Now I run the place for the new owners. When my Social Security kicks in, I'm going to retire and just work on my own garden."

Lancaster looked at Decker. "Anything else?"

He shook his head.

"How was he killed?" asked Richards.

"We're holding that back for now," said Lancaster.

"Am I free to go?"

"Yes."

She rose and looked at the pair. "I didn't kill him," she said quietly. "Years ago, I probably would have, no problem. But I guess time does help to heal you."

She walked out.

Lancaster looked at him. "You believe her?"

"I don't disbelieve her."

"There were no usable prints or other trace in Hawkins's room."

"I didn't expect there would be."

"So what now?"

"We do what we always did. We keep digging."

Lancaster checked her watch. "Well, right now I've got to get home and get some sleep or I'm going to keel over. I'll give you a call later. You should get some sleep too."

He rose and followed her out of the room.

Outside, Lancaster said, "I can drop you off where you're staying."

"I'd rather walk, thanks. It's not that far."

She smiled. "Nice to be working with you again."

"You might not think that much longer."

"I've gotten used to your ways."

"So you say."

He turned and walked off into the breaking dawn.

CHAPTER

6

A GENTLE RAIN KICKED IN as Decker trudged along the pavement.

It felt very odd to once more be investigating a crime in his hometown. The last time had involved the murder of his family. This one was different, but it still affected Decker personally.

If I was part of convicting an innocent man?

He looked around as he walked. He had decided not to come back for Cassie's birthday, or their wedding anniversary. That simply would have been too much for him to handle. Yet he would keep returning for their daughter's birthday. He had to be here for that milestone, though each visit was emotionally crippling for him.

His long feet carried him past where he was staying, and after a few miles he reached the long-established neighborhood. It was light now. He stopped walking and stood on the corner staring up at the place he used to call home.

The last time he'd been here was two years ago. It looked remarkably unchanged, as though time had stood still since his last visit. Although there were two unfamiliar cars in the driveway, a Ford pickup and a Nissan Sentra.

As he stood there, a man in his early thirties and a girl around seven came out of the side door. The girl was carrying a school backpack and the man was dressed in khakis and a white collared shirt with a windbreaker over it. He carried a slim briefcase in one hand. The girl yawned and rubbed her eyes.

They climbed into the pickup truck and backed out of the driveway. That's when the man spotted Decker standing there watching the house.

He rolled down his window. "Can I help you, buddy?"

Decker studied him more closely. "You must be Henderson."

The man eyed him suspiciously. "How do you know that?"

"A friend told me." He pointed at the house. "I used to live there a few years ago."

Henderson ran his gaze over Decker. "Okay. Did you leave something behind?"

"No, I, uh…" Decker's voice trailed off, and he looked confused.

Henderson said, "Look, don't get me wrong, but it's a little odd that you're standing out here this early in the morning watching my house."

Decker pulled his FBI creds out of his pocket and showed them to Henderson. "My friend on the police force told me you'd bought the house."

"Wait a minute," said Henderson, staring at the ID card. "Amos Decker?"

"Yeah."

Henderson nodded and looked anxious. "I heard about—" He snatched a glance at his daughter, who was paying close attention to this exchange.

"Right. Anyway, have a good day. Hope you enjoy the house and the neighborhood. Nice place to raise a family."

Decker turned and walked off as Henderson drove away.

It had been stupid coming back here. He'd rattled the guy unnecessarily. And for what? He didn't need to come here for a walk down memory lane. It was all in his head. Pristine. Forever.

And painfully so.

He retraced his steps and got to the hotel where he and Jamison were staying in time to see her exit the elevator and walk into the lobby.

"Christ, Decker, are you just getting in?" she said, eyeing his grungy, wet clothes.

"Good morning to you too. Would you like to get some breakfast?"

She followed him into the dining area off the lobby. They sat, ordered some food, and sipped their coffees.

"So?" said Jamison. "Was Susan Richards any help?"

"She didn't cop to the murder if that's what you're asking. She doesn't have a solid alibi. She was home asleep, she says."

"Well, considering the hour, that makes sense."

"We may be able to tighten the parameters on that by talking to her neighbors. But I don't think she's good for it. She says she didn't even know he was back in town. And that seems perfectly logical."

"Unless she saw him on the street."

"*I* saw him and didn't recognize him," said Decker. "And I spent a lot of time with the guy all those years ago."

"Have you called Bogart and gotten his permission to work on this?"

He said quietly, "We've, uh, talked. I'm surprised he hasn't called you."

"No, he didn't. So what did he say?"

At that moment their food arrived.

Decker said, "I'll fill you in later."

"Thank you for ordering a veggie omelet, by the way," said Jamison. "And avoiding the bacon."

"You must be growing on me."

"Well, I'm just happy that you're not *growing* anymore. You look good, Decker."

"That's a stretch, but thanks."

He put his knife and fork down and finished his coffee.

"What are you thinking?" asked Jamison.

"I'm thinking that there's a killer walking around town this morning thinking he or she got away with murder, and it's really pissing me off."

"Is that all?"

He looked at her curiously. "Isn't that enough?"

"I mean, do you feel guilty about what happened to Meryl Hawkins?"

"I didn't pull the trigger on the guy. I didn't ask him to come here and ignite this case again."

"But you think that the fact that someone killed him is evidence that he might have been innocent? I mean, you basically said that earlier."

"Meaning that I made a mistake?" said Decker slowly.

"I wouldn't look at it that way. You investigated the case and all the evidence pointed to that guy. I would have seen it the same way."

"Regardless, if he *was* innocent, I have to make it right."

Jamison hiked her eyebrows. "Because the weight of the world's problems always falls on your admittedly broad shoulders?"

"Not the weight of the world. The weight of one case that I handled. Responsibility comes with the territory. My actions took a guy's freedom away."

"No, I'd say *his* actions took his freedom away."

"Only if he did it," countered Decker. "If he didn't commit the crimes, it's a whole other ball game."

Jamison fingered her coffee cup. "If he was set up, whoever did it knew what they were doing. Who would have a beef against the guy that badly?"

Decker nodded. "Good point. And I have no idea. Hawkins was a skilled machinist but lost his job when the factory he worked at had layoffs. Then he went on the odd-job road. Doing what he could to make ends meet."

"Sounds like a lot of people these days."

He eyed the FBI badge that was clipped to her lapel. "How does it feel?"

She looked down at the badge and smiled. "Pretty damn good, actually. Did you ever think of taking the plunge?"

"I'm too old now. Age thirty-seven is the cutoff and I'm not a military veteran, so I can't seek that waiver. And even if I could still apply, I doubt I'd pass the physical."

"Don't underestimate yourself. And since you know the requirements, I take it you looked into it?"

Decker shrugged. "I can do my job without the federal badge. I'm still a sworn police officer. I can arrest people." He paused and added, "And you always have my back."

"Yes, I do."

"I went by my old house early this morning."

She looked startled by this admission. "Why?"

"I don't know. My feet pointed that way and suddenly I was there. Met the dad who lives there and saw his little girl. Lancaster had told me about them. I spooked them a little showing up like that, but the dad had heard about what had happened...there. It turned out okay."

Jamison leaned forward. "I know that you don't want to hear this, Decker, but I'm going to say it anyway." She paused, seeming to choose her words with great care. "At some point, you're going to have to let this go. I mean, I get coming back here to visit their graves and all. But you have your life left to live. That means you have to move forward and stop dwelling in the past so much. Cassie and Molly wouldn't want you to do that, you know that."

"Do I?" said Decker abruptly.

She sat back, looking saddened by this comment.

"They shouldn't be dead, Alex. If anyone should be dead, it should be me."

"But you're not. You're alive and you have to spend every day living for them and yourself. Otherwise, it's all wasted."

Decker rose. "I'm going to take a shower and change my clothes. And then we're going to go catch a killer. I'll meet you back down here in half an hour."

"Decker, you need to get some sleep!"

"No, that would just be *wasting* time, wouldn't it?"

As he walked off, Jamison just stared after him, the look on her face one of heartbreak.

7

Decker let the hot water run off his head for a full minute before soaping up. The next moment he had a brief panic attack because he couldn't recall Cassie's favorite color. Then his memory righted itself and the proper shade kicked out of his brain.

He rested his head against the shower tile. *Shit, more hiccups. No, more* malfunctions *because I'm a machine, after all. Right?*

Was his memory going to keep misfiring? Right when he needed it to work precisely? Or would there be a time when it simply stopped functioning altogether? Then a dreaded thought sprouted up: Was he developing complications from his brain injury all those years ago? Like CTE?

He finished in the shower, dried off, and put on fresh clothes. Mentally he still felt like crap, and physically he was tired, but at least he was clean.

Jamison was waiting for him in the lobby. They got into the car and from the driver's seat Jamison said, "Where to?"

"Our only viable suspect right now, Susan Richards."

On the way he phoned Lancaster and told her what they were going to do. He had to leave a message because the call went to voicemail. She was probably still sleeping, surmised Decker.

Richards's home on Primrose Avenue was a small single-story brick bungalow with old-fashioned green-and-white-striped metal awnings over the windows. The patch of yard was neatly laid out, with mature trees and well-shaped bushes and planting beds. An abundance of colorful fall flowers was displayed in pots on the covered front stoop.

"Nice landscaping," commented Jamison.

"She was a florist for years," explained Decker. "Into gardening. Runs the floral shop she sold to new owners a while back."

"Do you actually think she could have murdered Hawkins last night?"

"She could have. But I don't know if she did. That's what we have to find out."

They got out, but Decker didn't head up to the front door. He instead walked over to the house across the street.

"Verifying alibis?" said Jamison as she caught up to him.

He nodded and knocked on the door of the bungalow that was a twin of Richards's home, only with a screened-in porch on one end.

Answering the door was a tiny elderly woman with white hair so thin they could see her reddened scalp underneath.

"Yes?" she said, staring at them from behind thick glasses.

Jamison held out her FBI badge, which the woman scrutinized.

"FBI?" she said. "Have I done something wrong?"

"No," said Jamison hastily. "We were checking on a neighbor of yours, Ms.....?"

"Agatha Bates." She looked up at the towering Decker. "Are you FBI? You didn't show me a badge." She ran her gaze over him. "You look too big to be FBI. I watch a lot of TV. No FBI agent is as big as you."

Jamison said hastily, "He works as a consultant for us."

Bates slowly drew her gaze from Decker and settled it on Jamison. "Which neighbor?"

"Susan Richards."

"Oh, Susan, sure. Nice lady. Lived here a while. Not nearly so long as me. I've been here fifty-seven years." She looked at Decker again. "Don't I know you?"

"I worked here on the police force for twenty years."

"Oh, well, I don't have much contact with the police. I pay my taxes and I've never robbed anybody."

"I'm sure," said Jamison. "We were wondering if you could tell us when you last saw Ms. Richards."

"Well, I saw her this morning when the police came to get her. We don't usually have the police around here."

"That was pretty early," noted Jamison.

"Well, I get up pretty early. Only sleep maybe four hours a night. You get old, you don't sleep. I'll be sleeping all the time pretty soon."

"Excuse me?" said Jamison.

"When I *die*, honey. I'm ninety-three, how much longer do you expect me to be around?" She paused and adjusted her glasses. "So why did the police take her in the first place?"

"For some questions. Did you see her yesterday, in the evening, maybe?"

"I saw her come home. It was around quarter past eight."

"How can you be so certain?" asked Decker. "And have you spoken to her this morning?"

"No, I haven't talked to her. If she's home now she hasn't come out of her house, least that I saw. Usually takes a walk in the morning. I have my coffee on the screen porch. I wave, she waves back. I guess the police coming messed that up."

"So you didn't see her come back from the police station this morning?" asked Decker.

"No. I was probably in the kitchen making breakfast, or out in the backyard puttering. I like to putter. People my age, we putter, and we do it slow. I don't need a broken hip."

"So last night?" prompted Jamison.

"Quarter past eight," she said again, staring at Decker. "She volunteers at the homeless shelter. She always gets in around that time. And I know the time because *Jeopardy!* had been over about fifteen minutes. I got the Final Jeopardy question. The answer was Harry Truman. I remember Truman. Hell, I *voted* for him. All three of the contestants got it wrong. Not a single one was over thirty. What do they know about Harry Truman? I would have won enough to take a vacation somewhere."

"So, you saw her come home last night? Did she leave again? Would you have seen her if she did?"

"She didn't drive in her car if she did," said Bates. "That car of hers sounds like a bomb going off when she starts it up. It's an old Honda. Darn muffler's shot. Told her to get it fixed. Almost makes me wet my pants every time I hear it. My hearing's still good. I can hear pretty much everything and especially that damn car."

"But she could have left another way. Walked or called a cab?"

"Well, I was out on the screen porch doing the crosswords and reading until about ten-thirty or so. I would have seen her leave. After that, I went inside. Hit the hay about eleven or so."

"Okay, to be clear, at least until ten-thirty or so she hadn't left her house?" said Decker. "And you never heard the car start up, at least until you went to bed around eleven?"

"I thought I just said that. Are you *slow*?"

"That's great," said Jamison quickly. "Mrs. Bates, you've been very helpful."

"Okay, glad to do my civic duty." She jerked her thumb at Decker and said in a low voice to Jamison, "I think the FBI needs better consultants. But you keep doing what you're doing, honey. Nice to see a gal agent."

"Thanks," said Jamison, trying hard to suppress a smile.

They left Bates and headed back to the street.

Decker said, "If Richards walked, she could have gotten to the Residence Inn in time to kill Hawkins. And she clearly could have if she took a cab."

"If she took a cab, we'll be able to find any record of it. I suppose they don't have Uber here?"

"No, I don't think so."

They tried the other two homes, but no one answered their knocks.

"Bottom line is we haven't eliminated Richards as a suspect for Hawkins's murder," noted Decker.

"But do you really think she might have done it?"

"She has the most direct motive, but there are a lot of obstacles in the way. How she would know he was back in town being foremost among them."

"You don't think he would have gone to see her?"

"How would Hawkins even know where she lived? Lancaster

didn't tell him, I know that. And if he was innocent of the murders he wouldn't have gone there to apologize."

"You can Google someone's address easily enough," said Jamison.

"He just got out of prison and was terminally ill. I'm not sure I see the guy walking around with a computer and an Internet connection. Or finding one all that easily."

"But he might have gone to get some info from her, especially if he thought *she* did it."

Decker shook his head. "No, Hawkins knew from the trial that she had a firm alibi." He paused and added thoughtfully, "Theoretically, she could have hired someone to do it for her, though there was absolutely no evidence of that. But we still arrive back at the problem with motive. With her husband around, she could stay home and raise the kids. She never got remarried, there was no boyfriend waiting in the wings. She didn't get rich off her family's murders. I just don't see it. And no way she was going to kill her own kids."

"I agree," admitted Jamison.

"There's one guy we can talk to who might be able to tell us more."

"Who's that?"

"Ken Finger."

"Ken Finger? How does he figure into this?"

"He was Hawkins's public defender."

"Is he still around?"

"Let's go find out."

8

KEN FINGER WAS INDEED STILL AROUND.

Decker had finally reached Lancaster, and she arranged to meet them at Finger's office, which was located a block over from the downtown courthouse.

His secretary, Christine Burlin, a woman in her midforties, met their request with a stern look. "Mr. Finger is very busy at present," she said when confronted with Decker, Jamison, and Lancaster.

Lancaster took out her badge. "I think Ken can make some time for this."

Burlin stared at the badge far longer than was needed.

"Come on, Christine," said an exasperated Lancaster. "It's not like you don't know who I am. Some of your kids go to the same school as Sandy. And you know Decker as well from working with Ken."

"Well, I try to maintain a professional atmosphere at work, Detective Lancaster."

"I'm all for professional," said Decker. "So where's Ken?"

Burlin looked up at him. "I heard you were back in town for a few days," she said. "You still working for the FBI?" Decker nodded and she looked at Jamison. "I remember you too. I take it you're still consulting with the Bureau?"

"I'm actually a special agent now," said Jamison.

"That's a strange career change, from journalist to FBI agent."

"Not that strange," replied Jamison.

"Why?"

"An FBI agent looks to find the truth and make sure the right people are punished. A journalist digs to find the truth and makes sure the public knows about it, and that sometimes leads to bad people being punished."

"Hmmm," said Burlin, looking skeptical of this. "I guess that could be."

"Where's Ken?" said Decker impatiently. "We're wasting crucial time here."

Burlin frowned. "I see that *you* haven't changed one bit." She picked up her desk phone and made the call.

A few moments later she escorted them into Finger's office. It was large with ample windows. His desk was constructed of dark wood with a leather top. It was strewn with books, legal pads, files, and stapled pleadings. A large bookshelf held old law books and red file folders, neatly labeled. There were chairs set around a coffee table. A credenza against one wall was set up as a bar, and also held two large glass jars of M&M's. Ken Finger sat behind his desk.

Finger had only been about thirty when he had defended Hawkins against a capital murder charge. There apparently had been no other takers who wanted to defend in court the man charged with brutally murdering two men and two kids.

He was now in his forties and worked as a defense attorney for those who needed it. And in Burlington, like most towns, there were a great many who needed his services. His tidy brown hair was turning gray, as was his trim beard. His pleated trousers were held up by bright red braces and his white shirt had French cuffs. His striped bow tie was undone and hung limply around his wattled neck. His belly stuck out from between the braces.

He rose and greeted them, motioning them over to the seating area around the coffee table.

"I guess I know why you're here," he said, after Burlin closed the door behind her.

"Guess you do," replied Lancaster.

"How the hell are you, Decker?" Finger said.

"Okay," said Decker as he sat down. "So you've heard?"

"How could I not? Burlington's not that big. And although it's not like the attack on the high school when you lived here, it's still newsworthy when a convicted murderer comes back to town and then gets murdered."

Lancaster said, "Had he come to see you?"

Finger shook his head. "Hadn't seen hide nor hair of him since he went to prison."

"You never visited him there?" asked Jamison.

"Well, I take that back. I *did* go visit him there because we filed an appeal, but it was turned down flat. I mean, we didn't really have any grounds for an appeal. If anything, the judge went out of his way to accommodate us. And the jury could have returned a death sentence, but they didn't. I actually told Meryl that his escaping the death penalty was the best he could expect. Why make waves?"

"Were you convinced of his guilt?" asked Lancaster.

Finger shrugged. "It didn't matter to me one way or another. My job is to defend. It's the state's job to prove guilt. I live in the creases of reasonable doubt. All defense lawyers do."

"But did you *think* he was guilty?" persisted Decker.

Finger sat back and steepled his hands. "You know that the attorney-client privilege survives the death of a client."

"I'm not asking for you to reveal any privileged communications," Decker pointed out. "I'm just asking your opinion on the matter. That's not privileged and can in no way injure your client. He was already convicted and now he's dead."

Finger grinned. "You would've made a good lawyer, Decker. Okay, yeah, I thought he'd done it. I think he went over there just to steal some stuff and ran into a whole lot of trouble that he couldn't handle. It wasn't like the guy was a career criminal. Hell, he hadn't had so much as a parking ticket. I think that was one reason he didn't get the death penalty. I think he lost it and started shooting and strangling, and before he knew it, he had four dead bodies. Then he just got the hell out of there."

"And no one saw him drive up, enter the place and then leave, or hear the shots?" said Decker.

Finger shrugged. "Who knows? People said they heard nothing.

One house was playing loud music. In the other the folks said they were watching TV or sleeping. The third house the people weren't home that night, and the fourth house was abandoned. And the houses weren't that close. And then there was the noise from the storm." He gave Decker a funny look. "Hell, Amos, you and Mary are the ones that made the case against him. Prints. DNA. Motive. Opportunity. And the murder weapon found hidden in his home. I mean, as a defense lawyer, I had nothing really to work with. I considered it a miracle he only got life without parole."

"And the stolen goods?" said Lancaster.

"Hawkins didn't have an explanation for that because he said he didn't commit the crime. But if you want my opinion, I think he chucked it all when he knew he couldn't fence them without it tying him to four homicides."

Decker shook his head. "He had five hundred dollars in his wallet the night he was picked up."

"And the prosecution suggested that was the proceeds from his fencing the stolen goods. But the stuff that he was supposed to have stolen would have fetched more money than that, I think."

"And you postulated a theory that Hawkins was planning to use the five hundred bucks to purchase painkillers for his wife, Lisa, off the street. Did he tell you that, or did you just come up with it?"

"Hey, I don't just 'come up' with stuff, Decker," Finger said firmly. "That's what he told me."

"So where'd he get the money?" asked Lancaster.

"He never said."

"I wonder why," said Decker. "I mean if he could have come up with a viable explanation that would have taken a big chunk out of the prosecution's case."

"Believe me, I tried. But he wouldn't say."

Lancaster said, "He'd gotten laid off from his job a while back. They had no money."

"I'm just telling you what he told me about it, which was zip. And I wouldn't let him take the stand, so the prosecution was able to bring out the money during the trial. I tried to poke holes at it and brought up him wanting to buy drugs for his terminally ill wife to get some sympathy in the courtroom, but I could tell the jury wasn't buying it. They were connecting the dots on the money and the stolen goods. There was no way around that. And for all I know the five hundred bucks did come from that. Who's to say what a fence will pay for hot goods connected to a string of murders? And there was no way a fence would have come forward and gotten involved in the case. So there was no avenue for me to investigate unless Meryl opened up about it, which he never did."

Lancaster said, "But more to the point, why would he go to a house that early in the evening and that was full of people?"

Decker interjected, "There were no cars out front. David Katz's car was parked in the back of the house. And Hawkins wouldn't have been able to see that if he approached from the front, which he had to. The Richardses only had one car at the time and the wife had taken it. The other car was in for repairs."

"But there were lights on when the first responders got there," countered Lancaster. "Pretty stupid burglar to hit a house all lit up."

Finger spread his hands. "What can I tell you? That's what happened. Like I said, the guy wasn't an experienced criminal. And he had no alibi. You know that."

Decker said, "And Hawkins might have thought the lights were on just because of the storm. With no cars out front, and the house didn't have a garage, he might have thought it was empty."

Finger added, "And if he didn't do it, someone went to a lot of trouble to frame him. Why would they? He was a nobody. Blue-collar guy his whole life. I'm not saying that's bad. Hell, I admired him for that. My old man was a mechanic, could do stuff I never could. I'm just saying Meryl was a regular guy with a regular life. Not worth the trouble."

"And yet somebody went to the *trouble* of killing him," said Decker. "And his life wasn't exactly regular. His wife was dying and his daughter was a drug addict."

"That's true. Hey, did you check with Susan? She's still around."

"Gee, why didn't we think of that?" said Lancaster.

"So you don't think she's good for it?" said Finger.

"What I think about an active police investigation is none of your business, Ken."

Finger smiled. "Come on, Mary, I thought we were friends."

"We're also professional adversaries because I have to testify in court to put away your guilty clients, and you do your best to discredit my *truthful* testimony."

"Hey, it's called cross-examination. We don't have many arrows in our quiver, but that's one of the prime ones. And the state has all the resources. I'm just one guy."

"Keep telling yourself that. It's a good day when the Internet works at the police station. My computer's about fifteen years old. And I haven't had a raise in eight years."

He smiled impishly. "You can always come over to our side. Be an expert witness. Pays pretty well."

She returned the look. "Thanks, but no thanks. I have a hard enough time sleeping as it is."

"I sleep like a baby," retorted Finger, grinning.

Decker looked over at the bookshelf where a bunch of files were stacked. "We need to see your records on the case."

"Why?"

"Because there might be a clue in there as to who killed Hawkins."

"The privilege still applies, Decker."

Decker looked at the man. "Hawkins came to me and asked me to prove his innocence. He did the same to Mary."

Finger glanced sharply at Lancaster, who nodded. "That was the only reason he was back in town. To tell me and Decker that we got it wrong and he wanted us to make it right. We went to the Residence Inn to meet with him to go over that. That's when we found him dead."

Decker said, "So it seems to me that by his words and actions, Hawkins has waived his privilege, because how else can we prove his innocence if we can't look at your files?"

Finger sighed. "Well, you make a compelling argument, I'll give you that. And I guess it couldn't hurt at this point. But it's been a long time. You think I still have that stuff?"

"Most attorneys I know never throw anything away," replied Decker firmly.

"So you're thinking he's innocent now, after all this time?"

"Some people here thought I'd killed my family," said Decker.

"I wasn't one of them," said Finger quickly.

Decker rose. "So let's go get those files."

"What, you mean now? They're in storage probably."

"Yeah, now."

"But I've got to be in court in twenty minutes."

"Then I'm sure your secretary can help us. Now."

"What's your rush?"

"After all these years, I'm not waiting on the truth one second longer than I have to," replied Decker.

CHAPTER

9

"It's over here."

They were in a climate-controlled storage unit. After consulting the iPad she was holding, Christine Burlin pointed to a shelf in the far back of the space.

"You seem very well organized," said Lancaster appreciatively.

"Well, of course I am. Mr. Finger is not the best in that regard, so I have to make up for it. And I can assure you that I do."

Lancaster whispered to Jamison, "She has four kids, the oldest is in eighth grade, and I think she still dresses them in Garanimals."

There were only two boxes dealing with the case, Burlin told them. She made Lancaster sign an electronic receipt before she would allow them to take the containers. They trudged back to their cars with Decker schlepping both boxes.

Lancaster said, "You can take them back to the station. Captain Miller has arranged a room for you to use."

"How is Captain Miller?" said Decker.

"Ready to retire," said Lancaster. "But aren't we all. I'll meet you back there later."

"Wait a minute, where are you going?" asked Decker.

"I have other cases to work," she said incredulously. "And this one is not officially on my plate or even a case for the department."

"But Hawkins's murder is."

"And we don't know if it's connected to what's in those files. So, you go through them and let me know what you find out, if anything. And let me go about trying to solve some *new* crimes, like Hawkins's murder."

She got into her car and drove off. When Decker didn't climb into their rental, Jamison paused, her hand on the car door. "What's up?"

"That's what I want to know: What's up with Mary?"

"What do you mean?"

"I've known her a long time. She's not telling me something."

"Well, she has that right, Decker. But she might come around. And it's nice that you're worried about your old partner," she added.

They drove to the police station and were directed to the room reserved for their use. As they were heading down the hall a man in his early sixties stepped out of an office.

Captain MacKenzie Miller was still short, wide, and puffy, with an unhealthy tint to his skin. But his smile was broad and infectious. "Look what they let in the door," he said.

He put out his hand for Decker to shake. He nodded at Jamison and shook her hand too, then pointed to the badge on her jacket. "I heard. Congrats, Alex, I know that wasn't easy."

"Thanks, Mac."

Decker eyed the man who had been his superior his entire time on the police force. Miller was a good cop, tough, fair, and he didn't bullshit. He had actually stopped Decker from putting a bullet in his brain once. It would be impossible to dislike the man after that.

"Well, you've been establishing quite a rep for yourself at the Bureau. Ross Bogart keeps me updated."

"Didn't know that," said Decker, the boxes pressed against his wide chest.

"Nice to know there are some things you *don't* know," said Miller. He eyed the boxes. "Lawyer's files? Hawkins?"

"Yes," responded Jamison.

"We'll, I'll let you get to it, then. It's good to see you both. Let's grab a beer later if you're able."

Decker said, "Can I ask a question?"

"Would it matter if I said no?"

"What's going on with Mary?"

Miller folded his short arms over his thick chest. "Why do you think anything's going on with her, Amos?"

"We know each other. Something's off."

"You *knew* each other. It's been a couple of years. People change."

"People don't change that much," replied Decker.

"Then ask her." Miller wagged a finger at him. "Just be prepared for whatever answer she has. You up for that?"

Decker didn't answer, and Miller didn't look like he had expected a response.

"I appreciate your letting us work on the case."

"Well, I want to get to the bottom of it as much as you do. If we messed up, we have to make it right. You have my full backing."

"Thanks, Mac," said Jamison.

"I'll leave you to it, then." He disappeared back inside his office.

They proceeded to the room and Decker put the twin boxes down on the metal conference table. He took off his coat and slung it over a chair back.

Taking the top off one box, he said to Jamison, "I'll take this one. You go through the other." He slid it over to her.

"What exactly are we looking for?" she asked, opening the box.

"Hopefully you'll know it when you see it."

She sighed, sat down, and lifted out the first few files.

* * *

Four hours later they had each gone through both boxes.

"Not a whole lot here," noted Jamison.

"This is the defense's side of things. I've asked Mary to have someone pull the department's files."

"They keep things that long?"

"Probably only because nobody had the time to throw them out."

"Ken Finger didn't seem to have much evidence to go on."

"That's why the jury convicted his client after only two hours of deliberation. And an hour of that was spent at lunch."

"He was pretty tough on you on cross-examination," said Jamison, holding up a transcript of Decker's time in the witness box.

"That was his job."

"But you were quite firm in your statements."

"Because I believed them to be true."

"Meaning you no longer do?"

Decker looked at her over a piece of paper he was holding. "Meaning back then I didn't necessarily see the forest for the trees."

"Meaning?"

"Meaning I might have been so eager to get a conviction on my first homicide investigation that it didn't strike me as odd that a guy would burgle a house that early in the evening when it might be full of people."

"Well, maybe he wasn't that smart. As has been pointed out, he wasn't an experienced criminal. Maybe he didn't know how to properly case a target."

"Hawkins wasn't dumb. And the thing is, he had never been in any sort of trouble with the law before. That didn't mean much to me back then because the forensics were overwhelming. But to go from never having a parking ticket to four homicides is like going from hopping over a rain puddle to leaping across the Grand Canyon. It should have set off warning bells."

"But like everyone's been saying, he probably didn't go in there thinking he was going to kill anyone. Then it just went sideways."

"Granted, he was desperate. His wife needed pain medicine. His daughter was a drug addict he was trying to help. He might have felt he was up against a wall. He went there just to steal and, like you said, everything might have gone to hell after that."

"And he had the cash in his pocket."

"So if had the money, why was he still wandering around when he was picked up by the cops?"

"Maybe he was trying to score the drugs to help his wife."

"Maybe," said Decker. "But the thing is, there was a house next to the Richardses' that *was* empty that night. I'm not talking about the uninhabited one. I mean the Ballmers. They were out of town visiting relatives. Why not go there instead and break in and steal stuff, and avoid having to murder four people? And why did he pick that neighborhood of all places? It was a long way from where he lived."

"It was also isolated."

"I don't think that's a good enough reason."

"The guy who lived there was a banker. Maybe in Hawkins's mind that meant there would be valuable stuff to steal."

"I think that's a stretch. By no means was that the rich part of town. If you're a burglar, you don't go to skid row to do your business. You go where the money is."

"Well, rich people have security systems and extra locks and gates and sometimes private guards too. An area like where the Richardses lived might be more vulnerable."

He shook his head. "It doesn't make sense, Alex. Something is off."

"So despite your previous skepticism, now you're saying that you believe Hawkins to be innocent?"

"No, I'm just trying to get to the truth." He rose. "I'm going to check on the police files. You want some vending machine coffee? It sucks, but it's hot."

"Sure."

Decker walked out and down the hall. Two cops and one detective he'd worked with greeted him as he passed by. They didn't look happy to see him here, and he could understand why. Word had gotten around. If Hawkins had been wrongly convicted, it would be a slap in the face to the whole department.

It'll be a punch in the gut to me. My first real homicide. Did I want it too bad? And did I screw over Meryl Hawkins to get there?

He was so preoccupied with his thoughts that he almost bumped into her.

Sally Brimmer hadn't changed very much. Early thirties, pretty, efficient-looking. And as he had thought before, the woman's slacks were still a little too tight and too many buttons on her

blouse were undone, exhibiting enough cleavage to be intentionally suggestive. She was in public affairs at the police department.
Decker had scammed her once, pretending to be an attorney to
get a look-see at a prisoner being held here. That had placed her in
a bad light with Captain Miller, among others. Decker had taken
full responsibility for what he'd done and tried to make sure she
was held blameless. However, by the put-out look on her face at
seeing him, his actions had not been enough to soothe her harsh
feelings for him.

"Ms. Brimmer," said Decker amiably.

Her hands were on her slim hips and a pouty look was perched
on her lips. "I heard you were back. I hoped it was just a rumor
that would turn out not to be true."

"Uh, okay. Nice to see you too."

"What are you doing here?"

"Working a case. And I need some department files. I thought
I'd have them by now."

"You don't even work here anymore."

"I'm working with Mary Lancaster on a case. Captain Miller
authorized it."

"You're not bullshitting me again," she said defiantly.

"Actually, it's the truth."

"Right. Fool me once..."

"Agent Decker, do you want these in the small conference
room?"

They looked over to see a young uniformed officer wheeling
a hand truck down the hall on which were stacked four large
storage boxes.

"Yeah, thanks. My partner's in there now. I'm just on a
coffee run."

Brimmer watched incredulously as the man headed down the
hall to the conference room.

"So you *weren't* bullshitting me. Which case?"

"Meryl Hawkins."

"Don't remember it."

"Way before your time."

"Wait a minute. Wasn't that the guy who was just murdered?"

"Yep."

"But that's a current case."

"It is. The reason he was murdered probably goes back to four homicides that took place about thirteen years ago."

"How do you know that?"

"Because I was one who investigated it."

"Four homicides? Who was the killer?"

"Well, that's the question, isn't it?"

He walked on in search of coffee and found it in the break room. Instead of vending machines, however, they had a Keurig. Times did change, and incremental progress was made. Decker prepared two coffees and was about to head back when his attention was caught by something on the TV that was bolted to the wall of the break room.

It was a local station and the weather report was just now coming on. The forecast was for late afternoon storms.

As soon as Decker heard that, something clicked in his head.

Rain.

CHAPTER

10

"WHAT ARE WE DOING HERE, Decker?" asked Jamison. "You never said." She added under her breath, "As usual."

Decker didn't appear to have heard her. He was staring at various spots in the living room of the Richardses' old home, particularly the floor. In his mind he dialed back to that night and laid what was there on top of what he was seeing right now.

And they tallied pretty much exactly.

"Rain."

"What?" said Jamison, looking confused.

"It rained the night of the murders at the Richardses' home. Bucketed down. Started at around six-fifteen and continued until after Lancaster and I got there. It was a whopper of a storm. Lots of thunder and lightning."

"Yeah, his lawyer mentioned that. So what?"

Decker pointed to the floor. "There were no wet footprints inside the house other than those of the first responders. No traces of mud or gravel. And Mary and I and the techs put on booties."

"So how could the killer, who clearly came after the rain was pouring down, have not left any wet marks on the floor or carpet?" She paused. "Wait a minute, you didn't think of this until now?"

Decker's eyes kept roaming the room.

"Decker, I asked you…"

"I *know* what you asked, Alex," he said heatedly.

She stiffened at his harsh words.

Not meeting her gaze, Decker said, "I found the print and

the blood trace on the wall switch in the living room. It's where someone would put their hand if they were going to hit the light. We had the tech lift it. We ran the print through the databases and Hawkins's name got kicked out."

"Why was he in the system? Finger's files didn't say. You said he'd never been in trouble with the law before."

"His old job was with a company connected to a defense contractor. He'd had to pass a background check and have his prints on file because of his employment there."

"So from that point on?"

"Hawkins was our prime—well, really only—suspect."

"How long did all that take?"

"We got the ID on the print around one in the morning. We immediately went looking for Hawkins after getting his address. He wasn't home when we got there. But his wife and daughter were. They had no idea where he was."

"Where did you find him?"

"We put out a BOLO and a patrol car spotted him a couple hours later walking down a street over on the east side of town. They arrested him and brought him in to the station on suspicion of murder. Lancaster and I met him there."

"Walking? Didn't he have a car?"

"An old clunker. It was parked on the street in front of his house when we got there looking for him. We confirmed later it was the only car they owned. With the rain and cold temperatures, when we arrived, we couldn't tell if it had been driven recently or not. Although by the time we got there, it would have been hours after the murders were committed. The engine wouldn't have been warm anyway. But we later checked with neighbors and they told us the car had been there all day and night. Even so, we did check the car's exterior and tires for any trace from the Richardses' house, but if he had driven it back there after the murders the heavy rain would have washed anything like that away. We didn't have a warrant, so the interior of their house was going to have to wait to be searched."

"So what was Hawkins's story?"

In Decker's mind, he and Lancaster walked into the same inter-rogation room where they had interviewed Susan Richards. Same mustard yellow walls. Same sort of person sitting in that chair. The accused. A hunted animal looking for a way out.

"He knew his rights. He wanted a lawyer. We told him one was on the way, but that if he wanted to answer some questions, it would help us eliminate him as a suspect. But if he didn't, that was okay too. We needed to legally cover our butts."

"Did you tell him you had his print at the crime scene?"

"We were holding that back as a trap. We'd gotten search warrants by then, so another team was tearing his house and car apart looking for any trace, and the gun used in the murder. As you know, they later found it behind a wall in his closet."

"Meaning he had to go back home and hide it. And his wife and daughter didn't know about this how?"

"Lisa Hawkins was really sick, of course, and slept in another bedroom. The daughter, Mitzi, answered the door basically in her underwear. She looked like crap. High as a kite on something. She could tell us nothing. We had to go to Mrs. Hawkins's bedroom to see her. She couldn't even get out of bed. She was basically in in-home hospice."

"Damn," said Jamison. "Last thing she needed was for this to drop in her lap."

"She was really upset. Wanted to know what was going on. But she was making no sense, and I'm not sure she could even process what we were telling her. And her stoned daughter couldn't either. Between the two of them, Hawkins could have driven his car through the front of the house and I don't think they'd have noticed."

"Did Hawkins answer any questions?"

"The uniforms told him what he was charged with when they arrested him. But no other details. I told him basically what had gone down."

"What was his reaction?"

Now Decker's mind fully engaged with the memory. He was no longer in the Richardses' old home. He was in the interrogation room with the younger Lancaster sitting next to him and the still living Hawkins across from him. The man was tall and lean, but strongly built, before the cancer came to tear him down. His face was ruggedly handsome, and Decker remembered his hands being strong-looking and heavily callused. They could have easily strangled the life out of a young girl.

* * *

"Mr. Hawkins, while we're waiting for your PD to be assigned, can you clear up a few points for us?" said Decker. "It would be a big help, but you have the right to refuse to answer, just to be clear."

Hawkins settled his arms over his chest and said, "Like what?"

"Like where were you tonight between seven and nine-thirty or so?"

Hawkins scratched his cheek. "Taking a walk. Been walking all night. Was doing that when your boys picked me up. No law against walking."

"In the pouring rain?"

Hawkins touched his wet clothes. "And here's the proof. When they picked me up, that's what I was doing. Honest to God."

"Where were you walking?"

"All over. Had to think."

"What about?"

"None of your beeswax." He paused. "And, hold on, they never told me who was killed."

Lancaster told him who and where.

"Hell, I don't know those people."

Decker said casually, "So you've never been to that house?"

"Never. No reason to."

"You see anybody on your walk who can corroborate your story?"

"Nope. It was raining. Nobody was dumb enough to be outside, except me."

"You ever been to the American Grill on Franklin Street?" asked Lancaster.

"I don't eat out much. Can't afford it."

"You ever run into the owner?"

"And who's that?"

"David Katz."

"Never hearda him."

Lancaster described him.

"Nope, doesn't ring a bell with me."

A far slimmer Ken Finger, Hawkins's court-appointed attorney, arrived just then, and Hawkins was compelled to open his mouth and provide a court-ordered cheek swab of his DNA.

Hawkins asked Decker what he was going to do with that sample.

"None of your beeswax," Decker replied.

✻ ✻ ✻

Decker looked at Jamison after describing this back-and-forth to her. "And later that morning, the search team found the gun hidden behind a loose section of wall in Hawkins's closet. Ballistics matched the bullets taken out at the postmortem."

"And the DNA from the cheek swab?"

"It took a while to get the results back, but they matched the trace under Abigail Richards's fingernails.

"Case closed at that point."

"Apparently."

Decker looked at the floor again. "Except for no traces from the rain."

"He could have had another pair of shoes and socks with him. He could have taken off his shoes and left them outside. And changed into the dry shoes."

Decker shook his head. "No."

"Why not?"

"Look at the porch."

Jamison stepped to the window and looked at the small-roofed porch with open sides.

Decker said, "Mary and I got soaked going in, and that porch offered almost no protection. And I don't see Hawkins having the foresight to bring an extra pair of shoes and socks. And how could

he take the time to stop and change out of his shoes before breaking into a house with a bunch of people in it? Anybody could have
looked out the front door or window and seen him. And hell, he'd
have to have brought another set of clothes and a hair dryer before
he set foot inside. Otherwise, there would have been traces."

"Is there another way into the house that he could have used?"

"None that wouldn't leave us with the same problem as now."

"He could have cleaned up his wet traces on his way out."

"After murdering four people he's going to take the time to do
that? And from all the different places he had to be in the house
to kill them all? And there's carpet too, so he's going to what, get
out a steam cleaner and fire it up and get rid of every single bit of
mud, wet gravel, soaked blades of grass?"

"But, Decker, you know the alternative if that is the case."

Decker glanced over at her. "Yeah, that Hawkins was right, and
I was wrong. He was innocent. And I put him away in prison.
And now he's dead."

"That wasn't your fault."

"The hell it isn't," said Decker.

11

THERE WAS NO PLACE on earth colder than a morgue.

At least Decker was thinking that as he looked down at the body of Meryl Hawkins on the metal table. The ME had drawn back the sheet so that Hawkins's emaciated body was completely exposed. On one side of Decker stood Jamison. On the other was Lancaster.

The ME said, "As I noted, the cause of death was a small-caliber soft-nosed or dumdum bullet. It deformed after cleaving through the skull and then cartwheeled through the soft tissue, breaking up more as it did so, just as it's designed to do." He pointed to the man's brain that was sitting on another table. "You can see that it did considerable damage. Hawkins would have died instantly. Round was still in the soft tissue. In fragments. That's why I can't give you a more exact answer as to caliber."

"And no way to do a ballistics comparison if we do find a gun to test?" said Lancaster.

"Afraid not. As I said, it's just metal slivers and chunks dispersed over a wide area of the brain. Like a bomb exploded. Really no spiral lands or grooves from the gun barrel left to match it to, unfortunately." He added, "There were also traces of polyurethane foam and microbeads embedded in the wound and brain tissue."

"What?" said Jamison, looking puzzled.

Decker said, "The killer used a pillow to muffle the shot."

"Cheap version of a muzzle suppressor," added Lancaster. "The burn marks on his forehead would have been even more pronounced if the killer hadn't used the pillow. It was pretty close to a contact wound."

"They must've cleaned up the trace and taken the pillow with them," said Decker. "There was no sign of it in the room."

Decker pointed to the man's forearms. "They're healed now, of course, but that's where the scratches were, presumably from Abigail Richards trying to fight him off."

Lancaster added, "After he was arrested and jailed, we noted the wounds on his arms. Hawkins said he'd fallen down and scraped both arms. He'd cleaned them up and bandaged them before he was arrested. If any of Abigail Richards's DNA was on him, that probably would've removed it. In fact, we found none. But we did find his DNA on her."

Jamison said, "And that seems to be rock-solid evidence of his guilt. I mean, he was there. She tried to fight him off. He was good for the murders."

"Yeah," said Decker. "And all we have against that is a guy who said he was innocent and now he's dead."

Lancaster said, "Do you think it could be that Hawkins *did* commit the murders but wasn't alone? He had an accomplice and now that accomplice killed him before he could reveal his identity?"

"He's had thirteen years to do that," pointed out Decker. "And you'd think Hawkins would have fingered an accomplice at his trial, if for no other reason than to cut a deal. And there's something else." He told Lancaster about his rain theory. He added, "Rain residue and other trace from the storm should have been found at the crime scene but wasn't."

Lancaster seemed taken aback by this. "I...I never focused on that."

"Neither did I, until now."

"Crap, Decker."

"Yeah."

"What's that on his forearm?" asked Jamison.

The ME, a short, balding man in his fifties, pulled an overhead lamp on a long flex arm closer and turned it on, hitting that spot.

"Yes, I noted that," he said. "Let's take a closer look."

The marks on Hawkins's arm were black and dark green and

brown. A casual observer might have concluded that they were bruises. Only they weren't. Closer inspection under the intense light revealed clearly what they were.

"It's a tattoo," said Decker. "Or several tattoos."

"That's what I concluded too," said the ME. "But poorly done ones. I mean, my daughter has one and it's far nicer than these."

Decker opined, "That's because these were done in prison with very crude instruments and whatever they could find to use as ink."

"How do you know it wasn't done before he went to prison?" asked Jamison.

"Because I saw his forearms thirteen years ago. Several times. No tats." Decker leaned down and looked at the marks from a few inches away. "Looks like they used paper clips or maybe staples. That tat looks like they used soot mixed with shampoo for the ink. The other two seem to be Styrofoam that's been melted. Those are pretty popular choices for inmate tats."

"Didn't know you were such an expert on prison tattoos," said Jamison.

"Decker and I have visited our share of prisons over the years," noted Lancaster. "Seen a lot of convict skin with body art. Some cool, some hideous."

Decker was still looking at the tat. "It's a spiderweb."

"Trapped," said Lancaster.

"What?" asked Jamison.

"Symbolizes being trapped in prison," explained Decker. "It's referring to their prison sentence."

"That looks like a teardrop," observed Jamison, pointing to the mark near the crook of the elbow.

Decker nodded. "Right, it is."

"What does that mean?"

Lancaster and Decker exchanged a glance. He said in a subdued tone, "Sometimes, it denotes that the person has been raped in prison. Usually it's inked on the face, where everyone can see it."

"Damn," said Jamison.

Decker closed his eyes and felt sick to his stomach.

And I helped put you there because maybe I didn't do a thorough enough investigation.

Jamison was watching Decker and put a hand on his arm. His eyes popped open and he abruptly moved away from her. He didn't notice her hurt look at his reaction.

Lancaster examined the last mark that was to the right of the teardrop. "I've never seen one like that before, though," she said.

"Looks like a star with an arrow going through it," said Jamison. She looked at Decker. "Any ideas?"

"Not yet," he replied. He looked at the ME. "How far along was his cancer?"

The ME shuddered. "Advanced. If the bullet didn't get him, my guess is he had a few weeks left. Actually, I'm surprised he was still able to function."

"He said he was on street meds," said Jamison.

"The tox screens will show what was in his system. He had nothing in his stomach, no food or anything, I mean. I would imagine his appetite would have been negligible at that point. But he must have been a strong man to keep going with that level of cancer in him."

Decker said, "Well, maybe wanting to prove his innocence gave him that strength."

"Anything else of interest?" asked Lancaster.

"We've got his clothes over there in those evidence bags."

Lancaster looked at Decker. "He also had a small duffel. We've got it at the station. Nothing much in it, but you'll probably want to go through it."

Decker nodded as he continued to stare down at the body.

Three tats. The spiderweb looked to be the oldest. That made sense. When Hawkins had first got to prison, he was probably pissed beyond belief, if he was indeed innocent. The web tat would have been one of his few ways to vocalize that anger. The teardrop tat probably came soon thereafter. Fresh meat in prisons did not remain fresh for long.

Then there was the unidentified one. Star with an arrow through it. He would have to find out what that one meant. Because that one looked to be the most recent. Decker could tell because Hawkins had recently lost weight, probably because of his illness. The other two tats showed signs of his shrinking weight, and the corresponding change in the width of his forearm. The star, though, evinced no signs of this. And the markings looked fresher too. He might have had it done right before he left prison, in fact.

And if he'd had this tat put on close to when he was released it might have held some significance for him at that time.

And since Decker had missed there being no muddy footprints in the house, he was determined to not miss anything else on this case.

Homicide detectives rarely got do-overs. He wasn't going to screw this one up.

Again.

12

IT WASN'T MUCH.

Decker was at police headquarters staring at it. The duffel held a few items of clothing. A bus ticket for Hawkins's ride from prison. A wallet with some cash. Some paperwork from the prison that Hawkins had drawn graffiti over.

There was a dog-eared paperback book by a writer Decker had never heard of. It had a garish cover of a man holding a knife against a scantily clad woman's throat. It was straight out of a Mickey Spillane yarn from the 1950s, he thought.

There was also a photo in the wallet of Hawkins's daughter, Mitzi.

Her last name was now Gardiner, Lancaster had found out. She lived in Trammel, Ohio, about a two-hour car ride from Burlington. She'd been in her late twenties when her father went to prison. Lancaster had also learned that she was now married and the mother of a six-year-old boy.

The picture of Mitzi was from when she'd been in elementary school. Decker knew it was her because Hawkins had written his daughter's name and age on the back of the photo. And Hawkins had written there, "Daddy's Little Star." That might be the reason Hawkins had the star tat on his arm. The photo obviously represented far happier times for the Hawkins family. Mitzi looked bright and innocent, all cheeks and smiles, as kids did at that age.

And then the dream had shattered. She had grown up to be a drug addict and petty criminal to finance her habit. She'd done short stints in jail, and longer ones in rehab. The little girl with the limitless future was no more.

Yet apparently she had finally gotten her life together.

Good for you, thought Decker. But he also knew that he would have to talk to her. Her father might have gotten in touch with her after being released from prison.

Lancaster walked in and looked at the pile of items on the table. "Nothing?"

Decker shook his head. "Got a question."

"Okay."

Lancaster sat down and popped a stick of gum into her mouth.

"Stick to the gum and quit the smokes," advised Decker.

Her lips pursed. "Thanks *Dr.* Decker. So what's your question?"

"Who called it in?"

"What?"

"Who called in the disturbance at the Richardses' house that night?"

"You know we never found out the answer to that."

"Well, I think we need to find it out now."

"How?" she said incredulously. "It's been too long."

"At the time, I read the transcript of the call and listened to the recording as well. The caller was a female. She said she'd heard a disturbance at the house. The cops were sent out and arrived shortly thereafter. Then so did we once the homicides were confirmed."

"That we know."

"But how did the caller know there was a disturbance? The call didn't come from the landlines at the neighboring homes. It didn't come from any traceable cell phone. So where?"

"I guess we weren't too focused on that. We just thought it was a Good Samaritan passing by."

"A *convenient* Samaritan, anyway. And one who is passing by in a monsoon down a dead-end road? Why go down there unless you lived there?"

Lancaster thought about this for a few moments. "And then once we got there all signs pointed to Hawkins once you found the print."

Decker nodded because he knew this was true. And it was grating on him beyond belief.

"Okay," he said. "We need to go over this case from square one. No predisposition that Hawkins was good for it. Fresh eyes, wide open."

"Decker, it's been over thirteen years."

"I don't care if it's been thirteen hundred years, Mary," he snapped. "We need to make this right."

She studied him for a long moment. "You're never going to get over it, are you?"

"Don't know what you're talking about."

"Yes you do."

Decker stared at her moodily. "I need you one hundred percent on this."

"Okay, Decker, but please keep in mind that I've got a slew of other cases to work on, not just Hawkins's murder."

Decker scowled. "This has to be your priority, Mary. If the guy really didn't do it, we screwed his life up, sent him to prison where it looks like he was raped, and then let somebody murder him."

"We didn't *let* anyone murder him," she retorted.

"We might as well have," Decker shot back.

"Problem?"

They both looked over at Jamison standing in the doorway.

Lancaster finally drew her gaze from Decker. "Just two former partners having a discussion." She turned back to Decker. "I'm sorry, Amos. I will work this case as much as I can with you. But my plate is pretty damn full."

"What about your saying it was good working together, like old times?"

"We don't live in old times. We live in the present." She paused and added, "At least I do, because I don't have a choice."

Decker gazed at her stonily.

Jamison said, "Decker, have you heard back from Bogart?"

"He still hasn't called you?"

"No. But he's good with us staying here and working on the case?"

"No, he's not. So you better pack up and head back to D.C."

"When did you hear that?"

Decker didn't answer.

"Decker?"

"A while back."

"And you didn't think to mention it?"

"I'm mentioning it now. I'll see you back in D.C. at some point."

"But you mean you're staying? Decker, you can't."

"Watch me."

He stalked out.

Jamison looked down at Lancaster, who sat in the chair still slowly chewing her gum.

"What the hell is going on with him?" Jamison said. "If he disobeys orders he's going to blow up his career at the Bureau."

Lancaster stood. "Amos Decker has always had priorities. But his 'career' has never been one of them."

"I know, he just wants to find the truth. He always says that."

Lancaster glanced toward the door. "I actually think he just wants to find some peace. And all of this"—she paused and looked around the room—"all this is just how he survives with more guilt on his shoulders than any person has a right to bear. And what happened to Meryl Hawkins just added a shitload more, because he obviously blames himself for what happened. It's just how he's wired. God, I wish I'd never told Hawkins where Decker was." She touched Jamison on the shoulder. "It was good to see you, Alex."

Lancaster followed Decker out, leaving Jamison alone.

13

Decker sat on a red park bench in the town of his birth.

Burlington, Ohio, warts and all.

It had been crushed when most of the factories closed up decades before. Then it had made a comeback of sorts. Then the recession had come and knocked it down again.

Now it was slowly coming back.

He wondered when the next knockdown would come. It always seemed to.

Jamison had sent him a half dozen texts after she'd left town, and he'd ignored them all. Part of him felt bad about this. None of this was about Jamison. This was all about Amos Decker, he knew.

You're never going to get over it, are you?

Lancaster's words had ripped into him like that round into Hawkins's brain.

You never are going to get over their deaths, are you, Amos? How can you? It was your fault.

He had sat on this bench before, just as now, when fall was speedily giving over to winter in the Ohio Valley. Back then he'd been making a feeble living as a private investigator. He'd been sitting here awaiting a man and a woman who were headed toward a cocktail lounge that was no longer in business. He had been paid by the woman's wealthy father to convince the con artist creep who had won her heart to leave town. He had been successful. It wasn't that hard, since the man thought himself far smarter and slicker than he actually was. He never counted on running into Amos Decker, who finished him off in a few easy moves of chess play.

While waiting for the couple he had observed those moving around him, making deductions and grafting them onto his memory. He used to refer to his memory as his personal, wired-in DVR. Now he had updated the term to fit modern times.

I have a personal cloud in my head where all my data is kept safe and secure until I want to pull it out.

Two young men walked past arguing about something. Decker noted the clenched hand of the one on the left, in which years ago there would have been five-dollar bags of crack. Now he suspected the dude had some opioid pills that he was trying to sell. The dude on the right was arguing price, no doubt. In his hand was a fistful of Jacksons, in his back pocket a snort bottle of Narcan. In the event of overdose, which was pretty much inevitable, users were bringing their "back to life" medication with them so that a passerby could stick it up their nose and give it a squirt. Thus they would live another day to die once more.

Such was life in the twenty-first century.

He floated this image up to his personal cloud and went in search of others.

He found it in a woman pulling into a parking space on the street in front of what used to be a service station and was now a CrossFit facility. She climbed out dressed in tight workout clothes and slung a bag over her shoulder, her face glued to her smartphone screen and with ear buds in. He looked over her car. The parking permit on her front bumper identified where she lived, for any potential bad guy to see and follow.

He wanted to tell her to find another way to do the parking thing, and not to be so oblivious about her surroundings while she eagerly examined her critically important social media happenings. But he figured she'd just call the cops on him for harassing her.

This scene was dutifully uploaded to his cloud for no apparent reason other than it always went there.

Last shot. An elderly couple walked by, hand in hand. He looked a bit younger than she, perhaps in his early eighties. Her hand was trembling, and she had a tremor along one side of her face. The other side drooped. Either Bell's palsy or she'd previously suffered a stroke. The man had hearing aids in both ears and what looked to be a melanoma growing on his nose. And yet they shuffled slowly along together. Growing old, nearing the end, and still in love. That was the way it was supposed to work.

Decker tried but failed to *not* upload that to his cloud. But he did try to stick it in a particularly remote part of his memory.

So, with Jamison gone, he was alone again. In some ways, he preferred it. He had been on his own after his family had been taken from him. And he had survived.

Maybe it was for the best. Maybe he was destined for a solitary existence. It just felt more comfortable.

He shifted his sole focus to the problem at hand.

Meryl Hawkins. Decker had approximately one million questions and not nearly that many answers. In fact, he had none at all. But he was not parked on this bench merely for his health, or for the sake of nostalgia.

He had spoken to one widow, Susan Richards. Now he was awaiting another.

Rachel Katz walked down the pavement a few minutes later. She and David Katz had never had any children. She lived alone in a condo downtown. It was a luxury loft in an old factory building. Decker had learned that she still worked as a CPA and had her own practice. And she still owned the American Grill. Her office was a five-minute walk from her loft.

Several years younger than her late husband, she was now forty-four. A striking-looking woman when Decker had first met her all those years ago, she had aged exceptionally well. Her blonde hair was still long and skimmed her shoulders. She was tall and fit, with a swagger to her walk. She moved like she owned the world—or at least Burlington, Ohio.

She was dressed in a black jacket with a white cuffed shirt underneath and a long skirt. Her choice of lipstick was flaming red, her fingernails the same shade. The briefcase she carried lightly smacked against her thigh as she walked.

A couple of construction workers catcalled out to her as she passed by. Katz ignored them.

Decker heaved himself off the bench and went to work.

Just like old times.

14

SHE LOOKED UP AT HIM, recognition flitting across her features as he stopped her on the sidewalk.

"I remember you."

"Amos Decker. I investigated the death of your husband when I worked on the Burlington police force."

"That's right." She frowned. "And I heard on the news that the man who killed him came back to town. And that he was found murdered."

"That's right. Meryl Hawkins."

She shuddered. "Well, I can't say that I was sorry. But I thought he was in prison for life. What was he doing here? The news didn't say."

"They let him out because he was terminally ill with cancer."

She had no reaction to this. "And what are you doing here?" she asked.

"I just have some questions for you."

"Do you still work for the police? I thought I heard that you left town."

"I work for the FBI now. But I'm still a sworn officer in Ohio." He showed her his official credentials.

"And what exactly are you investigating?"

"Hawkins's murder. And that of your husband and the other victims at the Richardses' that night."

She shook her head, looking confused. "We *know* who killed my husband and the Richards family. Meryl Hawkins."

"We're taking another look at it."

"Why?"

"There are some anomalies we need to sort out."

"What sort of anomalies?"

"Do you want to go somewhere to discuss this rather than out on the street? Or we can go down to the police station."

She looked around at several passersby staring at them. "My condo is right over here."

He followed her into the building, which had a concierge, and they rode up in an elevator to her floor.

"Didn't know they had places like this in Burlington," noted Decker as they walked down the plush corridor. "At least they didn't when I lived here."

"We just completed this a year ago. I'm actually involved with the development company that renovated this building. We're working on two others. And I'm also working with another group in several new projects around town and a slew of businesses, including some restaurants. We have big plans for Burlington."

"Economy finally turning around?"

"Seems to be. We hope to get several large companies to come here. We're really rolling out the red carpet. Two Fortune 1000s have already started building regional headquarters in the area. And a high-tech start-up just opened its headquarters downtown, which brought in a lot of young, affluent people. It's a lot cheaper to live here than in, say, Chicago. And we enticed a hospital system to build a new facility. And we're well along to getting a parts supplier to the Big Three in Detroit to build a new factory on the north side of town. Those people have to live, shop, and eat out somewhere. New restaurants and places to live downtown are already popping up, in addition to what I'm working on. So, yes, things *are* looking up."

"Great."

They entered her condo, which had an open floor plan and lots of twenty-foot windows. Decker watched as Katz used a remote to open the shades to let in the fading light.

"Beautiful place," he observed, looking at all the expensive architectural details, like exposed beams and repointed brick walls, slate floors, high-dollar appliances in the kitchen, and oil and acrylic paintings on the wall. The furniture was big enough not to be overwhelmed by the large footprint, with several comfortable seating areas laid out.

"It was featured in *Luxe*," she said. "That's a design magazine," she added when Decker looked blankly at her. "Targeted to the very affluent." She paused. "Sorry if that sounded snooty."

"No problem. I'm just not very knowledgeable about that stuff. And I've never been affluent."

"Well, I wasn't born with a silver spoon. And being a CPA, I work about a hundred hours a week."

"You must have gotten off early today, then. It's not yet five. I was expecting to be waiting longer before I saw you coming home."

"This is just a little break for me. I head back to the office in a couple hours for a client meeting. And then I have an event later tonight. I was hoping to catch up on a few domestic chores right now, so if we could get down to what you wanted?"

She sat down on a couch and motioned for Decker to sit in a chair opposite.

"So what anomalies were you referring to?"

"I can't get into specifics because it's an ongoing investigation. I can tell you that Meryl Hawkins came back to town to ask the police to reopen the investigation."

"Reopen it. Why?"

"Because he said he was innocent."

Katz's features turned ugly. "So you're taking the word of a murderer to reopen the investigation? Are you kidding me?"

"No, not just that. There are the anomalies I mentioned."

"And that you won't specify. So what do you want with me?" she said abruptly.

"Can you tell me why your husband was there that night?"

"Good God, I already testified to this."

"It would just take a minute. And you might remember something you hadn't before."

Katz let out a long, annoyed sigh and crossed her arms and legs. "It was a long time ago."

"Just whatever you can remember," prompted Decker.

"Don Richards was the loan officer at the bank, so David knew him. He'd been instrumental in getting the loan for the American Grill construction. My husband was very ambitious. That was one trait that drew me to him. He wanted to make a lot of money and also do things to help bolster the community. I appreciated that."

"When did you two meet?"

"Shortly after the Grill opened." She got a far-off look on her face and smiled. "We were set up on a blind date, of all things. We were both so busy, it was hard to find time to meet people. We hit it off right away and were married six months later."

"And as you said, you still own the American Grill?"

"Yes. It was in both my and David's names. It passed to me after Hawkins *murdered* him."

"Has it been profitable for you?"

"We've had good and bad years. Right now it's doing okay."

"So, as far as you know, your husband was just there that night to shoot the breeze with Don Richards? Or was it about business?"

"I don't know. I told you that before. I didn't even know he was going over there that night. They might have been talking about some business projects, because David had several things going on at that time, and Don was his main contact at the bank. But I don't know why he would have done that at Don's home." She added icily, "As you know, David never came home alive, so he couldn't tell me what they discussed. I thought we'd be together for life. Turned out it was only for a short time."

"Had your husband become friends with Mr. Richards? Did you and his wife hang out with each other?"

"No, nothing like that. They had kids. We didn't. And they were older. And David and I were working all the time. We didn't have time for friends, really."

"And you were *working* that night, correct?"

"I'd just started my own CPA firm. I was burning the proverbial midnight oil." She frowned. "Until I got the call from the police. I couldn't believe it. I thought it was some awful prank." She paused and glanced up at Decker. "I had to identify his body. Have you ever had to do that? ID the body of someone you loved?"

"I'm sure it was very hard," Decker replied quietly.

She suddenly gazed hard at him. "Wait a minute. Oh my God, that happened to you. Your family. I remember now. It was all over the news."

"Doesn't matter," said Decker. "Your husband's wallet and wristwatch were missing. And a gold ring with encrusted diamonds he wore."

She nodded. "I gave that ring to him. For what turned out to be his *last* birthday," she added coldly.

"Anything else you can remember that might help me?"

"I don't want to help you," she said candidly. "Because Meryl Hawkins killed my husband. We were going to have a family. We were going places. We talked about moving to Chicago. I mean, a place like Burlington can only take you so far."

"Then why are you still here?" asked Decker just as bluntly.

"I...My husband is buried here."

Decker's features softened. "I can understand that."

She stood. "I really need to get going, so if there's nothing else?"

Decker rose from his chair. "Thank you for your time."

"I'm not going to wish you luck. And I'm glad that Hawkins is dead."

"One more question. Can you tell me where you were between eleven and midnight on the night Meryl Hawkins was murdered?"

She blanched. "Do you really believe I had anything to do with his murder?"

"I don't know. It's why I'm asking. But if you have an alibi, it would be good to get it out there. The police are going to ask you for one."

"Why?"

"Because he was back in town and you believe he killed your husband. If it makes you feel any better, we asked Susan Richards the same thing."

"And did *she* have an alibi?"

Decker didn't answer.

"When was it again?" she asked, evidently upset.

He told her.

She stood there rocking back and forth. "I'll have to check my schedule and see what I can find. I'm so busy I have a hard time remembering what I was doing an hour ago."

As he headed to the door, she called out after him.

"Why are you really doing this?"

He turned back, his hand on the doorknob. "There're enough guilty people in the world without us making an innocent person one."

"Do you really think Hawkins was innocent?" she said skeptically.

"That's what I'm going to find out."

"You sound confident. But it's been a long time. Memories fade."

"I don't have that problem," said Decker.

15

He finally answered the phone. He really had no choice. It had now been a while since she'd left town.

"Hello, Alex."

"Well, it's about damn time," she barked.

"I've been busy."

"So have I. The team's leaving to go work on a case in New Hampshire. Plane takes off in an hour."

"Good luck on it."

"Bogart is not happy."

"I'm sure he has every right to be pissed at me."

"You're just placating me. I was calling to see if you wanted to join us in New Hampshire. I checked on flights. There's one you can catch out of Cleveland, with a layover in Newark."

"I can't do that, Alex. I'm working the case here."

"Well, get in good with your old friends at the police force there. I'm not sure you'll have a job at the FBI when you get back."

"I guess I can understand that."

"Nobody wants that, Amos. I hope you know that."

"I do."

"Good luck, with *everything* you're doing up there."

She clicked off and Decker put down his phone and stared at it for a long moment. He was suddenly hungry. And he knew exactly where he wanted to eat.

* * *

The place was only about a quarter full when he got there, even though it was the dinner hour. He had noticed some new eateries that had opened up on his walk over here. Maybe they were taking business away from the American Grill.

He was shown to a table and sat down. He glanced at his menu and then scanned the interior.

Waiters and waitresses were making the rounds of the tables. Other wait staff stood against the wall conversing.

His gaze passed one table and then came back to it, his attention suddenly riveted on the couple sitting there. It was Earl Lancaster, Mary's husband. He was there with a woman, only it wasn't his wife. Earl had started out as a construction laborer before becoming a contractor. He had the build of a man who used his muscle for a living. He was about six feet tall, with a Marine buzz cut, thick arms, and a broad chest. He was dressed in an untucked white long-sleeved shirt and dress jeans. A pair of black loafers were on his feet. His companion was in her early forties with a slim build, long, soft brown hair, green eyes, and a pleasant smile as she peered lovingly into Earl's face.

Earl broke off looking at her, gazed around the restaurant, and flinched when he saw Decker staring at him. He said something to the woman, jumped up, and headed over to Decker's table. Decker noted that the woman watched him the whole way.

Earl sat down across from Decker.

"Amos, I heard you were in town. Mary told me."

"Is that right?" said Decker, letting his gaze linger for a moment longer on the woman before looking at Earl.

The man seemed embarrassed. He put his hands together on the tabletop and stared down at them.

"Guess you're wondering what's going on."

"I am, but it's also none of my business."

"Fact is, Mary and I are splitting up."

"Really?" said Decker. "I'm sorry to hear that. And who's your friend over there?"

Earl glanced up. "I know what you're thinking."

"I doubt it."

"Mary initiated this whole thing, Amos. It wasn't my idea. But I have a life to live."

"What about Sandy?"

"We're splitting custody, but I'll have her more. Mary's schedule is too crazy."

"And she's okay with that?"

"She suggested it."

"What's going on with her? Why the divorce? Why letting you get Sandy? This isn't making sense."

Earl looked uncomfortable. "She's a cop. She's got… It's a lot of pressure."

"Do you want to get divorced, Earl?"

"I don't have a choice, do I? It's not like I can stop her."

Decker glanced at the woman again. She smiled, but when he didn't return it, she abruptly looked away.

"Well, regardless, I think *you've* already made your choice."

Earl's features turned angry. "I don't need to be judged by you, okay?"

"I'm not judging anybody. I'm simply making an observation. If I'm wrong, tell me so and I'll say I'm sorry."

Earl's anger dissipated. "Look, it's true, Nancy and I are seeing each other. But Mary and I stopped… well, we stopped living really as husband and wife a while back. If you know what I mean. And I didn't start seeing her until Mary told me our marriage was over. I swear to God."

"I believe you. And how is Sandy taking it?"

"She doesn't really understand."

"I think she probably understands more than you think."

"We'll get by. We have to."

"No argument there. Hope everything works out for you. All of you," he added.

"I know why you're in town. Mary told me. The Hawkins case. You know one of the victims, David Katz, owned this place?"

Decker nodded. "And now his widow does. You know Rachel Katz?"

"Yeah, I know her. She's involved in lots of projects around town."

"She apparently has big plans for Burlington."

"Well, the town needs a shot of energy. Glad she's doing what she's doing."

"Okay," said Decker.

"I, uh, better be getting back. Good to see you, Amos."

"Yeah."

Earl retreated to his table, where Decker watched him and the woman named Nancy talking and snatching glances at him. He picked up his menu and waved the waitress over after he'd made his decision. She was in her thirties, tall and skinny. A young man was behind her. She introduced him as Daniel, a trainee. He looked to be in his twenties, with dark hair and sharply defined features. He smiled shyly and then watched the waitress, his order pad held out like hers.

When Decker ordered, she smiled and wrote it down. "That's a lot of food."

"Well, I'm a lot of guy," replied Decker.

Daniel laughed along with the waitress.

When his meal came, he ate it methodically, all the while looking around the restaurant. When Earl and his friend left, they did not look in his direction, for which Decker was glad. He was not adept at these moments. Things he could say before his brain injury were impossible to get out now, even if the underlying emotions were inside him. Or else he would blurt out the wrong thing and make everyone uncomfortable.

Mary divorcing. So that was the explanation for her odd behavior. He felt sorry for both Earl and her. Yet he felt sorriest of all for Sandy. He would like to talk to Mary about it but was afraid he would just botch it.

He finished his meal and ordered a cup of coffee. Whenever the door opened, a chilly wind leaked into the space. He would have to get a heavier coat if he was going to stay here much longer. He wasn't that far removed from the days when the only clothes he had were the ones he was wearing.

As he was drinking his coffee, a voice said, "Why do I think you're not really here for the food?"

Decker looked up to see Captain Miller standing next to his table. He was dressed in a suit, but his necktie was loosened. He might have just come from work.

He sat down across from Decker.

Decker said, "I saw Earl. And his lady friend, Nancy."

Miller slowly nodded. "Okay. Then you know."

"I know they're getting divorced. And I heard his side of things. Not Mary's."

"Then you need to ask Mary for her take, if you want to. I suggested that to you back at the police station. So, any startling revelations come to you about this restaurant since you were here last?"

"The coffee still sucks."

"Anything else?"

Decker looked around the mostly empty space.

"Why does Rachel Katz still own it?"

16

COCOON, THOUGHT DECKER.

At their meeting Rachel Katz had crossed her arms and legs before settling in to answer his more serious questions. People often cocooned like that when they were getting ready to lie, or at least be evasive. It was as though they were wrapping themselves in themselves, to keep everyone else out. It was an instinctual physical reaction with people, and even though it wasn't a foolproof indicator of someone lying, Decker had found it pretty accurate.

So, what was she lying or being evasive about?

He filed that query away since he had no way to answer it yet.

He was presently standing in front of the Richardses' old house. But he was looking at another house that was two homes over from the Richardses'. This was the only house that was still occupied by the people who had lived here when the murders occurred. Back then Decker had interviewed them and the other neighbors. Out of that he had gotten a big fat zero's worth of help. He hoped the second time was the charm, because Decker seriously doubted he would get a third bite at the apple.

"Mr. DeAngelo, do you remember me?"

Decker stared down at the short, balding, rotund man in his sixties who had opened the door at his knock. Though it was chilly outside he was dressed in a stained undershirt that emphasized his potbelly, and khaki pants with the zipper partially open. He had a cloth napkin in his hand and was wiping his mouth.

He looked quizzically at Decker before recognition breached his features.

"You're that detective. Pecker?"

"Decker. Amos Decker."

"Right, right."

Decker glanced at the napkin. "Looks like I interrupted your dinner."

"No, we were just finishing up. Come on in."

DeAngelo closed the door behind Decker, whose nostrils were immediately assailed with the mingled aromas of garlic and pesto.

"Smells good," he said as he glanced around the tidy interior.

"You want some? Ma made plenty. Always does." He playfully grabbed his belly. "Why I'm so fat."

"No, thanks. I already ate."

"Ma?" called out DeAngelo. "Look who's here."

A petite, gray-haired woman came out from the kitchen drying her hands on a dishtowel. She wore a full apron over her skirt and blouse.

"Mrs. DeAngelo, I'm Amos Decker. I used to work as a detective on the local police force."

"That's right. I remember." She looked him up and down. "Heard you moved."

"I did, but now I'm back. At least for a little while."

"Well, come in and sit, sit," said Mrs. DeAngelo. "Would you like some wine?"

"Sure, that'd be great. Thanks."

She brought the wine and poured out three glasses and they all sat in the small living room that held the exact same furniture as the last time Decker had been here.

"We're retired now," said DeAngelo. "Well, I am. Ma always took care of the kids and the house. Hell, worked harder than I ever did, taking care of them."

"Now I just have to look after you," said his wife with a knowing smile at Decker.

DeAngelo said, "We're thinking of selling the place. Kids are all grown and gone off with their own families. Maybe get a condo down in Florida. I can't take too many more Ohio winters. Gets into your bones."

"I hear you," said Decker.

The couple fell silent and looked at him, apparently waiting for him to explain what he was doing there. Decker felt this curious scrutiny while he sipped his wine.

"I suppose you heard about Meryl Hawkins?" he began.

DeAngelo nodded. "Strangest damn thing. Thought he was in prison for life. Then he's here and then he gets killed. Is that why you're back?"

"Sort of, yes."

"Are you looking for who killed him?" asked Mrs. DeAngelo anxiously.

"Yes, and I'm looking at something else too."

"What's that?" she asked.

"If Meryl Hawkins didn't kill your neighbors all those years ago, who did?"

The DeAngelos had both raised their wineglasses to take a sip. And both of them nearly spilled their drinks.

DeAngelo said, "I don't understand. That Hawkins fellow *did* kill them. That was proven."

"He was convicted of the murders, that's true," said Decker.

"But isn't that the same thing?" asked Mrs. DeAngelo.

"Usually yes," conceded Decker. "But not in all cases. I'm taking a fresh look at the case. You two are the only ones left who lived here when the killings took place."

DeAngelo nodded. "That's right. The Murphys moved to Georgia. And the Ballmers retired to, where was it again, hon?"

"Hilton Head."

"And the other house was empty," noted Decker.

"That's right. Been empty for a while. It's empty again, though a couple families have come and gone in between. There was a family moved into the Richards house, but they didn't stay all that long."

"Wouldn't catch me moving in there," said Mrs. DeAngelo. "I'd have nightmares all the time. I did anyway after what happened."

"So that night you reported you didn't hear or see anything," said Decker.

"That's right," replied DeAngelo. "Raining like crazy. Thunder and lightning, and the wind. Holy Jesus. I remember it clear as day. We were afraid we'd get a tornado."

"And yet you still managed to fall asleep in front of the TV," his wife reminded him. "We were watching some movie."

"*Blade Runner*," said Decker. "That's what you said."

"That's right," said DeAngelo, looking impressed. "You've got a good memory."

"So nothing you can remember from that night?"

Mrs. DeAngelo said, "Well, I saw that one car come in. Oh, it was before the storm. I was just finishing making dinner. Saw it pass by when I was looking out the window. I told you all that."

"That would be David Katz's car. A four-door Mercedes sedan. Silver."

"Yes, that's right. Beautiful car."

"Probably cost more than our house," commented DeAngelo.

"And you didn't see him get out of the car when he got to the Richardses'?"

"No. Where I was standing in the kitchen, my view is blocked by the house in between ours."

"And it was just you and your husband here that night?"

"Yes, our oldest was in college. Our two younger ones were out with friends."

"So, no other cars? No sounds from the Richardses'? I know you've been asked this before. But if you could think about it again."

"I didn't hear anything from the Richards house, no," said Mrs. DeAngelo.

Decker was about to move on to another question when something in her voice caught his attention. "What about one of the other houses?" he asked.

"Well, it was the empty one. Just to the left of us."

"So the one closest to the Richardses?"

"Yes. It had been abandoned for a long time. Sometimes you had teens over there doing things, drinking and smoking and—"

"Screwing," said DeAngelo.

"Anthony!" exclaimed his wife. "Language."

DeAngelo grinned and settled back in his recliner. "Well, they were."

"So it might have been the same that night?" said Decker. "Some teens over there? What exactly did you see or hear?"

"It was just a glimpse of movement, really." She rubbed her temples. "Oh, it was so long ago." She looked at her husband. "But I do think it was a teenager."

"Male or female?"

"Male. At least I think so. It really was just a glimpse."

"And do you remember what time that might have been?"

"Well, it was certainly after the storm had started. I was thinking to myself that they were getting soaked."

"But you don't have a certain time in mind?"

"No, I'm sorry."

Decker nodded. "Okay. I appreciate your making the effort."

He left them there and walked back outside. He didn't know what he could expect all this time later. Most witnesses couldn't remember what they saw yesterday, much less thirteen years ago. He walked over to the empty house to which Mrs. DeAngelo had just been referring.

He peered into one of the windows but couldn't see much. He tried the door. It was locked. He had no idea who even owned the house. Whoever did wasn't doing much with it.

He headed over to the Richardses' house and surveyed it.

David Katz had driven his car into the driveway and then past the front of the house and behind it, where he had pulled into a small grassy park-off situated there.

Decker looked back over his shoulder. From here it would have been impossible for DeAngelo to have seen him get out of the car and go into the house. The other neighbors had reported the same thing: They hadn't seen Katz go into the house where he would later die.

And yet it was indisputable that he had.

Decker looked down at the ground here. Katz's car's tires had sunk deeply into the ground, what with all the rain. He had driven in before the storm started, so there weren't really traces of his car tires coming onto the property. As Lancaster had earlier pointed out, the rain would have washed those away. But a car coming in *after* the rain had started should have left some traces. So had the killer walked here? In the driving rain? And left no traces of that inclemency when he had entered the house? It made no sense. But it had to, somehow, because it had happened.

His phone buzzed. It was Lancaster.

"I think we got a runner," she said. "We must've spooked her."

"*Her*? Who is it?"

"Susan Richards."

17

"Hold on, where's the FBI gal? I liked her."

Agatha Bates was staring up at Decker through the lenses of her thick glasses.

Mary Lancaster, who stood next to Decker in Bates's small living room, said, "She's on another assignment out of state. I'm working with Agent Decker now."

Bates nodded. "Well, so long as you got somebody to keep an eye on *him*. He's a strange one," she added, as though Decker couldn't hear her. "I think he's just too big for his own good, if you know what I mean."

Lancaster said to him, "I had gone over to Richards's house to question her again. The car was gone and there was no answer. Mrs. Bates was out in her yard, called me over, and told me what she saw last night."

Decker glanced out the window across the street at Susan Richards's house. "What can you tell us?" he said.

"What I told this lady. It was around nine-thirty last night. I heard that dang car start up."

"You mean Richards's car with the loud muffler?" said Decker.

She frowned up at him. "I thought I just said that."

"Tell him what happened next," said Lancaster quickly.

Bates slowly drew her gaze from Decker and said, "Saw Susan get out of the car while it was running and head into the house. She came out a few minutes later with a big old suitcase. One of them rolling ones. She leaned down and opened the car trunk and heaved it in. Then she slammed the trunk shut and got in the car."

"What was she wearing?" asked Decker.

"Long trench coat and a hat, all I could see."

"And you're sure it was her?" said Decker.

"'Course I am. I know Susan. Tall, thin, blonde hair and all."

Lancaster nodded. "And then she drove away?"

"That's right. She didn't tell me about taking a trip. But she must be going away for a while. That bag was stuffed."

Lancaster looked over at Decker, who was once more staring out the window. She said, "Richards must have left in a hurry. She didn't stop the newspaper or mail deliveries. I checked."

"So is she on the lam, then?" asked Bates. "What we used to call it when people go on the run. You know, like *The Fugitive*. I loved that show. Don't make 'em like that anymore." Her small face crinkled with pleasure. "And I had the biggest crush on David Janssen. What a hottie he was. He's dead now. Everybody I liked on TV is dead now."

"We're not sure of her reasons for leaving," said Lancaster.

"Well, if Susan killed that man, she probably would try to get away," said Bates. "I know I would."

Decker said, "Did you see anyone else over there last night?"

Bates's gaze swiveled back to him. "No. Woulda told you if I had."

"Nothing out of the ordinary?" he persisted.

Bates thought about this. "Not unless you count somebody going on the lam."

Decker and Lancaster left and walked across the street to Richards's home. A forensic team was inside looking around.

Decker looked to the sky where a storm was coming in.

Lancaster followed his gaze. "Weird weather this time of year. It was warm and humid and not a cloud in the sky last night. Now we're going to get a storm and the temp will drop twenty-five degrees."

Decker nodded absently. "You put out a BOLO, right?" he said.

"Of course. Nothing yet. We also tagged her credit cards and her phone. No charges, and she must have turned her phone off."

"Someone will probably spot the car. Or *hear* it."

"So does this confirm her guilt vis-à-vis Meryl Hawkins?"

"Did you check the rear door of the Residence Inn?"

"Hasn't changed since your time. Still broken. And no CCTV. So, did Richards exact her revenge on Hawkins?"

"I don't know."

"If she's innocent, why run?"

"Same answer."

"So how do we get answers?"

"We need to know more about Hawkins."

"Like what?"

"Everything."

"You mean after he was murdered?"

"No, before."

"How does that help us?"

"If he didn't kill the Richardses and David Katz, there must have been some reason why the real murderer would pick him to place the blame. We might find those reasons by looking at what he was doing *before* the murders."

They walked back to their cars. When they reached them Decker turned to his old partner.

"I saw Earl at the American Grill."

She looked surprised and popped in another piece of gum. "Did you? Was he alone?"

"No."

She nodded. "Did you speak to him?"

"He came over. We…talked about things."

"Nuance has never been your strong suit, Decker. And while you're a stone face when it comes to police work, your poker face sucks when it comes to personal matters. He told you about *us*."

Decker looked at her uncomfortably as the wind picked up around them.

"You have time for a drink?" she asked.

Decker nodded.

* * *

He followed her to a bar called Suds. Decker had frequented the place so often after the deaths of his family that the owner had used a Sharpie to write his name on the barstool on which he always sat.

The place was three-quarters full as folks drank and ate food from the bar menu. Music played in the background and some pinball machines lined up against one wall kept lighting up and dinging. The smack of pool balls came from another room where patrons could engage in billiards to their hearts' delight, so long as they kept ordering drinks and munchies.

Decker and Lancaster sat at a high table set against one wall. Decker ordered a beer and Lancaster a vodka tonic.

"You okay with your decision to join the Bureau?"

"I'm okay with it," said Decker tersely. "But I didn't think we came here to talk about me."

Lancaster took a sip of her drink and munched on some nuts from a bowl in front of her. "Life is complicated. At least mine is."

"How does that lead to divorce? I thought you and Earl cared for each other."

"We *do*, Decker. It's not really about that."

"What else is there?"

"What people want out of life, for one."

"What do you want that's different from what Earl wants?"

"I want to keep working in law enforcement."

"And Earl doesn't want that?"

"It's hard on him, Decker. It's hard on Sandy. I get that. But all I've ever wanted to be is a cop. I've worked my entire adult life to get to this point. I can't just chuck it, even if I do care for somebody."

"So it's an either/or?"

"It apparently is for Earl. But I'm not blaming him. You know when those monsters left those mannequins at our home dressed up to look like they'd been murdered two years ago? It scared the shit out of all of us, but Earl especially took it hard. He couldn't stop talking about it. What if it had been for real? Things changed after that between us. And they've never gone back to what they were."

"And what about Sandy? Earl said he's getting more custody than you."

"With my job, how could I have done that? It would be way too hard on Sandy. I'm not going to put her through that."

"She's your daughter."

"And she's Earl's daughter too. And she has special needs. His job is a lot more flexible than mine. I can't suddenly duck out of a homicide investigation or not show up for court so I can pick her up from school because she's having an episode. I know. I tried. It didn't work. You saw that for yourself."

"I did and I'm sorry."

She gave a weak smile. "Apologies? You going soft on me in your middle age?"

"Doubtful." He took a swig of beer. "I'm sorry that my problems intruded into your life. What happened to your family was because of me."

She reached over and gripped his hand. "Every problem in the world is not yours to solve. I know you have very broad shoulders, but no one can take on that sort of responsibility. And it wasn't your fault. It was the fault of a couple of very sick people. You know that's true."

"Do I?" he said. "It doesn't feel that way."

"You can't live this way, Amos. It's not sustainable."

"I never expected to live that long anyway."

She withdrew her hand and said coldly, "No one should wish for a shortened life."

"I'm not wishing for it. I'm just being realistic."

"You've lost weight. You're in a lot better shape than the last time I saw you."

"It's not my weight that concerns me."

She glanced at his head and frowned. "Problems there?"

"Does it matter? I'll just keep going until…I don't."

"I guess we can talk in circles all night."

"I'd rather move forward on this case."

"So, you mentioned Hawkins's past. Where do you start?"

"I start with before he allegedly became a murderer."

"You mean?"

"Exactly."

CHAPTER

18

TRAMMEL, OHIO.

Decker had never been here, though it was only a two-hour drive southwest of Burlington. It wasn't that far mileage-wise, but the only way there was mostly over state routes and rural back roads.

Trammel's downtown looked just like a photo of his hometown, right down to the dinginess and despair, alleviated by the glimpses of hope in the form of a new business opening and the foundation of a building being dug. And young faces on the sidewalks, and late-model cars on the streets.

Mitzi Gardiner lived in what Decker would call the upscale part of town, made up of large old homes where Trammel's elite had once lived, and where the new money had now congregated. They were large and brick with a past century's small windows, immaculately landscaped lawns with mature trees and bushes, and more modern additions tacked on by recent owners. Most had gated front entrances and luxury cars parked in the curved drives.

After being buzzed in through the gate, he walked up to the front door, noting the precisely laid-out planting beds, though the flowers had withered or else died out as fall deepened to winter. The house's windows were sparkling clean, the brick veneer seemed to have just been power-washed, and the front double doors looked like a fresh coat of paint had just been applied to them.

Neat, nice, monied. All the things Mitzi Gardiner had never been when Decker first met her. She'd been an unemployed drug addict and petty criminal who would steal and prostitute herself out to anyone to support her habit. He remembered her as tall, scrawny, and pasty, with needle-tracked arms and a deviated septum from all the snorted coke. Her pupils had been dilated, her movements jerky and largely out of her control. A wreck of a human being.

He knocked on the door and immediately heard footsteps approaching. He had phoned ahead. She knew he was coming.

When the door opened, Decker could hardly believe his own eyes. Or, even more incredibly, his infallible memory.

The woman gazing back at him was around forty, tall, shapely, her blonde hair done in such a way as to maximize both its fullness and attractiveness. She wore a pale blue dress that flattered her hips and showed a glimpse of cleavage, a simple necklace with one emerald at the throat, and a large diamond engagement ring and wedding band on her left hand. Her makeup and complexion were perfect. The once-destroyed septum had been fully repaired. The eyes held not a hint of dilation. The teeth were white and perfect and no doubt veneers, for her drug habit had left her own teeth gray and diseased, he recalled.

She must have registered his surprise. "It's been a long time, Detective Decker," she commented, her full lips curving into a self-satisfied smile at his amazed look.

"Yes, it has. I'm glad to see that you've..."

"Turned my life around? Yes, I have. Years of bad choices followed by some far better ones. Would you like to come in?"

She led him inside and then to an old-fashioned conservatory at the back of the house overlooking the pool and manicured rear grounds. A uniformed maid came in with a tray of coffee. Mitzi poured out the coffee after the maid departed.

"I assume you'd heard about your father before I contacted you?" said Decker, his cup cradled in one big hand.

"I saw the news, yes," she said.

"As next of kin you'll probably be called on to make a formal ID. I mean, we know it's him. It's just a formality."

"I would prefer not to. In fact, I would prefer to have nothing to do with it."

"He *is* your father."

"And he also killed four people."

"He has no other family left. And there's the matter of burial."

"They must have protocols for that when someone can't afford to be buried. Can't they just cremate him?"

Decker let his gaze wander around the sumptuous interior of the conservatory. "I guess so, for those who can't pay for it."

"I know you must think I'm a terrible person, Detective Decker. But the fact is I haven't seen my father since he went to prison for murdering those people."

"You never visited him there?"

"Why would I?" She leaned in closer to him. "I have a new life that I worked really hard on. Brad, my husband, doesn't know anything, really, of my past. I moved from Burlington, cleaned up my act, legally changed my last name, finished college, started working in the financial field, and met my husband. We married, and now I'm a full-time mom and loving it."

Decker looked around. "What does your husband do? It must pay well."

"It does. He runs his own high-end job placement platform."

"High-end?"

"Corporate executives, law and finance, manufacturing, Silicon Valley and all its high-tech positions, lobbying, defense industry, even government positions. He's been very successful."

"All that's way out of my league."

Mitzi paused to take a sip of her coffee. "So you see, I have no desire to revisit that part of my life. And I really don't want my family to know about my…struggles. In fact, as far as my husband knows, I'm an orphan. And I guess now I am."

"I recall that your mother died before your father even went on trial."

"Thank God. It would have crushed her."

"Did your father try to contact you, either while he was in prison or after he got out?"

"He wrote me letters when he was in prison. But I never wrote back. After I moved, I didn't leave a forwarding address."

"And after he left prison?"

"I had no idea. I thought he was in prison for life."

"So apparently did everyone else. Including him."

"Why was he released? The news didn't say."

"He was terminally ill. The state didn't want to foot the bill, apparently."

She nodded but made no comment.

"And you're sure he didn't try to contact you?"

"He'd have no way of knowing where I was. They said someone killed him? Are you sure it wasn't suicide? You said he was dying."

"No, couldn't be suicide. I can't tell you why, but just trust me on that."

She sat back. "That's so bizarre. Who would want to hurt him? It's been so many years."

"Some people carry long grudges."

"You mean the widows? What were their names again?"

"Susan Richards and Rachel Katz."

"I assume you've checked with them."

"We have."

"And?"

"And we're following up."

"So what do you want with me? On the phone you just said you wanted to talk. I know nothing about the murder of my father."

"I want to talk to you about the murders he was convicted of."

"Why?"

"What if your father didn't commit them?"

Her features sagged. "That's crazy. Of course he did."

"And you know for sure how?"

"Like you just said, he was *convicted* of them. *You* helped convict him. His fingerprints and DNA were found at the house."

"Would it surprise you to learn that he came back to Burlington proclaiming his innocence? That he wanted me to prove it?"

"Would it surprise me? No. But it *would* surprise me if you took it seriously."

"Maybe it would surprise me too. But he comes back

saying he's innocent and then somebody kills him, on the same day?"

"Like I said, you have two potential suspects."

"The widows. Did you know they still live in Burlington?"

"Why would I?" she said quickly.

"Well, you said they would be on your list of suspects. They'd sort of have to live in Burlington to make it happen that fast."

"Oh, well, I guess I assumed."

"Can I take you through the case again?"

"Do we really have to? I've worked hard to put this behind me."

"It's really important. And it won't take long."

She looked at her watch. "It *can't* take too long. My husband and I are going out to dinner later. I'd really prefer that you weren't here when he arrives. It would take too much explaining."

"I'll be as expeditious as I can."

She sighed, poured another cup of coffee, and sat back, looking at him expectantly.

"Your father went out that day around three, you said."

"I think that's right. It's been a long time."

"That's what your statement said."

She waved her hand dismissively. "Okay then, whatever."

"They found him very early the next morning walking along a part of town that I would have described back then as being pretty dangerous."

"Okay?"

"Had he ever been to that part of town before?"

"Not that I was aware."

"Had *you* ever been to that part of town?"

She frowned. "What, do you mean when I was looking for drugs to buy? I don't know. Maybe."

"He had the opportunity to give us an alibi but never did. He said he was just walking in the rain. Something no one could corroborate."

She spread her hands but said nothing.

"Before that we came to your house to find him. But he wasn't there. You said he'd gone out."

"That's right."

"And he never told you where he was going?"

"No. We didn't talk much back then."

"Yet you'd come back home to live."

"I had nowhere else to go. Look, I was a total druggie back then. You know that and I know that. My mother was dying and needed looking after and I couldn't even provide that."

"So your father looked after her?"

Gardiner hesitated.

"Your statement didn't really say one way or the other," Decker added helpfully.

"We didn't always see eye to eye, but I have to give credit where credit is due. My dad really cared about Mom. He did what he could. After he lost his job they had almost no money. And her pain was awful." She involuntarily shuddered.

"She was hooked up to a drip line that night," noted Decker. "I remember seeing it."

"Yeah, well, half the time there were no pain meds in that IV bag. They couldn't afford them. *Fucking* insurance companies." She caught herself, put a hand to her mouth, and added, "Sorry, it's still kind of a sore subject with me."

"So your mother *had* insurance?"

"Until my dad got laid off. Then they couldn't afford to stay on the insurance. And cancer was a preexisting condition. So they couldn't get another policy anyway."

"What did he do?"

"He worked every odd job he could and used the money to get what he could from local doctors."

"But then he was arrested and held until trial. What then?"

"She suffered incredibly," said Gardiner, her eyes filling with tears. "My mother was in terrible pain and there was nothing I could do about it."

"Until she passed away?"

"Yes. Fortunately, she died in her sleep soon after." She shook her head. "She worked so hard her whole life."

"What did she do?"

"She was born near Columbus. She was smart but never had a chance to go to college. She worked at OSU. In the cafeteria, when she was in her twenties."

"I actually played football there."

"Really?" She looked him over. "I guess you're plenty big enough. Then she met my dad and they got married. He was working at a manufacturing plant, I think, up near Toledo. They met on a blind date, or so my mom told me. Love at first sight, Meryl and Lisa. Then I came along soon after." She paused. "They had a nice life. Until I grew up and screwed everything up."

"With your drug addiction?"

She nodded. "Look, they tried to get me help, but I kept relapsing. Nothing I did seemed to work. I tried, but it was damn hard."

"It is damn hard, but give yourself some credit. You finally kicked it."

"Yeah, I did."

"Had your father ever mentioned the Richardses? Or David Katz?"

"No, never. I didn't even know he knew them."

"Well, he might not have."

"Well, then why did he go to that house?"

"That's the question, isn't it? Susan Richards and Rachel Katz also testified that neither of them knew him, and weren't aware that their husbands did either."

"So it was a random burglary, then? He just drove around—"

"Walked. He didn't have a car other than the one that was parked in front of your house all that day and well into the night. We confirmed that with witnesses from your old neighborhood."

"He could have stolen a car," she pointed out.

"That's true. But no car was seen approaching the Richardses' house that night except for David Katz's."

"Wasn't it raining like crazy that night? How could anyone say for sure they didn't see a car?"

"Fair point. Talk to me about the discovery of the murder weapon at your parents' home."

"What about it?"

"It was found behind a wall panel in your parents' closet?"

"Okay. So?"

"Did you know about that panel?"

"No. I'd never been in their closet. I never had any reason to."

"And one of the techs found it?"

"I think so."

"You were there?"

"I had to be. I couldn't leave my mother alone."

"So you were there on the day of the murders and then afterwards?"

"Yes. Again, I couldn't leave her alone."

"And you never saw your father after the time of the murders?"

"No. I never left the house. I answered the door when you and your partner showed up that night."

"That's right."

She looked at her watch. "Now, if there's nothing else?"

"There's just one thing."

"Yes?"

"How did the gun get in the closet?"

"What?"

"If your father didn't come home after the murders, how did the gun he used to kill those people end up behind the panel in the closet?"

"I...I don't know."

"Maybe you were asleep? Or...?"

"Or maybe I was stoned out of my mind?" she said, a bitter look on her face.

"When we came to interview you later that night, you were sort of out of it."

"Then there's your answer. My father came home, hid the gun, and then left again. And neither my mother nor I saw him."

"Right, that would explain it. And the stuff he stole never turned up."

"I don't know anything about that. You didn't find it in our house."

"No, we didn't. And we looked for it."

"Okay." She made a show of looking at her watch again.

"He had five hundred dollars in his pocket. Any idea where that came from?"

"I assumed from him selling the stuff he stole."

"Right, well, thanks for your time."

She showed him out. At the door Gardiner said, "I'm not really sure why you're putting yourself through this, Detective Decker."

"That thought had crossed my mind."

Decker walked down the drive and the gates automatically opened as he approached them. When he got to his car, he suddenly looked back at the house in time to see a curtain on one of the front windows flutter closed.

He got into the car thinking that people were interesting. Sometimes they just couldn't distinguish the truth from bullshit. Sometimes they didn't want to. It was often easier just to believe a lie.

He drove off with more questions than he'd started the trip with.

And for some reason, that made him happy.

Amos Decker actually smiled as he drove back to Burlington.

He stopped smiling when something rammed into his car on a back road in the middle of nowhere.

CHAPTER

19

DECKER HAD SEEN THE HEADLIGHTS coming up on him but figured the person would slow down and back off.

That was not how it played out. Not even close.

The first strike catapulted his big frame straight ahead. His front and side curtain airbags deployed, and he felt his skin tingle and then burn slightly from the released gases powering the safety devices.

Momentarily disoriented by the collision, Decker looked in the rearview mirror and saw the lights coming at him again. The headlights were set higher than his taillights.

Truck. A big one. He thought he could see the huge metal bumper right before...

The rear of his car was lifted completely off the road with the next impact.

His airbags having already burst open, Decker felt his chest hit the steering column after colliding with the airbag and crushing it. But the air pocket still prevented serious injury.

He cut the wheel to the right, and then the left. The truck mirrored those movements. He could smell gasoline.

Great, his tank must've gotten cracked.

He floored it and the car leapt forward.

The truck accelerated to match this burst of speed.

Decker dug in his pocket for his phone. His fingers tapped on the screen.

If he could just call 911...

Then the phone was flung out of his hand when the truck

smashed into him again. This sent his car into a sideways spin. He felt like a NASCAR driver who'd had his car's rear tapped by another at high speed. Fishtailing, totally out of control. It was not a great feeling.

But Decker had been in high-speed chases before as a cop. He knew what to do. He didn't fight the wheel but rather steered in the direction of the spin to regain control of the car.

He slid sideways down the asphalt, tires smoking, fuel leaking, and Decker fearful that heat from one would ignite the other.

He came to a stop about fifty feet later. He pushed the deployed airbag out of the way and looked out the window.

The monster truck was heading his way, a T-bone impact definitely in the works.

Well, screw that.

Decker pulled his weapon, rolled down the window, took aim, and unloaded his mag first at the radiator, then down to the tires, and finally up to the windshield. Three fractured circles were imprinted on the glass where his bullets hit.

The truck immediately veered off, ran into the grass shoulder, regained traction, shot back onto the road, and limped off, smoke now coming from its engine.

Decker didn't know if he'd hit the driver or not. He could only hope he had.

He was debating whether to go after the truck, when the smell of gas suddenly strengthened.

He quickly undid his seat belt, bent down and retrieved his phone, kicked open the door, and hustled away from the car. He dialed 911 and told them what had happened, giving his location as best he could. Then he watched with a sickening feeling as a lick of flames emerged at the rear of his ride.

He instantly turned and sprinted away from the car. When the explosion rocked the dark sky, he was flung forward by the concussive blast and drilled face first into the hard shoulder of dirt, grass, and gravel.

And that's where the cops found him when they showed up later.

* * *

"You just can't keep out of trouble, can you?"

Decker looked groggily up from his hospital bed at Lancaster hovering over him and furiously chewing her gum.

"Did they find the truck?"

She shook her head.

"I think I might have wounded the driver," said Decker as he touched his forehead and felt the bandage there. "I placed three shots in the windshield right in front of the driver's seat."

"State police are checking it all out. Dollars to donuts we'll be able to find the truck. So who do you think it was?"

Decker sat up a little. "Someone who either followed me to Trammel or picked up the tail after I left Mitzi Gardiner's house."

"And how did that go?"

Decker filled her in on his interview.

"You think she was telling the truth?"

"Almost nobody tells the entire truth. They slant facts to make themselves look better or blameless, or both."

"Sounds like she's really turned her life around, though," said Lancaster, a bit wistfully.

"Which means she has a lot to lose potentially," countered Decker.

"You think she called somebody after you left?"

"I guess you can pull her phone records and check. Although it would be a little obvious if as soon as I leave her somebody tries to kill me. She has to know she'd be on the suspect radar."

"And with her new, chic life, she might not have ready access to hired killers."

"They might have just wanted to warn me off, not kill me."

She looked him over. "I think you need to rethink that. From what I heard, you almost got French-fried in your car."

"It *was* close," conceded Decker. "Any developments on your end?"

"None worth mentioning."

"Well, this attempt on my life tells us one thing," said Decker.

"What's that?"

"It seems that Meryl Hawkins was telling the truth."

20

TALK ABOUT COMING FULL CIRCLE.

Decker dropped his duffel on the floor of his new digs.

It was the next evening and after a night's stay in the hospital he had moved into the Residence Inn. This was actually his old room when he'd lived there.

He'd gotten a new rental car after spending considerable time on the phone trying to explain to Hertz exactly what had happened to the other one.

"Someone was trying to kill you?" the customer service rep had said skeptically. "I've been doing this a long time and that's a first for me."

"Not for me," Decker had truthfully replied.

He sat in the one chair next to the window and overlooking the street. He popped the cold beer he had brought with him.

That was dinner. Well, really it wasn't, but after nearly getting blown up the night before, he didn't have much of an appetite.

He touched his head where the bandage still was. It was another knock up there to add to all the others. How many more could he endure without something major popping?

And he was tired of getting nearly blown up. He'd almost bought it in a similar way back in Baronville. The only good thing to come out of his almost being killed was the fact that someone was afraid of what he would find out. That meant there was a truth out there that needed to be discovered.

And Decker meant to find it.

One floor down was the room where Meryl Hawkins's life had ended, a bit prematurely.

And violently.

Sipping his beer, Decker walked down to the space. It was still off-limits and stickered with yellow tape, but the officer guarding the door knew Decker and let him pass.

"What happened to you?" the cop asked, eyeing the bandage around the big man's head.

"When I find out, I'll let you know."

Decker closed the door behind him and surveyed the space. Nothing had been touched other than Hawkins's body being removed. He wondered briefly about the man's burial, or cremation. Part of him wanted to haul his daughter down here to take care of her father's remains. Part of him understood why she wanted nothing to do with it.

At the end of the day that was really none of his concern.

He looked at the chair where Hawkins had been sitting. There were traces of blood on it, not from the exit wound since there hadn't been one. The splatter from the entry wound had been the source.

Pillow, gun, dead guy. No witnesses.

He looked around the rest of the room. It had already been thoroughly searched and nothing else had been found.

They'd gotten the postmortem report on Hawkins but not the tox screen yet. His stomach had been empty. But what was in his bloodstream?

Decker closed his eyes and dialed up his cloud. Hawkins had told him at the cemetery that he was going to take something to help him sleep, after spending a few hours throwing up. There had been no evidence of that in the bathroom, but he might have cleaned it up. But there had also been no sign of meds, either illegal or not.

They'd checked the Dumpster at the rear of the building and found nothing there either. Had whoever killed him taken the meds for some reason? Why would that be? What could they have revealed?

He went back to his room, put his few clothes away, cleaned up, and, suddenly hungry, went in search of dinner.

He chose Suds because it was close and cheap. He sat at the bar and ordered a beer, and a burger and fries with chili. He involuntarily looked over his shoulder once, thinking that Jamison might swoop in and chastise him for the cardiac killer meal plan.

He turned to his right when the person sat down next to him a few minutes later.

Rachel Katz eyed the bandage around his head. "What happened to you?"

"Cut myself shaving," replied Decker as he took a sip of beer.

She looked down at his plate. "Not into organics, I take it."

"What's more organic than meat and potatoes?"

She smiled. "You have a comeback for everything. I didn't see that in you all those years ago."

She ordered a glass of Prosecco.

He glanced sideways at her. "Somehow, I didn't figure you for a Suds patron."

"Oh, I'm full of surprises. But I'll let you in on a little secret." She leaned over next to him. "I'm the majority owner of this bar." She straightened and studied Decker for his reaction to this.

"I'm impressed at the diversity of your holdings. From penthouses to pubs."

She smiled. "Another quip. Good for you. If the detective thing doesn't work out, fall back on stand-up, no pun intended."

Her drink arrived, and she took a sip of it, filling her hand with nuts from a bowl in front of them.

"So, how's the investigation coming?"

"It's coming."

"I thought you would have solved the whole thing by now."

"Investigations don't work that way. They're on their own timetable."

"But you solved my husband's murder really fast."

"Did I?" he shot back.

She munched her almonds and peanuts and looked around the full bar. "It's good to see the town getting back on its feet, isn't it?" she asked.

"So when you finish rebuilding Burlington, what's next?"

She swiveled around and leaned back against the bar. "I'm not sure. There are lots of places like Burlington, but not all have the potential to make a comeback. I don't want to make a ton of money here and blow it on another place that will never make it out of the abyss."

"So how do you calculate that?"

"I won't bore you with the statistics, but a lot of number crunching goes into it. Luckily, as a CPA, my background is all about number crunching. And those numbers can be magic, a road map into the future, if you know how to read them right. All successful people do that."

"All *financially* successful people, you mean."

"Is there any other kind?" She added quickly, "Just kidding. I know we need more Mother Teresas in the world. I'm just not one of them. Not how I'm wired."

"And how are you wired?"

"Me first, I guess. And I'm not ashamed to admit it. I don't like hypocrites. I know enough people who pretend to care about others while they're stabbing them in the back. I stab people in the chest. They can see it coming from a mile away."

"Thing is, they're still dead," replied Decker.

"Yes, but at least they have a chance to defend themselves," she said sweetly, draining her drink and waving for another one, which was immediately delivered. "I hear Susan Richards has gone missing?"

Decker put down his burger and looked over at her. "And where did you hear that?"

"Oh, come on, I heard it on the town gossip network ages ago. I wonder why she would have disappeared like that?"

Decker said, "Guilt?"

Katz took a sip of her Prosecco. "I didn't say that, but the timing is awfully peculiar."

"Timing in homicide investigations often is."

"You're the expert on that, not me. So, do you think she killed Meryl Hawkins and took off before the cops found proof that she murdered him?"

"Speaking of proof, did you ever come up with an alibi for the time of his death?"

"I was at dinner with a business associate until eleven-thirty or so. Then he drove me home. We got to my place around midnight. I think that lets me off the hook."

"And the name of this business associate?"

She took out a pen and slip of paper from her purse, wrote something down, and handed it to Decker.

He glanced at the paper, his eyes hiking in surprise. "Earl Lancaster?"

"Yes. He's working on some projects for me. He's a first-rate general contractor. Why?"

"He's married to my old partner."

"Not for much longer," said Katz. When Decker again looked surprised, she added, "Small town, Detective." She swallowed the last of her drink. "Well, let me know if you need anything else."

With a whisk of blonde hair, she was gone.

After she left, Decker sat there and wondered one thing.

Why hadn't Earl mentioned that he was working with Katz when they had run into each other at the American Grill?

Because that development royally screwed his wife.

Or soon-to-be ex-wife.

21

"YOU MEAN YOU *KNEW*?"

Decker looked across at Lancaster. It was the next morning and they were sitting in her car outside the Residence Inn. He'd called her and told her he needed to speak with her but preferred to do it in person.

"I *knew* he was doing some work for Rachel Katz. I didn't know that he was her alibi. Earl didn't tell me that. We don't talk all that much anymore, particularly about his business."

"But why didn't you mention to me that he was working for a possible suspect in a murder we're both investigating?"

"He works with lots of people and I didn't think it was relevant."

"Well, it is. And now that he's her alibi?"

Lancaster said, "I might have to recuse myself from the investigation."

"There's no *might* about it, Mary. You have to."

"Earl wouldn't lie, if that's what you're implying. If he said he was with Katz, he was."

"I'm not implying anything. I just know that you have to get off this case. Any defense lawyer will tear the department a new one if you stay on now."

She popped a stick of gum into her mouth and started chewing furiously.

"And now I need to talk to Earl about this," said Decker.

"I know. And I think I need to talk to him too."

"No, Mary, you can't do that."

"He's still my husband, dammit."

"He's also a potential alibi for someone who had a pretty good motive to kill Meryl Hawkins."

"Shit!" She slapped the steering wheel. "And I didn't think my life could get any worse."

"You're the one asking for the divorce."

"That's what Earl told you."

"Is it not true? You just told me that Earl doesn't lie."

"Does it matter, Decker? Our marriage is over."

"And this woman he's seeing?"

"She's fine. Earl didn't start seeing Nancy until things were over between us."

"Yeah, he told me that. But you're really okay with Earl getting custody of Sandy?"

"We're *sharing* custody. But I told you before, his work is more flexible than mine. It's better and less disruptive for Sandy to have her spend the week with Earl. Her well-being is all I'm concerned about."

"Okay, give up your kid, then."

She looked at him, fury on her features. "What right do you have to tell me that? You don't know jack shit about my situation. It was your choice to leave here and go work for the FBI. So don't come back to *my* town and tell me how to run *my* life." She pointed to the door. "Now get the hell out of my car."

Decker got out, but he poked his head back in.

"The thing with kids, Mary, is that when you turn around for just a second and then look back, sometimes they aren't there anymore."

He shut the door and trudged off.

* * *

Later that day, the knock on Decker's door was unexpected.

When he opened it, his surprise instantly turned to exasperation.

"Long time, no see, Decker," said the smiling man on the other side of the doorway.

Blake Natty was a detective with the Burlington Police

Department. About six years older than Decker, and more senior at the department, he had been left in the dust by Decker's investigative prowess. And he had not bothered to hide his feelings about it.

He was about five-eight, one-sixty, and dressed in a way that matched his name, complete with pocket kerchief and golden links on his French-cuffed shirt.

"What are you doing here, Natty?" asked Decker.

Natty's smile broadened. "This is just a courtesy call. I'm taking over the investigation on the Hawkins case. Heard Mary got knocked off over some accusation from you. A little surprising considering you two were partners once."

"Well, you got everything about that wrong, which at least shows you're consistent."

Natty's smile vanished. "As I said, a courtesy call. And it's to tell you that we do not require your services in connection with the Meryl Hawkins case."

"Have you talked to Captain Miller about this? Because he was very much okay with me working the case."

"Miller has to answer to the superintendent. And the super has a different opinion."

"Right. Would that still be Peter Childress?"

"It would be. Didn't you call him an ignorant asshole one time?"

"It wasn't just the one time. And he earned it fair and square."

"Well, just do not involve yourself in the investigation. So, with that, I don't see anything keeping you in Burlington. You can just head on out."

"There's the crimes that Meryl Hawkins was convicted of."

"Right. That's also off-limits. It's a Burlington PD investigation, and in case you forgot, you're no longer part of the team."

"No law against me looking into a case if I want to."

"There is a law if you interfere with an active police investigation."

"So you *are* looking into whether Hawkins was innocent?"

"None of your concern. I can have one of my guys run you to the bus station. There's a bus to Pittsburgh that leaves in two hours. And you can catch a flight from there back to your precious D.C."

"Thanks, but I'm staying."

Natty drew closer, nearly chest to stomach, and looked up at the nine-inches-taller Decker. "You don't get a single pass on this, no get-out-of-jail-free card. I catch you in my way, the next room you inhabit is a jail cell. I want to make myself really clear on that."

"You've never had a problem making yourself clear, Blake. Even when you had it a hundred and eighty degrees wrong. Which was most of the time."

"Watch that ego, Decker. Even a guy as big as you won't be able to hold it in."

Decker closed the door in the man's face, went back to his chair, sat down, and turned his thoughts back to the case.

Natty, he was sure, would look for any opportunity to put bite to his threat and plant Decker's butt in jail. Yet Decker had spent much of his life swimming against the current. Natty was an irritant, nothing more. But Decker would have to watch himself.

A text dropped into his phone.

It was from Lancaster.

I'm really pissed at you, but I'm sorry about Natty being assigned to the case. Wouldn't wish that on my worst enemy. Which you're not. At least not yet. M

Decker dropped the phone into his pocket, sighed, and sat back in his chair.

His visit to the old hometown was turning into quite a nightmare.

22

GENTRIFICATION SOMETIMES SUCKED because it made homes unaffordable to those living there before their neighborhood was suddenly hot, and all the money wanted to move into new luxury residences after knocking the old stuff down.

Decker was thinking this as he looked around at the area where Hawkins had been picked up that night on suspicion of a quadruple homicide.

Back then it had been the equivalent of a war zone in Burlington. Drug deals had gone down here, and gangs had fought each other over turf and customers. Cars from the suburbs would line up on the streets, like parishioners to the offering basket, only the money they put in would bring not solace and help for others, but drugs and continued misery in return. Empty homes and businesses were used as needle and coke pipe hangouts or gang headquarters. As a cop and later detective, Decker had spent a lot of time in this part of town. In some years there had been a murder a week. Everybody had guns, and no one had a problem using them.

Now the place was full of upscale apartments and thriving small businesses. Hell, there was even a Starbucks. A park sat where once there had been an empty boarded-up warehouse. Decker had to admit it was a lot better than it had been.

They could film a Hallmark movie here and not change a thing.

He and Lancaster had come here after questioning Hawkins at the police station. In Decker's mind's eye, the area was returned to its miserable state thirteen years prior. The park was gone, the new residences vanished, the streets returned to trash-strewn and crumbling. Addicts staggered down the streets, dealers were lurking down dark alleys hustling their product. Users came in with cash and left with their drugs of choice.

There were hookers too, because they naturally went with the drugs, Decker had found. Almost all of the hookers were addicts too and scored tricks to pay for their daily doses. And the luxurious loft apartment building he was standing in front of once more became an abandoned shirt factory with mattresses strewn inside where the business of sex was negotiated and then consummated.

Through all of this Meryl Hawkins walked with the rain beating down on him, though because of the bad weather, they could find no one out and about to corroborate his story. Yet if he was telling the truth and he had been trudging through this downpour, why? And why wouldn't he tell Decker and Lancaster during their interrogation? Anything he told them could have helped his cause. Silence only hurt him. He could have named a person whom he had met with and they could have followed up on that, and he might have been a free man.

Decker dialed up something in his memory. Something far more recent.

"*She was hooked up to a drip line that night. I remember seeing it.*"

"*Yeah, well, half the time there were no pain meds in that IV bag, including that night. They couldn't afford them. Fucking insurance companies. Sorry, it's still kind of a sore subject with me.*"

"*So your mother had insurance?*"

"*Until my dad got laid off. Then they couldn't afford to stay on the insurance. And cancer was a preexisting condition. So they couldn't get another policy anyway.*"

"*What did he do?*"

"*He worked every odd job he could and used the money to get what he could from local doctors.*"

Had Meryl Hawkins really been out that night scrounging up illegal pain meds for his suffering wife? His lawyer had raised that possibility at the trial. If he had, he could still have committed the murders. There was plenty of time for him to do that and get to that part of town.

Yet if he had gotten the pain meds, none had been found on him. And how could he not have scored some in what was Burlington's premier open-air drug market? But then again, he would have to be careful with what he bought. Half the crap being sold here could kill you, even if you were healthy.

Morphine would have been the presumptive choice, Decker figured. It certainly would be what the hospice folks used with their patients. But Hawkins had to be damn sure of the provenance. He certainly wasn't going to give his wife some half-assed, kitchen-sink-concocted drug, and there had been plenty of those back then.

There were, Decker recalled, some sellers here who had pure stuff. They hadn't made it in kitchen labs; they'd stolen it from pharmacies and hospital supply rooms. They asked premium dollar for it, because of its purity. You got more pop for your dollar and you clearly knew what you were injecting. That meant chances were good that you'd live to be an addict another day.

That, Decker decided, would be the stuff Hawkins would be looking for. If he had learned one thing about the man during the investigation and trial, it was that Meryl Hawkins was completely devoted to his wife. Yet no drugs of any kind had been found on him.

Decker closed his eyes. Five hundred dollars *had* been found on Hawkins. Was it cash he'd gotten for the stolen goods?

But how could the guy have transported all the stuff he supposedly took when there was no accounting for a car being seen there? It was possible he could have driven a stolen car there and no one had noticed it. Then he could have simply driven away, come here, and tried to barter stolen goods for drugs. He had the cash, so maybe he had been trudging through the rain after fencing the stuff and was looking for the right kind of drugs for his wife when the police had picked him up.

Although given that the man had never even had a parking ticket before that, it seemed implausible that after killing four people

Hawkins could calmly go about his task of selling the stolen goods and shop for drugs in the middle of a monsoon. And he had to know the police would be looking for the killer.

Decker opened his eyes.

When they had questioned Hawkins late that night, he had seemed genuinely stunned that he was being accused of murder. Back then Decker and Lancaster had just assumed he was lying like any killer would.

Decker closed his eyes once more and he was back in that interrogation room sitting across from a man accused of four homicides, including two kids.

Decker had slid pictures across of the dead people.

"You recognize these, Mr. Hawkins?"

He hadn't looked at the photos.

"Look at them, Mr. Hawkins."

"I'm not and you can't make me."

But Decker had noticed the man glanced sideways at the photo of Abigail Richards and grimaced, almost looking like he might be sick to his stomach. Back then Decker had taken that as an indication of a guilty conscience.

But now?

"Give us a name, Mr. Hawkins," Lancaster had said. "Of anyone you might have seen or met with tonight. Or who might have seen you. We can follow that up, and if it checks out, you're a free man."

Hawkins had never given a name. And as Decker focused his memory on that exact moment, he recalled seeing something on the man's face that he hadn't necessarily seen before.

Resignation.

"Hey, Decker!"

Decker looked over at the car that had pulled up beside him. The driver had rolled down the window and called out to him.

Decker mouthed a curse under his breath.

It was Blake Natty looking cocksure, as usual.

"I thought I made myself clear, Decker."

"You're going to have to explain that, Natty."

Then he looked past Natty and was surprised to see Sally Brimmer in the passenger seat looking very uncomfortable.

Natty said, "I told you that you cannot investigate these cases."

"No, you told me I couldn't interfere with *your* investigation." Decker made a show of looking around. "Not seeing any interference. I'm just out for a stroll. How about you, Ms. Brimmer? You see any interference with a police investigation going on here?"

Brimmer looked like she wanted to melt into the car's floorboards. She smiled weakly and said, "I'm not getting in the middle of this, guys."

"Smart gal," said Natty with a slick grin before turning back to Decker. "Maybe you should be that smart. I don't want to have to lock you up."

"I'm sure. I mean why would you want a federal lawsuit landing on the department like a nuclear bomb? Even all the brown-nosing you've done with the superintendent all these years wouldn't be enough to save your butt."

"You better watch yourself, smart-ass."

"I do, Natty, every day of my life."

"And you give me any more lip, your fat ass is going into a cell. Guaranteed."

"Then you get a First Amendment lawsuit on top of the other one. I don't think the department has enough lawyers to cover all that crap, and it would probably hit the national news pipeline." Decker peered past him to look at Brimmer. "You do PR for the police. You care to wade into the middle of *that* one, Ms. Brimmer?"

She held up her hands in mock surrender and looked away.

Decker looked down at Natty's ring hand and then over at Brimmer. "Wait a minute, Natty, aren't you still married?"

Natty barked, "What's it to you?" He glanced quickly at Brimmer. "What the hell are you insinuating? I'm...I'm just giving her a ride to...her apartment."

Decker glanced at Brimmer again, who was staring out her window now. Then he made a show of checking his watch. It was nearly eight p.m.

"Well, tell Fran I said hello, when you get back from Brimmer's *apartment.*"

"Stay out of my damn way, Decker, or you *will* go down."

Natty hit the gas and the car sped off.

Decker stared after it and thought he saw Brimmer looking back at him through the rear glass. Though in the darkness, he couldn't be sure.

Natty and Brimmer. Who saw that coming?

23

The Hawkinses' old home.

It wasn't empty. There was a car parked in the driveway.

It was the next day and Decker trudged up the steps to the front door of the house, as he eyed the kids' toys in the front yard.

He knocked and instantly heard cries from young children, the scraping of animal claws on hardwood, and then the firm tread of grown-up feet coming toward the front door. It opened to reveal a young woman around thirty. Her brown hair was tied up in a ponytail and her face held the weary features of a mother with young children. This was confirmed when three small faces poked out from behind her.

"Yes?" she said, looking Decker up and down. "There's no solicitation in this neighborhood, just so you know."

"I'm not selling anything," he said as he held out his FBI credentials.

She took a step back after looking at his ID. "You're with the FBI?" she said skeptically. "I thought they wore suits."

"Some do, I'm just not one of them. And I'm kind of a hard size to fit."

She stared up at him and nodded. "I can see that. What can I do for you?"

"How long have you lived here?"

"Two years. What is this about?"

"Over a dozen years ago, a family named Hawkins lived here." He glanced down at the kids. "Can we speak privately?"

She looked back at her children, two twin boys and one girl, all between the ages of three and five. "I'm afraid I don't have any privacy," she said with a resigned smile. "Look, why don't you come in?" She led him inside and the children backed away, staring up at the giant Decker in fear.

"Hey kids," said the woman suddenly. "Cookies in the kitchen. One each only! And I *will* check."

The three took off. They were joined by a wire-haired terrier that shot out from behind a piece of furniture, where apparently he'd been cowering.

"Yeah, some watchdog, that Peaches," said the woman dryly. "Now, what about this other family?"

"I'll get right to the point since I doubt we have much time before your kids come back. A gun that was used in a serious crime years ago was found behind a wall in the master bedroom closet here. I wanted to take a look at that spot."

The woman's features collapsed. "Good Lord. Nobody told us about that when we bought the place. I thought the Realtor had to tell you stuff like that. When did it happen?"

"About thirteen years ago. And no crime was committed here, technically."

"And you still haven't found this person?"

"No, we did. He was in prison. Then he got out. And a few days ago someone murdered him."

"Oh my God," said the woman, putting a hand to her face. "But if he was convicted of the crime involving the gun, why do you need to see the place where it was found?"

"Because I'm not sure if he actually *did* commit those crimes."

Her features took on a look of understanding. "Oh, you mean this is like one of those cold case things? I like those shows. Not that I get a chance to watch much TV anymore."

"Right, exactly. A cold case." Decker heard a rush of footsteps coming their way. "I think the cavalry's returning. So if you could let me see it?"

"Sure, come on back."

She led him to the bedroom. "Excuse the mess. I barely have time to brush my teeth with three rug rats."

"I'm sure."

A crash came from somewhere within the house, and then the sounds of Peaches barking and someone crying.

"Um," said the woman, looking nervous.

"Go check it out. I won't be long."

"Thanks." She shot out of the room, yelling, "Good grief, what now!"

Decker pushed some hanging clothes out of the way and shone his Maglite over the back wall of the closet. Then he looked to the left, where the panel in question was situated. He rapped against it with his fist. It rang hollow. He rapped against the other two walls and got the same sound. It was just drywall over studs after all.

It had been repaired and painted over and there was nothing really for Decker to see. He thought back to the first time he'd seen this space. The panel had been taken off—it had been cut out and then wedged back into place. Not so very seamlessly, it appeared, which was one reason why it had been discovered so readily.

He remembered that behind the cutout was an open space in between the studs. The gun inside a box had been found there. There had been no prints found on either item. He looked down at the floor. The closet was carpeted, and it looked to be the same carpet as during the Hawkinses' time here. He got down on his knees and hit it with his light.

What are you doing, Decker? After all this time did you think you were going to find a smoking gun in the frigging carpet?

He straightened and finally admitted to himself that he was grasping at straws. He had not a sliver of a lead on this investigation. Either with the murders all those years ago, or with Meryl Hawkins's more recent one.

He rose and left the bedroom.

And that's where Decker ran right into a wall of police with a grinning Blake Natty bringing up the rear.

24

I T W A S T H E S A M E C E L L where Decker—pretending to be a lawyer—had scammed his way in to meet with a prisoner who had confessed to murdering Decker's family.

He didn't know if this cell selection had been made intentionally, but he doubted it was a coincidence. Someone was definitely trying to send a message.

The police waiting for him in Hawkinses' old house had been the first sign. His being read his Miranda rights for interfering with a police investigation had been his second, and more visceral, sign.

But Decker was nothing if not a patient man. He leaned back against the cinderblock wall and waited. They knew where he was. At some point they would have to come to him, because he could not come to them.

An hour later a surprising figure appeared in front of the steel bars.

To her credit, Sally Brimmer didn't look pleased to see him in a jail cell.

He glanced up at her.

"Ms. Brimmer. Having a nice day?"

"Apparently better than the one you're having."

"I wouldn't argue with that."

She drew closer to the bars and spoke in a low voice. "Why did you push it? You know Blake hates you."

"I don't care whether he hates me or not. I have a job to do and I'm going to do it."

"But you're not part of the police force anymore. This isn't your problem."

"It is my problem if I helped send an innocent man to prison."

"Do you really believe he was innocent?"

"Let's just put it this way: I have a lot more doubts about his guilt than I used to."

"Okay, but does it really matter? The guy's dead."

"It matters to me. It matters to his memory. He has a daughter who thinks her father killed four people."

Brimmer's cheeks reddened. "I really hated you for conning me that time."

"I took full responsibility for it. I didn't want you to suffer because of what I did."

"I know that man helped murder your family. I...I guess I was surprised you didn't kill him in the cell."

"I wasn't sure he'd done it. In fact, I had doubts." He paused. "I have to be sure, Ms. Brimmer. It's the way I'm wired."

"I guess I can see that. And I brought that up only because..." Her voice trailed off and she looked around nervously. "Because I would have done the same thing if it were me."

He rose and went over to the bars separating them. "Can you do something for me?"

She took a step back looking wary. "What?"

"I need to look at the files from the Richardses' and Katz's murders."

"But I thought you had. I saw the guy taking the boxes to the conference room that day."

"I got involved in running down potential witnesses and didn't get to the files before, well, before I ended up in here."

"But surely you read them all from when it happened." She glanced upward at his forehead. "And I heard you can't forget anything."

Now Decker took a step back and wouldn't meet her eye. "I didn't read them all back then. In particular the pathology report."

"Why not?"

"I didn't have to testify to that. The ME did."

She didn't look convinced.

He finally looked at her and said, "I screwed up, Ms. Brimmer. It was my first case as a homicide detective. I thought Hawkins was good for it pretty much right from the start. So I didn't dot all the i's or cross all the t's."

Surprisingly, she smiled at this.

"What?" he said in reaction to her look.

"That's actually comforting."

"How so?"

"I thought you were infallible, like a machine. Now I know you actually *are* human."

"Depends on who you ask, actually. Can you get me the files?"

"I guess I can make copies. But I can't bring them to you here."

"I won't be here much longer."

Her brow wrinkled. "How do you know that?"

"There *is* something known as a bail hearing. It's sort of required."

"Do you have a lawyer?"

"No, but I'm good on that."

"Are you sure?"

"Pretty sure."

"Blake is not going to make it easy."

"I never thought he would."

"I guess you're wondering why I'm…I mean, he and I…"

"It's none of my business. And I'm not judging anybody. I don't have the right."

"I appreciate that."

"But I will give you a piece of advice. I had a daughter once."

"I know," she said, looking pained.

"And if she had had a chance to grow up, I would never let her near Blake Natty. Take that for what it's worth. The fact that he's seeing you while he's still married should tell you all you need to know about the guy."

Brimmer looked at him sadly, then turned and hurried off.

CHAPTER

25

THE JUDGE DID a double take when he looked down first at the docket sheet and then up at Amos Decker, who stood behind the counsel table.

At the prosecutor's table stood Elizabeth Bailey, a veteran prosecutor who knew Decker quite well. They had worked numerous cases together while he'd been on the police force.

Behind the waist-high rail where the public could sit, there were only two people: Blake Natty and Superintendent Peter Childress, a tall portly man in his late fifties with gray hair cut short and a puffy, pockmarked face. He had on a dark suit, crisply starched white dress shirt, a blue-and-white-striped tie, and a white pocket square.

"Decker?" said the judge, a diminutive man in his late sixties with a reedy neck and an abundance of silvery hair that contrasted starkly with his dark robe. He peered at Decker through thick black-framed glasses. "Amos Decker?"

"Yes, Judge Dickerson. It's me."

"Obstruction of justice charge?" said Dickerson, glancing at the charging document. "Interfering with a police investigation? I thought you were *with* the police."

"I left to join the FBI a couple of years ago, but I'm still a sworn officer here in Burlington."

Dickerson moved his lips as he read something off the papers lying in front of him. Then he slid off his glasses, set them down, steepled his hands, and looked at the prosecutor.

She stood there looking quite anxious.

"Ms. Bailey, can you explain to me what in the world is going on here?" said Dickerson.

Bailey was in her forties, her frame big-boned. The woman's blonde hair had dark roots. She wore a beige suit and white blouse along with a small chain necklace. Bailey took a moment to deliver a quick scowl at Natty. She cleared her throat as she looked back at the judge.

"Mr. Decker is being charged with obstruction of justice and interfering with a police investigation."

For a moment it looked like she might continue, but Bailey set her lips in a firm line and said nothing more.

Dickerson looked perplexed. "Well, I *know* that. That's what I just read off the document. What I mean is, I would like more of an explanation."

"Mr. Decker was approached by a man named Meryl Hawkins."

"Meryl Hawkins? *The* Meryl Hawkins?"

"Yes, Your Honor. He was released from prison early because, well, because of medical issues. He met with Detective Mary Lancaster and Mr. Decker, proclaimed his innocence for the murders, and asked them to clear his name."

"And he was subsequently murdered?" said Dickerson.

"Yes."

"And how does that bring Mr. Decker here today?"

"Mr. Decker was asked by Captain Miller to look into the murder of Mr. Hawkins and also to reexamine the previous case against Mr. Hawkins."

Dickerson tapped his finger against the top of his bench and said patiently, "That in no way answers my question about why Mr. Decker is here today. Indeed, it only deepens my confusion, Ms. Bailey."

"Yes, Your Honor. I can understand that. But—"

Childress gripped the railing and abruptly stood. "Judge, please, if I may? I think I can clear this up."

Dickerson slid his gaze over to Childress, and Decker thought he could see a shadow pass over the jurist's features at the sight of Burlington's top cop.

Decker had not been the only one to think the superintendent of police was an arrogant, incompetent jerk who crossed the line when it suited him. There were many who had been stunned to see Childress leapfrog over the more senior Captain Miller for the superintendent job. But rumor was that Miller had declined the position because he wanted to remain closer to the people on the police force. And though he habitually treated underlings badly, Childress was polite and deferential to those above him in the pecking order. And he could make the biggest bunch of bullshit sound totally legit. Decker thought he might be about to get a sampling of that talent right now.

Dickerson said, "Superintendent Childress, I didn't see you over there. Can you explain what exactly is going on? If Captain Miller authorized Decker to—"

"That is absolutely true, Your Honor. However, after we looked at this matter again, we came to conclude that Mr. Decker, who is no longer a member of this department, could bring untold legal liability to the city of Burlington if he did something outside legal parameters while ostensibly acting on the department's behalf. Indeed, he was found searching the residence of Mr. Hawkins's old home without benefit of a search warrant."

"I didn't need a search warrant since I had the permission of the homeowner," interjected Decker.

Childress carried on smoothly, "Be that as it may, we can't run around behind Mr. Decker to make sure he follows the law. Indeed, he was formally told by this department not to involve himself in this investigation, and yet he disobeyed that request. We had no alternative but to take him into custody, and that's why we're here today."

Dickerson seemed to be wavering. "As I recall, didn't Detective Decker solve the case behind the terrible shootings at Burlington High School a couple of years ago?"

"Indeed, he did," said Childress. "In fact, the department awarded Mr. Decker a commendation for his work on the case, and I was there applauding as loud as anyone. This is clearly nothing personal, as I'm a big fan of Mr. Decker's. But we have a department to run and I can't sit by and see him do damage to it."

"All right, I see your point."

Bailey said, "Your Honor, this is simply a bail hearing and a chance for Mr. Decker to enter his plea."

"Not guilty," said Decker immediately.

"Are you represented by counsel, Mr. Decker?" asked the judge.

"Not yet, sir. I'm working on it, if it comes to that." He glanced over at Childress and saw the man staring at him with a grim expression.

Bailey quickly said, "Because of Mr. Decker's previous relationship with the department and his current work with the FBI, we're fine with him being released on his own recognizance."

Childress stepped forward. "I think Ms. Bailey's facts need to be somewhat updated, Your Honor. Mr. Decker no longer has ties to this community. He moved away over two years ago. And he obviously no longer works for the department, which is one of the reasons we're here today. And I have it on good authority that he may not even work for the FBI, so the points made by Ms. Bailey for his being released on his own recognizance fall away."

"Do you really consider Mr. Decker a flight risk?" asked Dickerson.

Childress spread his hands and said in a very sincere voice, "Again, when he was on the force, he had no bigger cheerleader than me, Judge. But he's been gone a long time now. I can't say that I know the man anymore. And, quite frankly, him going rogue like that after he was warned off the case, well, it does not inspire confidence, I have to say."

Dickerson looked over at Decker. "Is all that true?"

"I still work for the FBI. And I *do* have ties to the community."

Childress jumped in. "I'm afraid that's simply not true. He has no home here, or other property. Or job. Or—"

"My family is buried here," said Decker quietly, looking not at Childress, but staring directly at Dickerson. "That's why I came back to town. To visit the graves of my wife and my daughter. It would have been her fourteenth birthday." He paused. "So my ties to this community run very deep. About as deep as they can, in fact."

Natty clucked his tongue and rolled his eyes at this. Childress looked visibly put out by the statement. However, Bailey's eyes watered and she looked down at her hands.

Dickerson nodded. "Mr. Decker, I accept your not-guilty plea, and you are released without bond on your own recognizance. A trial date will be set. I just ask that if you are planning to leave the area that you let the court know."

"I'm not going anywhere, Your Honor, until *all* of this is settled."

Dickerson disappeared into his chambers. As soon as the door was closed, Childress stepped directly in front of Decker and looked him up and down. Now that the judge was no longer around, the man's entire demeanor had changed from professional and genuine to cocksure and mean.

"I can't tell you how thrilled I am that you're back in town, Decker. Because your ass is going down for this." He looked over at Natty. "What are the sentencing guidelines for this again, Natty?"

"One to three. Double that for aggravated circumstances."

Childress stared gleefully at Decker. "Here's hoping for aggravated circumstances, then."

Decker looked him over. "You must not want to solve Hawkins's murder."

"Why do you say that?" said Childress, the grin still planted on his face.

"You assigned Natty to it. He can't even solve the mystery of why you're a dick."

Bailey coughed and looked away, rubbing at her eye.

"You think you're so much smarter than everybody else, don't you?" barked Childress.

"No. But I know I screwed up the Richards and Katz murders. And I'm here to fix that."

"The only thing you should be working on are your obstruction and interference charges."

"I think that'll play itself out okay."

"Oh, you do, do you?" said Childress, his grin deepening as he shot a glance at Natty before looking back at Decker. "And why the hell is that?"

"I don't want to waste my time telling you, because you wouldn't understand."

Childress jammed a finger in Decker's chest. "I'm smart enough to be the superintendent of this fucking police department."

"No, you're really not. That's all due to you benefiting enormously from a principle."

"You're damn right I have principles."

"No, I said *principle*. Singular."

Childress looked at him strangely. "What the hell are you getting at?"

"It's actually named for you, Childress."

"What is?"

"The *Peter* Principle." Decker turned to Bailey. "I guess my lawyer, whenever I find one, will be in touch, Beth."

She nodded. "Thanks, Amos. I can give you some recommendations."

Decker looked over at Natty. "When I find Hawkins's and the Richardses' and Katz's murderers, I'll let you know."

"You're not to go anywhere near that," said Natty angrily.

"Somebody tried to kill me," said Decker. "I don't take kindly to that."

"We're working on that," said Natty.

"Any leads?" asked Decker.

"We're working on it," repeated Natty. "I don't like you, Decker. You know that. But I like even less people trying to take out a cop. I'm gonna get whoever did that."

Childress appeared to still be focused on what Decker had said to him.

"There's no law against an FBI agent investigating a crime," said Decker.

"I know you're not working this case for the FBI," said Natty.

"Based on what?" said Decker.

"Based on…based on…based on I damn well said so."

Bailey gave this comment a well-deserved eye roll, picked up her briefcase, and said in an incredulous tone to the still confused-looking Childress, "The *Peter* Principle?" When Childress still looked perplexed, she added, "For God's sake, just Google it."

She walked out.

Decker followed her.

"Where the hell do you think you're going?" snapped Childress.

Decker kept right on walking.

26

DECKER HAD JUST SETTLED into his bed.

His arrest and the bail hearing had shaken him more than he cared to show. With someone like Childress breathing down his neck, solving this case was going to be even harder. And it was difficult enough as it was.

He rolled over and punched his pillow, shaping it to be more comfortable.

Decker's memory—his albatross and gold mine all in one. It allowed him incredible tools to successfully do what he did, but also imprisoned him within an indestructible cell of recollections any other human being could simply allow time to extinguish.

He was actually glad Lancaster had had to recuse herself and Jamison had gone back to the FBI. Better to suffer this alone. After this case, he might just chuck the FBI and move off somewhere by himself. Well, he might not have a choice about that, actually. He knew Bogart was growing weary of his constantly going off on his own cases. The FBI was many things, and a bureaucracy with rules and ways of doing things was one of the main ones. Decker couldn't keep bucking that bureaucracy and those rules without suffering the consequences.

So it might just be me going it alone after this.

This admittedly self-pitying analysis came to an abrupt halt when the knock came at his door.

Groaning, he looked at his watch.

It was nearly eleven o'clock.

He turned over and closed his eyes.

Knock, knock.

He ignored it.

Then pounding followed.

He jumped out of bed, slid on his pants, padded across the small room to the door, and flung it open, ready to read the riot act to whoever was there. And if it was Natty, to perhaps do more than that.

It was not Natty.

Instead, there stood Melvin Mars—all nearly six-foot-three, two hundred and forty chiseled pounds of him.

Decker was so taken aback that he blinked and then closed his eyes for a full second. When he reopened them, Mars was still there.

Mars chuckled at this. "No, I'm not a dream, Decker, or a nightmare."

The pair, rivals from their college football days, had run into each other again when Mars, a Heisman Trophy finalist and lock to be a first-round NFL pick as a running back from Texas, had been sitting on death row for murder when another man had come forward claiming to have committed the crimes. This revelation had come on the very eve of Mars's execution.

Decker had helped to prove Mars's innocence, and Mars was given a full pardon and a huge monetary reward from both the federal government and the state of Texas as compensation for the erroneous guilty verdict as well as the racist and brutal treatment Mars had received at the hands of his prison guards. He owned the apartment building in D.C. where Decker and Jamison lived, leasing apartments out to those hardworking folks who otherwise could not afford rental prices in the capital with its high cost of living. He had been dating a woman whom they all had encountered during a previous investigation. Harper Brown worked for military intelligence. Unlike Mars, she came from money, but the two of them hit it off immediately. The last Decker had heard they were vacationing somewhere in the Mediterranean.

"What the hell are you doing here?" said Decker.

"Just happened to find myself in the area."

Decker looked at him skeptically. "Alex called you and told you to come here and watch over me, didn't she? Because she couldn't."

"If I lied and said no, would it matter?"

"Come on in." He closed the door behind Mars, who took a look around.

"Man, the FBI must have a pretty hefty per diem to let you stay in a luxury place like this. Couple levels above the Ritz."

"This actually used to be my home."

"I get that, Decker. My prison cell in Texas was a lot smaller and it didn't have a window."

"Do you have a place to stay? This only has the one bed."

"I'm actually staying here too. Just checked in. Exit date to be determined."

"You can afford to stay at the fanciest place in town."

"I've never needed fancy."

"I wish Alex hadn't done this."

"She cares about you. That's what friends do."

"Did she fill you in on what's been going on here?"

Mars sat down in the only chair in the room and nodded, as Decker perched on the edge of the bed. "She did. Sounds pretty messed up. What's happened since you two parted company?"

Decker started to explain. When he got to the part about being arrested, Mars put up his hand. "Whoa, whoa, wait a minute, your butt was in jail? I would've paid to see that."

"Depending on how things turn out, you might get to see it for free. On visitors' day."

"You're kidding, right?"

"I made some enemies in this town."

Mars's grin widened. "Not you, Decker. You're such a teddy bear. Never rub anyone the wrong way."

"You don't have to be here, Melvin."

"I don't go anywhere I don't want to. I spent twenty years

going nowhere, and I had no choice in the matter. Lots of catching up to do on that score. I'm here because I want to be, make no mistake."

"Where's Harper?"

"Back at work."

"How was the Mediterranean?"

"Magical. Never seen that much water in my whole life. West Texas is pretty damn dry."

"You two getting serious?"

"We're having fun, Amos. That's the gear we want to be in right now. No more, no less." He sat back and looked around. "So how do we do this? Looks like you got two mysteries. One from a long time ago. And one from right now."

"But they're connected. They have to be."

"So Meryl Hawkins gets out of prison, comes here, and tells you he's innocent. He wants you and your old partner to prove him right and clear his name. But that same night he gets killed."

"And the widow of one of his alleged victims has disappeared."

"So you think this Susan Richards shot him and now she's on the run?"

"I don't know, but it looks that way. They still haven't found her car or her. Which is pretty weird in this day and age."

"Well, it's a pretty big country too. Somebody can disappear if they want to. Look at my old man."

"Your father was a little more experienced with stuff like that than I suspect Susan Richards is. And he disappeared before there were smartphones with camera and video capabilities, and social media was nonexistent."

Mars shrugged. "Proof's in the pudding. Lady hasn't surfaced. And you still haven't answered my question. How do we attack this sucker?"

"Other things being equal, I think we need to solve the crime in the past to have any shot at figuring out who killed Meryl Hawkins."

"Well, you solved my cold case, and that one went back even further. So my money's on you."

"I'm not sure I'd take that bet."

"Going back in time. You know how you did it with me. So now?"

"I've spoken to the people involved back then. The widows. The daughter. The only remaining neighbors."

"How about the first responders? The ME?"

"The cops are no longer working. They've moved out of the area. The ME passed away three years ago."

"But you still got the records, though." Mars tapped his forehead. "Up here."

"Not all of them, because…because I didn't read everything. In particular the forensic file, at least not thoroughly."

Mars raised his eyebrows at this.

Decker did not miss this reaction. "I'd been a homicide detective all of five days when the call came in. That's not an excuse. But the print and DNA were slam dunks, or at least I thought they were. I wasn't as diligent about the rest of the stuff. And it might have cost Hawkins his freedom and then his life."

"Only thing that makes you, Decker, is human. And let me tell you I had my doubts about that." He tacked on a grin with this.

"I'm not supposed to make mistakes, at least not like that."

"And here you are trying to make up for it. Doing the best you can. That's all you can do."

When Decker didn't respond to this, Mars said, "What's wrong, Amos? This isn't the guy I know. Something is eating at you. And it's not just that you might have screwed up. So lay it out there, dude. Can't help if I can't follow."

"Some people are meant to be alone, work alone, just…alone."

"And you think you're one of them?"

"I *know* I am, Melvin."

"I was alone for twenty years, Amos. Just me and steel bars and concrete walls. And maybe a lethal needle waiting on my ass."

"Now I'm not following."

"Then let me lay it out clean for you. I was convinced I was a loner too. That that was just how life was going to be. But I made a mistake."

"How so?"

"I let circumstances beyond my control define me. That's not good. That's worse than lying to yourself. It's like you're lying to your soul."

"And you think that's where I am?"

"Alex told me why you two were here in the first place. Visiting your family at the cemetery."

Decker looked away.

"You feel tied to this place, and I get that. But see, you're not. You moved from here. Joined the FBI. And if you hadn't done that, I'd be rotting in a prison in Texas, or more likely dead. But this is not about me, it's about you."

"Maybe it was a mistake to move," said Decker.

"Maybe it was and maybe it wasn't. But the point is, you made that choice. You got the world's greatest memory, Amos. There's nothing you can't remember. Now I know that's a blessing and a curse. And with your family and what happened to them it's the worst of all possible things. But all the good stuff? All the happy times? You remember those too like they just happened. Hell, I can barely remember how my mom looked. I can't really remember her touch or her smile. I can't remember any of my birthdays when I was little. I just have to imagine how it was. But you *can* remember that stuff. So, you could move to Siberia and be out in a blizzard and you just got to close your eyes and you're right back here having dinner with your wife. Holding her hand. Getting Molly ready for school. Reading a book to her. It's all there, dude. It's *all* there."

Decker finally looked at him. "And that's what's so hard, Melvin." His voice slightly shook. "I will always very clearly know, like it was yesterday, how damn much I lost."

Mars rose, sat down next to his friend, and put his big arm around Decker's wide shoulders. "And that's what they call life, my friend. The good, the bad, and the ugly. But don't let the last two diminish the first one, 'cause the first one's the important one.

You keep that one alive, man, you can face down anything. That is the gospel truth."

The men sat there in silence, but still communicating exactly what they were feeling, as the best of friends often do.

27

"DON'T THINK ALEX WOULD APPROVE of this," said Mars.

He and Decker were standing in front of the breakfast bar in the lobby of the Residence Inn the next morning. It was laden with food constituting every cardiologist's nightmare.

"I used to love this part of the day," replied Decker, looking longingly at plates of bacon and plump sausages and scrambled eggs, and then over at stacks of pancakes, waffles, and jars of syrup.

"Well, it didn't love you back."

"Amos!"

They both looked over at the tiny, withered woman who was hurrying toward them carrying a plate of flaky biscuits. She was in her eighties, with sparkling white hair crammed under a hair net.

"Heard you were back in town." She held up the plate. "You want to just take this plate to your table, like you used to? Made 'em myself."

"Hello, June." He looked at the biscuits for a long moment, until Mars poked him in the side.

Decker started and said, "I think I'll pass, but thanks. I think I'll just get some, um, orange juice and a bowl of the oatmeal."

June eyed him suspiciously. "You've lost weight. I mean, you're almost skinny. You sick?"

"No, I'm actually healthier than I've been in a long time."

Her look said that she highly doubted this was true. "Well, if you change your mind, just give me the high sign." She glanced at Mars. "Your friend could use some fattening up too."

Mars cracked a smile. "Yes ma'am. I'll get right on that, *tomorrow*."

"Well, all right then." She scampered off.

Mars eyed all the food at the buffet and shook his head. "Man, how did you end up not stroking at your table when you lived here?"

* * *

They had just finished their meal when Decker's phone buzzed. It was Sally Brimmer.

"I copied all the files to a flash drive," she said, her voice barely above a whisper. "I don't want to email it to you because that could be traced, and I like my job."

"I can meet you somewhere and you can give me the flash."

"I get off work at six. You know McArthur Park on the east side of town?"

"Yeah."

"I can meet you at the little pond there, say six-thirty?"

"I'll be there. And I really appreciate this, Ms. Brimmer."

"Just make it Sally. Co-conspirators should be able to use first names, *Amos*."

The line went dead.

Mars eyed him. "Good news?"

"I think so, yeah."

His phone buzzed again. He thought it might be Brimmer calling back, but it was another number. One that Decker recognized.

"Captain Miller?"

"Amos, first I want to say that I'm sorry."

"For what?"

"For what happened to you. The arrest, and the bail hearing, where I heard from Beth that Natty and Childress made it crystal clear that they're unmitigated assholes."

"I already knew that. And none of this was your fault."

"No, it was, because I let Childress get the upper hand. He outmaneuvered me. But I played another hand last night. I went straight to the commissioner. And then he went to his boss. The result is that right now you are allowed to observe on the case."

"What does that mean exactly?"

"Pretty much like it sounds. Natty and Childress can't stop you from being there. You can look at clues, you can even talk to witnesses, and run down potential leads. You can't bring suspects in for questioning, though, but you will be privy to forensic testing and other results of the investigation."

"And Natty will still be working it?"

"Unfortunately, yes. I wish to God that Mary hadn't had to recuse herself."

"You're not alone on that. But I appreciate all that you did, Captain Miller. And at least I can be part of the case again." He glanced at Mars. "I do have a new assistant working with me. I assume he can tag along."

"You can try, Amos. Natty will probably blow a gasket, but I'll leave it to you to figure out a way. Now, there's one more thing."

"What's that?"

"They found Susan Richards's car."

"Where?"

Miller gave him the details.

"But no trace of her?" said Decker.

"None. I'm sure Natty is already up there checking it out. Tread carefully. I wish I could offer more, but the bureaucracy keeps getting in the way."

Again, the line went dead.

Decker quickly explained to Mars what had just happened.

"So they found her ride, but not her? What does that tell you?"

"Not much," replied Decker.

"So we head there now?"

"Yes, we do."

June was walking past and Decker grabbed a couple biscuits off the platter without the tiny woman even noticing. He flipped one to Mars before taking a bite out of his. "Don't say I never gave you anything."

Mars looked down at his biscuit before biting into it as well. "Yeah, like a heart attack."

* * *

Decker pulled his rental to a stop right on the other side of the police tape flapping in a stiff breeze. Cop cars were everywhere, along with state trooper vehicles.

The car was about two hours outside of Burlington. It had been discovered behind an abandoned motel that had closed its doors about forty years before. It was on a local road that had been shunned by travelers once a nearby interstate opened.

Decker and Mars climbed out of the car and looked around. An officer immediately came up to them. Decker pulled out his creds and held them up.

"FBI?" said the officer. "What are you doing here?"

"Same thing you are. Trying to find Susan Richards."

"Hey!"

Decker had expected this, and still his blood pressure started to rise.

Natty walked over to them. "I guess you talked to Miller."

"*Captain* Miller. Your superior."

Natty pointed a finger in Decker's face. "You *observe*, that's all. You step out of line, your ass is right back in the slammer again."

The cop looked between them and said, "You put an FBI agent in jail?"

"He's not a real FBI agent."

"Really?" said Mars sharply. "This dude saved the life of the president of the United States. Has a direct line to the man in the White House. Had his picture taken with him, got a medal and a letter of commendation." Mars crossed two of his fingers. "Dudes are like this."

The officer looked up at Decker in awe.

Natty bristled and gazed up at Mars. "Who the hell are you?"

"He's my assistant," said Decker.

"I thought you worked with Jamison."

"She's on another mission."

"Is he an FBI agent?"

"He operates under the auspices of my creds."

"What exactly does that mean?" said Natty.

"It means I go to the commissioner if you try to block me from observing, Natty."

"You are so full of shit."

"Who found the car?" asked Decker.

Natty looked like he might not answer.

"Look, Natty, I was being straight with you before. If I can find out who did this, the collar is yours."

"Like I need your help to do that."

"Okay, then I observe without your help. But if I make the collar, the FBI gets all the credit. But I don't see how Childress would want that. And he may be backing you right now, but that wasn't always the case, Natty. He'll throw you under the bus in a second if he thinks it'll make him look good. Remember the Hargrove case?"

At the mention of this name, Natty noticeably stiffened, and though his look was still sullen, he flipped open his notebook.

"Guy Dumpster diving found the car at around four o'clock this morning. Called in the locals. They pulled up our BOLO and notified us."

"Can we take a look at the vehicle?"

"The trace team's already been over it."

"Just observing."

Natty licked his lips, made a grunting sound, turned, and walked off. Decker and Mars followed.

Mars whispered, "Don't see why you thought this guy was an A-hole, Decker. He's a real pussycat."

"Minus the cat," replied Decker.

"So this Childress guy is even worse?"

"He's worse because, unlike Natty, he can slickly pretend to be what he's not, to the *right* people. And that's what makes him so dangerous."

28

THE SMALL OLD HONDA with the bad muffler was wedged next to a huge rusted construction Dumpster, like an enormous barnacle on a ship's metal hull.

Decker and Mars stood a few feet away. Decker's gaze swept over the car and the environs, before alighting on the blue-scrubbed tech collecting evidence.

"Hey again, Decker," said Kelly Fairweather. "Who's your friend?"

"Melvin Mars," said Mars, stepping forward and putting out his hand. "I'm, uh, assisting Agent Decker in this investigation."

"Cool," said Fairweather.

"What do you have so far?" asked Decker, keeping one eye on Natty, who was consulting with another tech on the other side of the Honda.

"Well, for starters, no prints other than Susan Richards's. Inside or out."

"Makes sense, it *is* her car," said Mars.

"Her luggage gone from the back?" asked Decker.

"Yep. Nothing there."

"Keys?"

"No keys."

"No meaningful trace?"

"No blood, semen, body parts, human tissue, or other significant biological remains."

"No sign of another person being in the car?"

"Nope. Just her."

"Mind if I take a look?" asked Decker.

"Go ahead. Use these."

He moved toward the car after slapping on the pair of latex gloves Fairweather had handed him. Mars followed behind him.

Natty looked up as Decker approached, but then returned to his conversation with the other tech.

All four doors of the Honda were open, and so was the trunk liftgate. Decker pointed to the Dumpster. "I'm assuming someone checked for a body in there."

Fairweather nodded and made a face. "We did. Nothing but trash. I'll need a tetanus booster."

"No evidence from her or the car in it?"

"Not that we could find."

Decker ran his eye over all of this and then poked his head inside the front driver's-side door and checked the seats there. He did the same for the rear seats as Mars hovered by his shoulder.

"Kelly, have you logged the positions for all prints you found, interior and exterior?"

She nodded and pulled out an electronic pad. "All on here. Lot easier than the way we used to do it years ago, right?"

"Right," said Decker absently as he looked over the different digital screens.

Fairweather said, "All the usual places. Steering wheel, cupholder, console, glove compartment, gearshift, control knobs, rearview mirror, dashboard, inside of the door and window."

"And outside?" asked Decker as he moved to that digital page.

"Door handle, driver's front side, and rear doors. And exterior driver's-side window. Again, the usual."

"And we've had no meaningful rain since she disappeared."

"Correct."

"So no recent prints would have been damaged or even washed off by a heavy rain."

"Right."

"How long do prints last on something?" asked Mars.

"Depends on the surface involved, what substance might have been on the fingers, the timing, the weather conditions, a whole host of factors," said Fairweather.

Decker handed her back the pad. "What else?"

"Not a lot. We don't know how far the car's been driven because we didn't know the odometer reading before she left. She did have an oil change sticker on her windshield. The car's been driven about four hundred miles since then, but the oil change happened over three weeks ago. Not much we can deduce from that."

"Insect debris on the front and the windshield?"

"Not too much. But she could have gotten it washed after she left town."

Decker nodded because he too had thought of this.

"So, Decker, have you solved it?" Natty had walked around the side of the car and was looking up at him.

"Just observing," said Decker.

Natty smirked. "Always knew you were overrated."

"Yeah, dude's been here ten seconds," said Mars. "How long you been here?"

Natty looked over at him. "Who the hell are you, really?"

"Decker's *assistant*. You might want to follow my lead on that, you know? *Assist* the man."

"You got a real comedian here, Decker," said Natty irritably.

"One thing I would draw your attention to," said Decker.

"What's that?"

"There's no print on the rear liftgate."

"So what? Richards got in the front seat."

"After she put a really heavy piece of luggage in the rear compartment."

"She used her key fob to open the trunk."

Decker shook his head. "Agatha Bates, her neighbor, said Richards started up the car and then went back inside and brought out a large piece of luggage that she put in the rear cargo hold. And she struggled to do so before slamming the liftgate shut." Decker paused and looked from Fairweather back to Natty.

"There were no prints anywhere on the liftgate," said Fairweather. "I went inch by inch."

"Pretty weird," said Mars.

"No, it's not," said Natty. "She used the button on her key fob to open it, like I just said."

"She couldn't," said Decker.

"Why?"

"The keys were in the ignition. This car is old enough, so you have to put the key *in* the ignition, not just have it with you to start the car. So the key and the fob already would have been in the vehicle." He eyed Natty. "Check out the ignition if you don't believe me."

"Okay, if that's the case, where's the print?" said Natty, looking confused.

"Good question."

"What does its absence tell us?" asked Natty.

"Another good question," said Decker. "And here's one more. Why did she start the car first and then go back into the house and bring the luggage out? Why not bring the luggage out, start the car, and drive off? The way she did it, the lady had to make two trips instead of one."

Natty's brow furrowed. "Okay, I give. Why would she—?"

But Decker had already turned and walked off.

"Damn it, I hate when the sonofabitch does that," exclaimed Natty.

Mars said, "Yeah, I get that. But second piece of advice, man?"

Natty eyed him. "Why should I listen to you? I don't even know you."

"Yeah, but I know Decker. You want to solve this sucker and get your next promotion, give the dude some room to work."

"I'm running this case!"

"But what you don't want to do is run it into the ground. Just my two cents."

Mars turned and followed Decker.

Natty looked at Fairweather, who was staring at him. "What?" he barked.

"I don't know that guy, but to me, he makes a lot of sense."

"Why does everybody think Amos Decker walks on water!" barked Natty.

"Hey, the guy's got his issues. We all know that. But when it comes to catching bad guys, do you know *anybody* who does it better?"

She went back to work, leaving Natty staring down at his shoes.

29

On the drive back to town, Decker said nothing.

Mars would look over at him occasionally, and several times appeared ready to ask something, but then he'd glance away and remain silent.

"You have something to say?" Decker finally asked.

Mars grinned. "Was I that obvious?"

"Apparently."

"That Natty guy has it in for you. What's that about?"

"He didn't like the fact that Lancaster and I solved most of the homicides in Burlington. Well, more than most. Basically all. He was the rising star in the department before I got bumped to detective. He got relegated to investigating lesser crimes, and I think he blames me. Then he made a big mistake on the Hargrove case. Missing person turned homicide. That sidetracked his career. Since I left I guess he's been attempting a comeback. And he kisses Pete Childress's ass, even though the guy hung him out to dry when the fallout came on the Hargrove matter."

"Is he any good at being a detective?"

"He's *competent*. But he always goes for the easiest solution. And he makes mistakes. Gets sloppy at times. Assumes things he shouldn't."

"Like you did with the murders all those years ago?"

Decker glanced over at him. "I deserved that."

"Come on, I was just pulling your chain. I'm telling you, you keep yourself under all that pressure, you're gonna pop one day."

"I think my popping days are over."

"What's on the agenda now?"

Decker looked at the clock on the dashboard.

"We've got some time before we meet Sally Brimmer and pick up the flash drive."

"So where?"

"Susan Richards's house."

* * *

Decker pulled his car into the driveway about two hours later and they got out. Decker glanced over at Agatha Bates's home and thought he could see the old woman on her screen porch reading a book.

Mars looked the house over. "You think Richards is dead?"

"No signs of violence in the car. Or outside it. No one's found a body. But still, she could be dead."

"How are we going to get in?"

"I've got a key. My old partner, Mary Lancaster, gave it to me while we were working Susan Richards's disappearance." Decker put the key in the lock and began to turn it.

"Wait a minute, Decker. Will this get you in trouble? Aren't you just supposed to be observing?"

"Well, when I go into the house, I'll just be *observing*."

Decker led Mars into the front part of the house.

"So, Richards packs a big bag and hightails it out of here after you bring her in for questioning on the Hawkins murder."

"And we couldn't confirm her alibi. The other neighbors weren't home during the time in question. And the old lady across the street, the one who saw Richards leaving, can't completely account for Richards's movements when Hawkins was killed."

"Which may explain why she ran for it. She killed the guy."

"But how would she even know he was back in town?" Decker wondered.

"Maybe she ran into him. Or saw him and followed him back to the Residence Inn. That's possible."

"It is *possible*, but not probable."

"Then what are we doing here?"

Decker led the way upstairs and into the woman's bedroom. He went straight for the closet. It had been reconfigured and enlarged, he figured, because the house was old enough not to have originally had such a spacious closet. It was packed with clothes on hangers, sweaters and shoes on shelves, and purses and handbags on hooks. He stood in the middle of the space and looked around.

Mars said, "Harper has a closet about four times the size of this one. And it's packed to the gills. Didn't know one person could need all that stuff."

"Society demands that women care more about their appearance than men."

"Wow, that's very enlightened of you."

"It's not me. My wife would always say that."

"Well, looks like Susan Richards took that to heart."

Decker noted several empty hangers, a space on a shelf where it looked like two pairs of shoes had been removed, and a hook without a corresponding bag.

He left the closet and went over to a chest of drawers. He went through each one. Then he walked into the bathroom and examined every inch of the space, including the bins under the sink.

He got up and opened the medicine cabinet and looked at the line of prescription bottles. He picked them up and examined each one in turn, holding one bottle for a beat longer before replacing it.

"Lady is on a lot of meds," said Mars.

"*America* is on a lot of meds," replied Decker.

They walked back down to the first floor and Decker headed over to the fireplace mantel. He looked over each of the photos lined up there.

"Her family?" asked Mars.

Decker nodded. "Husband and two kids. In an ideal world Susan Richards might be a grandmother by now."

Mars shook his head. "There's nothing ideal about this world."

Decker looked around the room, his eyes taking in everything and then processing it.

"What are you seeing, Decker?" asked Mars as he too stared around the space. "Is anything missing?'

"Not really. And that's the problem, Melvin."

30

It was dusk now and with the dropping of the sun, the temperature had lowered to a level where one could see one's breath.

Decker had left Mars in the car parked at the curb. His rationale was that Sally Brimmer would not appreciate another person being in the loop of her possibly illegal action in giving Decker the records he needed. He strode through the small park to the pond that lay near its rear, which one reached by traversing a winding brick path. There was no one else there that he could see.

When he turned the last corner and the pond came into view, so did Brimmer. She had on a long trench coat, a hat, and gloves. She looked over at Decker and hurried past the pond, which had an aerator in its middle, throwing off streams of water and affording a pleasing sound. That was also good, Decker thought, because it would be difficult for anyone to eavesdrop on them.

She reached him, her hand in her pocket. Brimmer suddenly shivered.

"Winter's definitely coming," noted Decker.

"It's not the weather," she said, a trace of bitterness in her tone. "I'm nervous. What I'm doing could cost me my job."

"No one will find out from me. And if it makes you feel any better, I'm only going to use the files to try to find the truth."

"I know that," she said, her voice now contrite. She looked around and pulled her hand out of her pocket. In her palm was a flash drive.

"How did you manage to scan all the files without anyone knowing?"

"I've been after the department to convert paper files to digital ones. I've actually been doing some of it myself, although it's not technically my responsibility. But I had the time, and it wasn't like some of the older people at the department had any interest, or would even know how to do it. I just included the files you wanted in a stack I was already doing." She handed him the flash drive.

"Ingenious," said Decker.

"High praise coming from you."

"Captain Miller managed to get a meeting with the commissioner, with the result that I'm officially back on the case, as an observer."

"Well, that's something."

"It's better than nothing," agreed Decker. "They found Susan Richards's car and I was able to go over it."

"What about Blake?"

"He was there but voiced no objections. He might be seeing that I could be useful, especially if he gets the credit if I do figure this out."

"He'll turn on you if he gets the chance," said Brimmer warningly.

"I'm under no illusions when it comes to Natty." He cocked his head. "How about you?"

"How about me what?" she said defensively.

"You've got a lot going for you, Sally. You could do a lot better than Natty. Someone your own age who's actually single, for instance. I guess I just don't see the attraction on your end."

"Why do you care? I always thought you were just this...machine." She suddenly looked chastened. "I'm sorry, that was really out of line. I didn't mean it."

"You're not the first to say that, and you won't be the last. As to you, I was a father with a daughter, like I said. I...I don't want you to be hurt or get in a situation you can't get out of."

Brimmer looked down at the brick pavers under her feet. "I work long hours. All I know are cops. I don't have any family here, and few friends. Blake...he took an interest. He even used that old line that his wife just doesn't get him or his work." She laughed hollowly. "And I fell for it, I guess. Just like a million other women. But he did make me feel special."

"*Did*?"

She smiled resignedly. "I've broken it off with him, Amos. It wasn't just what you said, although I needed to hear that too. He *is* married. And I wouldn't want that to happen to me if I were married. It's not fair. And it does speak to a person's character if they're willing to cheat like that, as you said."

"I'm glad you reached that decision."

"You never cheated on your wife, did you?"

"Never even thought about it. I had everything, Sally. A wife who I loved beyond anything I'd ever felt before. And a daughter who I would have sacrificed anything for. Now I don't have either one."

"But you have memories. Good ones."

"Yeah, I do. But it's not the same. Even for someone with a memory like mine. Memories don't keep you warm at night. And they don't make you laugh, not really." He paused. "But they can make you cry."

She put a hand on his arm and squeezed. "And to think, I used to believe that you were this gigantic jerk."

"I can be. As you well know."

"And you can be someone else too, Amos. Someone I would like to call a friend."

"We *are* friends, Sally. I know what it took for you to help me. Even if my memory sucked, I'd never forget that."

They grew silent until Brimmer said, "I better get going."

"I'll walk you out. It's pretty dark in here and there're a lot of places for creeps to hide."

"Never stop being a cop?"

"It's just how I'm wired."

They reached the street a couple of minutes later.

"Thank you again," said Decker.

"No, thank *you*, Amos." She spontaneously went over and hugged him. Decker bent down to hug her back.

Right as the shot hit.

CHAPTER

31

DECKER FELT THE WOMAN go limp in his arms at the same time as he felt something wet hit his face. He slumped to the pavement holding Brimmer, as he heard shouts and feet running. He looked up to see Mars sprinting toward him.

"Get down, Melvin!" he called out.

"Over there, Decker!" said Mars, pointing to his left, across the street.

Decker checked Brimmer. The bullet had entered the left side of her head and exited out the other side, in the direction of the park. Her glassy eyes were staring lifelessly up at him.

He knew she was dead, but he still checked her pulse. With no blood pumping through her body, the woman was already growing cold.

"Shit," Decker said, looking dazed and in disbelief. He touched his face where her blood had landed.

He looked over at Mars, and then across the street from where the shot had come. He pulled his gun, got up, and raced across the street, with Mars right behind him.

Decker pulled out his phone, dialed 911, identified himself, and told the dispatcher what had happened and the exact location. "We're in pursuit of the shooter. Get some cop cars out here now and we can box the sonofabitch in." He put the phone in his pocket and picked up his pace.

Mars took a slight lead because he had seen where the shot had come from. As they ran along, Decker said, "Did you see the person?"

Mars shook his head. "Just a silhouette, at the opening of that alley. I had no time to warn you. I just happened to glance that way right as he fired."

They reached the alley and peered down it. Decker checked the building. It was being rehabbed. Construction materials were all over the place, along with scaffolding.

"Think the asshole's still down there?" said Mars.

"Don't know. If he is, we'll get him."

As soon as Decker said this, they could hear the sirens.

"Cavalry's on the way," he noted.

"But if I'm the shooter, I'm getting the hell out of here," said Mars.

"Which is why we're not waiting. Stay behind me."

"You don't have to be my human shield, Decker."

"You're a running back, Melvin. I'm a blocker. But if he takes me out, do not let me die in vain."

They moved down the alley, intently listening for any sound of footsteps, breathing, or, more ominously, a trigger being cocked.

Decker held up a hand. He had heard something.

"What?" hissed Mars.

Decker put a finger to his lips.

Now Mars could hear it too. Heavy breathing, like someone had been running but had stopped.

As the sirens drew closer, Decker started to pick up his pace. Mars stayed right with him. They reached a spot about midway down the alley when Decker halted once more. The spot was brightly lit by overhead lights. The sound of breathing had grown stronger.

Decker pointed his gun straight ahead and then hustled forward.

The man was lying on the asphalt, his head on top of what looked to be a rolled-up bunch of rags. Next to him was a bag full of items. He was dressed in filthy clothing. The heavy breathing that they had heard was his snoring, apparently.

"Decker," whispered Mars. "Is that a gun?"

Lying on the ground next to the man and within reach of his outstretched hand was a rifle with a scope. Decker stepped forward and used his foot to slowly move the gun away from the man.

The next moment he was slammed against the brick wall. His face hit the rough brick and he felt several cuts opening on his face. His pistol smashed into the brick and he felt something snap. The collision had been so sudden that he felt sick to his stomach.

He turned, eyed the man still lying on the ground, dead asleep. The attack had not come from there.

"Decker!"

Decker regained his equilibrium, cleared his head, and looked back.

Mars was dodging out of the way of a knife strike, as the man who had clocked Decker moved in for the kill. He was small but wiry, and his movements were laser quick and precise.

Decker hurtled forward, and when the man turned the knife on him, he pointed his gun and fired at his leg.

Absolutely nothing happened. The impact with the wall must have damaged the weapon.

The next instant the man kicked the gun out of Decker's hand, then drove his fist into Decker's gut, doubling him over.

Decker staggered back at the same moment that Mars hit the man from behind so hard that he was lifted off his feet, flew forward, and slammed into the wall. He was up in an instant, though, and whirled around, the blade in his hand.

He charged after Mars and slashed him on the arm. Mars fell back and the man was about to cut him again when Decker launched forward and wrapped his big arms around the assailant, pinning his arms and the knife to his sides. Under the illumination of the lights attached to the buildings, he could see that, despite the cold, the man's muscled forearms were exposed, and covered in tats—words and symbols.

A few seconds of struggle later, the man slammed the back of his head against Decker's face. Blood flew out of Decker's nose and mouth. Then the man was able to point the knife downward and jam it into Decker's thigh. Decker cried out and released the man, who hit the ground running and soon disappeared from sight as the sirens grew closer. Decker put a hand over his leg wound.

Mars ran forward, took off his windbreaker, and wrapped it around Decker's thigh.

Decker said, "Are you okay?"

"He didn't get me bad. Who the hell was that guy?"

"He's the one who shot Sally Brimmer."

"You have any idea why?"

"The only idea I have is that he was trying to shoot me. And she just got in the way."

32

THE MORGUE AGAIN.

Decker had been in far too many of them.

And the electric blue light sensation was bombarding him almost like the night he had found his family. It was as if a strobe was attached to the ceiling of the room and was blasting the unsettling light into every pore of the place.

He touched his leg where underneath his pants a large butterfly bandage had been applied. The emergency room doctor had told him he'd been lucky. Another couple inches to the left and his femoral artery would have been nicked. And he might have bled out right there in that alley.

He next touched his face, which was covered in Band-Aids and bandages. He was stiff and sore and felt like he'd just played in an NFL game. Mars was next to him, his injured arm in a sling. But at least they were still alive. Lying in front of them was Sally Brimmer's pale body with a sheet pulled up to her neck.

The homeless man in the alley had turned out to be what he looked like—homeless. And strung out on so much crap that it had taken the EMTs an hour to wake him up. The gun had no usable prints, and Decker knew why. The shooter had been wearing gloves. He had probably flung the murder weapon next to the homeless man to simply get rid of it. He had attacked Decker and Mars because they had gotten to him before he reached the other end of the alley. Lying in wait, he had tried to add two more lives to the one he'd already taken. Unfortunately, he had managed to elude the police and get away.

The ME was in the room, washing a few of his instruments in the sink. There was only one overhead fluorescent light on, throwing the room into shadows and making an already disconcerting sensation worse.

A moment later the door clanged open and there was Blake Natty, his face white, his features screwed up in agony. He lurched over to Brimmer's sheet-draped body and looked down at it. He put a hand to his mouth, and Decker heard the man start to quietly sob.

No one said anything until Natty had composed himself and rubbed his eyes dry on his coat sleeve. He looked over at Decker and Mars. Next, he ran his gaze over their wounds. "Heard he almost got you both too."

"Almost," said Decker. "The guy was a lot smaller than we were."

"Small but lethal," said Mars. "I've seen guys with shivs, hardened cons, who couldn't wield a blade anything like that dude."

"Guys with shivs? Hardened cons?" said Natty. "Were you a prison guard or something?"

"Or something," said Mars quietly.

Decker rubbed his stomach. "And he had fists like bricks. And some crazy arm tats."

Natty said, "What were you and Sally even doing there?"

Decker knew this question was coming and had prepared several answers. One came tumbling out. It happened to be the truth.

"I arranged to meet Sally at McArthur Park. We were coming out to the street when the guy opened fire."

"Why did you want to meet with her?"

"Because I wanted to get her help on the case. I won't be able to help you solve it by merely *observing*, Blake. You know that, and I know that."

Decker had been prepared for Natty to explode at this comment, but to his surprise the detective merely nodded. He rubbed his nose and said, "I guess I can see that. Do you...do you think Sally was the target?"

"No. I was. Someone already tried to kill me once. We were

standing so close together that the shooter hit Sally and not me." He paused and looked at the disconsolate Natty. "I'm sorry, Blake. I really am. Sally was just trying to do the right thing."

Mars said, "Why is someone so desperate to kill you?"

"Someone doesn't want Decker to figure out the truth," replied Natty. "I mean, you worked on that case all those years ago. Hawkins came to you and Mary to clear his name. And now they're going to try to stop you. Mary got recused, but you're still on the trail."

"So are you," pointed out Decker. "I think we all have to watch our backs."

"So you think someone hired the guy to do this?" said Natty.

"I do. Which means that Hawkins was innocent. And that means the forensic evidence tying him to the scene was somehow forged."

Natty glanced at him incredulously. "Prints and DNA at a crime scene. Forged?"

"It can be done," responded Decker.

"It would be hard as hell," retorted Natty.

"But not impossible."

"Who would want to frame Meryl Hawkins?" asked Natty.

"Wrong way to look at it."

"What's the right way, then?"

"Someone wanted to get away with murder. Hawkins was the patsy they chose to hold the bag. It could have been anybody, but for some reason they chose him. *That's* how we have to look at it."

"But, Decker, that turns this whole case upside down," said Natty.

"No, the case has always been right side up. We've just been looking at it from the wrong angle."

"You mean we have to start from square one?" said Natty.

Decker pulled the flash drive out of his pocket and held it up. "Commencing with this." He looked over at Brimmer's body. "Because the dead deserve answers," he said. "Sometimes more than the living."

CHAPTER

33

MARS WAS SOUND ASLEEP on the bed in Decker's room. It was past two in the morning and yet Decker was wide awake sitting in a chair and studying his laptop. He was scrolling through all the information that had been on the thumb drive Brimmer had given him.

He had taken off his belt holster with his new pistol to replace the old one damaged in the fight in the alley and laid it on the nightstand. He was still upset that he had let the shooter get away.

He and Mars had been at this for hours, until Mars had grown exhausted and collapsed on Decker's bed instead of going to his own room. The rain was pouring outside, and Decker could hear the drops ramming his window like thrown handfuls of gravel. It was one of those Ohio Valley storms that sprang up out of nowhere and pounded the entire state for a while.

But right now, he had tuned out the storm and homed in on the critical facts of his case from over thirteen years ago.

The 911 call had come in at 9:35 about a disturbance at the Richardses' house. That should have been a red flag for him, as should many things, in retrospect.

Who made the call? And what was the disturbance?

Not even the neighbors had noticed anything unusual that night. And there were no tracks of any other car coming to the house that night, just David Katz's. With the rain and mud, there would have been fresh tire tracks. So no other car had been there.

And here was the kicker. Decker was looking at the times of death provided by the medical examiner who had done the posts on the four bodies. The ME had said that all four victims had been killed close to eight-thirty. The records showed that he had based his conclusion on several indicators, one being the temperature of the bodies when they were discovered. Although Decker knew that was very tricky and could be affected by numerous factors. But a one-and-a-half-degree Fahrenheit drop in body temperature per hour after death was the standard rule.

But principally the ME had based his conclusion on the contents of the Richards family's stomachs. Susan Richards had testified that she had made dinner for the family and then left it in the oven before she went out. She said the family usually ate dinner at around six. The autopsies of the Richardses had revealed that if they had indeed eaten around six, the state of digestion of their food demonstrated that around two and a half hours had passed between their eating the food and being killed. It was not an exact time, the ME had been careful to stress, but he felt confident. And he could not possibly have been off by a full hour, he said.

Katz had shown up around six-thirty, according to Mrs. De-Angelo's testimony. The meal presumably had been finished and the kitchen had been cleaned up by then. Decker had even checked the dishwasher and seen the three empty plates and accompanying glasses and utensils inside. That probably confirmed that the Richardses had indeed eaten at around six. If they had still been eating when Katz had shown up, they might have invited him to join them, but the contents of the dishwasher demonstrated this had not been the case. He had probably arrived when they were cleaning up after finishing dinner.

Richards had offered him a beer and the kids had gone upstairs. And then someone had come and killed them all.

But that's when things got weird.

Because that meant that four people lay dead in the house for a little over an hour before someone called 911, citing a disturbance. And they had called from a phone that no one had been able to trace.

Now that Decker was looking at all of this with a detached, objective eye, the holes in the story seemed obvious. He actually groaned at his ineptitude.

Okay, time of death does not jibe with the 911 call citing a disturbance. Four dead bodies could hardly cause a disturbance an hour after they died.

An alternative theory occurred to him suddenly. Had someone entered the house and stumbled upon the four bodies an hour later and that person had been the one to call 911? And had that person been Meryl Hawkins? That might explain how his fingerprints had been found on a light switch. But that could not explain his DNA ending up under Abigail Richards's fingernails. And how could Hawkins possess a phone that couldn't be traced?

Decker put those difficulties aside and focused on another. They really didn't know the order in which the victims had died. They had just assumed that the bodies on the first floor had been dealt with before the killer had gone upstairs to dispatch the two children.

That was problematic, Decker knew. And he had thought so all those years ago too, though he had finally discounted the significance of it. You shoot two people on the first floor, there's going to be some noise, and not just the gunshots. There will be people shouting, presumably, or a scuffle. The house was not that large. Those sounds would surely have carried upstairs.

There was one landline phone upstairs, in the parents' bedroom, and they had determined that neither of the Richards kids had cell phones. But still, they could have tried to reach the phone in the bedroom and call the police, then hide, or escape out a window. But they hadn't.

He could imagine the older Frankie Richards being a little more able to react to something like that than his younger sister. The kid was a drug user and also a small-time dealer, and was thus used to being around potentially bad actors and some level of risk. He kept cash and product at his house, they had found. He had to know that someone might come and try to take either one or both. Back in those days, you didn't have to have thousands of dollars or bricks of coke to warrant a theft like that. People would kill you for fifty bucks and a bag of weed.

Had the sounds of the storm covered the two deaths downstairs?

And had the children not known what was happening until it was too late?

Decker passed on to his next question as the rain continued to pound outside. Why had Abigail been strangled when all the other victims had been shot? Decker thought he knew the answer to that one.

But as his eyes hovered over the screen, his mind suddenly filled up with so many blinding images that he almost felt like he would vomit.

In his mind's eye he was at his house the night he'd found his family dead. Electric blue sensations were pounding him from all corners. He had always been able to push, or at least diminish, this memory by banishing it to a far recess of his mind. But now, stunningly enough, he was unable to do so. It was as if he was no longer in control of his own mind. It was like a spontaneous, uncontrolled data dump from a computer.

He stood on shaky legs and wondered whether he could make it to the bathroom before he threw up. But then his stomach cleared, yet his mind did not.

He glanced over at Mars, who was still sound asleep on the bed.

Part of Decker wanted to wake his friend, explain what was happening to him, and ask for help. But what sort of help could Mars possibly give him? And Decker would feel embarrassed even asking.

Instead, he stumbled out of the room, down the hall, and then down the stairs. He used the rear exit door that he had told Lancaster about. He lurched outside where the trash and recycling Dumpsters were located. The rain was still pouring, and in just a few seconds Decker was soaked to the skin.

He finally hunched down under a metal roof that covered part of the rear of the inn. Over and over in his mind he saw himself going through his old house, the one now occupied by the Hendersons. Step by step.

His brother-in-law in the kitchen.

His wife on the floor by the side of their bed, only her foot visible when he entered the room.

And finally, Molly tied to the toilet in the bathroom with the sash from her robe. She'd been strangled to death, just like Abigail Richards.

And they had all died because of—

Me.

Decker put his hands over his head and sat there on the cold asphalt as the rain pounded down on the metal roof above.

He thought he had hit rock bottom when he'd lost his family, his job, his home. He had nothing.

But this, he thought to himself as the images unspooled over and over in his head, beginning with his brother-in-law and ending with daughter.

This…this is rock bottom.

CHAPTER

34

"YOU OKAY?"

It was the next morning and Mars was staring at Decker from across the table in the Residence Inn's dining area.

"Fine, why?"

"Because when I woke up you were in the bathroom, sounding like you were throwing up."

"Must've imagined it. My stomach was a little rocky, but that's it."

"I knocked on the door, don't you remember that? Asking if you were okay?"

"Don't *you* remember? I told you I was good and then I guess you went to your room. But before that you'd fallen asleep on my bed. You were probably mentally out of it when you checked on me."

Mars studied him for a moment but then shrugged. "You were up late. I ran out of gas."

"I was going over stuff, trying to make sense of things that don't seem to make sense."

"Like what?"

Decker outlined for him what he had thought about last night.

"Okay, they probably died around eight-thirty. And the call comes in an hour later," said Mars. "Well, I know from experience that an hour means a lot in a criminal investigation."

"Actually, it's an hour and *five* minutes, because the 911 call came in at nine-thirty-five. But the ME couldn't nail the TOD to the minute, so it's at least an hour discrepancy."

"What exactly did the 911 call say?"

"That they heard suspicious noises from inside the Richardses' house. People screaming and then a gunshot."

"But that's impossible. They weren't killed at nine-thirty-five."

"We don't know if the person really heard a shot or something else. And we don't know if they heard a shot that killed someone or just a shot."

"Well, dead people don't scream."

"True, but who's to say someone else wasn't in the house screaming at that time and that's what the caller heard?"

"Who would that person be?"

"I have no idea. I have no idea if such a person exists. But I do have a thought about something else."

"What?"

"Abigail Richards was strangled, not shot. Why?"

"You mean why wasn't she shot like the others because it was easier than strangling somebody?"

"Right."

Mars thought about this for a few moments. "I give."

"When you shoot someone, you don't transfer your DNA to under their fingernails. When you strangle someone, that opportunity presents itself."

"Wait a minute, are you saying somebody somehow got some of Hawkins's DNA from his skin and placed that under the girl's nails?"

"Yes."

"So that can be done?"

"Sure. And Hawkins *had* scratches on his arms. So something happened to him. I think that's when his DNA was harvested to incriminate him."

"But if somebody else had scratched him, let's say, and then took that skin and, I guess, blood and hair and put it under Abigail's nails, wouldn't some of that person's DNA also end up under her nails?"

"Possibly but not necessarily. Depends on how it was done. In any event, the DNA screen done at the time confirmed it was Hawkins's DNA under her nails."

"And the fingerprint? Could that have been placed there too?"

"It could be. It's extraordinarily rare to find a forged print. It's far more likely to find a fabricated one at a crime scene."

"What's the difference?" asked Mars, looking curious.

"Cop finds a glass with a suspect's prints on it outside of the crime scene and then places the glass *at* the crime scene and swears he found it there. Or a third party could do the same thing. Person wasn't at the scene but the glass with his print was because it was intentionally placed there. That's a fabrication. A forgery is where you actually take someone's prints from one surface and transfer them to another surface at a crime scene."

"Is that hard to do?"

"Well, you certainly have to know what you're doing. You lift a print with tape, you're going to disturb ridge lines. And prints interact differently with different surfaces. You lift a print from a metal surface and transfer it to a wooden surface, chances are you're going to interject some anomalies into the picture that'll throw up a red flag."

"Then an expert would catch it every time?"

"No, unfortunately. I remember they did a test once to check that very thing. About half the time the forensics folks thought a forgery was a real print and a real print was a forgery. I don't like those odds."

"Gee, that's a little unsettling, particularly for someone like me who got wrongly convicted. Was there anything dicey about Hawkins's print at the crime scene?"

Decker shook his head. "And I checked it very closely. And we had another expert who I trusted come in at the time and do the same thing. He could find nothing that would lead him to believe it was forged."

"Then Hawkins *had* to be there."

"It seems so. But if he was, how could he be innocent? And if he was there and didn't kill them, he would know who did, presumably. Why didn't he finger that person after he was arrested?"

"I give," said Mars.

"He could have come upon the bodies *after* they were dead.

He could have been the one to call 911 at nine-thirty-five and then gotten the hell out of Dodge, although that leaves open the question of why we couldn't trace the call."

"So how did the murder weapon turn up at his house behind the wall?"

"Someone planted it there to frame him."

"Okay."

Decker shook his head. "No, it's not okay. If he happened upon the bodies *after* the real killer had left, how did the killer know to frame Hawkins?"

"Maybe he knew Hawkins was going to break into the house that night. Maybe that's why he killed them that night, because he knew Hawkins was planning to be there later. So he planted the DNA on the girl and then Hawkins hit that light switch himself, adding even more evidence against him." After he finished speaking, Mars smiled. "How's that theory?"

"You make some good points, Melvin. It doesn't explain everything, but it's still an interesting theory we have to explore."

"And it would explain the time discrepancy too," noted Mars as he sipped his coffee. "And Hawkins would have to describe something weird going on to get the cops to come out. He knew the people had been shot and had probably screamed when they were, so that's what he told the police dispatcher he heard, even though he couldn't have."

Decker nodded and forked some eggs into his mouth. The memories of his discovering his murdered family had finally stopped unspooling in his head at around four in the morning. He had come back to the room and gone right to the bathroom and stripped off his soaked clothes. That's when Mars had heard him retching in there, but he'd lied and told him he was fine.

But will it happen again?

He said, "So how did Hawkins get those scratches on his arms? He had to realize that the DNA taken from his arms was planted under Abigail's nails. Yet he never raised that as a defense. He never said a person had scratched him and presumably gotten his DNA that way. He maintained that he had slipped and injured himself. Even though naming the person might have raised reasonable doubt in the jury's minds."

"You think he was protecting somebody?"

"Possibly."

"You have anybody in mind?"

"Yes, I do."

CHAPTER

35

SHE DID NOT LOOK REMOTELY PLEASED to see him again.

"I'm going out now," Mitzi Gardiner said from the partially open front door of her beautiful home.

She was dressed immaculately in a pleated skirt, nylons, and low-heeled pumps. Her white blouse had an open collar. Around her neck was a string of small pearls. She had a dark, short-waisted jacket on over the blouse. Her hair had not a strand out of place. Her makeup and lipstick looked professionally applied. She could be presiding over a board meeting at a Fortune 500 company.

"We can wait then or come back another time," said Decker, who was once more struck by her transformation from an emaciated and perpetually strung-out drug addict. "But it won't take long if you can make the time now."

She eyed him and then Mars, who smiled pleasantly back at her.

She frowned and looked at her watch. "I can give you five minutes."

She led them through the house and into a book-lined library. She closed the doors behind them and indicated seats. They quickly sat down on a small couch.

She sat down across from them.

"Well?" she said, staring at him.

He said, "Thanks for agreeing to see us now."

"Five minutes," she said. "Then I have a meeting I need to get to. An important one."

Decker cleared his throat. The questioning would have to be delicate. It was hard because his preferred approach was to figuratively grab a suspect by the neck with a line of queries.

"We're running down some leads and it occurred to us that your father might have been framed."

Gardiner sat back and looked coolly at him. "So you intimated on your last visit. And I told you that you were barking up the wrong tree, if you remember."

"By the way, when I left here to drive back to Burlington after speaking with you before, someone tried to kill me."

She sat up, looking genuinely shocked. "I hope you don't think I had anything to do with that."

"No, not at all. I just wanted you to know because you may want to be on your guard."

"Thank you for your warning. But I carry a gun with me when I'm out."

"Really, why is that?"

"Because I'm wealthy, Agent Decker. And people who aren't want to take things away from you. I know that better than most, having once been on the other side of the glass looking in."

"Have you had problems with that in the past?"

"I don't think that has anything to do with your investigation." She tapped her watch. "And the clock is running on your time to question me."

Decker plunged in. "There is a substantial time discrepancy in what happened thirteen years ago. That has changed my understanding of the case."

"What time discrepancy? And why didn't someone see it back then?"

"It was just overlooked. But the time of the victims' deaths and the 911 call to police? It doesn't make sense."

She sat back. "All right. I guess I'll take your word for that. But why would that cause you to come to see me?"

"Your father had scratches on his arms. The police concluded that those scratches were caused by Abigail Richards fighting for her life while your father strangled her."

"Do we really have to go through this?" she said irritably.

"When your father was arrested, he was wearing a long-sleeved shirt and a jacket over it."

"So what?"

"If he was wearing that while attacking Abigail some hours earlier, how could she have scratched his arms and gotten his DNA under her skin? Her nails wouldn't have penetrated his clothing, even if she did manage to somehow break the skin. There would have been no transfer of DNA."

"I'm not a detective, so I don't know. Maybe he changed clothes between the time of the attack and when he was picked up."

"But he hadn't been home."

"That I know of. I told you before, I was probably high."

"It was rainy and chilly that night. I doubt he would have been wearing a short-sleeved shirt."

Gardiner was looking at her watch. "Okay, but isn't that beside the point? His DNA *was* found under her nails. That came out at the trial."

"Which leads me to this question. Can you think of anyone who would want to frame your father?"

"Frame him? How? By killing four people that he didn't even know? By putting his fingerprints and DNA at the crime scene? My father wasn't that important, Agent Decker. Why would anyone waste time incriminating him?"

"I take that as a no?"

She didn't bother to answer.

"Your father said the scrapes on his arms were from when he fell down, not from Abigail's fingernails."

"But again, his DNA was found under her nails. Isn't that conclusive?"

"We were also thinking that if your father *was* innocent, he could have raised any number of defenses, implicated other people. For instance, he could have said that another person had scratched his arms. And that that person had used the DNA from under *their* nails to plant under Abigail's fingernails."

Decker sat back slightly. This was the moment of truth.

Gardiner was sharp enough, he knew, to realize the implications of his question.

But she surprised him. "After my father lost his job, he started hanging around a bad lot, Agent Decker."

"That never came out at the trial."

"Well, he did. He was desperate for money. For all I know, he started committing crimes but was never caught until the murders. As I told you before, he did whatever he could to get money for my mother's pain medications. So maybe he was in a fight and got the injuries that way. He probably wouldn't tell anyone that, because he was afraid it might incriminate him, or the person might do him harm if he did tell the authorities."

Mars said incredulously, "He was on trial for murder. How much more danger could he be in?"

Gardiner didn't even deign to look at him. She kept her gaze on Decker. "He might have been trying to protect my mother and me. If he talked, his 'associates' might harm us."

It was at that moment that Decker realized he had seriously underestimated Mitzi Gardiner.

"That's an interesting theory," he said.

"Really?" she said. "I would think it was the *only* theory that would adequately answer your question." She looked at her watch again. "Well, time's up."

"And if we have any more questions?" said Decker.

"You can ask someone else for answers."

She walked out of the room, leaving them there.

A few moments later they heard a door open and close. After that, a garage door cranked up and a car drove out. From the window, they watched her drive down to the gate in a silver Porsche SUV. The gate opened, and a few moments later she was gone.

"Gentlemen?"

They turned to see a woman in a maid's uniform. "Mrs. Gardiner asked me to show you out."

As they left the house Mars said, "We just got our asses handed to us, didn't we?"

"Yes, we did."

36

It was six-thirty exactly when Decker and Mars pulled down the drive into the Richardses' old home. Decker drove into the parking area behind the house and they got out. It wasn't raining yet, but it was scheduled to start soon, and the dark clouds confirmed that prediction.

Mars looked up at the old house. "So this is where it all happened? And where you started your career as a homicide detective?"

"Apparently an inauspicious start," commented Decker moodily.

"Hey, it was your first time. You think the first time I ran the ball at Texas I was as good as the last time I ran it? You learn from your mistakes, Decker, you know that."

"Well, I made enough of them on this case to last a lifetime."

He led Mars to the side door. This presumably was where David Katz had gone into the house. Decker had a key that had been given him by Natty. He unlocked the door and stepped into a utility room. Up a short set of steps was the kitchen.

"So we're here to sort of walk through the crime scene?" said Mars.

Decker didn't answer right away. He gazed around at the small room. The HVAC equipment was in here, as well as hookups for a washer and dryer.

"Why would Katz have pulled around here to come into the house?" He was really saying this to himself more than Mars.

"Well, maybe this was the way he always came in."

"There's no record that he was ever here before."

Mars looked around the room. "Well, then I guess that is strange. Why come in here instead of through the front door?"

They walked up the stairs and into the kitchen.

"You think maybe Richards told him to come in that way?"

"I have no way of knowing that," replied Decker. "I don't know who arranged the meeting or why. Or even if it was a meeting or just a shoot-the-breeze sort of thing."

They arrived at the spot where David Katz had been shot.

"He fell here and the beer he was drinking hit the floor but didn't break."

"Okay. And then Don Richards was shot—"

Decker put up a hand. He had just downloaded something from his "cloud" that was not making sense.

"What?" said Mars, who had seen this expression before.

"Two things. The beer bottle was nearly empty when it hit the floor."

"How do you know that?"

"The spill pattern and volume of beer on the floor."

"Wouldn't some of it have dried?"

"We took that into account."

"Okay, so he drank the rest."

Decker shook his head. "He had almost no beer in his stomach when they did the autopsy."

"That doesn't make any sense. And the second point?"

Decker closed his eyes and brought two images up in his head.

"Katz was right-handed. The print of his we found on the beer bottle was from his left hand."

"Well, that's weird. You didn't see that before?"

"No, actually I did. But I didn't place any great importance on it because sometimes you hold a drink in your other hand. We've all done it."

"But now?"

"But now I'm looking at everything that doesn't seem to fit."

"And what does that tell you, looking at it that way?"

"That someone could have pressed his hand on the beer after he was dead, but used the wrong hand."

"To make it look like he was drinking beer? Why would that matter?"

"I don't know."

Mars looked at Decker nervously. "And if there was almost no beer in his stomach, that wasn't a red flag?"

"Should have been," admitted Decker. He looked down at the floor. "But if Katz didn't drink the beer, who did?" He eyed the kitchen sink. "Maybe it went down there."

"To make it look like he'd drunk most of what was in the bottle?"

"If that was their plan, they didn't know how postmortems work. Not that it made a difference since I completely missed that because I didn't fully read the PM report." He slammed his fist against the wall and then rubbed the cut the blow had produced. "The fact is, everything changed when we found the fingerprint, Melvin. I was really eager to get the person who'd done this. And that print led directly to Meryl Hawkins. Nothing else mattered at that point."

"I get that, Decker. And I know you want to beat yourself up over this, and maybe you're right to do it. But you got another chance to get it right, so clear your head, get rid of the guilt, and focus. I know you can do this, bro."

Decker took a couple of deep, calming breaths. "Okay, the problem has always been, how did the killer or killers get here? They had to come down that one road and pass the other houses. No one saw them. There was no trace of another car, and there would have been."

"Maybe they came on foot."

"They had to have come to the house *after* the rain started. Yet there was not a single trace of that in the house. They might have been meticulous in cleaning up, but to not leave a single mark?" Decker shook his head in disbelief. "Not going to happen."

"Well, what if the killers were in the house *before* the rain started. Then they ambushed Katz when he came in. And killed everybody else."

Decker thought about this. "That means they would have come to the house in broad daylight with no rain to give them cover. Someone would have seen them coming down the road."

"Maybe they came from behind the house and not down the road."

"And waited hours to kill everyone? Why?"

"I don't know," admitted Mars. "Maybe they were trying to get some information from them before they murdered them."

"That's a possibility, Melvin. And an intriguing one."

"So the only car found here was Katz's?"

"That's right. Susan Richards had one car and the other was in the shop for—"

Decker froze as another image dropped from his cloud to rest atop another.

"What is it, Decker?" asked Mars.

Decker came out of his reverie and said slowly, "Don Richards and his son, Frankie, were shot once in the chest, both through the heart. Nonsurvivable. But Katz was different. He was shot in the head, *twice*. Temple and the rear of the skull." He looked over at Mars. "Why would that be? Why change the scenario for Katz?"

"Maybe he struggled with them or he ran off, and they had to shoot him in the head. Got him in the back and then in the temple."

"The order of the wounds was actually the reverse of that. Temple first, then the back of the head. The temple shot un- doubtedly would have been fatal. He would have fallen to the floor. Why shoot him again in the head when they knew he was already dead?"

Mars shook his head. "Doesn't make sense."

"Abigail was strangled, I believe, because that was the most plausible way to get Hawkins's DNA under her fingernails. If they were that purpose-driven in the way they killed her, maybe there was a similar purpose behind shooting Katz twice in the head."

"But what would that purpose be?"

Decker pantomimed a gun with his hand and held it to his temple. "Bang. The guy drops. They bend over him and, bang, shot to the back of the head."

"Right, but why?"

Decker straightened and looked at his hand. "Because they wanted to cover something up that the temple shot didn't accomplish."

"What would that be?"

"Maybe a contusion on the back of his head."

"From what?"

"From when he was knocked out. *Before* he was brought here to die."

37

A PUZZLED MARS LOOKED at Decker. "Wait a minute, are you saying that he *didn't* drive his car here?"

"His *car* was driven here, certainly, but who's to say he was the one driving? We just assumed all along that it was him. I think it's possible he was in the trunk or the backseat unconscious, and the killer or killers drove him here. The neighbors only saw the car, not the driver. They didn't know Katz from Adam, so they couldn't have identified him even if they had seen him."

Mars said, "And that would explain why they parked the car in the back and came in that way."

"Right, they couldn't exactly carry an unconscious Katz in through the front door. And that would also explain his left-hand print on the beer. They just pressed his hand against it. They might not have known whether he was right- or left-handed. They just wanted it to look like he had come here of his own free will and was enjoying a beer when someone shot him."

"But you said there was *some* beer in his stomach."

"They could have revived him and made him drink some, or else they poured some down his throat while he was unconscious. And it would explain the absence of any marks by another car, and the lack of rain traces brought in by the killers. They were in the house *before* the rain started, not because they were here before Katz came as you speculated, but because they came *with* him. They left the house after the rain started and therefore wouldn't have left any traces of it inside."

"And if they left out the back on foot, the rain would have covered all those tracks."

Decker nodded. "And I missed all that because of this."

He led Mars back into the living room and pointed at the light switch on the wall. "That's where we found the fingerprint. My attention was drawn to it because there was a smear of blood on the light switch plate. No print associated with it. Like someone had rubbed their arm or hand against it or something. But right after I saw the blood, I checked for a print, and there it was. And it matched Hawkins perfectly. Far more than you need to hold up in court. This was a home run. And he said he'd never been here, so how else could it have gotten here unless he'd been here that night? It showed he was lying, and that pretty much sealed his fate. That and the DNA under Abigail's nails."

"And you said it would be hard to forge a print."

"Yes. But to do it really well, you need some knowledge of forensics and you need some special equipment deployed in a multistep process, and even with all that there are a lot of things that can go wrong."

"Damn, didn't know it was that complicated."

"You obviously never watched *CSI*."

"I was in prison for most of that time, Decker. And for obvious reasons, *CSI* wasn't a real popular show for the inmates."

"Bottom line is I have confidence in the expert who said he believed Hawkins's print was genuine."

"Then Hawkins had to be here, no way around it."

Decker wasn't listening. He was staring transfixed at the switch plate. Then he ran back into the kitchen and looked at the light switch there. Moments later he hustled into another room and did the same. Mars followed him into each new space with a bewildered look on his face.

"Decker, you okay?"

Decker returned to the living room, dug into his pocket, and pulled out a Swiss Army knife. He deployed the screwdriver.

"Dollars to donuts this is the same light switch plate that was on the wall that night."

"Okay, so what?"

"It's different from the switch plates in the other rooms."

Decker unscrewed the plate and removed it from the wall. Underneath was revealed the imprint of a smaller rectangle.

"Do you see that, Melvin?"

Mars looked at him. "Yeah, but what does that mean?"

"The original switch plate was *smaller*. That's the outline there between the painted area and what was underneath the plate. You can see where the paint faded because it was exposed to light all those years. They needed the same size or a bigger plate there to cover it."

"Wait a second, you're saying somebody got Hawkins's print on that plate and brought it here and replaced the other plate with this one?"

"Yes."

"Damn."

"That way his *real* print is on the *original* surface. That's why my expert swore it wasn't a forgery." He paused. "Instead it was a *fabrication*. They brought the print to the crime scene, but in a way that was beyond suspicion. A glass or other object introduced to a crime scene can easily be placed there. A light switch plate? It seems like part of the house. Immovable. But it's not. Just two screws, in fact. Like I just took out."

"Somebody went to a lot of effort to frame the guy."

"Which means the motivation was pretty significant. But this is not about Meryl Hawkins. He was a pawn. It could have been anybody. But they picked him for a variety of reasons. And this shows the murders weren't the result of a random burglary gone bad. The focus now should be the victims. Who would want them dead?"

"Well, there were four of them. I guess we can discount the kids. I don't see some middle schooler who got his feelings hurt doing this."

Decker nodded. "So David Katz and Don Richards. Either or both."

"You said they had done business together. Katz was the businessman and Richards was the banker."

"Right."

"Had they become friends?"

"Not that we could find. Rachel Katz said no. The Richardses were older and had kids, and they didn't. And they were both too busy with work to form friendships like that, at least that's what she told me."

"And did either of the wives say why Katz was coming over that night?"

"Neither of them knew that he was. Again, that's what they said. It doesn't make it true."

"Did Katz just pop in, then?"

"There *was* a phone call placed the day before from Katz's cell phone to Richards's cell phone. It might have been then that they arranged to meet."

"If Katz called Richards, maybe he initiated the meeting?"

"That could be, yes," agreed Decker. "But even though Katz called Richards, that doesn't mean he asked for the meeting. He might have just called out of the blue and then Richards asked him to come by."

"When he knew his wife would be out—is that significant?" asked Mars.

"It could be very significant, especially considering that Susan Richards has vanished."

Mars said, "Well, Richards worked at the bank. Maybe something fishy was going on there and he wanted Katz's advice."

"And then someone came here and killed them. And killed the kids too because they would be witnesses. But that would be risky. Why not kill whoever was the target while they were alone, not in a house filled with people?"

"Maybe they were running out of time and were afraid that someone was going to blow the whistle on what they were doing."

Decker was staring miserably at the switch plate. "It's only a small difference, but I should have noticed it before."

"They manipulated you and everybody else."

"Rookie mistake. I assumed things I shouldn't have."

"But now you figured it out and you get a second chance to get it right. Like you did with me. You gave me a second chance."

"You're cutting me a lot of slack."

"Well, sometimes friends have to do that. But then sometimes they have to kick you in the ass too. And trust me, if it comes to it, I will."

"I would expect nothing less, Melvin."

Decker's phone rang. He answered, and Captain Miller started speaking.

"They found Susan Richards."

"Where?"

"Two towns over."

"You bringing her in?"

"We are. In a meat wagon. She killed herself, Amos."

38

Decker was in the morgue looking at yet another body.

She looked like she was asleep, not dead.

"Bodies really piling up," said the ME as he laid the sheet back down on top of Susan Richards.

"Cause of death?"

"My best guess right now, drug overdose. Women usually go the overdose route when committing suicide. Guys like to blow their heads off with guns."

Richards had been found in an abandoned building by a construction worker working nearby who had noticed an odd smell.

"Time of death?" asked Decker.

"Rigor has resolved so she's been dead a while. I'll have a better time later."

"Could the time of her death be close to when she disappeared?"

The man looked over the body and rubbed his chin. "Yes, actually, it could."

Decker had already been told that the suitcase she had been seen putting in her car had not been found with the body.

"Any pill bottles found with her? Or a suicide note?"

The ME shook his head. "No, on both counts."

The door opened and Blake Natty walked in, looking shriveled and depressed. He eyed the body of Susan Richards with little interest. "So she killed herself?" he said.

"Unknown as yet," said Decker.

Natty said, "Well, if she did kill herself, we know why: She murdered Hawkins."

"If she did kill him, she got the wrong guy," said Decker.

Natty waved this off. "That's your theory."

"It's more than a theory now," replied Decker. He explained about the light switch plate at the Richardses' old house. "And they placed a smudge of Katz's blood on the plate to draw our attention to it and thus the print."

"Where do you think the print and the switch plate came from?"

"The easiest source would have been Hawkins's home. I think they didn't put Katz's blood on the print because that would have messed up the ridge lines."

"And the DNA under the girl's nails?" asked Natty.

"They picked her because she was physically smaller and weaker than the others. And they needed a plausible scenario to get the DNA under her nails. And a struggle during a strangulation plausibly fit that bill."

"But Decker," said the ME, "I pulled out those reports and went over them after I knew you were looking into the case again. If someone else had scratched Hawkins and then transferred what was under that person's nails to under Abigail Richards's nails, you would expect to find the other person's DNA as well."

"If the other person were a family member, would that make a difference?" asked Decker, who already knew the answer.

"Well, of course it would. All humans' DNA is ninety-nine point nine percent the same. But that one-tenth is dramatically different for all, except if you're a monozygotic or identical twin. But the testing that was done on Abigail's nails would not have picked up on a third party's DNA if the person were a family member of Hawkins. They would have had to do additional steps. Actually, they would have had to do extra steps to check for any third-party corruption, family or not."

Natty eyed Decker. "What family member are you talking about?"

"There really can only be one: his daughter, Mitzi."

"Why would she have set up her old man?" asked Natty.

"I don't know." He looked at the ME. "Is the DNA sample still available to do additional testing, to see if Mitzi's DNA or a third party's had corrupted it? I asked you to check earlier."

The ME nodded his head. "I did check. And there is some left. I'm having an expert in Cincinnati where they have much better equipment and protocols do sophisticated testing on it. They'll be able to differentiate between a father's and daughter's DNA, and also the presence of any third party. But it will take a little time."

"Let me know as soon as you have something."

"You really think his daughter was involved?" said Natty.

"If she were it would explain how the murder weapon came to be found in a panel behind the wall of his closet. I just reread the report of the search team that went over Hawkins's house. They wrote that Mitzi had drawn their attention to some unevenness of the wall. They didn't ask her why she knew about it."

"Are *you* going to ask her about it?" said Natty.

"I think if I go back to that well again, she's going to lawyer up. Probably already has. Right now, she's home free, or thinks she is."

Decker looked back at Susan Richards's body. He closed his eyes and thought back to something that a witness had told him. He put layer after layer of facts on top of that one, pulling them down from his cloud with ease. Until something did not make sense. It stood out, in fact, like a blinking red light.

Natty said, "So, you don't think she killed herself?"

Decker opened his eyes. "I'm almost sure she didn't."

"How?"

"Because I think she was already dead when she left her house."

CHAPTER

39

IT WAS THE NEXT DAY and Decker and Mars were standing in front of the late Susan Richards's house. Across the road, Decker could once more see Agatha Bates sitting on her screened porch.

"You're saying that Richards was in the rolling suitcase already dead?" said Mars.

Decker absently nodded.

"So that means another woman was impersonating her."

"Agatha Bates saw the person from a distance. And it was dark, and judging by the thickness of Bates's eyeglass lenses, her sight is far from perfect. And the person had on a long coat and a hat. That was one thing that made no sense to me. It was warm that night with not a cloud in the sky. So it was a disguise, because they wanted to take no chance that Bates might be able to see it *wasn't* her neighbor."

"But why do you think it wasn't Richards in the first place?"

"Richards's car muffler was really loud. That was why the person came out and started the car and then went *back* inside to get the suitcase."

"I'm not following."

In answer, Decker pointed across the street. "Think of it this way: This was all a show for Bates. The person wanted her to hear the car start up, knowing that she would look out the window and see who she thought was Susan Richards come out with the suitcase. If she had come out and put the bag in the car and then got in the car and started it, Bates would not have seen what she did. Bates said the person had trouble getting the suitcase in the car. That was probably because of Richards's weight." He paused. "And in addition to that, she barely took any clothes or shoes or other things. So why the big suitcase? And she was on a bunch of meds. I saw them in the medicine cabinet. Most weren't too critical, but one she left behind was: high blood pressure medication. She had to take that every day."

"So someone killed Richards because...?"

Decker said, "To place blame for Hawkins's murder on her. Then she's found, ostensibly having taken her own life out of guilt. Case closed. At least with respect to Hawkins's murder."

Mars nodded thoughtfully. "Gotta admit, it all hangs together."

"But it leaves a lot of questions unanswered and creates a lot of new ones. And it doesn't tell us who committed those murders thirteen years ago, or who really killed Meryl Hawkins."

"Well, you think his daughter is involved somehow."

"But I have no way to prove it. At least not yet."

"So you think it's all connected, then? What happened back then and now?"

"Well, we have one factor unaccounted for."

Mars thought for a moment. "The dude who took a shot at you."

"Right. Who is he? Was he hired to take a shot at me by someone? Was he the one who earlier tried to kill me by ramming his truck into my car?"

Mars rubbed his arm where the guy had slashed him. "Dude could fight, I'll give him that."

"And I have other questions."

"Like what?"

"Why would someone drive Katz over there and kill him, Don Richards, and his kids?"

"Because they knew something incriminating, something that could hurt whoever killed them."

"Right. But if Katz knew something, why drive him over there and kill the others?"

"Because Don Richards knew something too. They had to take them both out. And instead of doing it separately, they did it all at once."

"Right. But the thing is, Susan Richards wasn't there. If her husband knew something that could hurt somebody, you'd think she might know too."

Mars snapped his fingers. "Maybe she *did* know, because she was involved in whatever it was. And that may be the reason she wasn't there that night."

"I've covered that ground before. While I can see Susan letting her husband die, I just don't see her allowing her kids to die too."

"So maybe she was just lucky she wasn't there."

"But she's dead now, because she was a scapegoat for Hawkins's murder, because she had a motive to kill him."

"But what would David Katz or Don Richards know that would get them killed?"

"Rachel Katz has a lot of projects going on around town, with money behind her. She's obviously very ambitious. And she wasn't there that night either, which meant she got to live."

"That doesn't make her a murderer, Decker. In fact, it might make her a target now if people are tying up loose ends from thirteen years ago."

"Well, nine times out of ten, when a spouse dies, it's the other spouse doing the killing. I don't think that was the case with Susan Richards, but it could very well be the case with Rachel Katz."

"Good enough reason never to get married," quipped Mars.

"Don't tell Harper that."

"Like I said, we're just having fun. Don't need a marriage license to do that."

"Well, I think I need to have another talk with Rachel Katz."

"You want me to come along?"

Decker studied his friend. "Yeah, I do. It might really help."

"How?"

"You're a lot cooler than I am and far better-looking. And you're rich on top of it. So I think Rachel Katz will be thrilled to meet you."

40

"WINE?"

Rachel Katz was dressed in black slacks, a white blouse, and high heels. Her hair was done up in an elaborate French braid. It was nearly nine o'clock. She had arranged to meet them after work in her loft apartment. She held up an opened bottle of Cabernet.

Decker declined, but Mars accepted the offer. She poured out a glass and handed it to him. She turned back to the table and picked up her own wineglass.

"So you and Decker work together?"

"No, I'm just in town visiting him," said Mars, taking a sip of the wine and sitting down next to her on the couch, while Decker sat across from them.

She sat back, crossed her legs, took a drink of her wine, and said, "Well, I'm sorry that your visit coincided with murder. Now, what can I do for you?"

"You look like you're ready to go out somewhere," said Decker. "I hope we're not keeping you."

"I am going out, but not until a little later." She glanced at Mars. "It's a new nightclub I'm part owner of. Going to check out the groove. That's important. You do much clubbing?"

"Oh yeah. There's a nice scene in D.C. And I've been dabbling in real estate up there." He glanced at Decker and added, "Even thinking about opening a bar up there with a dance floor."

"Well, then you're welcome to join me tonight. This isn't D.C., but we've put a lot of thought into the business model and the layout of the place. You might see something that might help you in your venture."

"Thanks, I might just do that," said Mars with another quick glance at Decker.

"I guess you've heard about Susan Richards," said Decker. "I know it was on the news this morning."

Katz frowned, uncrossed her legs, and sat forward. "That was truly awful. Taking her own life like that. It's just hard to fathom. But I guess if she did kill Meryl Hawkins...?"

"So you think that she did?" asked Decker.

"I have no way of knowing for sure, do I? But it seems rather obvious."

"And you were with Earl Lancaster at the time Hawkins was killed?"

"As I told you before, and I'm sure he confirmed."

"His wife had to actually recuse herself from the investigation because of that," said Decker. He paused, waiting for her reaction to this.

"I guess I could see that," she said. "It's like an episode of *Law and Order* or something."

"Or something," said Decker. "The night your husband was killed, you said you had no idea why he would be meeting with Don Richards? Or that he was even meeting with him?"

"That's right."

"Did you normally know your husband's schedule?"

"Mostly. But not always. Especially if this was last-minute. He had an office and a secretary. She would have kept his schedule."

"We talked to her back then. But I was hoping you might remember something."

"Well, I can't help you there. And I don't know why you're continuing to bother with this. Hawkins committed the murders. That was clearly established at trial. Now, I have no proof of who killed him, but other things being equal it might be the woman who disappeared and then turned up dead from a suicide." She took another sip of wine. "I admire her, actually. At least she had the courage to finish the guy. I didn't."

"Well, we don't know that she did."

Katz made a careless wave with her hand. "Whatever. You have your job to do. Anything else?"

"Do you happen to know Mitzi Gardiner?"

Katz looked puzzled. "Mitzi Gardiner?"

"You might have known her as Mitzi Hawkins."

"God, do you mean his daughter?"

"Yes."

"No, I didn't know her. Why the hell would I?"

"You might have seen her at the trial. She had to testify."

"No, I don't recall that. But I remember her being mentioned by some of the other witnesses, including you. I'm not sure what she even looks like."

"Well, her looks have changed a lot since then. For the better. She's turned her life around."

"Well, good for her. Couldn't have been easy having a murderer for a father."

"So you never talked to her? Interacted with her?"

"Never."

"She lives in Trammel. Very nice place. Wealthy. She has a young child."

"Good for her. I wanted kids too."

Mars said, "You're still young. Not too late."

Katz smiled at him. "You're sweet, but I think that ship has sailed." She turned back to Decker. "Anything else?"

"Did you talk to your husband on the day of his death?"

"I'm sure I did. We did sleep together and get up together. Probably had coffee before we both left the house that morning."

"I mean after that. During the day?"

"I really can't recall. It's been a long time."

"But no mention of his going to meet with Richards?"

"No. I told you that before."

"Just verifying."

"Why do I feel like you're trying to trap me?" she said darkly. "That would not be very nice, particularly since I have nothing to hide."

"I'm just trying to figure out what happened."

Katz finished her wine in one long drink and set the empty glass on the table. "Well, let me help you out with that. Hawkins murdered my husband and three other people. And then Susan Richards killed him and then killed herself. Case closed. There, that wasn't hard."

She stood and looked down at Mars. "How about we grab a drink before we head over to the club? I know a place."

Mars stood. "Sounds good."

"Melvin, we have something to do first, and then you can meet her there," said Decker.

Mars eyed Katz. "You cool with that?"

"Absolutely." She wrote down an address on a slip of paper and handed it to Mars. "I think you'll have fun tonight, Mr. Mars."

"Make it Melvin."

"Just keep it professional," said Decker in a joking manner.

"I'm always professional," said Katz. "As your friend will find out tonight."

As they walked back to their car, Mars said, "What do we have to do?"

"We're going to wire you up for tonight."

"And where will you be?"

"Right outside listening."

"You sure you're doing this for the case, or to keep me from doing something dumb with that woman?"

"Maybe both, Melvin. Maybe both."

41

Decker was in the front seat of his rental car parked outside of a place called 10th and Main. That was also its literal location. It was the club Rachel Katz had referred to and of which she was a co-owner.

It seemed to be pretty popular, Decker noted. There was a bouncer out front who nearly equaled him in heft, and he had been vetting a long line of mostly younger and seemingly well-heeled men and women vying to get in.

Maybe his hometown *was* on the way back, he thought. Although he didn't know if what amounted to an overpriced bar for well-off millennials was actually a good barometer of an improving economy for the average person.

He reworked his earpiece, and the noise from inside the club, communicated to him by the wire that Mars was wearing, came through loud and clear.

He settled in for a long evening.

* * *

Inside 10th and Main, Mars and Katz were seated in a roped-off section of the club, apparently reserved for VIPs. The music was loud, the bar crammed, and the dance floor full of swaying, already partially drunk people.

"So what do you think so far?" said Katz.

"Good vibe, lots of energy, and I can see your cash flow skyrocketing at the bar right now."

"We put the bar there to maximize access to it from the tables and the dance floor."

"Right. That way you get a continuous flow of business. And dancing makes people hungry and thirsty. And your table-to-patron ratio is good too. Pack 'em in, but without seeming to."

"You sound like you know business."

"Like I said, I dabble. Got some properties here and there. I like to work with low-income folks for the most part, give them a shot. Don't make as much profit, but I don't need the money."

She sipped her cocktail and moved her head rhythmically to the music. "That's very generous of you. I have a slightly different business model."

"What's that?"

"To get as rich as I possibly can." She laughed and rattled the ice in her glass.

"Different strokes," said Mars, grinning.

"How long have you worked with Decker?"

"Well, like I told you before, I don't work with him. I'm not with the FBI or anything. But he and I are buds. We played college football against each other. I was a Texas Longhorn; he was an Ohio State Buckeye. I ran the ball and he tried to tackle me."

"Did he?"

"He did as well as anybody did back then. Which wasn't all that good."

She laughed. "I respect a man who has confidence in himself."

"I was up for the Heisman my senior year but lost out to a quarterback."

Her eyes widened. "Wow. The Heisman? Did you play in the NFL?"

"I would have. But my career took a detour."

"How so?"

"Death row in a Texas prison."

Katz gaped until Mars grinned. She pointed at him. "Good one. I almost believed you for a second."

Mars looked around. "This is an expensive buildout. Did you finance it, or do you have your own cash?"

"I have partners with their own cash. They bring the money, I bring the local know-how. I put the deals together and execute on the plan. My background as a CPA really comes in handy. This is our eighth project together in just the last three years. And we're going to be expanding this same club concept to other cities in other states."

"Long-range strategy. That's a good thing. If you can streamline supply chains and consolidate your backroom and marketing operations, you can gain some economies of scale as you grow the business."

She looked at him with a new level of respect. "Exactly. So, you're here as Decker's friend, but are you helping him with the investigation?"

"I guess I'm a sounding board for the guy. He's Sherlock Holmes and I'm his Dr. Watson."

"Is he really that good?"

"The FBI thinks so. And I've seen him do some incredible things. And somebody tried to kill the guy, twice. So there must be something to hide, right?"

"God, I didn't know that."

Mars flexed his injured arm. "Dude cut me up too before he got away."

"Oh my God, you poor thing."

"Nothing too bad. I'm good to go."

"Any idea who the man is?"

"Not yet. But they'll keep looking till they find him."

"You want another drink? On the house."

"You don't have to do that."

"Yes I do, Melvin."

He grinned. "Okay, thanks. Same, straight up."

She rose and walked over to the bar.

Mars sat there, his head swaying to the music, seemingly not having a care in the world. He moved his mouth as though singing the lyrics of the song being played. "You hear everything okay, Decker?"

"Loud and clear. She seems to really like you."

"She's a beautiful, sexy lady, but she's not my type."

"What's your type?"

"She just seems a little too ruthless for my tastes. Money is her thing. But it's not mine."

"Easy to say since you have so much of it."

"Okay, you got me there. She's coming back now. Over and out."

Katz put the fresh drinks down and sat next to him, this time closer than before.

Mars said, "You ever think about coming to the D.C. area? Maybe you and me can do some business together."

"Now that would be wonderful," she said, flashing him a smile.

"You can use your original partners too, I'm not looking to cut anybody out. If you want me to meet with them, you know vet me and all. I'm cool with that."

"Yeah, let me think about that." She cradled her drink. "You know Decker keeps coming back to ask me questions. I think he might believe I had something to do with all this. And I didn't. I swear."

"Don't worry about that. He's just dotting his i's and crossing his t's."

"Does he suspect anybody yet?"

"Well, he thought Susan Richards might be good for the Hawkins murder, but now I don't know."

"He doesn't confide in you?"

"Not everything. You know Holmes kept stuff back from Watson too," he added with a grin.

She didn't return the look. "It was awful losing my husband like that."

Mars touched her arm and his features grew solemn. "Hey, sure it was. Nobody should have to go through that. Nobody."

She squeezed his arm. "Thanks."

Mars looked around. "So you got this place and you got the American Grill. Decker told me about the place. Now that's some broad bandwidth." He chuckled.

She smiled. "It was David's first project. I've kept the place to, I don't know, honor his memory, I guess. It's not like the restaurant makes a lot of money. In fact, based on tonight, I'll probably make more in one month here than that place does in six months."

Mars held up his cocktail. "Just start selling some of these fifteen-dollar highballs at the American Grill and you'll see your profit margins soar."

"I'm not sure how big that would go over with the Grill's clientele. They're more into pitchers of beer for five bucks."

"Not to change the subject, but did your husband have any business associates?"

She crossed her arms and her cheery disposition faded. "Why?"

"I'm back to playing Watson, see?"

"I guess I see. To answer your question, no, he was a solo operation. He got his financing from traditional sources."

"Like the local bank? Don Richards?"

"That's right."

"Anybody else in his past who might have had something against him?"

"Why are you asking these questions? Meryl Hawkins killed him."

"But if he didn't?"

"Why, because he said he was innocent?" she said skeptically. "His prints and DNA were found at the crime scene."

"You can fabricate that stuff."

Katz looked taken aback by this. "I didn't know that. Is that what Decker thinks?"

"Maybe. So, did your husband have enemies?"

"No, nobody I could think of. He was a nice guy," she added quietly. "He treated people well. He treated me well. He wasn't the type to screw people over and make them hate him or hold a grudge."

"So maybe they were targeting Don Richards."

"They?"

"In the event Hawkins is not the guy, there's a murderer out there."

"Do you have evidence that the fingerprints and such *were* fabricated?"

"This is where I pull out my official handbook and tell you that it's an ongoing police investigation."

"But you said you weren't with the FBI."

"Doesn't matter, still can't divulge anything, but you're smart enough to read between the lines, right?"

She nervously drank her cocktail and didn't answer right away. "If Hawkins didn't do it, the real killer might still be out there? Any idea who he is?"

"He, or she?"

She gave him a withering look. "I have an alibi for when it happened."

"Not my meaning. Lots of other 'shes' out there."

"Wait a minute, what about Mitzi, what was her last name?"

"Mitzi *Gardiner*."

"Did she have alibis for the murders?"

"Not sure."

"Well, don't you think you should check that?"

"I'm sure Decker is all over that."

"I remember from some of the testimony at the trial that she was an addict back then."

"I think she had problems in that area, yeah."

"So maybe she needed money for drugs and tried to rob them."

"And Susan Richards?"

"Seems obvious. She killed herself because she killed Meryl Hawkins."

He looked at her doubtfully.

"You don't think so?" she said.

"From how Decker described her to me, Mitzi was a skinny drug addict mostly stoned out of her mind. No way she killed four people, including two grown men. Besides, her DNA and prints weren't found at the scene."

"But you said that could be fabricated."

"It's easier to add stuff to a crime scene than it is to take stuff away, especially prints and DNA. Taking stuff away, you miss one little thing, you're screwed. Trust me, I speak from experience."

"So where does that leave us?"

"Investigating a series of murders."

"Do you think you'll find out who did it, after all this time?"

"I bet once against Amos Decker. And I lost that bet."

"Bad for you, then."

"No, actually he saved my life."

"Seriously?"

"As serious as it gets." He rose. "Thanks for showing me the place. You got a real winner here."

"Wait, do you have time for a nightcap? We could go back to my place."

"Thanks, but it's been a long day. Take a rain check?"

"Sure, okay," Katz said, the disappointment clear on her features. "And it was great meeting you."

"Same here. You gave me a lot to think about, and maybe I did the same for you."

Her expression changed, becoming somber and detached. She recovered from this a moment later, stood, and held out her hand with a forced smile. "Until next time, Melvin."

They shook hands and Mars said, "Look forward to it, Rachel."

He left her there gazing at all the partiers, but perhaps not really seeing a single one.

42

"So what do you think?" asked Mars. He and Decker were driving together back to the Residence Inn.

"I think you'd make a great interrogator."

"I didn't want Katz to think I was drilling down on her."

"That's not what I meant. The really good questioners don't seem like they're prying at all. That's what you did. You did a good job of gaining her confidence and not trying too hard."

Mars fist-bumped Decker. "Thanks. So what else? You think she's in on whatever this is?"

"She's hiding something, I just don't know what. And so is Mitzi Gardiner. And maybe so was Susan Richards, for that matter."

"Lot of people hiding shit in this town."

"Nothing new there," grumbled Decker. "Happens in every town."

Mars checked his watch. "It's midnight. How about some sleep? We're not as young as we used to be, you know."

"Sure," said Decker, although sleep was the last thing on his mind.

* * *

After Mars went to his room at the Residence Inn, Decker came back down to the parking lot, climbed into his car, and set off. He drove out of the downtown area and, his mind on autopilot, made his way to the neighborhood and house that he had called home for over a decade.

He pulled to the curb, rolled down the driver's-side window, and cut his engine and lights. He looked out the window at his old house, which was dark, the only illumination a single streetlight and the moon.

He had no real understanding of why he was here. It was punishing to see the place. Memories flooded back to him as easily as drawing breath. He closed his eyes as the images suddenly careened out of control just like last time; they were coming at him like flocks of hurtling birds or fired bullets. He couldn't make them stop. He felt his heart flutter, his gut lurch.

The sweat started to pool on his forehead, his skin grew clammy, and his armpits were suddenly soaked with sweat, the sudden stink assailing his nostrils.

His heart was now racing, and he thought he might be having a coronary. But slowly, ever so slowly, as he gripped the steering wheel as though that might allow some semblance of control over what was happening to him, things settled down in his mind. He finally lay back against his seat, exhausted without having moved at all. He hung his head out the window and sucked in the crisp air as the moisture evaporated off his skin.

This is getting old. And so am I.

He waggled his head, spit some stomach bile out the window, and kept taking deep breaths. He remembered when he'd come out of the coma at the hospital after getting crunched on the football field on opening day. A bunch of people he didn't know were hovering over him, asking him questions. He had IV and monitoring lines running all over him. He felt like Gulliver just awoken as a prisoner of the Lilliputians.

He had come to learn that he had died on the field, twice, only to be resuscitated each time by the team trainer. He'd been hit so hard his helmet had flown off and was lying in the grass far away from his body. The crowd had been cheering the blindside hit until they realized he was not getting up. When the trainer started pounding on his chest, the crowd of seventy thousand people quieted. The network had cut away to another game. It was not good for the NFL brand to show dead football players lying on the turf.

He learned he'd suffered a traumatic brain injury. Later, he discovered his brain had rewired itself around the damaged areas, accessing domains that had never been triggered before. This had left him with the twin conditions of hyperthymesia and synesthesia.

But he didn't know he had them until later. It wasn't like an X-ray could reveal this. The first time he had seen a color burst into his head, associated with something as incongruous as a number, Decker had seriously thought he was going insane.

Then, when he was able to recall things he never had been able to before, the doctors had started testing his cognitive abilities. He had looked at sheets of numbers and words and was able to regurgitate them all, because he could see them in his head, just as they had lain on the page. Then off he had gone to a special cognitive institute in Chicago that dealt exclusively with people like him.

Decker didn't know what was more amazing—his newfound abilities, or the realization that he was far from the only one who possessed them.

Now he snatched one more glimpse at his old home, briefly imagining that it was five years ago and Molly and Cassie were still alive, waiting for him to come home from being a cop. He would play with Molly, kiss Cassie, and...be a family.

He held on to that image for another few seconds and then let it go, a phantom that had to be released into the ether where it would simply vanish, because it was no longer real.

You can live in the past, or you can live in the present, but you really can't live in both, Amos.

He started the car, rolled the window back up, put his rental in gear, and drove off.

He was a loner, had always been a loner after he'd died on the field. Cassie, though, had been the one to make sure he did not shrivel up inside his cocoon and keep everyone away. After she died, there had been no one to do that.

Then Alex Jamison had come into his life and somewhat filled Cassie's role.

Decker didn't know where his thirst for justice, for right over wrong, had come from. He did know that he had possessed it long before his family was taken from him.

Maybe because that hit on the field stole me from me. And I've been looking for something to fill that hole all these years. And catching killers seems to be the only thing that cuts it. Because they steal the most precious thing of all: somebody's life.

He had no idea if that was the whole story or not. He just knew that right now, that's all he had to hold on to.

As he drove, he focused on the problem at hand. What he desperately wanted to know was, if David Katz had arranged to meet with Don Richards, and that had been communicated by a phone call that had involved only the two men, how had their killers known the men were going to be meeting that night?

He couldn't believe that Susan Richards had been party to it, because that would necessitate Decker's believing that she would sacrifice both her kids as well. Decker had seen the woman that night. As Lancaster had said, Susan had been hysterical, utterly out of her mind with disbelief and rage. She was a woman who had been truly shocked to learn that she had gone out for the evening and come home to find out she had no family left.

Decker slowed the car down as he thought back over all these points.

He settled on the phone call between Katz and Richards.

There was actually no way to know that it was Katz who had called Richards. It was just Katz's phone. Anyone could have made that call. And there was no guarantee that it was Richards who had answered, for the same reason.

The possibility was obvious: There could have been no scheduled meeting between the men. Decker had just assumed there was. The killer could have orchestrated all that to make it look like there was a meeting, or just Katz coming over for a beer. The fact that Decker believed that the killer or killers had driven an unconscious Katz over there made sense under that scenario. They could have gone in, held the Richardses hostage, brought in Katz, methodically killed them, laid their evidence casting guilt on Meryl Hawkins, departed the house through the back, and an hour later called in a disturbance.

So now the question was, who was really meant to be killed? Richards or Katz? The banker or the borrower?

And why?

And why did their killers pick that night to do it?

Decker knew if he could find an answer to any or all of those three questions, he might be able to blow this sucker wide open.

But he wasn't there yet. Maybe not even close.

He drove to a very familiar place: Burlington High School, where a little over two years before, a horrific mass shooting had stunned the town.

Decker parked his car and made his way to the dilapidated football field. Burlington no longer fielded a football team— they didn't have enough guys interested in playing the game. He climbed up into the bleachers as a light drizzle began to fall.

He took a seat and stared down at the field where he had been a superstar many years before. The only player in Burlington High history to go on to play in the NFL, if only for one play. He wrapped himself in his coat and stared moodily out.

As his gaze drifted to the right, he flinched as he saw her coming toward him. Mary Lancaster slowly made her way up the metal steps and sat down next to him.

"Didn't we do this before?" she said.

He nodded. "In the rain. After the school shootings. How'd you know I was here?"

"I didn't. You know my house backs up to the school. I take walks late at night. I saw you."

He nodded again. "But it's after one in the morning. It's not really safe for you to be out alone."

"And it is for you?"

"Well," he said. "I'm a lot bigger than you."

She opened her coat and he saw her pistol riding in its holster. "Someone wants to try to mug me, they'll be eating a round."

"I can see that. So, how's it going?"

"It's going. I hear you're making progress on the case."

"From who do you hear that?"

"Of all people, Natty. He seems to have had a change of heart about you after Sally was killed."

Decker said, "Did you know they were seeing each other?"

Lancaster looked stunned. "What? No, I didn't. Natty's married."

"Sally had ended it with him. She knew it wasn't right."

Lancaster shook her head. "I never saw that coming. And I still can't believe she's dead."

He glanced at her as the rain picked up. She had on a long trench coat and a ball cap. Her gray hair flowed out from underneath it. She looked to Decker like she was carrying an enormous weight on her slender shoulders.

"Are you ill, Mary? I mean really ill?"

She didn't look at him, but kept her gaze on the field. "Why do you ask that?"

"Because you're not the same. You've changed. And I don't think it's just because of what's happening with you and Earl."

She clenched her hands and then flexed them straight. "I'm not terminal, if that's what you want to know. I don't have cancer, despite my smoking."

"What, then?"

She didn't answer right away. When Lancaster did respond, her voice held a resigned tone. "Ever heard of early onset dementia?"

Decker gaped. "Dementia? You're still young, same age as me."

She gave him a sad smile. "That's why they call it 'early,' Amos."

"Are they sure? When were you diagnosed?"

"About six months ago. And they are sure. Brain scans, more MRIs than I can remember, blood work, biopsies, everything. I'm on meds, treatment."

"Then they can turn it around?" he said, with a small measure of relief in his voice.

She shook her head. "No, there is no cure. It's just holding the progression back as long as possible."

"What's the prognosis, then?" he said quietly.

"Hard to say. It's not like there are a million cases like me. And everyone's reaction is apparently different."

"Can they give you an estimate?"

She drew a long breath and her face quivered with emotion. "In a year I might not be able to recognize myself or anyone else. Or it could be five years. But not much beyond that. I won't even be fifty."

A long moment of silence passed, as tears slid down her cheeks. "I'm so sorry, Mary."

She wiped her eyes and waved this off. "I don't need sympathy, Decker, least of all from you. I know it's not your thing." She patted his shoulder and added in a kinder tone, "But I appreciate the effort."

"How did you know something was wrong?"

"When I woke up one morning and couldn't remember Sandy's name for about a minute. I blew that off, chalked it up to overwork. But little things like that started to happen with more frequency. That's when I went to the doctor."

Decker sat back and thought about his momentary inability to remember Cassie's favorite color. "Is that the reason for you and Earl splitting up?"

"Earl is a good guy, couldn't ask for a better one. But he has enough to do taking care of Sandy. I do not need to add to his burden."

"A good guy would not see it as a burden."

She looked at him. "Cassie never saw you as a burden, I hope you know that."

Decker looked away, his gaze drifting over the field where he had run like the wind, opposing players bouncing off him like pebbles flung against a mighty oak, people cheering him on, a normal kid with abnormal, even freakish athletic talent. Those had been some of the happiest times of his life, only to be dwarfed on the happiness scale by his time as a husband and father.

"I know that," he said quietly. "But I don't think you should give up on Earl that easily. The words *are* 'in sickness and in health.'"

"'Till death do us part.' Those vows are easy to make when you're young, healthy and happy and in love, your whole life ahead of you."

"Are you still in love with Earl?"

She looked at him, startled. "What?"

"I'm still in love with Cassie. I'll always love her. I don't care if she's dead. But Earl isn't dead. Earl is right here. I would give anything for Cassie to be here. And nothing, not early onset dementia or anything else, would keep me from her. Any second without her would be a waste of my life."

Decker rose and walked down the steps as the rain picked up.

Mary Lancaster watched him every step of the way.

43

"You look tired. Didn't you sleep okay?"

Mars asked this as he and Decker sat in the dining area of the Residence Inn the next morning having coffee.

"Slept like a baby," lied Decker. He sat back and fiddled with his paper napkin. "Planning went into this. They had to get the print, the DNA, and come up with the light switch plate. They had to kidnap David Katz. They had to commit the murders, leave the evidence, and flee the crime scene. This was clearly premeditated."

"I agree."

"So why did they pick that night, then? To do it? Was it just a coincidence that it was around the time of the only known phone call between the two men for a long while?"

"Maybe they found out about the phone call another way. What time did it happen?"

"Twelve-ten p.m."

"And Richards got the call at work?"

"It was his cell phone, but because of the time presumably it was—" Decker sat up straighter, his eyes wide.

"What?" said Mars, looking a bit alarmed.

"It was on a Monday in October."

"Okay."

"It was actually also Columbus Day."

"A holiday, then."

"Yes, and that meant two things. There was no school and the bank was closed."

"So where was Richards when he got the call, if not at the bank?"

"He could very well have been at home," said Decker.

"With his kids. And his wife. Do you think one of them might have overheard something, and then told someone?"

"That's certainly possible. But regardless, they would have had to act fast. Get the print on the switch plate and take it with them to the Richardses'. Then someone scratches Hawkins's arms and collects his DNA that way."

"And you think it was his daughter, Mitzi."

"It would explain why he kept quiet. He would obviously know who scratched him."

Mars said thoughtfully, "I see what you mean. His wife was dying, and he didn't want their daughter to get into trouble, even if it cost him his freedom."

Decker nodded. "When they finish testing the DNA sample, I bet it will show that Mitzi's DNA is also mixed up in what we found under Abigail's nails."

Mars said, "But why would she frame her own father?"

"She was a drug addict. Out of her mind half the time. She could have been easily persuaded to do it."

"But what would be the motive of somebody doing all that to kill Katz and Richards? And how does that tie into David Katz going over to Don Richards's house? Wait, do you think those guys were into drugs too?"

"Not that we know—" Decker stopped. "But Richards's son, Frankie, was. And we found out he was also dealing."

"But again, what's the connection?"

Decker closed his eyes and dialed up his cloud. After a few seconds he shook his head. "It's not in the case file."

"What's not?"

"The name of Mitzi's drug dealer."

44

NATTY WAS SITTING SULKILY behind his desk in the open room of the homicide department. Four other detectives were there working away, including Mary Lancaster.

A moment later Decker and Mars burst into the space. Decker glanced at Lancaster, who had a questioning look on her face, before marching over to stand in front of Natty.

"Karl Stevens," he said.

"Who?"

"He was the dealer who'd sold some stuff to Frankie Richards."

Lancaster had risen from her chair and approached. "We know that, but he had an alibi for the time of the murders. We checked that back then."

"Not the point," said Decker brusquely.

"So, what *is* the point?" snapped Natty.

"Did he also deal to Mitzi Hawkins?"

Lancaster and Natty exchanged a look. Natty said, "I don't know. It's been a long time. Does it matter?"

"It could."

Natty sighed. "I can check. No guarantees that it's in the records anywhere. And Karl Stevens sold to a lot of people."

Mars said, "Where is he now?"

Lancaster answered. "I can tell you that. He's at Travis Correctional Center. It's a private prison now. Stevens is serving ten to twenty on a second-degree murder conviction. He killed a guy over a heroin transaction. He's five years into his term. I was the one who busted him."

Decker said, "Travis Correctional? Isn't that where Meryl Hawkins ended up serving his time?"

Natty got on his computer and tapped some more keys. When he reached the page, his jaw fell. He looked up.

"You're right."

"Were they both in gen pop?" asked Decker, referring to the prison's general population.

"I don't know. But that's usually the case. They don't have the space to segregate prisoners. They're way beyond capacity as it is."

Lancaster said, "They could have interacted at the prison, then." She looked at Decker. "What are you thinking?"

"If they did interact, Stevens could have told him something that led Hawkins to come back here asking us to prove his innocence. I wondered about the timing of all this. I mean, did Hawkins just learn something that made him believe we could prove his innocence? He wanted to meet with me. Maybe it was then that he was going to tell me what he knew."

Lancaster said, "He must have learned it recently, otherwise why wouldn't he have raised it while he was still in prison?"

"What could Stevens have told him?" asked Natty.

"For one thing, that he was Mitzi's dealer," replied Decker.

"So what?"

"That could mean a connection between Frankie Richards and Mitzi."

"What kind of connection?" persisted Natty. "You're not making sense."

"Can you get us permission to visit Stevens?" asked Decker, ignoring the question. "Today?"

"I can try. But what could he possibly tell you?"

"I won't know that until I ask him." He paused. "You, um, you want to come along, Natty?"

The man didn't answer right away. He glanced at Lancaster and then said in a low voice, "I'm…I'm actually taking my wife out to lunch today."

Decker gazed at him for a few moments. "I think that's a better use of your time. I'll fill you in when we get back." He pointed at the phone on Natty's desk. "Make the call and tell them it'll be two of us."

"Make that three," said Lancaster.

"Mary, you're recused from—"

"Screw recusal, Amos. This doesn't have to do with Meryl Hawkins's murder where Earl is providing an alibi."

Decker glanced at Natty, who shrugged. "I have no problem with that."

Lancaster said, "Let's go." She walked out of the room without another word.

"Hey, Decker," said Mars, grinning. "She just did a really good impression of you."

* * *

It was a two-hour drive, and Mars dozed in the backseat. Decker had introduced Mars to Lancaster as they headed out.

Lancaster checked the backseat and then glanced at Decker. "At the football field?" she said quietly.

Decker kept his eyes on the road. "Yeah?"

"What you said made a lot of sense."

Decker just kept staring at the road and the approaching storm.

"I talked to Earl this morning."

Now Decker glanced at her, his expression prompting.

"I think we're going to...give it another shot."

"And his lady friend?" asked Decker.

"I don't think it would be an untruth to say that I pushed him into that relationship. Don't get me wrong. Nancy's nice and Earl likes her. Hell, I like her."

"But it's not what Earl wants?"

"No. He made that clear this morning. What he wants..."

"Is you."

Lancaster touched her wrinkled face and ran a hand down her stringy hair. "Can't really understand why. I look like shit. Nancy, on the other hand, is a real babe."

"Who's being shallow now?"

Lancaster looked embarrassed and dropped her hands in her lap. "I have to say I was surprised that you thought enough about my situation to tell me what I needed to hear."

"Meaning that I only look inward?"

"Meaning that I know those situations are very difficult for you with your special—"

"Maybe I'm growing out of it," interrupted Decker.

Lancaster absently touched her temple. "What did it feel like, when your... when your brain changed?"

He glanced over to see Lancaster staring at him with such intensity that he instantly felt anxious in trying to answer her query. He could sense that she was counting on him to tell her it would be somehow okay, or at least not terrible.

"I didn't have much time to make the transition, Mary. I woke up in a hospital and I was different. My mind was doing things it had never done before."

"I, um, I guess you were scared."

He glanced at her again to see the woman now staring at her hands.

"I won't lie to you, Mary. It was *unsettling*. But I got professional help and I was able to adapt. I won't tell you that it gets any easier. I will tell you that I was able to manage it. To live my life."

"It will be a bit different for me, I imagine."

"There's no cure for what you and I have, though they are very different things. But every day they make progress. In five years, who's to say they won't have beat what you have?"

She nodded but her look of anxiety remained. "If I live that long."

Decker reached over and gripped her shoulder.

She looked startled by this personal touch. It was not something that Amos Decker normally would ever do. She knew he didn't like being touched by others.

"You have Earl and Sandy and me to help you through this, Mary."

"You don't live here anymore."

"I'm here right now. And you know I'm going to keep coming back to Burlington."

"Because of your family."

"And now, also because of you."

This declaration caught Lancaster off guard. A small sob escaped from her lips and she suddenly seized his hand with both of hers and squeezed, as the tears, like released water over a damn, broke free and slid down her cheeks.

"You're a good friend, Amos. Sometimes I have trouble remembering that."

"You put up with me for a lot of years, Mary. Longer than anyone else other than Cassie. You probably deserve a medal for that. But all I can offer you is my friendship."

"I'll take that over any medal."

They drove the rest of the way in silence.

CHAPTER

45

WITH ITS CONCRETE WALLS, concertina wire, attack dogs, and guards with sniper rifles on towers, Travis Correctional Center rose out of the Ohio soil looking every bit the max prison that it was.

Decker drove up to the entrance and they cleared security, right as the heavens opened up and the rain poured down, forcing them to sprint for cover. Natty had secured an interview with Karl Stevens, and they were escorted to the visitors' room.

All three, Decker, Lancaster, and Mars, were well acquainted with prisons, for starkly different reasons. Catcalls, screams, the smells of over two thousand men kept in close proximity to each other in a facility designed for half that number, together with the comingled aromas of dozens of types of illicit contraband.

They sat at a table and awaited the arrival of Karl Stevens. He was brought in a few minutes later. Decker remembered him as tall and thin with long, dirty hair tied back in a ponytail, and a scruffy beard. The man appearing before them in his orange prison jumpsuit and shackles was thickened with dumbbell-driven muscle. His head was shaved, his facial hair gone. His knotted forearms were bedecked with tats that continued on his neck and up the back of his bald head.

He smiled at the trio as he was seated in front of them and his shackles locked into an eyebolt on the floor.

The guards stepped away but kept a watchful eye from across the room.

Stevens looked at Decker. "I remember you. Decker, right?"

Decker nodded.

Then the inmate turned to Lancaster. "Sure as hell remember you. You're the reason I'm here."

"No, let's keep to the facts, Karl. The reason you're here is because you killed a guy."

"Details, details," said Stevens with a smirk. He glanced at Mars and his expression soured. "Don't know you."

"No, you don't," said Mars.

"You a cop too?"

"He's helping us on a case," said Decker.

Stevens kept his gaze on Mars. "You got the look of somebody who's done time."

"You ever been locked up in Texas?" said Mars.

"No, why?"

"I wouldn't recommend it."

Stevens looked at Decker. "What do you want? I was going to work out, then I got the word you wanted to see me."

Decker said dryly, "Sorry to interrupt your exercise. We wanted to know if you were Mitzi Hawkins's dealer."

"Who's Mitzi Hawkins?"

"Meryl Hawkins's daughter."

Stevens shrugged. "That doesn't mean shit to me. I dealt to a lot of people." He laughed. "I didn't ask for fuckin' ID."

Decker described Mitzi to him.

Stevens chuckled. "You got to be shitting me. You just described every whacked-out bitch I ever sold to."

"How about Frankie Richards? You remember him? He was only fourteen. He died at his home along with his father and sister and a man named David Katz. They were murdered."

"Nah, can't say that I do. Anything else?"

Decker was looking at the tats on the man's forearms. Words and symbols.

When Stevens noticed this, he lowered his arms to below the tabletop, his shackles rattling as he did so.

"Which gangs do you belong to in here, Karl?" asked Decker.

Stevens grinned. "Hell, I'm Switzerland, man. Neutral. Most guys in here are Hispanic, or they got his skin color." He pointed at Mars. "*They* belong to the gangs, not the white guys. We're in the minority."

"You're not the only white guy in here," pointed out Lancaster. "Not by a long shot."

"Well, most days it seems like I'm in the minority. We got to do something about that." He grinned. "Take back our country."

"How? Lock up more white guys?" said Mars.

Stevens's lips curled back. "No. Just keep your kind out."

"I was born here."

"Ways around that," said Stevens, with another smirk. "We done here?"

Lancaster said, "If you're straight with us, Karl, we might be able to help you out."

He glanced up at her, all attention now. "Help me out, how?"

"Your sentence? It has some flexibility."

"I've done five on a ten to twenty. What can you do about that?"

"That depends on what you can do for us."

He rolled his eyes. "It's always the same old shit with you people. I got to tell what I know, if anything, and then you tell me the deal, take it or leave it. What other businesses negotiate that way?"

Decker said, "This isn't a business. This is you marking fewer years in here than you otherwise would."

Stevens said, "I can lie and tell you anything you want. Then you cut me a sweetheart deal. How about that?"

"Lies don't cut it. We need the truth, corroborated."

"It happened a long time ago. How do you expect me to remember anything?" As soon as Stevens said this, his features tightened.

Decker said, "*What* happened a long time ago?" When Stevens didn't answer, he added, "I thought you didn't remember anything about Frankie Richards or Meryl Hawkins."

"Just making conversation," said Stevens uncomfortably, his swagger now gone.

Lancaster interjected, "You want to deal or not? We can leave right now, but we'll be sure to note in the record how uncooperative you were. That way you go to the max twenty."

Stevens lunged forward and might have leapt across the table but for his restraints. The look on his face was that of a snarling wild animal. "You screw me like that, bitch, and you're gonna regret it. I didn't ask for you to come here."

"Is that right, Karl?" said Lancaster. "You got friends on the outside?"

"I got friends all over."

"So where were your friends when your ass ended up in here?" She paused. "Some friends. Why do you think you owe them?"

"Who said anything about owing anybody?" he barked.

The guards made a move to step forward, but Decker waved them off. He said, "Because guys like you are a dime a dozen, and Mary and I have seen it all a hundred times. You got stupid and you got caught and your 'friends' ran away from you as fast as they could. The result: You're in here and they're not."

"You got no idea who you're dealing with."

"Then tell us," replied Decker. "I always like to know who's on the opposing team."

Stevens waved this off with a rattle of his shackles. "I'm just spouting, man. Just bullshit."

"Getting back to Richards and Hawkins: You dealt for them both, I'm betting. Maybe you heard something from one of them that might tie into what happened?"

Lancaster added, "And maybe you saw Meryl Hawkins here and you two talked. About stuff? And then he got released."

"That was bullshit. I'm sick too. I got a liver thing."

"So, you *knew* he was released because of his cancer being terminal?" said Decker.

When the inmate once more looked chagrined at his own words, Decker said, "That's the second time you've screwed up talking with us, Karl. I think you need to tell us what you know, and we'll work a deal for you. You'll be out of here sooner than you otherwise would."

"You think it's that easy?"

"I don't know. Why don't you try us?"

"I gotta think about it."

Lancaster said, "What's to think about? You help us, we help you."

Stevens shook his head.

"Tell us this, did you talk to Hawkins?" asked Decker.

"I might have seen him around."

"And might you have discussed the murders with him?"

"Why don't you ask him?"

Lancaster said, "We would, but somebody killed him."

Stevens turned pale and looked like he might be sick. "I gotta go." He looked at the guards. "Hey, I'm done here."

Decker said, "It doesn't have to be this way, Karl."

"Yeah, it does. Now leave me the hell alone."

As he was being led away, Lancaster said to Decker, "I screwed up. I shouldn't have told him what happened to Hawkins."

"I don't think it would have mattered, Mary, but we did get one lead."

"What?"

"The tats on Stevens's arms were very close to the tats I saw on the shooter who killed Sally Brimmer."

"What? Are you sure?"

"Yes, I'm sure."

* * *

When they got back to Burlington, Natty met them in the detectives' room. "What the hell happened up there?"

"What do you mean?" asked Lancaster.

"They just found Karl Stevens with a shiv in his neck. He's dead."

46

Decker, Lancaster, and Mars were holding a powwow in the empty dining area of the Residence Inn as the rain beat down outside in the darkness.

"Well, that tells us your theory was right, Amos," said Lancaster. "Stevens was involved in this somehow."

"And by talking to us, he got the death penalty," added Mars bitterly. "I know the guy was scum, but nobody deserves that crap."

Decker sat there, his hands in his lap, his gaze centered on a spot on the ceiling. "The shooter who killed Sally Brimmer had the same tats. There's apparently a connection between him and Stevens."

"Are you really sure they're the same?" asked Lancaster.

"I got a clear look at them in the alley, and at Stevens's back at the prison. I think Stevens knew that, because when he caught me looking, he put his arms under the table so I couldn't see the tats anymore."

"Membership in the same gang," said Lancaster. "That's certainly possible."

"They moved quickly," said Decker. "He was dead within two hours of our meeting him."

"How could they possibly have acted that quickly?" asked Lancaster. "Unless it was unrelated to our visit. Inmates do kill other inmates, all the time."

"That would have to be the biggest coincidence in the world."

"And you don't believe in even small coincidences," said Mars.

"And you saw how Stevens clammed up when he found out

Meryl Hawkins had been murdered. He was afraid for his safety. He tried to shut it down, but it was too late."

"With him gone, how do we get to the truth?" asked Lancaster. "Our leads keep dying. And, hell, we don't even know how whoever killed the Richards family and David Katz got there or left."

"No, I think we do know that," said Decker.

He explained to her his theory on Katz being kidnapped and driven to the Richardses' home in his car. And also about the light switch plate change-out and the DNA possibly coming from Mitzi. "I told Natty about it all too."

"So that's why you wanted to talk to Stevens," said Lancaster.

Decker nodded. "I think Frankie Richards overheard the conversation between his father and Katz, and told Stevens about it when he saw him, or maybe he phoned him. The call came in on a holiday and both father and son were presumably home. Whatever Frankie told Stevens about that phone call, Stevens then told others. And they arranged things and the very next night they came and killed them all. That's how they picked that night and also the location, since Richards was probably expecting Katz to come over anyway. That seems to be what the phone call between the two was about."

Mars said, "And maybe they picked that night because they knew Susan Richards *wouldn't* be home. It might be that she knew nothing about what they were planning to discuss."

Lancaster said, "So we figure out what they were planning to discuss, this whole thing unravels."

"They only had one known connection. The American Grill restaurant."

"Which Rachel Katz still owns and operates," said Mars. "And that's puzzling, since she told me she'll probably make more in a month at her nightclub than the American Grill does in six months."

"And she's got all these other projects going, so it's a wonder she wants to keep the place," said Decker.

Mars said, "She told me it was because it was her husband's first deal. But the lady didn't strike me as being all that nostalgic."

"And she also told you she brings the local know-how and her partners bring the cash," noted Decker.

"You think her money partners are involved in all this?" asked Lancaster.

"I don't know. But if they are, they would have had to have been around thirteen years ago. It might be worthwhile digging into who they are."

"Whoever it is, they must have some serious connections inside Travis Correctional," commented Lancaster.

"How do you want to go about doing this with Rachel?" asked Decker. "They already know we're snooping around from our meeting with Stevens. I don't want to spook them even more."

Mars said, "What about me?"

"What about you what?" asked Lancaster.

"Lady clearly likes me."

"The lady also knows you work with us," said Decker.

"She told me a lot last night. Maybe she'll tell me some more."

"I don't like it," said Lancaster.

"I don't like it either," said Decker. "But it might be our best shot. And at the same time, we can find out who her partners are. There has to be paperwork filed with all of her projects."

"Okay, I'll get rolling on that," said Lancaster. She pointed her finger at Mars. "This is not fun and games. These people are killers."

"Yeah," said Mars. "Which is why we're going after them."

"You think you know a lot about killers?"

"Well, I was on death row all those years."

Lancaster looked at Decker. "Will you tell him to be serious?"

"He *is* being serious, Mary."

Lancaster whirled back around to stare suspiciously at Mars.

"Don't worry," he said. "Turns out I was innocent. Only cost me twenty years of my life and ruined any shot I had at playing in the NFL."

"Damn," said Lancaster. "That sucks."

"Oh, it more than sucks, trust me."

"How are you going to approach it with Katz?" asked Decker.

"Look, she probably thinks she can work on me and get details about the investigation. She tried doing that last night. I didn't give her much, but I did give her a taste here and there. I can let her think she's making inroads. And I'll do the same with her." He paused. "And there's something off with her."

"What do you mean?" asked Lancaster.

"I'm not sure. She's attractive, she's got money, education. But she feels like a loner to me. How come she never remarried? And why is she always so guarded about everything? When I asked about meeting her business partners, she didn't look comfortable with that at all."

"You could be right," remarked Lancaster.

"And if we end up in a place where I can snoop around, I will."

"Whoa, now you think you're some kind of, what, spy?" said Lancaster.

"Well, my girlfriend *is* a spy."

"Now you're bullshitting me, right?"

Mars held up his right hand. "God's honest truth."

She looked at Decker, who nodded. "Military intelligence."

"Sonofabitch," exclaimed Lancaster. "You have a whole new class of friends, Amos."

"Hey, if you don't grow, you wither, right?" said Mars.

Decker put a hand on his shoulder. "All that aside, this *is* dangerous, Melvin. You're not going into this clean. They know what side you're on. Things can go sideways fast. If you sense any of that happening, you need to get out, pronto."

"I've always been fast, Decker, you know that from our college football days."

Lancaster said, "Wait a minute, you two played football against each other?"

"Longhorn versus Buckeye," said Mars. "And guess who won?"

"You did," said Decker. "And I hope you win again. Because unlike our college football matchup, I'm rooting for you."

Mars smiled, but when he saw the look Decker was giving him he gripped his shoulder and said, "Look, I know this isn't a game. But people have been killed. For no reason other than some assholes decided they didn't get to live anymore, and that included kids. If I can help you take them down, then I will."

Lancaster exchanged a glance with Decker. "You have seriously upgraded your friends, Amos."

"I know," he said. "And I want to keep them."

47

"WHAT THE HELL is he doing here?"

Decker, Mars, and Lancaster were walking into the police station the next morning when Childress stormed across the front lobby to confront them.

Decker eyed the police superintendent, who was attempting to stare him down. "I'm observing," he replied. "Like I was told I could. Natty's on board with it."

"I don't give a damn if Natty's on board with it." Childress put a finger in Decker's face. "And I know damn well that you're hardly just 'observing.' You're working this case, I know you are, because I know you."

"Then you know that I want to get to the truth."

In a scoffing tone, Childress said, "You think you can just waltz back in here and try to do our work for us? We're perfectly capable of investigating this case ourselves. We don't need you or the FBI to help us." He glanced at Mars. "Are you FBI?"

"No, just your friendly neighborhood vigilante."

"Nothing wrong with cooperation," interjected Decker. "Happens all the time." He glanced at Lancaster but was not surprised to see her remain silent. This was her job, this was how she supported her family. And with her health issues, Childress could make her life miserable.

Now Childress got right in Decker's face. "Just remember that we are still pressing charges against you. And you still have a court date to keep. Hired that lawyer yet? Because you're going to need one."

"Well, I won't be hiring Ken Finger."

Childress drew back. "Why not? He's got a good reputation."

"Yeah, he did such a bang-up job for Meryl Hawkins."

"Hell! The world's greatest lawyer couldn't have gotten Hawkins off. The forensic case was overwhelming."

"You think so?"

"You built that damn case, Decker," snapped Childress.

"Only I built it *wrong*."

Childress was about to say something but seemed to swallow his words. "What are you talking about?"

"We were all had, that's what I'm talking about."

"You're nuts. Forensics don't lie."

"No, they don't. But people do. All the time."

"You're making no damn sense at all." Childress glared at Lancaster. "How the hell can you work with this guy, Mary?"

"He gets results. You know that as well as I do."

Childress turned back to Decker. "One step out of line. One. And your ass is mine."

"Well, that's quite tempting," replied Decker.

Childress looked like he was about to throw a punch, but he somehow marshaled his anger and marched off.

"Is he always that mellow?" asked Mars.

"He's actually gotten better," said Lancaster. "He went from Satan to just being an asshole."

"You're really being prosecuted, Decker?" asked Mars. "I thought it was just a joke."

"For now, I am. I doubt it will ever get to an actual trial."

"Don't believe that, if Childress has anything to do with it," said Lancaster.

"He'll keep. And we need to 'keep' our focus on the case."

"What's the next move?" asked Lancaster.

"Someone impersonated Susan Richards on the day she disappeared."

"That's still not been proven," pointed out Lancaster. "It's just speculation."

"Fine, but speculation or not, we have to follow the theory up."

Mars said, "Why don't you two run that down? I'm going to try to connect with Rachel. She left me her cell phone number."

"We want to be around when you do," said Decker.

"Okay, but you can't be hovering over me. I'll let you know what I set up."

"We can wire you up again."

Mars shook his head. "No, I don't want to chance her finding a wire on me. That will blow everything."

"Okay," said Decker reluctantly. "But be careful."

Mars gave him a thumbs-up as he left them.

Lancaster watched him go. "Don't worry, Decker. He looks like he can take care of himself."

"I'd worry less if he were going into a bar fight with five big guys. Melvin would win that battle for sure."

"Then what are you worried about? He's not going into a fight with five guys. He's meeting up with *one* woman."

"*That's* what I'm worried about."

"So, what are we going to do next?"

"Something you can't help me with."

"Why not?"

"Like I said, it has to do with Susan Richards. And what I want to check also involves Rachel Katz. You can't work that part of the case because of Earl."

"Earl was Rachel Katz's alibi for Meryl Hawkins's murder. *Not* for what happened to Richards."

"But do you think Childress will see it that way?"

"Who gives a shit?" In a bit of gallows humor, she added, "Next year I might not even remember who he is."

"Okay, if you're sure."

"I am. But how is Katz involved in Richards's disappearance and murder?"

"Someone impersonated Richards so Agatha Bates could ID her. And both Rachel Katz and Mitzi Gardiner are the right height and build. From a distance and with a long coat and hat on, they could be mistaken for Susan Richards. Especially by someone whose eyesight isn't the best, like Bates."

"You really think that one of them killed Richards and took her place after sticking the woman in that suitcase?"

"Either we prove it is true or we don't."

"Who's first? Katz or Gardiner?"

"We'll leave Katz for Melvin right now. Let's go talk to Gardiner."

"She's not obligated to tell us anything."

"Then let's hear that from her."

"Are you going to just point-blank accuse the woman?"

"You've never appreciated the subtle side of my personality, Mary."

Lancaster looked surprised. "That may be because I've never seen it, Amos."

"Well, hang on, because you're about to."

48

"Okay, this is harassment, damn it."

Decker and Lancaster were standing on the front porch of Mitzi Gardiner's home, while the woman stared angrily across at them over the width of the doorway.

"I can understand your feeling that way, Ms. Gardiner. But the fact is, we're doing our best to solve multiple homicides connected to your father, and, like it or not, you're one of the best resources we have. We just have some questions for you, and we'll make them as painless as possible. I promise."

Lancaster looked incredulously at Decker, having obviously never seen him talk this way to any suspect or person of interest.

Gardiner eyed Lancaster. "I remember you. You two worked the case together."

"We did, yes. And I have to say I doubt I would have recognized you." Lancaster ran her eye over Gardiner's long, healthy frame, her elegant clothes, her perfectly coiffed hair, and her blemish-free complexion.

"I know that I've changed quite a bit from when you last saw me."

"You look great."

"Thank you."

"And I have to say I never thought we'd end up revisiting this case. But then your father came back to town proclaiming his innocence."

Gardiner pointed at Decker. "I already told him that was crap. My father just wanted to mess with you. Make you doubt his guilt."

"We still haven't found out who killed him," said Decker.

"You said you were checking with the two widows."

"Right. Well, one of them was murdered."

Gardiner gaped and Decker saw her fingers on the door tremble. "Murdered? Which one?"

"Susan Richards. We believe she was abducted from her home and then killed."

When Gardiner didn't respond, Decker added, "Can we come in?"

She led them down the hall to the conservatory. She motioned for them to sit while she stood there clasping and unclasping her hands.

"You look pretty surprised," said Decker.

"Of course I'm surprised. First my father and now Susan Richards." She abruptly sat down across from them and stared at her lap.

Lancaster looked around the graceful lines of the room. "You have a lovely home."

Gardiner nodded absently, but still wouldn't meet their eyes.

Decker took something from his pocket and held it out to her. "I thought you might want to have this."

Gardiner looked up but did not reach for the photo.

"It's you as a little girl. We found it in your dad's wallet. There wasn't much else in there. I know you said you never visited him in prison, but he evidently kept this photo all these years."

Gardiner shook her head. "I…I don't want it."

Decker put the photo down on the table, face up.

"What are your questions?" said Gardiner, glancing at the photo and then quickly looking away.

"Well, and don't be offended by this, because we're asking everyone connected to this case. We need to know where you were when Susan Richards was last seen."

"You can't possibly believe I had anything to do with her death?"

"Look, I don't want to believe that anyone is capable of murder. However, some people clearly are. But I'm not accusing you of anything. I'm just eliminating suspects right now, and we can do that with you if you can tell us where you were."

"What time are we talking about?"

Decker told her the day and the time in the evening.

Gardiner sat back and closed her eyes. Then she reached into her pocket and pulled out her phone. She brought up her calendar and ran through some screens. Then she seemed to breathe a sigh of relief. "I was at a dinner with my husband. A business dinner. There were six other people with us. It's here in Trammel. At a restaurant. From seven o'clock until well after midnight."

"And your husband can verify that?" said Lancaster.

"Do you have to talk to him?" Gardiner said worriedly. "He knows nothing about any of this...of my past life."

"Well, if you give us the names of some of the other people there?"

"That's as good as telling him," she snapped. "He's built up a great reputation in this area and people trust him. Something like this could ruin him."

"Well, can you think of someone else who can corroborate your whereabouts?" asked Lancaster.

Gardiner suddenly looked animated. "Wait, I know the owner of the restaurant. She could verify it. We had a private room and we paid with a credit card. You can check the receipt."

"That works."

Lancaster pulled out a notebook and took this information down.

"Is that all?" asked Gardiner, still clearly distracted.

"You need to tell us where you were when your father was killed."

"My father? Now you're accusing me of murdering my own father?"

"Again, I'm not accusing you of anything. I'm eliminating suspects, like we did for you just now with Susan Richards's death."

She looked at her calendar after Decker told her the time parameters. "I was home with my family. In fact, I was probably asleep at that hour. Like most people," she added.

"And your husband can corroborate that?"

"If necessary," she said between clenched teeth. "Is that all?"

"There's another discrepancy," said Decker. "But I'm sure you can clear it up."

Gardiner looked wearily at him. "I remember that you never seemed to stop asking questions all those years ago."

"And I'm afraid I haven't changed. It just comes with the territory."

"What discrepancy?"

"You said you'd never been in your father's closet."

Gardiner seemed instantly on the defensive. "Who told you that?"

"Actually, you did. The first time I was here to question you."

"Oh, okay. But I don't understand the discrepancy."

"The police report indicates that you were the one to show the forensic techs the panel in the closet."

Gardiner frowned. "I don't remember doing that."

"It was in the report."

"Then the report is wrong. It can be, can't it?"

Decker said, "So you're saying you didn't show them the panel?"

"I'm telling you I don't *remember* doing that."

"Okay. So they might have been searching and found it on their own."

"I guess."

"But why would they say that you told them about it?" asked Lancaster.

Gardiner was very pale now. "I…I don't know. Maybe I did. I might have been helping them look or something. It's possible. It was a long time ago. And I was not in a good frame of mind. I didn't remember things very well."

Decker said, "Understood. Well, thanks for your time."

He stood. Lancaster quickly did as well, looking surprised that Decker was already done.

"That's…that's it?" said Gardiner, looking as surprised as Lancaster.

"For now, yes." Decker slid the photo of her as a child toward her.

"I told you I didn't want it."

"I know. But sometimes people change their minds, don't they?"

Gardiner made no move to pick up the photo.

Decker said, "We'll find our own way out."

* * *

As they got into their car Lancaster said, "Okay, I approve of your new 'subtle' nature, Decker. But you really closed out the interview fast. I thought it was just getting good."

"It *was* just getting good. But you can also push someone too far."

"She's scared."

"She *is* scared. Because she knows more than she's telling us. And she's very concerned that someone else will realize that too."

"Are you saying she might be in danger?"

"Everyone connected with this case might be in danger, including you and me."

"We're cops, we signed up for that. Mitzi Gardiner didn't."

"Didn't she?" said Decker as he put the car in drive.

49

Posh.

That was the word that occurred to Mars as he pulled to a stop in the parking lot of the Silver Oak Grill. He didn't know what it used to be, but its old bones had been given new life. He looked around at the other cars parked there and saw a sprinkling of late-model expensive rides. There was even a Maserati convertible parked near the awninged entrance.

He walked in and looked around. The buildout here had definitely been expensive. Mars had learned about construction costs from investing in real estate in the D.C. market. Old beams, pricey stone flooring, an elaborately carved bar, expensive wallpaper, coexisting with contemporary seating.

The place was nearly full with folks having lunch, and there were three people ahead of Mars waiting to be seated.

"Melvin?"

He looked to his right and saw Rachel Katz waving to him from a table in the corner. He walked over and joined her.

She stood and had to rise up on her toes to give him a hug and a peck on the cheek. Then she took a moment to appraise his attire. Gray jacket, black turtleneck, charcoal slacks, and black loafers.

"Terrific outfit."

"Thank you. You're looking quite sharp yourself," he said, noting her slacks, blouse, jacket, and flats.

"Well, I came straight from work."

As they sat, he saw that she had nearly finished her cocktail.

"Drink?" she said.

He eyed the almost empty glass. "What are you having?"

"Dewar's and water. I'm ready for a refill."

"Hitting the hard stuff in the afternoon, are we?"

"We are."

He grinned. "Sounds good to me."

They ordered their drinks and sat back.

"When you called, I was surprised you wanted to see me again," she said.

"Why's that?"

"Well, we left things a little, I don't know, flat."

"I'm into long-range forecasting. Date to date doesn't mean much."

"I'm flattered you referred to it as a date."

Their drinks arrived, and they tapped glasses.

Katz took a sip and said, "And I guess I'm also surprised that Decker is letting you see me. I mean, he is investigating, and despite all the facts to the contrary, I guess I remain a person of interest or something like that."

"You know the lingo," he said, grinning.

"I watch crime shows, what can I say?"

"Surprised you have the time what with work and all your other projects."

She leaned forward. "What would you say if I told you that most nights, I go home, change into my PJs, eat a peanut butter and jelly sandwich with chips on top, and watch old movies?"   .

He studied her. "I *would* believe that." He quickly added, "Not because you don't have options. I imagine you could have your pick of guys around here."

She made a face. "Thing is, I don't want the guys around here."

"Which raises the question of why you don't just move somewhere else. Chicago's not that far away."

"David and I were thinking of moving there. And then he died."

"So you feel tied to this place?"

"In a way, I guess. He's buried here. What he started to build is here."

"Right."

"You don't believe me?" she said, her mouth creasing into a frown.

"No, I *do* believe you. Look at Decker. He doesn't live here anymore, but he's still tied to the place. Comes back to visit his family's graves. Different people have different motivations. You want to stay here, you stay here. It's your decision, no one else's."

She was about to say something but then took a quick sip of her drink instead. "You want to order? The salmon is really good, but I'm going for the tuna tartare."

He glanced at the menu. "How's the wagyu?"

"It's great. We get it fresh every day."

"We?"

She smiled. "I guess I didn't tell you. I have an interest in this place too."

"A lady with lots of interests. Makes the world go round."

They ordered, and Mars looked around the place before resettling his gaze on Katz. "Lot of money in the parking lot and at these tables. Even saw a Maserati out there."

"The Maserati belongs to that gentleman." She pointed to a shortish man in his late sixties with thick gray hair. He wore a three-piece suit with no tie, crocodile skin loafers, and, despite the chilly weather, no socks. At his table were six other people. Four men and two women.

"Money man?"

"Yes. Duncan Marks."

"Is he one of your partners?"

"No, not really. But he does a lot of projects around town. And we *have* done a couple deals together. But I'm a small fry compared to him."

"Well, you're a big fry where I'm concerned."

She smiled at his statement. "How's the investigation coming?"

"Decker's interviewing Mitzi right about now. Checking alibis and stuff like that."

"You mean for Susan Richards's murder?"

"Yeah, among other things."

"Getting back to my earlier thought. How come Decker is letting you hang out with me? Is he hoping you'll learn some stuff so he can arrest me?" She said this last part in a cavalier way, but Mars could detect an undertone of apprehension.

"Like I said, I'm not law enforcement. I'm his friend. I don't tell him what to do and he doesn't tell me."

"But you still want to help him."

"Sure I do." He spread his arms wide. "And if there's anything you can tell me that will help, let me have it."

She laughed. "You're an interesting man. There aren't that many around this town, at least that I can find."

"You lost one when Decker moved away, that's a fact."

Their food came a few minutes later. Mars tasted his steak and his eyes widened. "Okay, that right there should be illegal, it's so damn good. I don't smoke, but I might just make an exception after eating this."

"We were lucky to get our chef. He's from Indianapolis. Trained under one of those master chefs you see on TV."

"Well, the dude can cook."

"Yes, he can. So, do you think Mitzi Hawkins will have an alibi for Susan's murder?" asked Katz abruptly.

Mars looked up from his plate. "I don't know. Decker must have it by now. If she had one. Then he'll need to check it out."

"Like he will mine."

"That's right." He put down his fork and knife. "You look concerned."

"Are you waiting for my confession?"

"No, because while I don't know you well, you don't strike me as the murdering type. I have a pretty good nose for that. But still, there may be something else weighing on your mind."

"No, I'm good. Just tired, I guess. Been burning the midnight oil lately." She rubbed her temples. "After you left the club, I did a little business. It wasn't nearly as much fun as I had with you."

"You flatter me."

"Not to beat around the bush, Melvin, but I do find you very attractive."

"Hey, you're beautiful, smart, ambitious, sensitive, the whole package."

"Why do I sense a 'but' coming?"

"I'm seeing someone right now."

"Lucky girl."

"I hope she thinks that. And I hope I didn't lead you on."

"No, you made things pretty clear, actually. But a lady can always dream."

Mars sat forward. "Look, Rachel, I like you. I really do. And while I'm not officially working with Decker, I am helping him any way I can, like I said."

Katz leaned back and picked up her drink. "Okay."

"The undeniable fact is there are a lot of people dying around here. You had four people thirteen years ago, including your husband. Then Meryl Hawkins. Then Sally Brimmer, although Decker was the target there. And then Susan Richards."

"And your point?"

"If you know anything, anything at all, you need to tell us. Last thing I want is for something to happen to you."

Katz's spine seemed to stiffen. "Thanks for your concern, Melvin. But I can take care of myself. And I don't know anything, so I have nothing to worry about."

Mars nodded slowly. "Okay, if you're sure about that."

"Very sure."

"Because there's been another murder you might not have heard of."

Katz had picked up her fork. She slowly put it down as she absorbed this news. "What? Who?"

"Man named Karl Stevens. He dealt drugs here. He sold stuff to Mitzi and to Frankie Richards. Decker thinks he might be involved."

"And he's dead?"

"He was in prison. We went to see him. He said he knew nothing either. By the time we got back to Burlington the man had a knife in his neck." Mars picked up his Dewar's and took a sip. "So, apparently, some people don't care if folks know anything or not. They just kill them."

"But how could...I mean, he was in prison. People get killed in prison all the time."

"You're right about that. But the thing is, the tats that Stevens had on his arms?"

"What about them?" Katz said in a trembling voice.

"They matched the tats on the guy who shot Sally Brimmer. Decker was really sure about that, and nobody's memory beats his."

"And you don't think that might be a coincidence?"

"Do you?"

Katz sat back and composed herself. "Well, I'm sorry about this Mr. Stevens, but that has nothing to do with me."

"Okay, if you're sure."

"I *am* sure."

"Then let's just get back to this lovely meal."

Mars finished all of his steak. Katz barely touched her food. She finished her second Dewar's, though.

As they were leaving, they passed Marks's table. Duncan Marks put out a hand and gripped Katz's arm. "Rachel, I thought that was you over there."

"Hello, Duncan."

"The place is doing fabulous. Another home run for you."

"Thanks."

Marks looked at Mars. "And I don't believe I know your friend."

Mars put out a hand. "Melvin Mars. Nice to meet you, sir."

They shook hands as the other people at the table stared dully at them.

"Rachel said that was your Maserati out there. Beautiful car."

"Yes, it is. German engineering and Italian design, a match made in heaven."

They all laughed.

They walked out of the restaurant and Katz turned to Mars.

He said, "Seems like a nice guy."

"Yeah, look, um, I know we just had lunch, but can we have dinner tonight?"

"Okay, sure. Where?"

She hesitated. "My place. I can actually cook."

When he looked uncomfortable, she gripped his arm. "I promise, it won't be like that. I...I just need to have a home-cooked meal and someone to talk to. And I'd like that someone to be you."

Mars squeezed her hand and nodded. "Sure, sounds good."

"Seven okay?"

"I'll be there. Anything I can bring?"

"Just yourself, Melvin, that will be enough."

50

DECKER AND LANCASTER WERE SITTING in the detectives' room when the door opened. It was the ME. He had taken off his white lab coat and was now dressed in a suit. He held up some paperwork.

"Got some results for you," he said. He joined them at Lancaster's desk and thumbed through the pages. "First up, Meryl Hawkins had some painkillers in his system. Oxycodone."

"Would that have incapacitated him?" asked Decker. "Could he have been unconscious when he was shot?"

"He could very well have been," replied the ME. "And Susan Richards. She died of an overdose of fentanyl. Doesn't take much with that drug. Nasty, powerful stuff."

"Any sign during the post that she was a regular drug user?"

"No, nothing like that at all. She was in good shape, actually. Would have lived a lot longer."

"And time of death?" asked Decker.

"She'd been dead a while, Amos."

"I asked you this before. Could she have been dead from the moment she allegedly left her house that night?"

"Well, I can tell you that her probable time of death would coincide with your theory." He paused. "So you think she was murdered at her house?"

"Something like that."

The ME shook his head. "This case grows more complex by the minute. Glad it's not my job to figure it out."

After the ME left, Lancaster said, "Well, if you're right, then someone killed her and took her body out in that suitcase and then dumped it. That means the person that Agatha Bates saw leaving that night was not Susan Richards."

"Tall, lean, and blonde," said Decker.

"Mitzi Gardiner or Rachel Katz, like you said before. But I checked Mitzi's alibi for the time Richards was allegedly abducted. The restaurant verified that she was there all evening, long after Richards went missing."

"So Rachel Katz, then?"

"Speaking of, any word from your buddy on her?"

"He emailed. They finished lunch. Said Katz was acting weird. Wants to have dinner at her place tonight. He said he thinks she's going to open up to him. He also said he told her about Karl Stevens being killed, and though she tried to hide it, she got really freaked out." Decker added, "Duncan Marks was also at the restaurant. Melvin talked to him. And Katz said he was involved with some of her projects."

"I didn't know that. But you remember Marks, surely."

"I actually did some work for him when his daughter, Jenny, got involved with a con artist. Marks came into Burlington way back and started buying up stuff. Took a little hit with the recession, but then came roaring back, acquiring properties on the cheap. He's made a lot of money. Had the biggest home in the area when I lived here."

"Still does," said Lancaster. "On that hill outside of town. It's like the guy is looking down on the rest of us."

"Reminds me of another guy with a big house on the hill in Pennsylvania. But he was broke, and wasn't looking down on anyone, actually."

"Well, Marks isn't broke. He's got money coming out of every pore of his skin. I heard he actually made a lot of money before coming to Burlington. Investments or some such. IPOs and other crap I'll never understand and never make a dime off."

"Why'd he pick Burlington? I never knew."

"I heard that his father was from here. Worked in the old shoe factory before moving away, I believe. Marks bought that and turned it into luxury condos."

"That's also where Rachel Katz lives."

Lancaster snapped her fingers. "That's right."

"So according to Melvin, Katz was freaked out by the news of Stevens's murder. And now she might want to talk to him. And he's having dinner with her tonight."

"Hawkins wanted to talk to you too, and he's dead now. And who knows, maybe the same for Susan Richards."

They looked at each other.

"Maybe we need to keep an eye on your buddy tonight."

"That's exactly what I was thinking."

51

WHEN RACHEL KATZ OPENED THE DOOR, Mars filled the doorway of her condo.

He was dressed in light gray slacks and an open-collared white shirt with a dark blue jacket over it. He had a bottle of red in one hand and a bouquet of flowers in the other.

Katz was dressed casually in jeans and a long-sleeved shirt, and she was barefoot.

"I feel overdressed," commented a smiling Mars as he walked in.

"You look great. I just felt like a jeans-and-no-shoes night."

She thanked him for the flowers and wine and gave him a kiss on the cheek. "You didn't have to do that," she said as she got out a vase and filled it with water, then set the flowers in it after snipping off the ends of the stalks.

"My mom taught me it was always polite and respectful to bring something."

"Well, your mother taught you right. Do you see her much?"

"No, she and my father both passed away."

"Oh, I'm sorry."

He shrugged. "It happens. You want me to get this wine going?"

"Yes, please. My Dewar's seems ages ago. The opener's in that drawer."

He poured out two glasses and handed one to her as he sniffed the air. "Something smells good. What's for dinner?"

"Caprese to start, chicken parm with my own secret sauce for the main, and cannoli to finish. Call it my Italian extravaganza."

"You did that after working all day?"

"I like to cook. But I admit the cannoli is store-bought."

"Still, damn impressive. You need any help?"

"You did your job by opening the wine and bringing the flowers."

"Guys always get cut slack."

"You are a wise man, Mr. Mars."

* * *

They ate about a half hour later. After they were finished, Mars insisted on clearing and cleaning. "You cooked and now it's my turn," he said firmly.

As she watched him collect the dishes, she stroked the stem of her wineglass and said, "I hope the woman you're seeing appreciates what she has."

"I think she does. But in a relationship, you gotta keep working it, from both sides."

"David used to say the same thing."

Mars rinsed the plates, glasses, and utensils and put them in the dishwasher. "Sounds like you two had a great relationship."

"We did. Only it was cut short."

Mars finished up and joined her in the living area, sitting next to her on the couch. She drew her legs up under her, holding out her glass as he refreshed her wine.

"Right. That was beyond tragic."

"But at least I thought it was over. And now Decker is back opening the whole thing up because he's convinced Meryl Hawkins didn't do it. But if he didn't, who did?"

"Did your husband have any enemies?"

"No, nothing like that. I told Decker the same thing."

"Maybe Don Richards had enemies. Or your husband was in the wrong place at the wrong time."

"That's what I *thought* had happened, but I also thought that Hawkins had committed the murders. And it *was* a robbery or a burglary. Things *were* taken."

"That could have just been a cover."

She nodded slowly but hardly seemed convinced of this.

Mars said, "When you invited me here tonight, it seemed that you had something on your mind. You said you wanted to talk."

Katz set her glass down and looked over at him. "I'm afraid."

"Of what?"

"Like you said at lunch, people are dying, Melvin. Hawkins. Susan Richards. That woman from the police department."

"I know, Rachel. It *is* scary."

"And someone murdered my husband. And…everything from the past just seems to be coming back. It's like I'm being haunted by ghosts I thought were long buried." She put a hand to her face and wiped at her suddenly teary eyes.

He put an arm around her shoulders. "Let me tell you something. Not that long ago, I was in a world of trouble. I mean bad, bad stuff. Then Decker came along. And he got to the truth and the man changed my life. After twenty years of people believing that a lie was the truth. But not him. Not Decker. He just keeps digging. Dude never stops."

Katz shivered a bit. "He sounds like a man to be reckoned with."

"Oh, he is. And people have tried. And he just keeps rolling."

"Does…does he understand that there can be different shades of truth?"

He drew a bit away from her, watching the woman closely. "Such as?"

"I mean, there are times when you can tell the truth, but people may not see it as the truth, not the same way that the person telling it does. And…and sometimes people feel they have to do things for, you know, reasons that might seem…"

"Seem what?"

"Wrong, I guess. But not to the person having to do the things. They might think it's the only thing they can do."

Mars looked confused by all this. "You've lost me."

"I…look, never mind. I know I'm not making much sense."

"Take your time. I've got nowhere to go."

She changed the subject. "So, Decker really believes that Hawkins was innocent?"

Mars looked at her for a long moment, clearly disappointed in the change in direction of the conversation. "Let's put it this way. Hawkins didn't try to kill Decker twice, because the man was already dead when those events occurred."

"You mean someone doesn't want the truth to come out? They're trying to stop Decker. And they silenced Hawkins because he might know something?"

"That's the way we see it, yeah." He paused. "So, do *you* know something that could help us?"

"If I did, I would've told you. I would've told people thirteen years ago."

"But there are shades of truth, that's what you just said."

She moved slightly away from him, as though symbolically distancing herself from this conversation. "It's amazing what a few drinks will do to loosen someone up," she said, tacking on a brief smile.

"I'm just trying to get to the truth, Rachel. That's all."

"But sometimes the truth doesn't set us free, does it? Sometimes it traps us."

"Is the truth trapping you?"

"No, of course not. I was just…speculating. Talking off the top of my head."

He took her hand. "I want to help you, Rachel."

"But you work with Decker."

"That shouldn't matter. I already told you I don't think you killed anybody."

"But…" she said quickly, and then stopped.

"But what?"

She abruptly rose. "I'm really tired all of a sudden. I think I'm going to call it a night."

Mars stared up at her, and then his expression changed. He leapt up and tackled her as one of the large glass windows shattered. They both fell heavily to the floor, as the shot fired through the window hit its intended target.

52

"SON OF A BITCH!" cried out Decker.

He and Lancaster leapt out of his car, which was parked down the street and across from Katz's building. They drew their guns and hunkered down next to the vehicle.

"There," said Lancaster, pointing to the opposite building. "The shot came from there. I saw the muzzle flash."

"Call in reinforcements," bellowed Decker as he punched in Mars's number.

It rang and rang, with no answer.

"Shit."

"Do you think the shooter's still there?" said Lancaster, putting away her phone after making the call. "If we go to check on Mars and Katz?"

"Right, he'll pick us off." He glanced at Lancaster. "It could be the same guy who killed Brimmer. You wait here for the cops to show. Keep trying to call Melvin." He texted the number to her phone.

"What are you going to do?"

"I'm going after the shooter."

"Amos—"

But he was already running down the street, keeping right next to the building where the shot came from, to make it difficult for whoever was in there to draw a bead on him.

He reached the front entrance of the building and looked it over. Plywood on the lower windows. The place looked abandoned. But it had a perfect sightline into Katz's apartment from the upper floors.

He raced up the steps to the front entrance and noted that the large double doors were chained shut. He heaved his bulk against them, but not even his size and strength could budge them.

He hustled on down the street, turned left at the next intersection, and raced down it. He was listening at the same time for a car starting up or footsteps running away. The night air was brisk and the sky clear for once.

He could hear nothing except his own breathing.

He reached the next corner and peered down it.

Nothing. No one and no car waiting to take the shooter away.

He forced himself not to think about Mars's fate. He had said a simple prayer that his friend was okay. And if he wasn't, Decker was going to risk his life to avenge him.

He raced over to the rear entrance, and that was where his luck turned. The door was open. And Decker well knew why.

The shooter had entered this way.

He eased the door open and stepped through. He knew he was a big target, and he squatted down to make himself less of one.

He took stock of the situation. The shooter might have already fled, out the door, and either driven off or used his own two feet to get away.

Only Decker had heard nothing that would indicate either had happened. And he doubted enough time had elapsed for the shooter to make his exit.

That would leave the person still inside an empty building, probably with a long-range, high-powered rifle, while Decker only had his new pistol, which he had never once fired, and would not be that accurate over any meaningful distance. The shooter could nail him from a lot farther away than Decker could the shooter.

He saw a bank of elevators but knew there probably was no power turned on in the building. That left the stairs. He used his Maglite to show the way and reached the door to the stairwell.

Like Lancaster, he'd seen the muzzle flash and downloaded the image in his head, counting up the floors.

Sixth.

He cautiously opened the door and made his way up, slowly.

He might meet the shooter coming down. Or the person could be up there waiting for him.

He counted the floors until he reached number six, understanding that the shooter could have gone to a lower floor, let him pass by, and then made his escape out the rear.

A moment later, he heard the sirens. Okay, the good guys were on their way. And an ambulance too, depending on what had happened in Katz's apartment.

He opened the door to the sixth floor and peered inside.

He hesitated to use his Maglite because it would just make him a target. There was enough light from the windows to allow his eyes to adjust rapidly. The floor plan was open, which was good and bad. It cut down on the places Decker would have to look, but it also allowed him no cover while he did so.

He closed the door quietly behind him and skittered over to behind an old metal desk.

Take your time, focus, and listen.

All he heard were the sirens coming closer.

That could be drowning out any sound of movement up here. He redoubled his efforts to hear any noise the gunman might be making.

His position had been chosen wisely. If the shooter wanted to escape, he would have to leave through the door Decker had come through.

He decided to try to move the needle.

"Police. You're surrounded. Put down your weapon and come out into the open where we can see you. Hands over your head, fingers interlocked. Do it now!"

He fell silent and waited.

The sirens outside had stopped. Any moment he expected to hear the front door being knocked open, followed by feet pounding into the building.

All he had to do was hold his position.

Come on, come on, show yourself.

If it was the same shooter, Decker didn't fancy getting into another hand-to-hand battle with the guy. If it was the same man, he probably outweighed him by well over a hundred pounds. Yet he had grave doubts that he would win such an encounter.

That's when he saw it.

The red dot swooping over the space, looking for him.

The guy had a laser scope.

That gave him the advantage over Decker, at least in some respects. But as Decker watched the dot flit around, the dust in the abandoned building was doing something quite remarkable. It was gathering around the light beam emanating from the scope, as though someone had clapped chalk erasers around it.

Decker quietly slid to his left, moving out into the open briefly before taking cover behind some crates. He peered over the top of the crates, but didn't see the red dot anywhere.

He ducked back down as the shot came his way, smacking the wall behind him. The dot had apparently been on his head.

He kept moving, keeping behind the limited cover until he had worked his way to the far side of the room. He lay on his side and peered around the leg of a desk. He could see the red beam again.

This time he followed the thing to its source.

He lined up his shot. A large wooden box.

He fired five times, four through the wood, and when those shots flushed the guy, he unloaded his fifth shot at the exposed flesh.

He heard a grunt of pain.

Okay, he'd hit the guy. But it wasn't over yet.

He looked for more red dots, but saw none. He slid forward on his belly until he had halved the distance between them.

He heard footsteps coming up the stairs.

He was sure the other guy could too. That might draw him out, make him desperate.

It did, only not in the way Decker was expecting.

A blur came out of nowhere, leaping through the air and landing on top of him before he had a chance to fire.

The pair rolled around on the floor, struggling for the upper hand. Decker collapsed on top of the guy, trying to use his far heavier weight to crush him. He felt something on his face and realized it was the other man's blood.

Then a wedge of elbow slammed into the side of his face, stunning him.

He gripped the man's chin with his hand and forced it back, trying to take the neck to a place necks were not designed to go.

He had not accounted for the man's other hand, though. The fist hit him once and then twice, both pummeling shots. Decker's grip was broken and he was forced to roll off the guy.

He saw the flash of blade and put up an arm to protect himself.

Two shots rang out.

He saw the man above him flinch once, and then a second time.

He dropped the knife. And then he fell to the floor with a thud.

Decker sat up to see Lancaster slowly lower her gun.

53

It was morgue time again.

Decker still felt slightly queasy from his fight.

He stared over at the body on the gurney. *I'd be on this slab instead of him but for Mary.*

Decker had been tremendously relieved to learn that Mars was unharmed, though Rachel Katz had been shot and was still in surgery.

He lifted the sheet to stare down at the man. The tats on his arms *were* nearly identical to the ones Karl Stevens had. Decker had had the prison take pictures of Stevens's tats for comparison just to be sure.

He looked at them more closely and was once more struck by the unusual variety of images inked there. But they all had something in common: They were symbols of hate groups. He looked over them, starting with the right forearm and going over to the left arm. Decker knew many of these symbols from his work with the police and later with the FBI. The folks represented by these tats were not exactly law-abiding.

The number 88. That was the numerical equivalent (the eighth letter of the alphabet being H) of "Heil Hitler."

Then the shamrock and the swastika, taken together, was often the mark of the Aryan Brotherhood.

The Blood Drop Cross, which was the primary insignia of the KKK and known by the acronym MIOAK, meaning "mystic insignia of a Klansman."

And the initials KI, which might refer to another hate group, though Decker didn't recognize them.

Still, there were some Decker had had to Google. The Aryan Terror Brigade symbol, and *Weiss Macht*, which was German for "white power." The sonnenrad, which was an ancient Indo-European sun-wheel and had been co-opted by the Nazis, who had placed the swastika dead center.

Then there were the SS bolts, another Nazi symbol, and the triangular Klan symbol, which looked like three triangles within a triangle, but upon closer inspection would show itself to be three letter k's in the triangle facing inward.

All in all, it was quite the smorgasbord of ink. Decker had no idea why the man had all this on him, but he had obviously been one seriously demented man.

The guy looked tough, even in death. A man with no scruples about ending someone else's life. As Decker's eyes traveled over the body, he saw scars and old wounds and other indicia of a violent life.

He thought about Mitzi Gardiner. She'd had a rough life growing up. And then she'd turned it around. She'd once more become her father's little star, of sorts. Like on the back of the photo he'd found in Hawkins's wallet. Her star had fallen. And then she had been reborn. Or had she?

Decker glanced over at the wall of slide-out cabinets where the corpses were kept. He strode over to the last one on the left. He opened the door and slid the rack out. He lifted the sheet and looked down at the body of Meryl Hawkins. He reached down and lifted up the man's arm.

The tattoo with the arrow piercing the star.

Symbolic of what? Then it clicked.

He phoned Lancaster. She was still at the office filling out forms.

"Hawkins told us the prison initiated his compassionate care release."

"I know he did," said Lancaster.

"I think he was lying."

"Why?"

"His daughter was his star. He drew stars on the back of his photo of her that he carried around. The latest tat he got was the arrow through the star. I think he ran into Karl Stevens and Stevens told him the reason why his daughter framed him. And then Hawkins applied for a compassionate care release, got his tat, and got out of prison to come back here."

"But he said the prison people came to him," countered Lancaster.

"I think when we check into that, we'll find out that's not how the system works. The inmate files for it, not the prison authorities."

"Okay, but you believed that he suspected that his daughter helped set him up from the get-go. And he did nothing back then."

"Only then he didn't know the real reason. The people behind it. Maybe he just thought she was stoned and had screwed up somehow. It could have been some of her drug addict friends looking to do a robbery and he didn't want to implicate her. Then he found out the truth."

"You mean you think he found that out from Stevens?"

Decker said, "That's right. And maybe Stevens knew somehow that Mitzi was now living high on the hog. At that point Hawkins didn't care about his daughter. She'd cashed in big-time by framing him. Before he died, he wanted his name cleared. He put an arrow through his little 'star,' got out of prison, and came to us."

"If his daughter knew that, she would be a prime suspect in killing him."

"She didn't have an alibi for his murder, so we're going to have to dig deeper on that." He paused. "Oh, and Mary?"

"Yeah."

"Thanks for saving my butt tonight."

After Decker clicked off, he looked back down at Hawkins's shriveled body. The man had gone to prison for a crime he hadn't committed. Then he'd found out that he had been set up and he wanted the truth to come out, as his last act before dying.

Well, Decker was going to carry the ball forward now.

"I'm sorry, Meryl. You deserved better. From me and everybody else."

He rolled Hawkins's remains back into the cabinet and closed the door.

It was too late to see Mitzi Gardiner now, but he had somewhere else he needed to go.

54

HE DROVE OVER to the spot where he'd nearly lost his life tonight. But he didn't go back into the abandoned building. He ventured inside Rachel Katz's condo building and took the elevator up after flashing his creds at the officer guarding the crime scene's perimeter.

The forensic team was still processing the area. Decker nodded at Kelly Fairweather, who was doing a bloodstain pattern analysis by the couch. In another corner of the apartment, Natty was talking with a second tech. He saw Decker and quickly headed over.

"Boy, close call for you tonight," said Natty.

Decker nodded. "Mary really saved my butt."

"And she nailed the bastard who killed Sally," said Natty with a grim smile.

"Any word on Rachel Katz?"

"Still in surgery. Last I heard, she's going to make it. Close, though, bullet nearly hit an artery. Your friend saved her life."

"I know. Melvin's over at the hospital now with her, probably adding another layer of protection."

"Guy had a fancy sniper rifle with a sophisticated scope."

"That laser scope gave me a bit of an advantage."

"Yeah, well, the guy could have made that shot from triple the distance away and still nailed his target, easy. Or so my firearms guy tells me."

"Any luck on identifying him?"

"We're running his prints through the system."

"He had pretty much the same tats as Karl Stevens had."

"Yeah, Mary texted me and told me. You think there's a connection, obviously."

"We talk to Stevens and he's dead. The shooter kills Sally and then tries to kill Katz. Yeah, I think we can definitely say there's a connection. But the tats may help us narrow this down to a gang. They look to be some oddball collection of neo-Nazis and Klansmen."

"Great combo," said Natty sarcastically. "But the thing is, Decker, would that sort of gang have been operating here thirteen years ago? I mean, I don't remember anything like that going on in Burlington then."

"Neither do I. But keep in mind they could be muscle brought in now by the folks who *were* doing all this crap thirteen years ago."

"Right."

Decker eyed him. "How did your lunch go with your wife?"

At first, Natty looked like he might erupt in anger, but when he focused on Decker's sincere expression, he said, "It went okay."

"Did she know…anything?"

"No. I don't think so. She might have suspected. But look, Decker. Sally and me, we never, you know. We were just friends. Okay, maybe more than friends." He let out an exasperated breath. "It's this damn job. It gets to you. I'm not trying to make excuses."

Decker thought of Lancaster and her marriage. "The job gets to a lot of people, Natty."

"So, what are we supposed to do? How do we handle it?"

"If I knew the answer to that, I'd be a consultant to cops. A rich one. But spending time with your wife is a good first step. You mind if I look around?"

"Help yourself. Just don't keep your 'observations' to yourself."

Decker nodded and went exploring.

He entered the bedroom and gazed around the space. He wasn't exactly sure what he was looking for. He doubted Katz would have left a box with the word *Secret* engraved on it for him to find, revealing all.

But Katz was an accountant with a precise turn of mind. She was organized, paid attention to the details. You just had to look around her home to tell that. So there might be something she had that she felt she needed to keep. If only for protection from someone.

He went through all of her drawers and then did the same methodical examination of her closet. She had a lot of clothes and shoes, like Susan Richards, but even Decker could tell that the stuff Katz owned was far more expensive than the items in Richards's closet.

He dug back in the very rear of the closet and went through boxes and bags, but came away a half hour later with nothing to show for his efforts.

He went into the bathroom and searched. When he got to the medicine cabinet, he found that Rachel Katz was on prescription anti-anxiety medication. That was not unusual. Lots of people were on meds like these. But still. He wondered what exactly she was so anxious about.

Well, the fact that someone tried to kill her demonstrated that she was certainly right to be anxious.

He picked up her purse, which was on the nightstand. Inside were her wallet, a set of keys, and a building security access card. He pocketed those items and walked back into the main area to find that Natty had left to go back to the police station. The forensic team was finishing up and Kelly Fairweather was packing up her kit.

"Find anything of interest?" asked Decker.

"Just blood. And the bullet. It went into the couch." She held up a small plastic container with a lid on top.

Decker took it and looked at the bullet, which was in pristine condition.

"Seven point six two," observed Decker of the round's caliber.

She nodded. "Right. It's called the NATO round. Lots of military forces use it, including ours. If that had hit her in the head instead of the shoulder, she'd be in the morgue, not the hospital."

Decker looked at her strangely.

"You okay?" she asked.

"I'll be okay once we solve this case."

He left and hit the street. He had another place left to check where Katz might have kept something of value. Her office. It was only a few blocks from her apartment, so Decker was just going to walk.

When he got there, he found the door to the building locked. He took out the key card, held it over the card reader pad, and the door clicked open. He checked the lobby marquee for Katz's office number and rode the elevator up. He strode quickly down the hall to her office door. All the other offices he'd passed had standard metal doors. Katz's office had a far more expensive solid wood door with matching trim. Knowing how she liked things just so, he wasn't surprised.

He tried several keys he had taken from her purse until one worked. He unlocked the door and went in. He decided to use his Maglite instead of turning on the office lights. There was a front reception desk, and a short hall off to the left. Two offices were off this hall and then a kitchen/workroom with a door that opened back into the reception area. The security pad was hung on the wall next to this door, its light glowing green.

He went back to the first office and opened the door. This was clearly Katz's office. It was larger than the other one and outfitted with custom shelves, a seating area with plush chairs, and a handsome partners desk. The shelves were lined with business memorabilia, photos of Katz with various city officials and others he assumed were her business partners. There were also photos of what looked to be her various properties and commercial projects. In each photo, Katz was smiling broadly, looking triumphant and happy.

And yet as Decker peered more closely, it appeared to him that the looks were hollow, that an underlying melancholy was present in each image. Maybe that was just him imposing what he knew now onto the woman's photos. Or maybe not.

Then he noticed the power cord lying on top of the desk. It was for a laptop, but there was no computer there. And there hadn't been one at Katz's home either. He opened some file drawers and his suspicions were heightened.

Someone had done a very good job of searching the office without seeming to have done so. He closed the drawer and looked at the shelving system built into the wall. He recognized it, since Katz had an exact duplicate in her condo.

But not exactly exact.

He stepped closer and noted a panel set between two open shelves. This same type of panel had been in her condo as well. But there was a difference. The one in her condo had a knob on it. Decker had presumed that was because the panel was actually a door and there was storage behind it. He had found this actually to be the case because he had looked inside it.

Yet there was no knob on this panel. He stepped back and looked at the unit again. He took the template from his memory of the one in Katz's condo and laid it over what he was seeing now. The absence of the knob was the only difference.

He strode forward and felt around the perimeter of the panel, probing with his fingers. Then he pressed down on the lower left-hand side of the wood and the door popped open. Behind it was a space filled with documents and files.

He pulled them out and set them on the desk. He was about to go over them when he stopped, rose, left the office, and walked into the kitchen area. On the wall was the security pad.

Why had it been turned off?

Decker hadn't done it. He didn't have the code. He had known of the possibility that Katz would have her own independent security system for her office. The exterior of the building had security. The front door to her office had been locked. But the security system had not been engaged.

An oversight, or...?

The whooshing sound of something igniting and the resulting smell of smoke that reached him a few moments later definitively answered the question for Decker.

55

OKAY, THAT'S A PROBLEM.

The reception area was on fire, which meant the only way out was blocked.

Decker called 911 and reported the fire and calmly asked for the fire department to get there before he was burned to nothing.

He peered around the edge of the hall to see the reception area filling up with smoke. Next, he looked to the ceiling. There were sprinkler heads mounted there. So why the hell weren't they going off?

He coughed and fell back from the flames.

Well, this told him that he'd been right. There was something here that someone didn't want discovered. They had searched the place, but out of an abundance of caution, they'd decided to then burn it down and somehow had disengaged the sprinkler system.

He retreated to Katz's office and looked desperately around. He was on the fifth floor, so breaking the window and going out that way was not going to cut it.

He put all the items he'd found behind the panel in a cardboard box, ran into the workroom with it, grabbed bubble wrap off the shelf, and taped it all around the box. He rushed back into Katz's office, ran to the window, and looked out, to make sure no one was walking down below on the sidewalk. He picked up her chair, carried it over to the window, and pounded it against the glass until the window shattered and fell away. He used the chair to scrape the rest of the glass away.

He looked down to make sure it was still clear and dropped

the box. It fell to the sidewalk. He could hear the bubble wrap air pouches collectively pop when it hit the pavement. He hadn't been concerned about anything in the box shattering on impact. Paper didn't break. But it was very windy outside and if the box had burst open, he would have been running around the city trying to find the contents.

The problem was, his opening the window had let the wind and, with it, enormous amounts of oxygen into the space from the outside.

He turned and saw the flames right at the door of the office.

Okay, this was getting damn tight.

He heard sirens and the screech of brakes from below and saw two fire engines pull up. He leaned out of the window and cried out, "The fire's coming into this space. I need to get out. Now!"

The fireman signaled to him and four of them rushed to one of the trucks and pulled out an inflatable jump cushion, which they quickly pumped up and positioned under the window.

Decker looked down at it. From up here it seemed about the size of a twin bed.

Shit!

"Jump!" yelled one of the firemen.

"I'm a big guy. Will that hold me, or do you have a larger size?" Decker called back.

"This will hold you, don't worry," the fireman yelled back. "Just jump away from the building. Back to the ground. We'll reposition if need be."

Reposition if need be. Well that's comforting.

He wondered when these guys had done their last refresher course on catching huge guys falling from great heights. He hoped it was this morning.

Decker turned to look at the flames.

Do I take my chances there?

Suddenly an explosion racked the office space and a gust of hot air blew embers over him.

Here goes nothing.

He climbed up on the windowsill, looked down to make sure

he was lined up as best he could be with the cushion, said a silent prayer, and jumped.

He was looking up at the sky, which was better than looking at where he was going. Were they repositioning right now? Or were they freaking out because they'd totally screwed up? Was he about to slam into the pavement?

Unsettling thoughts, but he needed something to pass the time because it felt like he was falling for about five miles, instead of five floors.

When he hit the cushion instead of the pavement, all the air was still knocked out of him. Hands grabbed at him and hoisted him quickly to his feet.

"You okay?" asked one of the firemen.

"I am now."

"Anybody else in there?"

"Not in the office I was in now. I don't know about the rest of the building."

"Any idea how it started?"

"Yeah, which is why I'm calling in the arson squad." Decker showed the stunned firemen his creds. "Someone turned off the sprinkler system in the building," he said.

Another fireman came up with the box Decker had dropped. "We found this on the street."

Decker took the box from him. "Right where I dropped it. Thanks."

As the men were fighting the fire, Decker sat on the opposite curb and called up Burlington's arson squad and filled them in. Then he called Lancaster and did the same.

"You *jumped* out of a building?" she said.

"Well, not by choice. It was either that or be quick fried. I wouldn't recommend either, actually."

"What the hell is going on, Decker?" she said. "It feels like the whole town is under siege."

"That's because I think it is."

"I'm still filling out forms. I'm starting to regret shooting the guy."

"I'm heading back with a box of stuff I collected from Katz's office. I'll meet you at the station."

Decker hefted the box and looked at the ladders and hoses and men combatting the fire. He set off down the street, climbed into his car, and drove to the police station.

Decker met Lancaster inside. He followed her into the same small conference room, set the box on the table, cut away the bubble wrap, and opened it. He handed Lancaster a stack of stuff and put another stack in front of himself.

"Her laptop wasn't there. I think whoever searched her office took it. Or maybe she has it somewhere else. When she comes out of surgery and regains consciousness, we can ask her."

Lancaster looked at him doubtfully. "You think she's going to cooperate?"

"Considering somebody just tried to kill her, what choice does she have?"

"You might be surprised."

"Well, life is just full of surprises. That's why we play the game."

He turned his attention to the stack in front of him. Financial documents, construction plans, Excel spreadsheets.

"She had a lot of business going on," commented Lancaster as she started going over her set of files.

"Did you have any luck running down any of her backers?"

"Not really. But we did find out that they were shell companies for the most part with locations in countries where they believe transparency is a bad word."

"I wonder why that is."

"It would seem that her financial backers don't want to be publicly known. But they might still be legit."

"And I *might* be short and skinny," said Decker. "Is there any way we can find out who's behind those companies?"

"How about your people at the FBI?"

"I'm not sure they're *my* people anymore."

"Then you're stuck with the resources of a small-town police force."

"Great."

Lancaster glanced up. "I heard you shoot when I was coming up the stairs. How'd you get a sightline on the guy?"

"His laser worked against him in that environment. I followed it back to its source thanks to a bunch of dust in the air. Katz was lucky that Melvin knocked her down when he did. I saw the guy's scope. Sucker was super sophisticated. He could have made that shot from a mile away—"

Lancaster looked up from what she was doing. "What is it? You okay?"

"I'll be right back," said Decker, who was not even looking at her. He got up and hustled out of the room.

He hurried down the hall to the evidence room and checked in with the officer manning it. He told the man what he wanted and was let into the cage, where the officer took him over to a shelf against the wall. The officer held up the rifle with the scope still attached. It was in a large plastic evidence bag with the department tag.

Decker looked at the rifle and scope. Then he thought back to the moment it had been used.

He rushed back to the room where Lancaster was.

"What is going on with you?" said Lancaster.

"*I* wasn't the target, Mary, that night outside McArthur Park."

"What are you talking about?"

"Sally Brimmer was."

56

"ERIC TYSON. FORMER MILITARY. Washed out of Ranger School and then out of the Army."

Lancaster looked up from her report the next morning. Decker sat across from her at her desk.

"We just got this back from the Army. We ran his prints through all the criminal databases and got a hit. Tyson was arrested on an assault charge about ten years ago, while he was in the military. It was off base against a civilian. That's why we were able to access his prints. We checked in with the Army, told them what had happened, and they sent us this file."

"Special skills?"

"Trained as a sniper. So you were right. The shot he took that killed Sally wasn't meant for you. He could have shot her from a mile away. Tyson was barely fifty yards from his target."

"How'd he wash out of the Army?" asked Decker.

"Got in with some bad company, apparently. Earned him a DD."

"So he leaves with a dishonorable discharge. What's he been doing since his military days?"

Lancaster shrugged. "Not sure. We're looking into it. Hope to have something soon. We can't find anything that shows he's been in prison."

"Well, considering all his tats, it was not anything good that he was up to, despite never having been in prison."

Lancaster sat back in her chair. "Okay, but why kill Sally Brimmer? You never said last night."

"I don't know. But I'm a huge target. He could hardly miss me.

Sally was going to give me a hug when the shot came. But I'm nine inches taller than she was. And a lot wider. Doesn't matter how close she was to me, he couldn't have missed, if I'd been the target." He slapped the top of the desk with his palm. "I should have seen that a long time ago."

"Same goes for me. But that doesn't tell us why she was the target."

"She had gotten me the files I'd asked for, after you got knocked off the case."

"How'd you even connect with her?"

"She came by to see me when my butt was sitting in jail. I asked her to do that for me and she agreed. We met in the park. As we were leaving, that's when she got shot."

"If they knew she was passing you information, why not shoot the both of you and take that information?"

"I don't think that was the reason," said Decker.

"Why?"

"Because if they knew she was giving me information, they probably knew what it was: police files. Big deal. Why would that be a death warrant for her? I could have gotten those any number of ways. Killing her wasn't going to stop that."

"So you're saying she was, what, complicit in something?"

"Or she knew something that was dangerous to other people."

Lancaster glanced up at him. "What people?"

Decker looked around the confines of the empty room. "She worked here."

Lancaster's voice sank to a whisper. "Decker, do you know what you're saying?"

"There are bad people everywhere, Mary. Cops are not immune, you know that."

She shook her head. "Granted, but none of this makes sense."

"It *does* make sense. We just haven't figured out how yet. Any word yet on the fire at Rachel Katz's office?"

"We got a prelim from the arson squad. They found an incendiary device attached to a timer. They must have placed it there after they searched her office. You just picked the wrong time to make your visit."

He rose.

"Where are you going?"

"To the hospital to check on Katz and Melvin."

"Is that all?"

"Then I'm going to see Mitzi Gardiner."

"You want me to tag along?"

"Aren't you deskbound after the shooting?"

"Well…"

"I'll talk to you when I get back."

* * *

"They think she's going to be okay," said Mars.

He and Decker were sitting in the visitors' room outside the critical care unit at the hospital.

"They *think?*"

"Well, she's stable, *critically* stable, but at least she's stable."

"Okay."

Mars rubbed his eyes.

"You look beat, Melvin. Why don't you go get some rest?"

"No, I'm good. I napped on the couch." He stretched his long arms. "They got cops outside her room."

"Yeah, I know."

Mars shook his head. "Why do I feel like it's my fault she's lying in that hospital bed?"

"Your fault? How do you figure?"

Mars said, "The people who shot her? They knew she was talking to me. They were afraid she might open up. So they decided to kill her. I don't push it, she's okay."

"That's pretty convoluted, Melvin. And wrong. You saved her life. She'd be on a slab but for you."

"I saw this red dot hovering over her face. Man, it scared the crap out of me. Then I just grabbed her and down we went right as I heard the glass break. I thought she was okay. You know? Then…then I had her blood all over me."

"What did she tell you, before she was shot?" asked Decker.

"She was really nervous. Afraid for her life."

"Well, she turned out to be right about that. What else?"

"I think she wanted to talk. But couldn't bring herself to do it. She said something about there being 'shades of truth.'"

"Shades of truth? What does that mean?"

"I don't know."

"Maybe a guilty conscience?"

Mars looked pained by this possibility. "Maybe. And she said that sometimes people have to do things that might look wrong to other people, but just seem like the only way to go for the person. And also that the truth could trap you."

Decker took all this in and said, "You know she might have been the one to impersonate Susan Richards. Mitzi Gardiner was the other possibility, but she has an alibi."

"If she did, then Rachel knew about her murder. That would qualify as a guilty conscience."

"Yes, it would. We'll need to talk to her when she's able."

"Now maybe she'll tell us the truth."

"Well, almost getting killed should be a great motivator," replied Decker. "And they burned her office down after searching it. So, they mean business."

Mars stared goggle-eyed at him. "Burned her office down?"

"While I happened to be in it. I had to jump out the window."

Mars gaped. "You jumped out a window?"

"From five flights up. Point is, I don't think Katz has an option now."

"And if she is guilty of something?"

"We'll work a deal. She who talks first gets the best one."

Decker stood to leave. "You need anything?"

"A little less excitement in my life would be nice."

"Then you're going to have to stay away from me, apparently."

57

WHEN DECKER PULLED UP to the Gardiners' home, the gate was open, so he pulled through. This time a man answered the door. He was in his forties, tall, broad-shouldered, and good-looking, and dressed in a suit that might have cost more than Decker's entire wardrobe. No, there was no *might* about it.

"Yes?" said the man.

"I'm here to speak to Mitzi Gardiner."

"What about?" the man asked suspiciously. "This is a no-solicitation area," he added warningly. "How did you even get inside the gate?"

"It was open." Decker took out his creds. "But I'm not selling anything. She'll know about this. I've been by before."

The man looked puzzled. "Here? You've been here?"

"Yes. Are you her husband?"

"I'm Brad Gardiner."

"Is she in?"

"She's not up yet. In fact, she's not feeling well."

"I can wait."

"No, that doesn't work. She...she's ill."

"Mr. Gardiner, I can understand that, but the fact is, this is a murder investigation. So time is of the essence."

"Murder! What the hell are you talking about?"

"It's okay, Brad."

Decker looked past Gardiner to see his wife standing there in a bathrobe and slippers. She scowled at Decker. "I can handle this. Why don't you get to work? You have that meeting."

"But, Mitzi."

She kissed him on the cheek. "It's okay, sweetie, I've got this. Trust me."

"If you're sure."

"I am very sure."

After her husband left, Gardiner looked at Decker. "You just won't leave it alone, will you?"

"I'm just trying to do my job."

"Isn't that what all cops say?"

"I don't know. I'm just one cop."

She led him back to the conservatory, where they sat down across from each other.

"What?" she said expectantly.

"Some recent developments I thought you might want to be made aware of."

"Such as?"

"Someone tried to kill Rachel Katz. Took a shot at her through her condo window."

To her credit, Gardiner didn't visibly react to this. "Is she all right?"

"She was shot with a sniper round. She's out of surgery and is critically stable. Another inch to the right and they'd be making funeral arrangements."

"Well, I'm glad they're not."

"The man who tried to kill her was then killed by police."

"Do they know who he is?"

"Yes." But Decker would go no further.

"What does any of that have to do with me?"

"You have the picture I left you?"

She appeared startled by this and sat up. "Um, no, I think I threw it away. Why?"

"Good thing I took a picture of it." Decker took out his phone and held it up.

She looked at the screen. "But that's the wrong side. That's the *back* of the picture."

"Well, for my purposes, *this* is the relevant side." He pointed at the writing. "Daddy's little star. He was a very proud papa."

Gardiner looked up at him from under hooded eyes. "That was a long time ago."

"Yes, it was. Things change. People change. I have another picture to show you." He flipped through the screens. "This is a picture of your father's forearm taken during the autopsy."

"Oh, please, God, I am not looking at that," she said in disgust.

"There's nothing gruesome about it, Ms. Gardiner. I just want you to look at the tattoos on the forearm."

"My father did not have tattoos."

"He got these after he went to prison."

She became subdued. "After?"

"Yeah. Here's the first one. A spiderweb." He explained the symbolism.

"I'm sure lots of prisoners get that one because even though they're guilty they can't accept what they did," she said defiantly.

"Here's the second one." He showed her the teardrop and looked at her expectantly.

"What does that one mean?" she asked dully.

"Travis Correctional is an all-male facility. And some of the men there get...lonely. And they take out that loneliness on other men, like your father."

She blinked rapidly as she processed this. "You...you mean?"

"Yes. I do. Now, here's the third one. And this is the one I really want you to focus on." He brought up the screen with the arrow through the star. "I've seen a lot of prison tats. I've never seen that one before." He looked at her for a reaction.

For a moment it looked like the woman had stopped breathing. Then she licked her lips, dabbed at her eyes, and looked away.

"Any idea what that might mean?" he asked.

"I know what you're getting at."

"What's that?"

"The photo! The writing on the back." She waved her shaky hand at the photo of the tattoo on his phone screen. "And...that."

He sat back and studied her.

She dabbed at her eyes again with her sleeve. Finally, she looked up at him. "What exactly do you want from me?"

"The truth would be fine."

"I've told you everything."

"No you haven't."

"This happened a long time ago. What the hell does it matter? Everyone has moved on with their lives. I know I have."

"Tell that to Susan Richards and Rachel Katz…And your father."

She shook her head and looked down.

"I'm not here to send you on a guilt trip, Ms. Gardiner."

She barked, "Oh, just call me Mitzi. That's all I'll ever be. Ditzy Mitzi. An addict who was always a disappointment to her father." She looked up at him and said coldly, "You put lipstick on a pig, it's still a fucking pig."

"Turning your life around could not have been easy."

She waved this off. "Doesn't matter now."

"I'm also here to make something as clear as possible."

"What?"

"People connected to this case are dying or in the hospital fighting for their life. By my count, you're the only one left."

"I told you before I could take care of myself."

"I'm sure the others thought the same. But the guy who shot Katz was a real pro. Ex-Army turned bad guy white supremacist type. Trained sniper. Hired to do the hit. He's dead, but who's to say another one won't replace him? And maybe you go out armed, but a pistol isn't going to save you from a long-range rifle shot you won't ever hear or see coming before it kills you."

"You're just trying to scare me," she said offhandedly, though her voice shook.

"I *am* trying to scare you. For your own good."

"I don't see how I can possibly help you."

"Can't or won't?"

"As far as I know, my father killed those people."

"How did your father feel about your drug use?"

"He hated it. Why?"

"I understand he was trying to get you into rehab."

"He'd done it before, but I could never make it stick. He kept trying."

"So he never did drugs himself?"

"Are you crazy? He was as straight as they came on that. He attacked a guy who came to our house trying to sell me some stupid weed."

"Okay. Your dad was picked up in a bad area of town. At his trial the defense laid out the possibility that he was there trying to get drugs for your mother's pain."

"We've already been over this. He might have. I mean, I told you before that he did his best to take care of her." She unexpectedly smiled. "He could build anything, really. Make anything work. He built a little scooter for me when I was ten, for my birthday. I mean, he made it out of scrap parts. It had a little battery and a motor. He made those too. Only went about five miles an hour but I rode it everywhere." Her smile faded. "But he couldn't build anything to help Mom. That was beyond him."

"How did he know to go to that area to get drugs?" asked Decker.

He saw Gardiner flinch slightly.

"What?"

"You just told me that your father didn't do drugs. Hated them. So how'd he know where to go? Or who to talk to, to buy the stuff? And where did he get the five hundred bucks he had in his pocket when the police picked him up?"

"I...I don't know where he got the money. And it was pretty easy to tell back then where the bad areas were if you wanted to score drugs. I already told you that. And you know that too from being a cop here back then."

"Well, Mitzi, the thing is, he didn't want just *any* drugs for your mother. He wanted something like pure morphine. Stuff that had been stolen from a hospital or pharmacy, not off-the-street crap. And having worked the narcotics detail as a cop here, I know that there were very few people in that particular market. And you really had to know your shit to get to them."

Mitzi looked extremely apprehensive in the face of all this. "I...I don't know what to tell you."

"And on top of that, your old man was still walking around quite a few hours after allegedly killing four people. You'd think the guy would have been running for the hills."

She licked her lips nervously. "Maybe...maybe he was confused or shocked at what he'd done. Or he was just trying to lie low. And hope that the police would conclude what you just did."

"But if he *had* committed the murders, he would know his DNA was likely to be under a dead girl's fingernails. It was just a matter of time before we came knocking on his door."

She let out a quick breath. "I can't explain it. It's just what happened."

Decker rose. "I'm sorry."

She glanced up at him, trepidation on her features. "Sorry about what?"

"Your life must have truly been in the gutter for you to have done this to your father."

"I don't know what—"

He put up his hand. "Don't bother. I don't have the patience or time for more bullshit from you." He lowered his hand. "I think you gave him the five hundred bucks after someone gave it to you. Then you managed to scratch the shit out of him at some point and passed his DNA off to whoever paid you. Maybe your father just chalked it up to you being in a drug-induced fit. He'd probably seen that many times before. And then you told your old man where to go to get the stolen hospital drugs. Only the person wasn't there because there was no person. You probably told him to keep trying, to go to lots of different places, where there was nobody either. But it was for his wife, after all. And so he did. That way he'd have no alibi for the murders, and we'd end up finding him in a bad part of town with a chunk of money in his pocket. And when we showed up that night, you pretended to be whacked out. You'd probably already been given the gun and stashed it behind the closet wall."

The whole time Decker was talking Gardiner's eyes kept widening and her jaw kept falling.

Decker continued, "I can only imagine the look on your old

man's face in prison when he ran into that scumbag Karl Stevens. And Stevens tells him what his 'little star' did to her own father." He took a moment to gaze around at the beautiful room.

"I hope it was worth it, Mitzi. But I can't possibly see how it could be."

CHAPTER

58

THE HOUSE.

The rain.

Decker sat in his car and watched his old home from across the street.

The gloom of the night was actually brighter than what he was feeling.

He had told himself that he could live in either the past or the present, but he couldn't do both.

Which do I choose? It should be an easy decision. So why isn't it?

His case was at a dead end, in more than one way. Gardiner was the key and it didn't look as though she was going to cooperate. Unless Rachel Katz regained consciousness with a willingness to help them, Decker wasn't sure they would ever get to the truth.

So he had come here. Back to where many things had begun for him.

He saw the lights on in the front room. Someone would pass back and forth every so often. The little girl he'd seen. Then her parents.

The Henderson family. Really just starting out in life, like Decker and his family had once done. Building dreams and burnishing memories that would last a lifetime for all of them.

His last Christmas with his family had been a memorable one. Decker had gotten a couple days off, and thankfully no one had decided to murder someone else that close to the holiday.

They had gone to see Molly perform in her school play. It had been a Christmas version of *Peter Pan*. Molly had played Wendy.

She had worked on her lines for two weeks, reciting them to whichever parent was around to listen to her, barging in on Decker when he'd been shaving, or even dressing.

She had carried it off without a hitch, helping others to perform their roles too because she'd apparently memorized everyone else's lines as well.

Great memory.

She didn't get that from her dad. Before his injury Decker had been pretty normal with his recall. And he couldn't imagine he could pass on the elements of a traumatic brain injury to his kid.

He sat next to Cassie in the audience that night watching their little girl act her heart out, surprising him with little things, tiny nuances that she seemed to instinctively add to her performance. She might have grown up to be a great actress.

Now no one would ever know.

Yes, it had been a great Christmas. They'd gone out to dinner after the play and celebrated Molly's performance. They'd toasted her with vanilla sundaes.

Decker had relished every moment but had of course believed there would be many, many more just like them. Enough to fill a lifetime of memories, even for someone like him. She would grow up, marry, have kids, and he would become the doting grandfather, or as close to that as someone like him could be.

He glanced over at the window again as he saw the little girl sit on the sofa next to her mom. A book was opened. A story was commenced.

Decker started up the car and drove off.

He could barely see the road for the tears.

He should never have come back here. It was literally tearing him apart, when he could least afford it.

It's always about the next case, though, right? Even when Cassie and Molly were alive. He had never dwelled much on all the time he had missed with them because there was always some bad person he had to track down. All the nights getting home long after they both had gone to bed. And then getting up and leaving before they awoke.

I just thought I'd have more time. Just…more time.

But then again, another sunrise was guaranteed to no one. Certainly not to his family.

And by association, not to him.

Thankfully, the farther away he drove, the faster these thoughts left him. For now.

He drove downtown and stopped in front of the building where he'd almost died. Across the street was where Rachel Katz had nearly perished, lending a macabre symmetry.

He checked in with the officer guarding her apartment and started to look around. He glanced across at the broken window, the blood on the couch and carpet. That told a story he already knew.

Katz had mysterious backers, offshore shell companies funneling the money for her myriad projects in little old Burlington, Ohio. What was the attraction?

It did make one wonder.

And then there was the American Grill. There were thousands of places just like it all over the country. Thick piled-high burgers, mammoth mounds of fries, chicken wings, pitchers of beer, large-screen TVs for sports. There would always be a clientele for that, but no one was getting rich off it, like Katz had told Mars.

He had done another search of her apartment and came away not knowing any more than he had on entering the place.

They would just have to wait until she woke up.

This was a frustrating case because he could not seem to make traction on any lead. He could not make Mitzi Gardiner talk. And he had nothing to charge her with. There was absolutely not enough evidence. He knew that she had worked to frame her father, but he couldn't prove it. She had been amply rewarded, with a new life. And yet as he'd left her home, he'd also left behind a woman who was clearly racked by guilt.

But that meant nothing in building a case. He would have to find a road to the legal truth somewhere else. It would not apparently go through Mitzi Gardiner.

He sat down on a chair in the kitchen and studied his possibilities. There weren't many, so they didn't take him long. He quickly settled on one.

Sally Brimmer.

She'd been killed for a reason. He had to find out what that reason was.

And he could start in one of two places.

He picked one, called Lancaster to meet him there, and set off.

CHAPTER

59

LANCASTER MET DECKER OUTSIDE of Sally Brimmer's apartment building on the west side of town. It was a nondescript six-story structure wrapped in dull brick.

"How's Katz?" Lancaster asked as she walked up to him.

"Still not conscious, but apparently out of danger."

"Well, that's good."

"Yeah, and it'll turn into *great* if she wakes up and tells us everything."

They walked into the building and rode the elevator up to the fourth floor. Lancaster had a key to Brimmer's apartment.

"It's already been gone over, and nothing was found. But I'm not sure how thoroughly it was done. After all, we thought *you* were the target."

"I did too until I stopped thinking I was."

They entered the apartment and looked around. Brimmer's job had not paid all that much, they both knew, but her apartment was well laid out and nicely furnished, with pillows and curtains and sturdy furniture and lovely oriental rugs over the hardwood floors.

Decker looked at Lancaster. She said, "Her parents have money. I was over here once for a holiday party and met them. Very nice people. They helped her out financially, I came to understand."

"Okay."

"They were devastated, obviously. They came to get her remains. The family's from the East Coast."

"How'd Brimmer end up here?"

"She went to college up the road from Burlington. Had a couple of PR jobs out of school. Her brother's a cop in Boston. I guess she got interested in that field from him. The department had an opening. She moved here and was doing some really good work. I doubt she would have stayed here long-term, though. She had a lot of potential. And she was still so young."

"We all have a lot of potential, until we don't," noted Decker grimly.

"So what are we looking for?"

"Anything that seems to be relevant."

"Great, thanks for the hint."

They went methodically from room to room, ending up in Brimmer's bedroom. Decker checked the attached bathroom while Lancaster went into the closet.

After a few minutes, Lancaster called out, "Hey, Decker?"

He walked into the large closet to see Lancaster holding something up.

"What?" he asked.

She held the item up higher. It was a short-haired wig.

Blonde.

Decker lifted his gaze to Lancaster's. "You think *Sally* impersonated Susan Richards?" he said.

"I think she might have. It wasn't Gardiner. And if it wasn't Katz, who else fits the description?"

"Sally was the right height and build," conceded Decker.

Lancaster fingered the wig. "And this is nearly the cut and style of Susan Richards's hairdo. And from a distance, with her back turned and an old woman looking out into the darkness? She could have been fooled."

Decker took the wig in his hand and looked it over. The memory came back to him effortlessly. Sally at the park. She had on a trench coat, gloves, and a hat. Exactly what the person leaving Richards's house was seen wearing.

"So if she participated in that, did she know Richards might be in that suitcase, either already dead or drugged?" he said.

"I can't believe she didn't know," replied Lancaster. "But then the question becomes why would she do it?"

"She was acting funny," said Decker. "When she interacted with me. Before and after Richards went missing."

"Funny how?"

"Guilty, maybe. But then I just associated that with her having a fling with Natty."

"Guilt, then, but of a different nature." Lancaster shook her head. "Brimmer was such a straight arrow in my book. Why in the hell would she have become involved in something like this?"

"Well, we don't know for sure that she was. We found a wig that looks like Richards's hair, but that could be a coincidence. Women do have wigs in their closets."

"That's true. And even if we find evidence of Sally's hair inside this wig, it'll prove nothing. If she's not involved, she presumably bought the wig to wear it."

"We have to find other proof. If she was paid off, we might be able to find a record of that in her financial accounts."

"And if she wasn't paid off?"

"Then someone might have coerced her into doing this."

"How?"

"Maybe someone who knew about her relationship with Natty?"

"Well, that could be. They kept it pretty secret. Hell, I didn't know."

Lancaster took back the wig and placed it into an evidence bag she drew from her coat pocket. "And you still think the motivation to kill Richards was to place blame for Hawkins's murder on her?"

"They had to cut that investigation off, Mary. The police start looking into Hawkins's claims, things could get dicey for whoever's behind all this. Her seeming to commit suicide was a good way to do that."

"Only it didn't work."

"They couldn't know that. They had to try. And Richards was their best bet for that."

"Why not Rachel Katz? She had a motive to kill Hawkins too."

"That's right, she did. But I don't think they could afford to kill Katz."

"Why not? Someone ended up trying to kill her."

"That was later."

"So how'd they choose between the two women?"

"Look at it this way: Katz has prospered since the death of her husband. Richards hasn't."

"So you think Katz was involved with the murders thirteen years ago?"

"I'm not going to go that far, Mary. But I think Katz ended up being useful. Richards didn't. So she was dispensable."

"What in the world is going on here, Decker?"

"Well, whatever it is, it's been going on for at least thirteen years."

"Dating back to the murders?"

"Actually sometime before them, probably."

Lancaster looked at the bagged evidence. "I'm going to have to tell Natty about this. He's in charge of the investigation now."

"I don't think he's going to take us suspecting Sally of being an accomplice in Richards's murder very well."

"That's an understatement. Unless he's involved as well," she added with a sudden thought. "Do you think he might be?"

"I think everybody's a suspect until they're not."

"How's it going down there?" Alex Jamison asked.

It was the next evening and Decker was in his room at the Residence Inn, on his phone.

"It's going. How about you?"

"Long road ahead, I'm afraid. Not making much headway. Bogart is missing your horsepower."

"Did he say that?"

"I can tell."

"He laid down the law to me when we last spoke. I'm not sure I'll have a place on the task force when I'm done here." He said this in part to get it off his chest, but also to get Jamison's reaction.

"I'm not sure about that either, Decker."

His spirits plunged. It had occurred to him that he did want to go back to the FBI after this was over. Now that might not be possible.

"I guess I can see that," he said.

"Look, if it were up to Bogart, I think you'd be okay. But he's got bosses too. And they know you're still in Burlington despite orders to the contrary. And they're not happy about it. Bogart went out on a limb for you, Decker, on a number of occasions. He shielded you from heat from the higher-ups. Now, we all know what you've done for the Bureau, and the number of lives you've saved in the past. But that will not always save you, I guess is what I'm saying."

"Thanks for your candor, Alex. I appreciate it."

"I'd expect the same from you if our positions were reversed."

"Not to change the subject, but if I send you a list of companies, could you find time to check them out?"

"Decker! Are you kidding me?"

"I know, Alex. I know. But it's really important."

"And what I'm currently doing isn't?"

"No, I didn't mean it that way. Only we don't have the resources that the FBI does."

There was such a pregnant pause that he thought she might have hung up on him. Then, finally, "Email them to me and I'll see what I can do."

"Thanks, Alex, I appreciate it."

He sent her the names of the companies and then lay down on his bed. The wind was picking up outside, which probably meant another storm was coming. Since it was getting colder, they might get some sleet or a dusting of snow with it.

Decker wrapped himself more tightly in his coat because the Residence Inn didn't have the best heating system in the world. It was like it only had the capacity to push heat a certain distance into the hotel before giving up and letting the majority of the unfortunate guests fend for themselves.

He didn't miss the Ohio winters. The East Coast had its share of cold weather, for sure. But there was nothing to stop the wind here; it beat relentlessly across the land.

But still, this was his hometown, his home state. He had played for the mighty Buckeyes and then, albeit briefly, the Cleveland Browns. He was a product of the Midwest. He never got too high and never got too low. He looked at the world realistically. He was a jeans and beer kind of guy. He could never fit inside a Ferrari, not that he would ever want to. He always tried to do the right thing. He helped others when they needed it.

And he tracked down killers nonstop.

And that was pretty much the sum total of Amos Decker.

He lifted his hands from his pockets and rubbed his temples. He scrunched his eyes closed. Something was funny up there. He felt a pang of anxiety start up from deep within him. He lurched up and went into the bathroom and drank handfuls of water in an effort to calm himself down.

He tried to push back visions of volcanic masses of memory loops cascading down on him, but he was powerless to stop his own mind from tormenting him.

He lay back on the bed, shuddered once as though he might be sick, and then drew a long, deep breath. With that one physical machination, the anxiety left him.

Maybe I should take up yoga. A downward dog every morning might do the trick.

He glanced out the window and decided that he was hungry. And he only had one place in mind to go.

He drove to the American Grill.

He had never answered the question of why Rachel Katz still owned it. And he didn't believe it was because it was her husband's first business venture.

He walked in, got a table, and sat and perused the menu. The place was about three-quarters full at seven o'clock. Most of the clientele seemed to be blue collar, some with spouses, some with kids. There were a few teens wolfing down burgers and wings. On the big-screen TV was an ESPN show where the panel was talking about the upcoming Sunday of football.

Decker looked out the window at the building across the street. It was a bank. The one where Don Richards had worked. On the other side of the Grill was an apartment building. Decker knew this because he had briefly lived there when he returned to Burlington after his football career ended.

He eyed the interior of the Grill. Large model prop planes and ships and cars suspended from the ceiling. Pictures of old movie stars framed on the walls. Humorous signs dotted in between them. Dusty fake plants standing in corners. A buffet bar set up in the middle of the place. The wait staff wore white shirts and black pants.

The kitchen was through a set of double swing doors. Restrooms on the right for men and the left for women. Greeter station right at the front door. Computer stands at the back where the wait staff logged in their orders. Full bar at the very back of the restaurant where multiple TV screens were bolted to the wall. The carpet underneath was a dull green, designed not to show dirt or stains. The tables were a heavy wood. There were four-topper tables set up along the perimeter. He could smell an alchemy of fried foods, cheap beer, and sweet desserts.

It was Americana at its monotone finest.

It wasn't all that profitable. And yet it was still in business when Katz had far more glamorous projects on which to spend her time.

Decker ordered his food, a Reuben and fries, and a Michelob to top it off. He once more almost looked around guiltily for Jamison to suddenly pop up and reprimand him.

The sandwich was good, juicy enough without being all over the place. The fries were warm and crisp. The beer tasted fine going down.

He eyed the table where he'd seen Earl Lancaster with his "friend." He hadn't expected his talk with Mary at the football field to have carried the day, but he was happy that they were giving it another shot.

This happy thought receded when he dwelled for a few moments on what the next few years of his former partner's life might be like.

The brain was the most unique organ humans possessed. Decker knew that better than most. When it failed you, it was unlike any other breakdown in your body. If your heart went, so did you, six feet under. Gone but remembered, hopefully fondly, for who you had been.

But if your brain went, you were also gone, though your body lingered and became dependent on someone else to take care of it. And that would be your loved ones' last impression of you, even though it wasn't really you, at least not anymore.

Decker came out of these musings in time to glance up. Through the window of the door going into the kitchen, he caught a man watching him. It was just a quick look, and then the man was gone. The only thing Decker could really observe was dark hair and a pair of penetrating eyes.

Decker, the cop, was instantly intrigued. He had spent almost his entire adult life as a policeman. Reading people's faces, separating the bad from the good, the scared from those trying to hide something. It was not a skill he could teach someone else. It really had become almost instinctual over time. It was a million little things processed together to spit out something close to a useful deduction.

And his antennae were quivering.

He slowly eased his phone out of his pocket, turned the flash off, and, while ostensibly checking his phone screen, snapped a series of pictures of the wait staff flitting around the restaurant. He recognized the waitress from the last time he was here. And trailing behind her was the young man named Daniel, who was learning the craft of being a waiter.

When he put the phone away, he glanced over at the kitchen double doors and thought he had seen someone at the window there.

Had it been the same guy watching him?

Decker motioned to the young woman who had been serving him. Daniel had gone into the kitchen.

She came over. "You want anything else?"

"No, the food was great."

"I'll get your bill."

"Looks like you're hustling tonight."

"Yeah, it gets a little crazy sometimes."

"Been working here long?"

"About a year."

"Last time I was in, you had a trainee following you around."

"Oh, right, yeah, well, that's how we learn the job."

"So, you did that too?"

"No, I already had several years of waitressing experience. Only reason I got the job. But it's kind of silly, if you ask me."

"What is?"

"Training all these people. They never stay. Two or three months on the job and then they're gone. I guess some people don't respect hard work or the time and money it takes to train somebody."

"Yeah, you're right. That doesn't make much sense."

"I won't be working here much longer, so it doesn't matter to me. I got another job offer and I'm taking it. Better pay, and benefits."

"Great."

"My mother used to work here, oh, about ten years ago. She was the one who told me to apply. Pay's not great, not that any wait job's is, but the tips aren't bad, especially on the weekends when the guys get drunk and open their wallets. Makes up a little for all the stupid stuff they say, but if they get handsy, and a lot of them do, I bring the hammer down."

"Good for you. Did your mother work here long?"

"No. I mean, she wanted to. But after about a year they let her go."

"Why's that?"

"They never told her. Then later, a friend of hers was hired to be a waitress here. About a year after that, they let her go too. No reason."

"That is really odd."

"Well, it's not my problem. I'll be out of here. Come to think of it, I've been here about a year. I guess if I wasn't leaving, they might fire me too."

"Maybe the management has changed since your mom's time."

"No, it hasn't."

"Come again."

"Bill Peyton is the manager now. And he was the manager when my mom was here. She didn't like him. He was always watching everything so closely."

"I guess that's what managers get paid to do."

"I guess. And the kitchen staff, they haven't changed either all that time."

"How do you know that?"

"Because they're the same people when my mom was here. I told her some of their names when I first started working, and she recognized them all. They were here from when the place opened, for all I know."

"You mean the cooks and busboys and all that?"

"Right."

"What are they like?"

"What do you mean?"

"Old, young, men, women, Ohio farm stock?"

"All guys. And, no, I don't think any of them are from Ohio. To tell the truth, I'm not sure where they're from. They don't interact with us much. Age-wise, they're probably in their fifties."

"Long time to be a short order cook or a busboy."

"I guess they're content with what they have. You get in a rut, you know? That's why I'm getting out. And I'm taking coding classes too. I don't want to be a waitress my whole life."

"Hey, well, good luck with your new gig."

"Thanks. I'll bring your check."

He gave her a nice tip and left.

On the way out, he looked at the plaque next to the door. It read: *Manager: Bill Peyton.*

He looked back into the restaurant.

He had never been a regular here. But he'd been here a few times before his life had fallen apart. He had never considered it anything special until now.

And now something that he had found at Katz's office took on a heightened importance.

61

"WHAT ARE YOU DOING, DECKER?"

It wasn't Lancaster asking him this question as he looked up from the document he was studying in the small conference room at the police station.

It was Blake Natty, looking disheveled and exhausted.

"Just the nuts and bolts of detective work. Nothing personal, Natty, but you look like shit."

Natty wiped his stubbly chin, ran a hand through his unkempt hair, and attempted to tighten the knot on his tie before giving up. He sat down across from Decker and clasped his hands in front of him.

"Fran threw me out."

Decker sat back and slowly took this in. "What happened?"

"She found out."

"About you and Brimmer?"

Natty nodded.

"How?"

"Some bastard emailed her pictures of us together in my car."

"You could have just been driving somewhere."

"We weren't...driving."

"Right. But she has to know what happened to Sally."

"She does. But I don't think it mattered. You see..." He stopped, looking nervous.

"Was Sally not the first time?" asked Decker.

"No. I screwed up...before. Fran took me back. But I don't think she's going to do it this time."

"I heard Sally's family came to take her remains."

Natty nodded. "I wanted to go to her funeral. But I didn't think it would be appropriate."

"You're probably right about that." Decker shifted in his seat. "I'm sorry about all this, Natty."

Natty said nothing. He just stared down at the table.

"Look, had Sally been acting, I don't know, weird lately?"

Natty glanced up. "Weird? What do you mean by weird?"

"Like she had something on her mind?"

"We were having a fling, Decker. She probably had *that* on her mind."

"I don't mean just that. The thing is, when she agreed to help me, I could tell there was something on her mind. And it wasn't her relationship with you. I already knew about that."

"What else could it be?"

"I just thought she might have mentioned something to you."

Decker would have much preferred to come straight out and ask the guy, but he couldn't. Right now, he didn't know who was involved in what, and he didn't want to give any of his suspicions away unnecessarily.

Natty rubbed the back of his neck and seemed to mull over the question. "She seemed a little jumpy lately. I just thought it was because you saw us together that day."

"Well, you made it pretty easy for me. You just drove up and started yelling at me while she was in the car."

At first Decker thought Natty might snap back at this comment, but he didn't. Maybe Brimmer's death and his wife's kicking him out had changed the man.

"I was the big dog here, Decker, before you came along. I made detective grade before you, and great things were expected of me."

"You did your job, Natty. You worked your cases, caught bad guys. Just like I did."

"Come on. There was no comparison. You were born for this."

"I'm not sure I was born for it, but right now it's the only thing I have in my life."

Natty looked pained by this simple, straightforward admission. "When your family got killed, I couldn't believe it. I really couldn't. Nothing like that had ever happened here. And then, and I'm ashamed to admit it, I relished watching you hit rock bottom. Every day you went lower and lower. And more to the point, you were no longer competition for me in the department."

Decker said nothing to this. *He* could have erupted over this baldly cynical statement, but he chose not to.

"And then a funny thing happened. We weren't closing nearly the number of cases we used to. And then the shooting at the high school happened. And we couldn't make a dent in finding out who did it. And then you came and solved the whole thing."

"I didn't have much choice, Natty. Seeing as how I was directly connected to the 'whole thing.'"

"But then you got the gig with the FBI and you were gone again. I did some cases with Mary and things were going okay. Maybe I'd get promoted up the ladder." He paused and chewed on his tongue for a moment. "And then this thing with Sally started. It was stupid. We both knew it was, but we couldn't stop." He glanced up at Decker. "We only had sex a couple of times. I wanted to do it more. But Sally, well, she was funny about that."

"You don't owe me an explanation on any of this, Natty."

"And then you came back to town and this whole shit with Hawkins started up again. When I saw you back, I just freaked. To be honest, I thought I was rid of you forever. And then there you were."

"I came back to visit my family's graves. I didn't ask for Hawkins to walk up to me and say he was innocent. But for that, I'd be long gone from here, for at least another year."

Natty cleared his throat and sat back. "I've been a cop longer than I haven't been a cop. It's become my whole life. I'm good at it, I think. But I'm not you."

"No one ever said you were," replied Decker. "And you wouldn't want to be me."

"Well, now Sally's dead and my wife is gone. Luckily, the kids are pretty much grown. So, all I got is…this," he added, looking around the room.

"When this case is done, Natty, I'll be gone. You can have it all to yourself."

Natty grunted and gave a hollow chuckle. "I'm finding out that my problems run a lot deeper than my jealousy of you, Decker."

"Then face them and try to work through them. You've seen a lot of shit in your life. So have I. Life is never perfect. You make the most of what you have. You can sink into self-pity or you can rise above it. Why don't you choose to rise above it, starting right now? And really think about my question about Sally. Was anything bothering her?"

Natty looked at him suspiciously. "Why do you keep asking that? Did you find something that…?"

"Sally had reddish hair."

"I know that," said Natty, looking confused.

"She ever wear a wig?"

"A wig? What, are you being funny?"

"No. A blonde wig, cut short."

"No, why? Why would she wear a wig? Do women even wear wigs anymore?"

"I don't know. Maybe some do."

"Well, not Sally. At least not that I ever saw. She had really nice hair. Why are you asking me that? Did you find a wig?"

"In her closet."

"What were you doing in her closet?"

"Lancaster actually found it. We were searching her place looking for a motive for murder."

"But you were the target, not her!"

Decker shook his head. "The guy who shot Katz was the same guy who shot Brimmer. We recently found out he was a trained sniper. He had a laser scope that could have nailed me from a thousand yards away. No way the guy misses a shot from a twentieth that distance. Look at me, Natty. I'm the size of a barn. *You* could've made that shot with your damn pistol."

Natty slumped back in his chair. "But why in the hell would anyone want to kill Sally? She was...she was a good person. She had no enemies."

"That you know of."

Natty glanced sharply up at him. "And what does the wig have to do with this?"

"The wig pretty much exactly matches Susan Richards's hairdo."

It took a few moments for this to connect with Natty. "Wait a minute. Are you saying that—"

"That Brimmer put on a wig to impersonate Richards? Yeah, I am. I think Richards's body was in that suitcase. It was all a show for Richards's neighbor. To make us think she'd done a runner. And then committed suicide."

"You're saying that Sally killed Richards? No fucking way. I've run into a lot of murderers, Decker. So have you. Sally couldn't have hurt a fly."

"I don't think she killed Richards. She might not have even known what was in the suitcase. It might have been locked. But I think she was forced to impersonate Richards and leave in her car with the suitcase. At some point others took the suitcase and then left the body where we found it."

"Why would Sally be part of something like that?"

"Maybe somebody was blackmailing her."

"About what?"

"One guess, Natty."

Realization spread over his features. "Our...fling?"

"Someone tells her they'll spill the truth to your wife unless Sally puts on the wig. Otherwise, she'd be ruined professionally. They didn't have to tell her that Richards was dead, or in the suitcase. She just had to drive it away in the car." Decker paused. "So, that's why I want to know if Brimmer was acting funny."

"But Sally was killed *before* they found Richards."

"But Sally could have already known she was dead."

Natty took a few moments to process all this. Then the detective in him seemed to win out and he sat forward.

"I thought it was just her being nervous about our relationship.

But we were having a drink at her place one night, this was shortly after Richards disappeared."

Decker sat forward. "And?"

"And she wanted to know what I thought about Richards's disappearance. I told her maybe she'd killed Hawkins and had gone on the run."

"What was her reaction to that?"

"She didn't seem to buy it, if you want the truth. I actually picked up on that and asked her if she had any theories."

"Did she?"

"She...she said that sometimes people looked at things from the wrong way round. Almost like looking in a mirror. She even gave an example. In a mirror you lift up your right hand, but in the reflection, your mind tricks you into thinking—"

"That it's your left," finished Decker.

Natty nodded. "What do you think she meant by that?"

Decker didn't answer.

Though he had an idea of exactly what the dead woman might have meant.

ON HIS BED at the Residence Inn, Decker laid out all the construction plans for the American Grill that David Katz had built about fifteen years ago. The plans seemed pretty normal for such a restaurant buildout, but he didn't recognize the name of the architect set forth on the plans. In fact, the address of the business showed that it was from out of state.

He called Lancaster. She was at home. He asked her to put Earl on.

"What's up, Amos?" said the man when he got on the phone.

"Got some construction-related questions for you."

Earl seemed relieved that the questions were not of a more personal nature. "Okay, shoot."

"You remember the American Grill project?"

"The Katzes' restaurant?"

"Right."

"Yeah. I mean, I didn't work on it, but I remember it going up."

"Did you try to work on it?"

"I didn't have my GC license back then, but I had my finish carpentry business. I put in a bid to do some of the interior work. Didn't get it."

"Do you know who the GC was?"

"Funny thing you mention that. I didn't know the GC. Nobody did, because Katz used a company from out of town. Hell, out of state, I think."

"What, you mean the workers too?"

"Yeah. Nobody local that I know worked on that project."

"Why would he have done it that way? Wouldn't it have been more costly?"

"Well, you'd think so. Bringing guys in like that, they have to live and eat somewhere. Guys who live here, we just go home at night. So, yeah, you'd have to pay more."

"Was there no capacity back then? Did he *have* to go out of state?"

"Hell no. That was one of the slackest periods I can remember. Everyone was looking for work. When they rejected my proposal, I even went around to Katz's office to see if there was anything else I could do. Mary and I hadn't been married all that long and we wanted to have a family. I was trying to build up my business. And Katz had blown into town with a lot of money and ambition and I was anxious to get on that train."

"And what happened when you met with him?"

"I didn't actually meet with him. I met with one of his people. Forget the name. He told me in not such polite terms that Mr. Katz had his own crew. Well, that pissed me off a little bit. I mean, why ask for proposals from local people if you're going to use your own crew?"

"What did that guy say?"

"I gotta tell you, Decker, I'm no wallflower. I'm a big, strong guy, but this guy scared the bejesus out of me just the way he was looking at me."

"Can you describe him? I know it's been a long time."

"No, I can. That's the sort of impression he made on me. He was about my height and weight. Dark hair, dark eyes, and, I don't mean this to sound un-PC or anything, but, well, he just didn't seem to be American. At least not in my mind."

"Did he have an accent?"

"Not that I could tell, but I'm not real good about picking up on things like that."

"So you left it there?"

"What else could I do? I couldn't force the guy to use me."

"So all the work was done with nonlocal people?"

"Far as I know. Well, I take that back. The excavation work was done by Fred Palmer, he's local."

"Excavation?"

"Yeah, for the foundation and everything. That can involve some heavy equipment. Katz may not have wanted to truck that in."

"Palmer still around?"

"Oh yeah, I got his number. I use him on projects. He's a good guy. Does first-rate work." Earl gave him the contact info.

"Thanks. Do you remember the construction work going on for the Grill?"

"Yeah, I'd drive by it every once in a while."

"Anything strike you as unusual about it?"

"Well, they had a high fence and security around the place."

"That's not unusual at a construction site, is it? I mean it's to keep people out and stop theft of equipment and materials."

"Yeah, but they had it there from day one. Before they had any materials on site. And you can't really steal a ten-ton piece of equipment and drive it off down the street." He paused. "And they tarped everything."

"What do you mean?"

"They covered everything up."

"You mean so no one could see in?"

"Right. I thought that was strange."

At that moment, apparently Mary Lancaster snatched the phone from her husband. "Why all this interest in the American Grill?"

"Just a theory."

"What's your theory?"

"I'm still forming it. But I think we made a mistake."

"What mistake?"

"By commencing our investigation at the point of the murders."

"Where else should we have started it?"

"Why did David Katz choose to come to Burlington, Ohio? Or did someone else make that decision for him?"

CHAPTER

63

Fʀᴇᴅ Pᴀʟᴍᴇʀ ᴡᴀs ɪɴ ʜɪs sᴇᴠᴇɴᴛɪᴇs, overweight and bald, with a cheerful face and ruddy complexion. His office had one window, one desk with a chair, and two chairs fronting the desk. There were no pictures on the wall. No carpet underfoot.

He was leisurely turning the pages of a file on his desk while Decker and Lancaster sat impatiently across from him.

"Been in business nearly forty-five years," he said.

"Right, you told us that. Have you found what you're looking for?" asked Lancaster.

"Okay, here it is. Thought so. The American Grill. Don't eat there myself. I've got acid reflux. Everything they serve gives me reflux."

"And the construction? My husband said you worked on it."

"Earl, now there's a nice guy. Nice guy. You're lucky, ma'am, to have him."

"Yes, very. The file? You said you had it?"

Palmer planted a thick thumb down in the middle of the page. "Heavy equipment rental."

"*Rental?*" said Decker. "Did you not do the work?"

"No, that's what *rental* means." Palmer laughed and gave Lancaster a funny look. "Can tell he doesn't know shit about construction."

"What sort of equipment?" asked Decker.

"Excavator, dump truck, front loader, bulldozer. It's all there." He tapped the file.

"How long did they rent it?"

Palmer looked over the page. "Says here two weeks."

"Did you normally rent out equipment like that, or did you also typically do the work?"

Palmer sat back and closed the file. "We like to do the work, of course. But that was an odd project."

"Why do you say that?" asked Decker.

"This Katz guy. Darren?"

"David," corrected Decker.

"Right, David Katz. He later got murdered, you know."

"Do tell," said Lancaster, nearly rolling her eyes.

"Oh, yeah. Killed. Him and some others. Anyways, he came into town and got this loan and wanted to build this restaurant. Okay, fine. Lots of people here could have done that for him."

"But he got a company from outside the area to do it," said Decker. "We know that."

"And he tarped things off and had really tight security around the construction area," added Lancaster.

"That *was* odd. I tried to get the work, but we got turned down. We were the biggest outfit back then. Still one of the biggest today. Surprised me, but it was his money."

"Was that the only thing odd about it that you found?" asked Lancaster.

"Well, no." He tapped the file. "That was."

Lancaster looked confused. "You've lost me."

"What I mean is, what do you need all that heavy equipment for, if you're just digging a foundation for a restaurant? I mean, how much excavation is there to do? Most projects like that, there's none. You just grade the property, lay your foundation, and build up from there. Hell, what they rented from me, they could've dug down to China, nearly." He laughed. "China, get it?"

"And did you ever ask them why they'd rented so much equipment like that?" asked Decker.

Palmer gaped at him. "What, are you serious? 'Course not. It was more money to me. None of my business what he does, so long as he pays. And he did. I will tell you that the construction took longer than it should have. And they had to pay some additional fees to me because of it. I remember driving by some days and wondering when the hell they were going to finish up."

"Why do you think it took extra time?" asked Lancaster.

"Not sure. But it did, that's all I know." He laughed. "I do remember one thing."

"What?"

"When we got the equipment back, they'd washed it all. Clean as a whistle. Now, I can never remember that happening before. Most times it comes back all crapped up and we have to clean it up. But not that time. I could've eaten my lunch off the stuff." He laughed heartily. "Eaten my lunch. Get it?"

"Yeah," said Decker. "I get it."

* * *

After leaving Palmer's office Lancaster looked up at Decker. "So what did we just learn?"

"That David Katz undertook, apparently, the strangest construction project in the history of Burlington."

"And what does that tell us?"

"That it's time for us to find out who the hell David Katz really was."

They were walking down the street when a car drove past and then stopped. The window came down.

"Amos Decker?"

Decker glanced over at the expensive car. Duncan Marks was sitting in the driver's seat.

"Mr. Marks, how are you?"

"Well, I'm fine, but you look great. Lot different from the last time I saw you."

"Yeah, things have looked up for me."

"Heard you were back in town."

"Yeah, for a bit."

"Never forgot what you did for my daughter."

"Hope she's doing okay."

"She is, actually. I think Jenny finally figured it out."

"Good to know."

"God, I heard what happened to Rachel Katz. That was awful. Is she going to be okay?"

"We hope so," said Lancaster.

"We've done some projects together. She's quite a business-person. Very smart."

Decker slowly nodded. "Would it be okay if we asked you a few questions about Katz? We're trying to dig into who attempted to murder her, and you might be helpful."

"Sure. Absolutely. Hey, come to dinner tonight at my house." He looked at Lancaster. "Bring your friend here too."

"You don't have to do that," said Decker.

"No, I insist. Least I could do after your help with Jenny. Say around seven?"

Decker nodded, and Marks drove off.

Lancaster looked over at him. "Might be an interesting dinner."

"Let's hope it's something more than interesting."

64

DECKER AND MARS LOOKED DOWN at the woman. She was so covered in tubes and monitoring lines that it was almost difficult to discern the living person under this medical canopy.

But it was Rachel Katz. Still alive. And still critically stable.

"What do the doctors say?" asked Decker.

"That she'll wake up at some point. They just don't know when."

"You've been in here most of the time. Has she come to at all? Made any sounds? Talked in her sleep?"

"No, nothing like that."

"You need to take a break from here, Melvin. She's got great care. And she's well protected."

"I don't know, Decker," he said doubtfully.

"I *do* know. And I've got some place I want you to go with me tonight."

"Where?"

"Duncan Marks's house. He invited me and Lancaster to dinner. I don't think he'll mind you tagging along. He was asking about Rachel today."

"Okay, but why are you having dinner with the guy?"

"Because he did some business with her. And I need to know more about the history there."

"Okay, if you think it will help."

"At this point, Melvin, anything will help."

* * *

They drove in Decker's car up the long, winding road to Marks's home, or, more aptly, his estate. They pulled in front of the mansion and parked in a stone-paved motor court.

Decker looked in the direction of Burlington and saw the lights of the town winking down below. Marks certainly had a fine view from up here.

When they got out, Lancaster tugged self-consciously at her dress and then prodded a few stray hairs back into place. "I didn't really have anything in my closet for something like this," she said, staring up at the enormous stone and stucco house, which looked like it belonged in the French or Italian countryside. "And I had no time to get my hair done."

Decker said, "You look fine."

"It's different for guys, Decker," she said in an annoyed tone.

"Just so long as you have your gun," he said.

"I hope you're joking," she said, grinning.

He didn't smile back.

Decker wore a corduroy jacket that looked like it had been new about thirty years ago, and khaki pants. And the cleanest shirt he had left.

Mars looked resplendent in a tailored wool jacket, white button-down shirt, slacks, and a pocket square.

"You, on the other hand, look like you could be in *GQ*," Lancaster said to Mars.

"Thanks. For twenty years I wore the same clothes, white prison jumpsuit, so this is a nice change."

They walked up to the massive double front doors and Decker rang the bell. A few moments later it was opened by a man in butler's livery, who escorted them through to the library, where he said Marks and the rest of his party had gathered for cocktails before dinner.

It was a long wood-paneled room with few books but a roaring fire in the fireplace and clusters of seating areas full of plush furniture that looked custom made and probably was.

Marks was standing near the fire with a drink in hand, with two other men and three women clustered around him. Decker recognized his daughter, Jenny. She was in her twenties, tall and blonde and vapid, at least in his estimation. She'd already done more falling in love than most people did in a lifetime. Her only problem had been that all these men had loved her father's money far more than they'd loved her.

She looked at Decker with unfriendly eyes, he thought. She was probably pissed that he knew more about her and her failed relationships than she wanted him to. Jenny was the product of Duncan Marks's second marriage to a younger woman who had called it quits and left after Jenny was only three years old. To his credit, Marks had raised her. But he'd given her more than he should have, was Decker's opinion. And with that, he had taken away any ambition she might have had.

"Decker," called out Marks, waving them over.

"This is my friend, Melvin Mars," said Decker. "I think you've met. I didn't think you'd mind if he came too."

"Right, right. You were with Rachel." Marks shook his head sadly. "That was so tragic. I hope she's going to be okay."

"She's hanging tough," replied Mars. "I've been with her at the hospital and things are looking up."

"Good, good." He waved to the others in his group. "Decker, I think you know Jenny, my daughter."

Jenny Marks gave Decker a small nod.

"And these are some of my business associates."

Decker ran his eye over the small group of men and women. They all looked intense, well-heeled, and unimpressed by him and his appearance. The women were elegantly slender and dressed expensively with earring-draped ears and necklace-draped necks, and they looked condescendingly at the plain Lancaster. One of them leaned into her friend and said something to make the other woman smile.

Decker saw Lancaster clutch her jacket more closely around her.

They were served drinks and gathered closer by the fire. They could hear the wind whistling down the chimney.

"God, Ohio winters, here we go again." Marks laughed. "Gets right into my bones."

"Dad, you spend winters either in Palm Beach or Palm Springs," his daughter pointed out.

"Well, I spent enough of them *here* in the past," he retorted with a smile. "You ever been to Palm Beach, Decker?" he asked.

"No, I never have."

"It's beautiful there."

"If you have a lot of money," said Jenny.

Her father said, "No, it's beautiful even without money. The scenery and weather are free. But the money makes it a lot more fun, I'll grant you that." Marks turned back to Decker. "Now, do you have any leads on what happened to Rachel? I mean, what sick bastard would have done something like this?"

"We *have* the sick bastard who did it." Decker pointed to Lancaster. "Thanks to my partner here, who shot him dead before he could kill me, at great personal risk to herself."

Now the other women looked at Lancaster quite differently. The one who had made the joke, probably at Lancaster's expense, paled and took a step back, staring at the detective with far more respect.

"Now *that's* impressive," said Marks. "The only *killing* I've ever made is in the real estate business," he added, without a trace of humor. He raised his glass to her. "Thank you for your bravery, Detective Lancaster."

The others followed suit. She smiled, blushed, and took a quick sip of her gin and tonic.

Decker continued, "We believe it was a murder for hire."

Marks snapped, "A murder for hire! Who in the hell would want Rachel dead?"

"I don't know." He looked around at the group. "You did business with her. Did she have any enemies?" He looked at each of them as they slowly shook their heads.

"I'm really the one who had the business relationship with her, Decker," said Marks. "Although we don't do much together anymore. She has her financial backers and really doesn't need someone like me. I can't say that I knew everything about the woman. But it never occurred to me that she had enemies. I mean,

I know what happened to her husband, but that was a long time ago. And he was just in the wrong place at the wrong time, if I remember correctly."

The butler came in and announced dinner.

Marks grinned at Decker as they filed into the dining room. "I know, it's quite British, the butler thing, I guess. And silly. But what the hell. I like it."

In the long dining room, Marks placed Decker next to him, while he put Mars in between the other two women and Lancaster between the other two men. Jenny Marks sat across from Decker, while her father took his place at the head of the table.

As they were eating, Decker asked, "So what did you know about David Katz?"

"David?" Marks rubbed his mouth with his napkin. "Well, he came to town years ago, young and smart and ambitious as hell."

"I understand he had already made money doing something."

"That's right. I heard that too."

Marks chewed on a bit of steak.

"Do you know exactly what he made his money in?" asked Decker.

"Not really. I thought it was the stock market, or the bond market, but I can't tell you definitively."

Meanwhile, the women next to Mars were asking him about himself.

"You look like an athlete," said the brunette on his left. "Were you in the pros?"

"Played some college ball. Wanted to play in the NFL, but never made it."

"You look like you could still play right now."

"Don't know about that. Those boys are a lot bigger and faster than when I played."

The woman on his right, indicating Decker, said, "How do you know that guy?"

"Dude saved my life once."

"Isn't he a detective or something?" said the woman.

"One of the best."

"He doesn't look like a detective."

"What are they supposed to look like?"

"I don't know. Like on TV, I guess."

"I'd take Decker over all those guys."

* * *

The man on Lancaster's left nibbled at his bread while watching her out of the corner of his eye. She sensed this and turned to him. "You been working with Mr. Marks for a long time?"

"Does it matter?" asked the man. He changed expressions when the guy on the other side of Lancaster made a face. "I mean, yeah, about fifteen years now. He's a good boss."

"What do you do for him?"

"Basically, whatever he wants me to do for him." The man gave what he probably thought was a disarming smile.

Lancaster didn't return it. She focused on her meal and asked the attendant for a top-off on her wine.

* * *

"Why all the interest in David Katz?" Marks asked Decker.

"You ever been to the American Grill?"

Marks laughed. "Not my sort of place. I can't eat burgers and fries anymore. And I'm more into wine than beer."

Jenny was sitting across from Decker. "You said you think someone hired a person to kill Rachel?"

Decker nodded and focused on her, as her father sat up straighter in his chair. "That's right."

"But why would anyone do that? Rachel has never hurt anyone."

"You know her well?"

"I would consider us friends. She's actually taught me a lot about handling myself. I've started to work with Dad, and she's been in the business world for a long time. I consider her a mentor."

"And you've been doing a good job too," said Marks proudly.

Decker's surprise must have shown on his face, because Jenny smiled sardonically and said, "I've grown a little since you last knew me, Detective Decker. Even earned my MBA."

"Glad to hear it, Ms. Marks."

"Oh, just make it Jenny. You saved me from that low-life jerk over two years ago. You deserve a first-name relationship."

"Okay, Jenny. When was the last time you talked to Katz?"

"Oh, probably about a week or so ago. We had lunch, just a catch-up sort of thing."

"She seem okay?"

"Yes, nothing out of the ordinary."

Marks said, "What do you think is going on, Decker?"

"I'm not sure. Someone wanted her dead. And her husband was murdered too."

"But that was a long time ago. And they caught the guy who did it."

"No, we didn't. A man was convicted, but he didn't kill David Katz and the others. He ended up coming back to town and being murdered too."

Marks said, "Wait a minute, that's right. I remember hearing about that. What was his name again?"

"Meryl Hawkins."

"That's right. It was all over the news. Those murders all those years ago cast a long shadow on this town, I can tell you that. And now you say he's innocent?"

Decker noticed that Jenny Marks had flinched at her father's remark. "What is it?" he asked her.

"Just something that Rachel said."

"When?"

"The last time I talked to her. We were discussing business and that's when she said it."

"What?"

"It was really weird." She paused to recall it. "Something about sins and *long shadows*."

"*Old* sins cast long shadows?" said Lancaster, who had been raptly listening to this exchange.

Jenny pointed at her. "Yes, exactly. Old sins cast long shadows."

Lancaster said, "Sounds like something out of a British detective novel."

Decker caught Mars's eye. He said, "Shades of truth."

"What?" asked Marks.

"Just something else that Rachel told someone. Do you know anything else about David Katz's background?"

"Well, I had him checked out when we were talking about doing some deals together. They never came to fruition because he was killed. Everything seemed to check out okay."

"How far back did your check go?"

"Um, I'm not sure. George?" He looked at the man on the right of Lancaster. He was small and slightly built, with thinning dark hair and a bony face.

George said, "We usually do a financial dig on the person. Go back about five years. I didn't do the one on this Mr. Katz, but that's generally the drill."

"Five years," said Decker, really to himself.

"Do you think that's far enough?" asked Marks.

"Apparently not," replied Decker.

CHAPTER

65

IT WAS SEVEN A.M. and Decker sat on his bed at the Residence Inn, once more going over the construction plans for the American Grill. He had sent off texts to Jamison asking her for help on a variety of questions. He hadn't gotten responses yet on those, or the research he had asked her to do about the shell companies backing Rachel Katz's projects. He didn't know if he ever would.

He was slowly turning the pages of the construction drawings when he stopped and peered more closely at a particular page. Then he flipped back a few pages and studied the information there. Next, he grabbed another handful of documents and went down the list of line items. Finally, he picked up his phone and made a call.

Lancaster answered. "I'm just about to step into the shower, Decker, can I call you back? And I had too much to drink last night. My head is splitting."

"It's actually Earl I want to talk to."

"Hang on."

A few moments later Earl's voice came on the line. "What's up, Amos?"

"Got another construction question for you."

"Okay. Shoot."

"I'm looking at the construction plans for the American Grill and invoices for construction materials."

"All right."

"You know the size of the place, right?"

"Generally. It's a typical footprint for a retail restaurant operation."

"Talk some more about that."

"Well, I mean a four-exterior-wall, one-story basic rectangle. Cinderblock construction with brick veneer and a flat tarred and pebble-topped roof where the outside HVAC units are housed."

"What sort of square footage are we talking?"

"For a sit-down restaurant as opposed to a fast-food place, about sixty percent of the space goes to the dining and bar area and forty percent to the kitchen, prep areas, and storage. The Grill, I would estimate, is about five thousand square feet, so about three thousand of that would be the dining and bar and the rest for kitchen, prep, and storage. Then you have your enclosed Dumpster area out back. The interior layout allows about fifteen square feet of space per patron seat. That's the general rule of thumb in the industry. That way, the Grill could comfortably accommodate a couple hundred diners at a time. Which I think is around its fire code limit of customers at any one time."

"Okay, how much concrete are we talking about for a place that size?"

"You'd pour your footers. That's not all that much. Then you'd lay your block walls." He gave Decker an estimate of the concrete, and the blocks required.

Decker looked at the line item on the page he was looking at. "The cinderblock count is pretty much spot on. But what if I told you the concrete outlay was way over quadruple what you just said?"

"That's impossible."

"Tell me a way that it wouldn't be impossible."

Earl was silent for a few moments. "Well, the only way to justify that much concrete is if they built a full basement, so their pour obviously would be a lot more. But why would a restaurant want a full basement instead of just footers and foundation you build on? You couldn't possibly need that much storage."

"Good question," said Decker. "Hope I find the answer."

He thanked Earl, told him to have his wife call back when she was done, clicked off, and looked down at the plans.

The American Grill was turning out to be far more special than he had previously thought.

A full basement for what?

And maybe whatever *that* was would explain why David Katz had built it, and why Rachel Katz had kept it all these years.

He went on his laptop and loaded in the name William Peyton and added the qualifier "the American Grill." Nothing remotely relevant came up in connection with the longtime manager of the restaurant.

He took out his phone and pulled up the photos he'd taken of the trainees including the one named Daniel. The trainees who never stayed very long. Then his memories shifted to the guy who'd been staring at him from the kitchen. There clearly had been suspicion in that look.

He glanced back at the construction plans and then focused on Earl Lancaster's words:

The only way to justify that much concrete is if they built a full basement.

But as he'd also pointed out, why would David Katz have gone to the additional time, trouble, and expense for more storage area than he could possibly ever need? And if there was an underground room, it would have to be accessible somehow. There would have to be a door down there. And steps. And what would be down there?

Mary Lancaster called him back twenty minutes later.

"Long shower," he grumbled.

"I had to dress and dry my hair too, and do it all with a friggin' hangover," she snapped. "Earl told me about your questions. Where are you headed with this?"

"I think there's another room under the American Grill."

"Why would that be?"

"I have no idea. But Earl couldn't think of another reason why so much concrete would have been used. And maybe that's why Rachel Katz hid the documents I found. That's where the additional concrete was listed."

"Meaning she knew about a possible underground room?"

"Katz told me that she and her husband met on a blind date. And six months later they were married. This was *after* the American Grill opened."

"So maybe she didn't know about the underground room, then?"

"At least not at that point. And that might explain why they used tarps over the construction site and used outside contractors and rented equipment. They didn't want anyone to know what they were doing."

"And Fred Palmer told us that the equipment they rented was a lot more horsepower than was needed. But they might need all of that if they were going to remove enough dirt to make way for a full basement."

"Right. Although I guess somewhere in the permitting process, they'd have to tell the folks in government about their plans and get approvals. Code compliance and inspections and all that. But I guess there's also no law against having a basement underneath your restaurant."

"But you would have to have a way to access it," said Lancaster.

"A waitress at the restaurant told me some interesting things." He quickly told her about the trainees and wait staff, the longtime manager, and the seemingly one-year turnover for all except the kitchen staff.

"Okay, this is just getting weirder and weirder," noted Lancaster. "What is going on in this alleged room underneath the restaurant? Do you think it might be a drug operation?"

"If so, it's certainly an odd one."

"And that would mean that instead of an innocent citizen who was murdered for being in the wrong place at the wrong time, Katz was dirty. Maybe that's what led to his getting killed."

"That could certainly be the case if somebody wanted him out of the way."

"But why kill the Richards family too?"

"Don Richards gave him the loan for the Grill. Maybe that ties in somehow." He paused. "I wonder about something."

"What?"

"I'm wondering if the loan was ever paid off," said Decker.

CHAPTER

66

"Okay, I've got bad news and bad news, which do you want first?" Decker was talking to Alex Jamison on his cell phone.

"Well, I guess it doesn't matter, does it?" he said.

"Okay, we struck out on the shell companies you gave us. We can't penetrate them."

"Okay."

"And the tattoos on the two dead guys? I ran them through the relevant databases and came up with zip. I mean, most of the tats taken separately are well known. But the Bureau has never seen them all strung together like that before. It's quite a mix of hate groups. Nazi, Aryan, Klansmen."

"Well, thanks for checking."

"No, you don't understand, Decker. I've got people freaking out here. When the FBI can't find out something, that's news. And they're also afraid that maybe these different hate groups are starting to come together, sharing resources, coordinating terrorist actions, accomplishing more terrible things together than they can separately."

"You mean the shell companies are unusually hardened, and the tats may reflect some new sort of new terrorist threat?"

"Bingo. When I told Bogart, he was really concerned."

"Well, I share that concern."

"Anything from Rachel Katz yet?"

"She hasn't regained consciousness. The doctors are getting worried."

"What else can you do?"

"I can find out what's in the basement of the American Grill."

"Haven't you seen the movies? You *never* go down to the basement."

"I did in Baronville."

"My point exactly."

Decker clicked off and went in search of Lancaster, finding her getting some coffee in the break room.

"You want a cup?" she asked.

He shook his head. "We need to go to the bank."

"Why, do you need money?"

"No, answers."

* * *

On the drive over to Don Richards's old bank, Decker said, "David Katz owned a late-model Mercedes sedan when he was killed. It's the car I think his murderer drove over in. Katz and his wife were living in a very nice apartment in town. He owned the American Grill after building it with a construction and operating loan. And he might have had other loans."

"So?"

"So how do you get a big loan like that without putting up collateral?"

"Maybe he put up collateral."

"Meaning he had money of his own."

"Well, yeah. He came to town with money. You know that. Duncan Marks mentioned it at dinner."

"Yeah, everybody keeps telling me that. But no one can tell me *where* the money came from."

"Well, maybe the bank can help."

"Only reason we're going there. Otherwise I wouldn't set foot in one."

"You don't like banks?"

"Not since they foreclosed on my house here and repossessed my car. And with my shitty credit score, *they* don't like *me* either," replied Decker.

* * *

Bart Tinsdale was the bank's vice president. He had been at the institution long enough to have known Don Richards. Tinsdale was tall and lanky but his suit was ill-fitting, the pants and coat sleeves too short for his limbs. His shoes were old and battered, and his socks seemed to have lost their elasticity.

However, he had an alert eye and firm handshake, and quickly guided them back to his small glass-enclosed office area off the main lobby, where they all sat around his desk.

He pointed out the window. "Every time I look out that window and see the Grill, I think about Don and David."

"So you knew them both?" asked Decker.

Tinsdale nodded. "I was just a bank clerk back then."

Lancaster said, "Well, you worked your way up. VP now."

Tinsdale's face crinkled. "I'm a little fish in a little pond. And I'm perfectly happy about that. Good place to raise kids, and I've got five."

"Wow, I've got one and some days it's more than I can handle."

The banker nodded appreciatively. "My wife is a saint. And if the kids turn out well, it's more because of her than me. But I do the coaching bit. Soccer and baseball. And I'm an assistant coach for basketball. I played in high school. Pretty full schedule."

"I can see that."

He sat forward. "But you didn't come about that."

Decker said, "No. We've reopened the investigation into David Katz's and Don Richards's murders. And we're also investigating the attempted murder of Rachel Katz."

Tinsdale involuntarily shuddered. "Been way too many killings around here." He gazed at Decker. "You were here when the shootings happened at the high school. My oldest daughter was a freshman when that happened. Thank God she was okay."

"Yeah, thank God," said Lancaster.

"So what can I do for you?" asked Tinsdale.

"For starters, we'd like to know more about the loan that Richards made to David Katz. Do you have those records?"

"Well, they'd be on the computer. Everything's on the computer. Even the old stuff now." He looked at his keyboard before glancing up. "Do you need to get a warrant for that?"

"Katz is dead. I don't see what harm there is in looking at old bank records."

"I guess that's true." Tinsdale tapped some keys and maneuvered through some screens. "Okay, what exactly do you want to know?"

"How much was the loan for?" asked Decker.

Tinsdale read off the screen. "Two point five million."

Lancaster gaped. "That's a pretty big loan, isn't it?"

"Well, I've done bigger. But it is fairly substantial for a restaurant in Burlington, I'll grant you that, particularly since it was so many years ago. But it was apparently an expensive buildout."

"Have you been to the Grill?" asked Decker.

"I have in fact, yes."

"It seemed like a million other restaurants I've been in. Not particularly high-end."

Tinsdale was nodding before he finished speaking. "I have to admit that I thought the same thing, actually. But the loan *was* granted."

"Did he have to put up any collateral for the loan?"

"Well, we put a mortgage on the property, of course, and the improvements. That's standard. And, yes, I would imagine he had to put up some money of his own. We don't generally fully fund projects like this. We want the borrower to have some skin in the game, so to speak. He was applying for money for the construction and also operating funds to get the business up and going. It's not like he could start paying down the loan from day one while they're still building the thing. The interest would be wrapped into the principal and payments calculated off that. Let me just check on a few items." He read down several more screens. "Okay, yes, he did put up some money of his own. A little over five hundred thousand. That went into the land purchase. And he also personally guaranteed the loan."

"Is that typical?" asked Lancaster.

Tinsdale gave her a knowing look. "Oh, yes. Especially with a restaurant. Failure rates on those are really high. And if the customer defaults, the bank doesn't just want to have to look to the collateral. We're not in the business of running a restaurant. And the resale rates on a failed restaurant operation are not very good. Pennies on the dollar. People figure if a location failed, why would a second try succeed?"

"So, if he personally guaranteed the loan, he must have had some wealth," said Lancaster.

"Assuredly yes. We would have done a complete financial due diligence on him. And he would have had to show proof of collateral funds and we would have filed a security interest on those assets. Stocks or bonds or cash accounts or whatever the collateral was, giving the bank a secured interest in those assets in case of default."

"Could you tell us what his net worth was back then?" asked Decker.

Tinsdale hit some more keys. "Let's see. Okay, we took an interest in some CDs that he had that were worth eighty percent of the loan amount. All told, it shows that his net worth back then was about nine million dollars."

"Wow," said Lancaster. "With all that money, why not just fund the construction out of his own pocket?"

Tinsdale smiled knowingly. "First rule of business, when you can, use someone else's money."

"Right."

"What was the main source of his wealth?" asked Decker.

"Seemed to be stocks and bonds mostly. Couple of annuities. It was all liquid."

"But does it show where his wealth initially came from?"

"No, it doesn't. But all the assets were legally in his name."

"And he was the only borrower?"

"Yes, he wasn't married when he did this deal."

"And Don Richards did everything by the book?" asked Lancaster.

"Absolutely. All done in accordance with the bank's loan requirements."

"What was Katz's background? Education? Birthplace? History?"

Tinsdale looked over the screens. "Says here on his loan app that he had a BA and an MBA. He listed his occupation as entrepreneur."

"But again, no source for his wealth other than the net worth figure?"

"Well, it was *his* money. That was verified. He might have inherited it."

"I assumed when he died that the loan rolled over to his widow?"

"No, it didn't."

"Why not?"

"It was a construction loan that was rolled into a five-year loan with a fixed interest rate. But Katz paid the whole thing off about six months after the restaurant opened."

"How did he do that?" asked Decker.

Tinsdale studied the screens once more. "It's not entirely clear, but it seems like he raised some private money from investors and used that to pay off the loan completely."

"And did he take out any more loans with the bank?"

"There were two lines of credit for a million each that he took out around the same time. He fully drew down on both and then paid them off. Then he bought an old factory building for about three million with an eye to turning it into retail and living space. He took out a loan for that too. It was finished after he died."

"Is the loan still outstanding on that one?"

Tinsdale moved through some more screens. "No. Katz paid that one off too."

"When?"

"Let me see. It says here it was paid in full one year after he took it out."

"But you said the building was finished *after* he died," said Decker.

"That's right. They were only about halfway done when he was killed." Tinsdale shrugged. "Apparently he had another round of investment money come in and they took the loan out."

"And did Don Richards work on all these deals?"

"That's right. He was sort of Katz's go-to person."

"Has Rachel Katz applied for any loans from the bank?"

"No. She doesn't even have a personal account with us. I think she has some deep pockets behind her. Doesn't need a commercial lending source anymore. She seems to be rolling in money right now."

"Nice job if you can get it," said Lancaster dryly.

* * *

Outside, Decker looked to the sky. "We were led to believe that the only deal Katz and Richards worked on was for the American Grill. But that wasn't the case. There were the lines of credit and the old factory building."

"Okay, but what did we get out of all that except that some people have all the friggin' luck, *and* all the money?" asked Lancaster.

"When somebody keeps paying off big loans unusually early because they got 'investment money' rolling in from shell companies, it tells me one thing." He looked at his partner.

Lancaster nodded. "David Katz was cleaning money."

"Exactly. And I wonder if Rachel Katz took over the *laundry* business when he died."

67

DECKER AND LANCASTER WERE SEATED across from Bill Peyton in his small office at the American Grill. Peyton was a big man, about six-two, two-twenty, with thick shoulders and muscular arms. His gray hair was cut in a bristly flattop turning silver at the temples. In his early sixties now, he looked like he could bench-press a truck.

"Thanks for meeting with us," said Lancaster.

"No problem. How is Ms. Katz doing?"

"She hasn't regained consciousness," said Lancaster. "But the doctors are still hopeful."

Decker slid a photo out of a slip of plastic and handed it across to Peyton. "Do you recognize this man?"

Peyton fingered the photo. "No, who is he?"

"The man who attempted to murder your boss. He was killed during the encounter. His name is Eric Tyson. Former military."

"No, never seen him before, certainly not here. I can ask around to the staff and see. But the fact is, Ms. Katz didn't come here much."

"But she still owns the place," pointed out Lancaster.

"She does. But in the grand scheme of her empire here, we're small potatoes." He grinned briefly. "And she trusted me to run the place, just like her husband did."

"You've been here from the get-go," said Decker.

"That's right. David Katz hired me."

"I guess you've run restaurants before?"

"I know my way around the business."

"It can be challenging. Lots of restaurants fail."

"Yes, they can. And we've had some new competition come in. But we're holding our own."

"Were you around when the place was being built?" asked Decker.

"I was, yes. David brought me on early enough, so I could have input in the process."

"How was David Katz to work for?"

"I always found him professional and focused. Later, I found his wife to be the same." He looked at his watch. "Anything else?"

"What will happen to the business if Rachel Katz doesn't recover?" asked Decker.

"I have no idea," said Peyton. "I guess that depends on what's in her will and what her relatives want to do. I hope we don't get to that point."

"Absolutely," said Decker. "Well, thanks for your time." He pulled out another photo of Eric Tyson from his pocket and handed it to Peyton. "And let us know if anyone remembers seeing that guy around."

Peyton took the photo without looking at it. "Will do."

They left and went outside.

"Well?" said Lancaster.

Decker took out the plastic slip with the photo inside. "Looks like a beautiful print on the photo. We'll run it and see if Mr. Peyton is who he says he is."

* * *

Decker dropped Lancaster and the photo off at the station and continued on to the hospital, where Mars was once more ensconced in Katz's hospital room.

"Nothing?" said Decker as he sat down next to him.

Mars shook his head.

"Got something to tell you." He filled Mars in on his theory of money laundering.

"So you think she was in on it?" asked Mars as he glanced at Katz.

"I don't know for sure, but it would be a stretch to conclude that she didn't know about it. She's got financial backers that even the FBI can't pierce."

Mars slowly nodded. "Could be the reason for her guilty conscience and all the weird stuff she was saying to me."

"Could be. We met with the guy who manages the American Grill. We got his prints through a bit of sleight of hand, and Mary's running them through the database."

"What could that tell you?"

"I don't think this is just about money laundering, Melvin. I think something else is going on. You don't need to build a basement under a restaurant to run a money laundering business. You just need legitimate businesses to flush bad money through and turn that bad money into other assets and a clean line of cash flow. That's what all of Katz's businesses could allow them to do."

"But you don't think that's all. So what else could there be?"

Decker shrugged. "I don't know. But I believe that David Katz and Don Richards were killed because something went wrong."

"Went wrong. Like what?"

"Something in the business. Someone felt threatened somehow, by one or both of them. They killed them and pinned it on Meryl Hawkins, with his daughter's help."

"And her payoff?"

"She got remade, new life, new everything. From the bottom to the top in a flash."

"Like Audrey Hepburn in *My Fair Lady*. One of my favorite films."

Decker looked at him in a bemused way. "Didn't see you as a *My Fair Lady* kind of guy."

"Hell, I could relate, Decker. I had to remake myself every second of every day, when I was growing up in West Texas and then when I was in prison. And when I got out of prison."

"Why not just be yourself?"

"Easy for you to say."

Decker sat back. "I guess you're right about that."

"Yeah, I was the high school and college sports star back then.

Whole damn state loved me. I was a hero. But God forbid I eat at their table. Or date their daughters."

Decker suddenly glanced at Katz. "Jenny Marks said that Katz had been a real mentor to her. Showing her the ropes of being in business."

"I heard that. So?"

"So, even though Katz said she didn't know her, I wonder if she did the same thing for Mitzi Gardiner?"

"Wait a minute, you think Gardiner was Hepburn?"

"And that means Rachel Katz might have been in the role played by Rex Harrison."

68

"WE...LOOK, UM, I think there's a problem."

Decker stared at Brad Gardiner, who was standing, pale and shaking, in the doorway of his home. Decker had just knocked on the door and Gardiner had flung it open.

"What sort of problem?" asked Decker.

"Mitzi...she's locked herself in our bedroom and she won't come out. And...and I think she has a gun. She's threatening to shoot herself, or anyone who comes through that door."

"Have you called the police?"

"I...no. I don't know what to do."

"Is anyone in the room with her? Your son?"

"No, he's at school, thank God."

"Anybody else?"

"I had the maid leave when...when things got weird."

"Why are you home at this time of day?"

"I forgot some papers. I came back for them. That's when Mitzi screamed at me when I tried to open the bedroom door."

"Okay, is she on something? Has she been drinking?"

Gardiner seemed to be on the verge of tears. "I don't know. What the hell is going on?"

"Show me to the bedroom."

Decker followed him down the hall and they arrived at the door.

"Honey, I have Mr. Decker here."

"Get him the fuck out of my house!" screamed Mitzi.

"Ms. Gardiner?" said Decker.

The next moment they both leapt back because she fired a round right through the wood. The slug missed both men and embedded in the far wall.

"Jesus Christ!" cried out Gardiner as he dropped to the floor shaking.

Decker slid over to him, keeping low. "What kind of gun does she have?"

"It's...it's a Sig Sauer. I bought it for her. But she picked it out."

"What model?"

"Um..."

"Think!"

"P238."

"What's it look like?"

"Small. She can carry it in her clutch purse."

"P238 Micro Compact chambered in .380 auto?"

"Yes, that's it. Exactly."

"Standard mag with it, or did she do something special?"

"No, standard."

Decker nodded. "Call the police and wait for them by the front door."

"What the hell are you two doing out there?" screamed Mitzi, followed by another shot through the door.

With one backward glance at the door, Gardiner did as Decker requested, sliding down the hall on his hands and knees. Then he rose and sprinted off. Decker straightened and, keeping well away from the bedroom door, said, "Mitzi, it's Amos Decker."

"I said to get out of my house, you bastard."

"We need to talk."

"About what? You've ruined my life. What the hell else is there to talk about, you shit!"

"How exactly did I do that?"

Another round blew through the wood and hit the opposite wall about a foot below the other two bullets.

"You know damn well how. You just...you just had to dig all this shit up, didn't you? From all that time ago. You couldn't give a crap how it might affect people. How it might affect me! You asshole!" she shrieked.

Another shot came through the door. Decker flinched with the impact against the wood but held his ground.

"That was not my intent."

"Don't you dare bullshit me. That's *exactly* what you wanted."

She fired another round through the door, ripping a big chunk off it as the wood around the other holes gave way.

"Look, if you stop shooting, we can have a conversation."

"I'm not talking to you. I'm going to kill myself."

"Why would you want to do that?"

"Because my life is over!"

"Your husband doesn't think that. Or your son."

"Don't you dare talk about my son. He's the only good thing I've ever done in my miserable excuse for a life."

"I think we *have* to talk about him if you're planning on leaving him motherless."

Now she started to sob. He could hear the gut-wrenching noises coming through the door.

He took a chance and peeped through one of the holes. She was lying in bed, wearing only a long T-shirt; her uncovered legs were long and pale. The gun was in her right hand.

"Mitzi, I can help you if you let me."

"N-nobody can help me. Not now."

"I don't see it that way."

"I told you to get out."

He ducked down as the shot came through not the door, but the wall. It must have hit a nail in the stud under the drywall, because it careened into the hall at a weird angle, nearly hitting Decker in the face.

He stayed low, breathing heavily and wondering where the hell the cops were.

"I can't leave you like this. I'm afraid you're going to hurt yourself."

"Fuckin' A, Sherlock. I'm going to do more than hurt myself, you idiot!"

"Rachel Katz wouldn't want that, Mitzi. She was the one who helped you to turn your life around. And now she's fighting for her life."

Silence.

A few moments passed.

"What do you know about anything?"

"I know a lot, Mitzi. I'd like to know more."

"You came here and…and accused me of framing my own father."

"So tell me that you didn't. Tell me that you're innocent."

"You wouldn't believe me if I did."

"Try me."

In a more subdued tone she said, "Look, it's…it's complicated."

"Believe me, I know that. But why do I think that Rachel Katz was blindsided by what happened? And you didn't really know what was going to happen either, Mitzi, did you? I think you were both used. I think you both thought you had no way out."

"I…I don't want to talk about it."

"At this point, you're going to have to."

"Screw you, Decker!"

He flattened himself to the hallway floor right as the bullet blasted through the door. The next instant he was up and had smashed into the door, breaking it open.

An astonished Mitzi gaped at him as he charged toward the bed. She aimed her pistol at him and fired.

Click. Click.

Decker wrenched the gun out of her hand and pocketed it. He looked down at her. "P238 Micro Compact has a seven-round standard mag." He looked at the bullet-pocked door and wall. "And you just fired your last bullet."

He turned back to her, as she covered herself with a sheet. "Get out!" she screamed.

"I can't do that. The police are on their way."

She looked confused. "Why?"

"Well, for starters you tried to kill me and your husband."

"No I didn't. I was just trying to make you leave me alone."

"Not sure the court will see it that way. You fire a gun at someone, deadly intent is pretty much implied."

Her lips trembled. "Do you mean I could go to jail? But I'm innocent."

"Like your father? He *was* innocent. And he still went to jail. Then someone put a bullet in his head. They didn't even let him die peacefully."

Decker sat on the edge of the bed and gazed at her.

"This is the moment, Mitzi. The crossroads. Now is the time where you can make the right decision instead of the selfish one. You can correct a lot of wrongs. Will you do it? Do you have the courage to do that?"

"What if I don't?" she said, drawing her legs up and gathering the covers around her.

"Then you go to jail. It's as simple as that."

"I'm going to jail regardless."

"Not necessarily. Or you could hang out here until someone tries to kill you, like they did with Rachel Katz."

He glanced at her nightstand and started when he eyed the half-empty prescription pill bottle. "How many pills did you take?" he snapped.

"Not that many," she said hesitantly.

"How many is that?"

"Four or five."

He snatched up the bottle and read the label. "Christ, Mitzi."

He called 911 and requested an ambulance, pronto, for a possible drug overdose.

She lay back against the headboard and looked around the room. She smiled. "I have a perfect life; did you know that?"

"Tell me about it."

"Can't you see for yourself? Perfect home, perfect husband. Perfect child." She uncovered her bare legs. "Perfect body." She tapped her teeth. "First-rate veneers to hide the shitty, ugly gray." She covered herself back up as her smile faded. "But the shitty, ugly gray is right below the surface. Right underneath. They couldn't take that away. It'll always be with me."

"But you made the change. That was a lot of work. You had to be determined. It wasn't easy kicking what you kicked."

"It...it was either do that or end up dead." She looked at him defiantly. "I chose to live."

"I'm glad you did. Now you have a family. A son who's counting on you. So choose to live this time too."

Her lips trembled when he said this. She rubbed at her eyes. "But now, it's...a-all effed up. I don't k-know what to..."

As Decker listened to this, he saw her eyes becoming droopy, her features more and more listless. He let a few seconds pass and, trying to keep his voice calm, asked, "Do you have any Narcan here?"

She smiled and shook her head. "That's for druggies. I'm not a druggie. Not anymore. I am the princess of the manor. The lady is perfect. Everybody says so."

"Are you sure it was just four or five pills?" he said quickly.

She stretched out like a cat. "Maybe it was more. I don't remember." She lay back and closed her eyes.

"Stay with me, Mitzi. Come on now." He sat down next to her and slapped her face. It was a poor substitute for Narcan, but he had to do something.

"Hey," she said angrily, swatting at him. "Y-you a-assaulted m-me."

"You framed your father. Why?"

She didn't answer.

"Why?" he said, shaking her. "Come on, talk to me."

"I did it for drugs."

"For drugs? You mean for you?"

She waved this comment off. "No, stupid. For Mom. Morphine. For her drip line. Pure stuff. Right from the hospital. Gave it to her t-till she died. And she died p-peacefully. All I could do for her. But it was s-something, right?"

"Right. Who got it for you?"

"They did."

"Who's they?"

She waved her hand around the room. "You know. Them!"

She yawned and closed her eyes.

He slapped her again. This time, she didn't complain. Or open her eyes.

Shit.

He could hear the sirens now.

Decker gripped Mitzi's shoulders to keep her upright as she started to slump sideways. "What did they promise you, Mitzi? A new life? A new everything? Did Rachel Katz help you out? Did she become your mentor?"

Mitzi mumbled, "She's a n-nice person. H-helped me."

"I bet she did. So they killed her husband and Don Richards. And the others. And set up your dad."

"Set him…up."

"And how did they approach you?"

"Ka, Kar…"

"Karl Stevens. Right. He was the go-between. Who was he working with?"

"He's dead. You tol' me…d-dead."

The sirens were growing closer.

"That's right, he's dead. But you're not. You can tell me all about it."

She shook her head. "Too l-late for th-that."

"It's never too late for the truth."

She started to fall sideways. He slapped her again. To no effect. The sirens had been growing louder and louder all this time. Then the sound died. They were in the driveway.

"Karl Stevens is dead, that's right. But who was he working with? Did it have something to do with the American Grill? Bill Peyton? Do you know him? Peyton?"

She opened her eyes.

"Pey-ton."

"Right. The manager at the American Grill. Did he come to you? Did he ask you to help frame Meryl?" He shook her violently. "Did he?"

She closed her eyes again and went limp in his arms.

He could hear footsteps pounding down the hall. The door burst open and three EMTs were there.

Decker called out, "Amos Decker with the FBI. She took pills from that bottle. More than five. I'm starting to lose her. I think she's unconscious."

One of the EMTs grabbed the bottle and looked at the label. "Okay, step back."

Decker moved away from the bed as the EMTs crowded around Mitzi, who had started to shake violently and then suddenly slumped over. One of the EMTs sprayed Narcan into her nostril. She didn't move for a long moment, and then she sat straight up and let out a lungful of air.

"Okay, ma'am, just relax. We're going to take you to the hospital to get checked out."

"W-what?"

Then she went limp again and fell over sideways.

"Shit," said the EMT. He sprayed another shot of Narcan up her other nostril.

She stirred but did not come fully back.

They started a saline drip line and put a blood pressure cuff and pulse monitor on her.

"Her pressure and respiration are really low," said one of the EMTs. "Critically low. I think she took something more than was in that bottle. Let's roll. Now!"

They were loading her onto a gurney when Decker noticed something.

"Wait a minute, where's her husband?"

"Who?" said one of the EMTs.

"Her husband. Tall guy. He let you in."

"Nobody let us in. The front door was open. We just followed the noise to back here."

Decker ran out of the room, down the hall, and out the front door. A late-model Audi 8 had been parked in front when he'd gotten here. It was no longer there.

He looked up and down the road fronting the house.

Brad Gardiner was gone.

And Decker had no clue why.

Am I ever going to get out ahead of this damn case?

"I DON'T LIKE GETTING PLAYED," grumbled Decker.

He was sitting alongside Lancaster and Mars in the visitors' waiting room at the local hospital in Trammel, where Mitzi Gardiner had been admitted into the critical care unit. As with Rachel Katz, they had armed guards stationed 24/7 outside her room.

Though the doctors were hopeful that she would recover, they could not guarantee what her mental state might be when she regained consciousness. One of the doctors had told them, "When abused, the drug she took can have a particularly destructive impact on certain areas of the brain having to do with memory."

"Well, that's great," Decker had replied. "Since we need for her to remember a lot of stuff."

Lancaster now said, "We found Brad Gardiner's car abandoned about two miles from his house. He might have been picked up there and taken somewhere else."

"It never occurred to me that her husband might be a part of all this," said Decker miserably.

"Playing a role all these years?" said Mars. "That's a commitment and then some."

"Agreed," said Lancaster. "I mean, they had a kid together."

"I'm not saying the guy doesn't love her or didn't want to marry her and have a child," said Decker. "But I can't think of another reason why he would have vanished like that, unless he was afraid we were going to find out something."

"This goes way beyond money laundering, Decker," said Lancaster.

"We need to find out all we can about Brad Gardiner."

Lancaster said, "I've already started digging. He went to college in Illinois. Moved here about fifteen years ago. Worked at a variety of jobs in the financial sector. Now he specializes in an upscale placement market."

"Mitzi told me a little about that. She called it a high-end job placement platform."

"That's right," said Lancaster. "Apparently he's not placing people in low-paying jobs. He focuses on finance, law, high tech, manufacturing, energy, those sorts of fields. They pay the big bucks and he gets big commissions."

"I wonder how he hooked up with Mitzi," said Decker.

"You really think this was all arranged after the murders thirteen years ago?"

"She didn't marry him thirteen years ago. She had to go through her big makeover. She told me that Katz helped her with that. Then Gardiner steps in and marries Mitzi and they have a kid and a wonderful life."

"And Gardiner came to the area about the same time as David Katz was opening the American Grill," noted Lancaster.

"Right. Mitzi said her husband knew nothing about her past. Now, either she was lying, or she didn't know that her marriage might have been a setup."

"Assuming it was, why would they go to all those lengths to give Mitzi a second shot at life?" wondered Lancaster.

"She helped them by framing her father for four murders. They wanted to keep her in line."

Lancaster shook her head and said, "Okay, but if they were afraid she might talk, why not just kill her? These folks don't seem to mind solving their problems with violence. And it's not like she was a major player in whatever they're doing."

"Maybe they were afraid with another murder so soon after the others that people would get suspicious and start digging. With Meryl fingered as the killer, no one looked anywhere else. I know that better than anyone."

Mars said, "And it worked, apparently, all this time."

Decker looked thoughtful. "But now, with Gardiner and Katz in the fold, we may be able to find out what's going on."

"Well, Katz hasn't woken up yet, despite what the doctors told us, and Gardiner isn't out of danger yet," said Lancaster. "And you heard the doctor about the state of her memory if she does come out of it. I'm not sure we can rely on either one."

"I agree," replied Decker. "Ground zero for us is the American Grill. We have to find out what's inside there."

"Okay, but we have no probable cause whatsoever to search the place for an underground room," pointed out his old partner.

"We can ask nicely," said Mars.

Decker shook his head. "And this Bill Peyton will be within his rights to say that the only person who can properly grant that request is lying in a hospital bed unconscious. And if we tip him off, and he is in on whatever's going on, that would not be good. The guy struck me as really cagey."

"So what do we do, then?" asked Mars.

Decker looked at Lancaster. "Did you run Peyton's print?"

"We did. And got nothing back. He's not in the system."

"Just because he has no criminal history doesn't mean much. Can we do a deeper dive on him? Try to find out his background? What he was up to prior to coming here?"

"We can. I just don't know how far we'll get. If he's not in the system, it might be hard to build a profile on the guy. I presume that there are a lot of Bill Peytons in this country."

"Yeah, I did a preliminary search online and found squat. But we have to find a way to search for that secret room," said Decker.

"I agree. I just don't know how we can."

"If Katz wakes up, we can get her consent."

"Right, but that might be *never*," retorted Lancaster.

"Then we have to try something else," said Decker.

"I get that, but what?"

"Up to this point, we've been entirely reactive. They've been leading us around by the nose. And I'm getting sick of it."

"Okay, so?"

"So, let's jerk their chain for once."

70

THE CALL CAME IN at one in the morning. Smoke coming from the American Grill. A fire, apparently. Two fire companies responded, along with the police.

Decker, Mars, and Lancaster followed on the heels of the arson squad as they approached the smoke-engulfed restaurant. The firefighters reported that it was only smoke and no fire.

That made sense, because the smoke bombs that had been placed earlier on the roof of the Grill and in the Dumpster in the rear could produce no flames.

Decker looked at the arson boss, Chuck Walters. "That's very suspicious, Chuck. I think we need to look inside for a point of origin. This might be some sort of feint, with the real fire to come once we leave."

The notion was fairly nonsensical, but Chuck nodded and said, "I think that's a good idea. Never know what might be on the inside."

"Never know," agreed Decker.

But hopefully we're about to find out.

They forced open the front door of the restaurant, which immediately set off the alarm. One of the firefighters hastened to turn it off using a special code he inputted into the alarm panel.

"A call will go out to whoever's on the notification list," said Lancaster.

"What I'm hoping for," replied Decker.

The firefighters went in first and gave the all-clear about twenty minutes later.

"Okay," said Decker, turning on the lights. "We need to search this place for possible arson materials. No stone unturned. Let's hit it."

The officers fanned out.

Decker immediately went into the kitchen area, followed by Lancaster and Mars.

The kitchen was spacious, scrupulously clean and organized, and virtually everything in the place looked made of stainless steel. They spent an hour going over every inch of it.

Afterward, Decker leaned against one of the counters and looked around, his thick arms folded over his chest.

"They're not making this easy," said Lancaster.

"Lots of people come in and out of this kitchen, including people who have no connection to any of this. So it can't be apparent. But even so, it has to be somewhat accessible."

Lancaster looked around. "I don't see anything that fits the bill unless we're talking a trapdoor in the floor."

Mars looked down. "It's tiled. With no breaks. A trapdoor would be pretty obvious."

Decker pushed off the counter and went back into the large freezer room. It was about ten feet deep and eight feet across. He shivered slightly as he moved around the space, examining all the shelves and food stacked on them. He came back out and looked at the outside of the freezer compartment.

"Anybody got a tape measure?" he asked.

Neither Lancaster nor Mars did, but one of the cops had a rolling distance tracker in his trunk. He used it to measure distances during traffic accident reconstructions.

Decker took the roller and paced off the depth of the freezer, going in between the shelving at the rear to tap his wheel against the back wall. Then he measured the width.

He checked the measurement and then went outside the freezer and measured the distance from the front of the freezer to the back wall of the kitchen. And then from the side of the freezer to the far wall.

He checked the measurement. "I'm two feet short. This wall is two feet longer on the outside than the depth of the freezer on the inside. And the width is off by over eighteen inches."

"How could that be?" asked Lancaster. "Maybe a load-bearing wall at the back or the side?"

"Why would it just be in the freezer and not out here?" said Mars.

Decker hustled into the freezer, followed by Mars and Lancaster. He went straight to the back.

"Melvin, help me with these shelves."

Together the two big men moved the heavy shelves out of the way with the food still stacked on them. When they were done, they were staring at a seemingly blank wall.

Decker hit every angle and corner of the wall with his light. He got down on his hands and knees and felt along the bottom where the wall met the floor.

Lancaster was shivering. "Can we hurry this up before I get hypothermia?"

Decker stood and faced the wall. "I don't see a button or anything like that. That would be too risky anyway. Someone comes in here, sees it, and pushes it to see what happens. Your secret is out."

"Like the floor, I don't see any break in the wall, Decker," observed Mars. "If there's a door hidden in here I just don't see it."

Decker looked back at the shelves they had moved. "With those shelves in front and food stacked on them, no one would be able to even get close to the wall."

"And what exactly does that mean?"

Decker put his palms against the wall. "It means that maybe the wall *is* the door."

He set his feet and pushed. The entire wall easily rolled back. Revealed off to the left was a door. He opened the door: there was a set of narrow steps going down.

"Open sesame," quipped Mars.

They went single file down the stairs and came out into a darkened space. Decker shone his flashlight around, as did the others.

The space held desks, maps on the wall, computers, telephones, racks of clothing, thick binders, and other pieces of equipment. On one side of the room, a long curtain had been drawn around a space about six by ten feet. The lights suddenly came on and Mars and Decker looked around to see Lancaster standing by a light switch.

"I don't like the dark," she said, turning off her flashlight.

Mars and Decker put away their flashlights and gazed around.

"Holy shit, what is this place?" asked Mars.

Decker strode over to a desk and looked down at the items lying there, next to a piece of machinery.

"They're making IDs here." He picked one up to see a young man staring out from what was a Virginia driver's license. The name on the license was Frank Saunders. Born in 1993 and with an address in McLean, Virginia.

"This guy I saw working at the restaurant as a wait staff 'trainee.' Only his name, I was told, was Daniel, not Frank."

Mars held up a stack of credit cards in one hand and sets of American passports and birth certificates in the other. "Okay, I'm no expert, but these damn things look genuine."

Lancaster had drawn back the curtain to reveal what looked like a rudimentary operating room and was now standing next to a gurney. She pointed to an array of surgical instruments lined up on a table. Next to that was a portable high-intensity light. And next to that were oxygen tanks and an IV stand with empty bags hanging from it. Lined up against the wall were a variety of medical monitoring instruments.

Lancaster exclaimed, "Okay, this is freaking me out. They're operating on people down here?" She pointed to the large sink set against the wall. "Maybe that's where they scrub up before doing whatever the hell they do."

Mars was looking at the racks of clothes. "They got everything here, for both men and women." He picked up a wig. "Including these."

Computers were set on each desk. Stacks of paper sat next to the computers. Decker picked up the top page of a stack.

"What is that?" asked Lancaster, coming over to him.

"It's a list of forty cities across the country. There's an X next to each city."

He pointed to the maps on the wall. "These documents might correspond to the red and green pins on those maps. Looks like they have pretty much every major metro area covered."

He picked up another piece of paper. "This reads like someone's bio. Birth information, background. Work experience. Marital status."

He looked down at the bottom of the page. He read off, "Gardiner and Associates."

Lancaster said, "Brad Gardiner?"

"Well, he runs a job placement business."

"But that's not illegal," said Mars. He looked around the space. "Now *this* place definitely looks illegal."

"Whether it's illegal or not depends on who you're placing in those jobs," said Decker.

He looked over at the gurney and surgical instruments. "That's obviously to change someone's appearance. The clothes, wigs, fake IDs, credit cards, passports, birth certificates, and fabricated backgrounds all work to complete a new identity. And then Brad Gardiner places them in positions around the country. And he's not placing people as waiters or maids. He's placing them in finance, the high-tech field, lobbying, government, and other sectors. That's what Mitzi said."

"Yeah, but what sorts of people?" asked Lancaster. Decker looked around the room. "People created here?"

"But they must have experience in those fields," said Mars. "I mean, you can't walk into Goldman Sachs or Google or GE or the U.S. government without knowing what you're doing."

"Oh, I'm sure they know what they're doing," said Decker. "And now we know this place wasn't really just laundering money."

"What do you mean?" asked Lancaster.

"They were laundering people."

"WHAT IN THE HELL do you mean, you lost him?" said Lancaster.

She was staring at a pair of plainclothes detectives who she'd assigned to watch Bill Peyton's apartment. They were back at the police station after thoroughly going over the lower-level room at the American Grill.

"He was there, Detective Lancaster," said the larger of the pair. "And then he was gone."

His partner added, "When you called and told us to bring him in, we knocked and knocked on the door. Then, when there was no answer, we forced the door and searched the whole place, top to bottom. There was no sign of him."

"He lives in an apartment building," said Decker. "Did you think to search the building?"

"But we had the front and back entrances covered."

"He could have gone into another apartment when you came into the building, and then left while you were searching his place," pointed out Decker. "If he was watching you watching him."

"Well, I guess he could have," said one of the detectives.

"There's no *guessing* about it," barked Lancaster. "He did."

After the men left them, Lancaster said, "Idiots. We had him, Decker. We had him. And now, poof, he's gone. You knew he was going to be on the security call list. That was supposed to flush him out. And then these morons lose him."

"Vanishing people seems to be a recurring theme with this case," said Decker sardonically.

"So now what?"

"We have a lot of information to process."

"My team is collecting all the evidence from that underground room. It's a ton. But the computers all are password protected. And my tech guy says the hard drives are clean. Which means everything is kept in some cloud somewhere that we can't access."

"But there's other evidence in there. The IDs, the documents, and the rest."

"You said they were laundering people?"

"The 'trainees' at the Grill. I think they came to Burlington to be processed. Given new identities, maybe some had their features changed through plastic surgery, then they were sent out into the world, probably at positions gotten for them by Brad Gardiner."

"But for what purpose?"

"I don't know."

"And why Burlington, Ohio?"

"I think this has been going on for as long as the American Grill has been in business. That underground room would explain the need for the additional concrete and the way they tried to hide it during the construction process."

"So David Katz was involved in this from the get-go?"

"I don't see how he couldn't be. And he paid off his loans early with fresh money."

"And Bill Peyton?"

"He's been there since the inception too. He had to know about the room. That's why he disappeared. I think he's a smart enough guy to see what we were doing. Using a 'fire' to get in and search the place."

"But a smart defense counsel could get all the fruits of our search thrown out as tainted. We didn't have a warrant and the fire explanation may not hold up at trial."

"We'll cross that bridge when we come to it. But I'm less worried about that than I am about stopping what's been going on here, Mary."

"So why was David Katz killed? And the Richardses?"

"Bad guys kill other bad guys when they feel threatened. It could be that Katz wanted more money to do what he was doing.

Or maybe he got cold feet and was thinking of going to the cops and telling them what was going on."

"And the Richardses?"

"The banker told us that Don Richards was Katz's go-to person there. Maybe the people behind this were afraid that Katz had told Richards too much. We've already speculated that Karl Stevens learned through his drug deals with Richards's son about some communication between Katz and Richards. Stevens must have told someone and then they struck on the idea of pinning all this on Meryl Hawkins."

"Because Stevens knew Mitzi."

"Right. Hell, Stevens might have been the one to suggest pinning it on Hawkins. He certainly knew about Mitzi's drug addiction and probably also about her mother and her need for pain meds. But Meryl wasn't stupid. He must have figured out that his daughter set him up. But he didn't know why. Maybe he just thought she'd gotten in trouble. He said nothing because he didn't want to add to her grief, and to his wife's."

"But then he runs into Karl Stevens in prison. And Stevens maybe runs his mouth. He lets Hawkins know the truth, or close to it."

"So he gets that tat of the arrow through his little star, symbolically killing his daughter. And comes back here trying to prove his innocence."

"And somebody kills him," said Lancaster. "But how would they have known what he was up to?"

"Stevens might have tipped off someone on the outside about Meryl getting out of prison. When he shows up back here, they decide they need to get rid of him before he can start making waves."

"Fortunately, he reached us before they could kill him," pointed out Lancaster.

"It won't be *fortunate* if we can't figure out the truth," Decker retorted.

"So Gardiner and Peyton are both on the run. You think they're going to hook up at some point?"

"Anything's possible. Gardiner really outsmarted me. But the guy was scared, Mary. And he wasn't scared of his wife, even though she was shooting at both of us."

"He was scared because of the people he's involved with."

"Well, considering what they've done so far, who can blame him?"

His phone buzzed. It was Jamison.

"Hey, Alex, I'm a little busy ri—"

She interrupted, "The team's coming to Burlington."

"What? I thought you were in New Hampshire."

"We were. But another case is suddenly taking precedence."

"What case?"

"Yours."

72

Ross Bogart looked every inch the FBI agent someone would expect to see on TV. Tall, physically fit, good-looking, with sharp features, alert eyes, and a quiet competency. But it was more than looking the part. The man was a gifted investigator and worked exceedingly long hours at his job.

Todd Milligan was nearly a carbon copy of his boss, albeit a bit shorter and about a decade younger. He and Decker had been at cross-purposes early on in their professional relationship but had long since reached common ground. The fact that Decker had saved his life once hadn't hurt either.

The FBI team had flown into the nearest regional airport and driven straight to Burlington, telling Decker that they preferred to meet at his place rather than the police station. Now they were standing in Decker's room at the Residence Inn. Melvin Mars was there as well, as was Mary Lancaster. The male FBI agents were dressed in matching dark suits, starched white shirts, and striped ties, and they sported impassive features. Alex Jamison had on a black pantsuit with a white shirt and low heels. Her expression was equally serious.

"Detective Lancaster, it's been a while, good to see you," said Bogart.

She replied, "Well, looks like we're hunting with Decker again. Like old times."

Decker said, "Why are you here, Ross? You didn't say."

Bogart leaned back against the wall and folded his arms over his chest. "We cracked the wall around two of those shell companies that you sent to Alex."

"Meaning the backers for Rachel Katz?"

"Yes. Although the financial relationships apparently go back farther than that. To the time of David Katz's being in charge of the business."

"And what did you find?" asked Lancaster.

"Both companies were set up by a businessman with known ties to a Russian oligarch. That's why we're here."

Lancaster gaped. "A Russian oligarch is bankrolling a business in Burlington, Ohio? How does that make sense?"

Bogart said, "It's a fact, so somehow it makes sense. We just have to figure out how."

Lancaster looked over at Decker. "I didn't see that one coming."

"The room underneath the American Grill," said Decker. "We speculated that it was laundering people. Giving them new identities, and then sending them off into the American workforce in places of influence through Brad Gardiner's placement business."

"But what they're really doing is spying on us?" said Jamison.

Lancaster nodded. "Exactly. And let's face it, legit businesses don't have ID mills hidden under restaurants. Their intent is clearly nefarious."

Decker had been typing in something on his phone. He looked up and said, "We need to find Gardiner and Peyton. And we need to dig into Gardiner's business."

"We didn't know about Brad Gardiner," said Bogart. "But now that we do, we'll get going on that. You said he's disappeared?"

"Along with Bill Peyton, the manager of the American Grill. Ironic, isn't it?"

"What?" said Bogart.

"That they called it the *American* Grill, since it was apparently financed by a Russian oligarch." He thought of something else. "The tats on the two dead guys, Tyson and Stevens."

"What about them?" said Bogart.

"Aryan Nation, Nazi, and KKK."

"Right."

"But there was one more."

Bogart thought for a moment but then shook his head. "Which one?"

"KI."

"I thought that was something to do with the Klan," said Jamison.

"I did too. And there is actually a Klan symbol close to that." He held up his phone. "But I just did some digging after you told us about the Russian connection."

"And?" said Bogart.

"Back in the forties, KI was sort of a foreign intelligence agency in Russia. KI apparently stands for 'Committee of Information.'"

"Damn," said Jamison, while Bogart looked intensely interested.

"How does an old and presumably now-defunct spy agency figure into this?" he asked.

"I look forward to asking Bill Peyton, or whatever his real name is, for the answer," replied Decker.

"But David Katz built the Grill fifteen years ago," said Lancaster. "Are you telling me that the Russians were involved in this stuff here all that time ago?"

Bogart said, "People think the Russians just started messing with us. It was long before that. They've had spies all over this country ever since the Cold War started."

"But a spy operation in Burlington?" said Lancaster.

"Softer target," said Bogart. "Not as many resources. And for a lot of these people, I imagine they don't end up working in Burlington. I imagine that Gardiner places them all over the country. This is just the launch pad."

"The map we found in the underground room confirms that," noted Decker. "These tentacles go all over the country, and to the largest metro areas."

"So, Gardiner's a traitor," exclaimed Lancaster. "And so is Peyton."

"If they're even American," pointed out Bogart. "Now we just have to find them and prove it. I'm calling in more assets, but we want to do this on the QT. We have no idea who else might be involved in this. That's why I didn't want to come to the station initially."

Lancaster looked stunned. "Wait a minute. Are you saying…?"

"What he's saying, Mary, is that no one is above suspicion," said Decker. "And I agree with him."

Lancaster looked put out by this but remained silent.

Bogart gazed at Decker. "You've been in the trenches here. And know the territory better. How do you want to do this?"

"BOLOs on both Peyton and Gardiner. Maintain round-the-clock protection on Katz and Mitzi Gardiner. Right now, they're the only witnesses we have." He paused. "We need to get a search warrant for Gardiner's business. Hopefully we'll be able to find out who he's placed and where."

Decker eyed Mars. "And I'm afraid that Rachel Katz would have had to know about all this at some point."

"But she kept quiet and played along," said Mars.

"Looks that way."

"Maybe she had no choice," said Mars defensively.

"People always have the choice to either be a traitor or do the right thing," said Milligan sternly.

"And Mitzi Gardiner?" asked Lancaster.

Decker said, "She was an addict who set up her father. She probably didn't know about the possible spy operation, and she didn't need to know."

"But why have Gardiner marry her?" said Lancaster.

"What better way to make sure she doesn't do anything stupid than by having one of the people involved right there every day? And Mitzi turned out to be a great mom and doting wife. For Brad Gardiner it was probably a win-win. He was playing a role and I'm sure he was well compensated for it. There are worse ways to spend your life than being rich."

Jamison said, "I think I'd rather stay single."

Bogart said, "We'll run those leads down and search Gardiner's business. What else?"

"Bag and tag everything that was in the Grill's underground room."

Bogart said, "You were lucky that an *apparent* fire broke out, so you could search the place and find that room." He stared pointedly at Decker.

"I'll always take luck when I can get it," replied Decker. "Even if I have to make it myself."

CHAPTER

73

"STRIPPED CLEAN," Bogart said over the phone to Decker. "Gardiner's office didn't have a thing left in it. He must have had an exit plan in place. As soon as you spooked him, he probably had the place wiped. Same thing for Peyton's apartment. Nothing left, if there was anything ever there."

Decker said, "We need to find out all we can about them, Ross. And his house and office have to be full of the guy's prints. Same for Peyton's apartment."

"I already have a team looking for that. Now, these 'trainees' you told me about at the American Grill?"

"Yeah?"

"I doubt any of them will show up for work. Peyton would have given them a heads-up. But I'll have people there just in case they do. And we'll track down where they were staying and search all those places too."

"Let me know if you turn up anything," said Decker.

"What are you going to do?"

"I'm going to take a little trip down memory lane."

* * *

Decker sat across from Lancaster at her house. In the background he could hear Earl and Sandy getting ready to go out.

Sandy burst into the room. She was a fireball of energy, always in a good mood, until she dropped into the blackness of despair, something that could occur within seconds. Her coat was half on and a ski cap covered her eyes.

She pulled it up and announced herself. "I know you," she said to Decker. "You're my mommy's partner. You're Amos Decker."

"And you're Sandra Lancaster." This was a little ritual that the pair had always engaged in.

Earl hustled in and grabbed Sandy's hand.

"We'll be back later," he said, glancing first at Decker and then at his wife.

"Right, hon, thanks," said Lancaster.

After the pair left, Decker refocused on his old partner. "Things going okay?" he asked.

"We're taking it day by day, hour by hour. I have to tell you that Earl teared up when I told him what you said to me on those bleachers that night. He's very grateful for your talking some sense into me."

"It was just my opinion, Mary. I can't judge you, because I haven't walked in your shoes."

"Well, I think you stopped me from making a big mistake. When things go bad, you need your family. You don't push them away."

"No disagreement from me."

"Okay, the case?"

"It's starting to make sense, but there are some gaps."

"*Some* gaps?"

"We know that Meryl Hawkins was set up. His daughter helped to frame him for the four murders. We don't know the exact motivation for the killings, but the fact that Katz had some sort of spy ring going on underneath his restaurant gets us close to it. He either had a falling-out or demanded more money, or whoever killed him was feeling threatened by him."

"Okay."

"Fast forward to today. Hawkins learns the truth from Karl Stevens. He gets out of prison and comes back here to enlist our aid to prove his innocence. Someone kills him that same night."

"And we still have no idea who that is."

"Since we've learned that the spy ring or whatever it is was still operating in Burlington, it seems to me that the spy ring's the likeliest culprits. Now we have Rachel Katz. She was the point person for a consortium of shell companies that Bogart has discovered have a Russian connection. Now, Rachel was waffling some. Look at her discussion with Melvin. They might have been afraid that she was going to turn on them. So they tried to kill her. They tried to kill me too. And they *did* kill Sally Brimmer."

"Because she impersonated Susan Richards. But we still don't know how someone got her to do that."

"No, we don't. That's still an open question, but they might have blackmailed her by threatening to tell Natty's wife about their affair. Now Mitzi Gardiner, overcome with guilt, tries to kill herself with pills. I think she was lucky she had a gun."

"Why?"

"Otherwise, her hubby might have saved her the trouble."

"You think he would have killed her?"

"I can't really assume otherwise. We found the underground room and all the evidence there pointing to some sort of spy ring. Peyton has made a run for it, as has Brad Gardiner. Now we've got two women in hospital beds and we're waiting for them to wake up to tell us what they know."

"*If* they wake up. And if they do, we have no guarantee they'll tell us anything."

"We have leverage over them. Mitzi tried to kill me. And there's no way that Rachel can plausibly argue that she had no knowledge of that room under the American Grill. If they talk, they can work a deal. If they won't they go to prison for a long time. But I don't want to count on them. We have to keep pushing."

"The FBI may find out some stuff that could help us."

"Maybe. But they also might end up with a big fat zero. These people obviously had an exit plan in place, and they executed it pretty damn well."

"So we may be back at square one then, after all this time."

"Maybe not," he said.

"What do you mean?"

"It's occurred to me that this whole thing runs deeper than I previously thought. It seems to me that someone connected to this is hiding in plain sight."

"Okay, how do we find out who that is?"

"We let them do it for us," Decker said cryptically.

74

THEY HAD BROUGHT MITZI GARDINER from the hospital in Trammel to the one in Burlington. Both women were in the same room so that their protection could be consolidated. Policemen and state troopers were arrayed around the hospital and outside their room. Across the street, counter-snipers were posted to prevent anyone from taking a long-range shot at the women.

Decker, Lancaster, and Mars were waiting outside the room because they had been told that Rachel Katz seemed to be coming around.

A few moments later, Natty showed up with Pete Childress and Captain Miller. Childress looked chastened and anxious, Miller grim and focused. Childress glanced at Lancaster, but would not look at Decker.

"Natty told me all the work you've done on this, Mary. Good job. In Burlington! I can hardly believe this crap is going on."

Lancaster said firmly, "Decker's done most of it, Superintendent. Without him, we'd be in the dark about everything." Childress seemed to wince a bit at her words.

He finally looked at Decker and nodded curtly. "Right, yes. Well, that's good, Decker. I'm, uh, I'm glad to see that you've been of assistance to the department."

"Maybe you can put a good word in for me with my obstruction case," replied Decker.

This time Childress perceptibly flinched. "Yes, well." He cleared his throat heavily. "I think that won't be a problem."

Miller added, "I'm *sure* it won't be. We're dismissing the charges, Amos."

"Good to know."

"Okay," said Childress. "Is she ready to talk yet?"

"Let's go see," said Decker.

They all trooped into the room. The beds were right next to each other, with Katz on the left and Gardiner on the right.

Gardiner had not regained consciousness. She looked like she was resting peacefully. Decker glanced at Katz. She was moaning slightly and seemed to be moving around a bit, as though she were in pain.

"Well?" said Childress sharply. He was pacing nervously around the room. "Is she going to talk, or did I get called down here for no reason?"

"The doctor's heading in momentarily," said Lancaster.

Childress kept pacing and shaking his head. He looked up at Decker. "I know the FBI's in town. Have they made any progress on this?"

"Not that I know of," said Decker. "The spy ring got flushed out but had exit plans in place, it seems."

"I understand that Brad Gardiner managed to slip away from you," said Childress, a note of gleeful triumph in his tone.

"He managed to slip away from a lot of people," said Lancaster defensively.

Childress glared at her. "I don't think Decker, of all people, needs anyone to stand up for him, Mary."

"I made a mistake," conceded Decker. "But in my defense, Mitzi Gardiner was shooting at me at the time."

This statement seemed to take all the fire out of Childress. "Yeah, I guess I would have probably lost him too under those circumstances." He looked at Lancaster. "Where's the doctor?"

A moment later a female physician dressed in blue scrubs walked in and greeted them.

Decker said, "How is she?"

"Ms. Katz is stable. And we're weaning her off the pain medication slowly. There was a great amount of internal damage done. More than we thought initially. She had a very close call." She glanced at the monitor next to Katz's bed. "I can't guarantee anything as far as her being communicative. But let me just make clear that her physical well-being is my chief concern. And if I see any adverse reaction in my patient, I will cut this off instantly. Understood?"

Childress didn't seem pleased by this but nodded and said gruffly, "Understood. Can we push forward, then? Because this is important."

The doctor went over to the machine hooked to the IV and manipulated some of the controls. A minute went by and nothing happened. Then Katz began to stir. Everyone drew closer when her eyes fluttered open, though they nearly instantly closed.

While the doctor was watching her closely, Katz opened her eyes once more and slowly looked around. When her gaze alighted on Mars she smiled tenderly.

"You...you saved..." Her voice trailed off and her eyes drooped.

Mars gripped her hand and smiled back. "You're getting better every day, Rachel. Doc says you're doing good. Real good."

Decker stepped forward to stand next to Mars. "Rachel, do you feel up to answering some questions?"

She looked up at him, her brow furrowed. "Questions?"

"Yes. Do you know what happened to you?"

Katz reached up and touched her shoulder. "Sh-shot."

"Yes. Someone tried to kill you."

"W-who?"

"We don't believe he has any personal connection to you. We think he was hired to try to kill you."

"I-I don't understand."

Mars gripped her hand again. "You were telling me about shades of truth, Rachel. Remember?"

She nodded slowly.

"Well, in this case I think shades of truth *will* set you free."

Decker said, "We found the room under the American Grill." He wanted to see her reaction to this, muddled as it might be because of the meds she was on.

She swallowed with difficulty and her eyes fluttered.

Natty came to stand next to Decker, with Childress next to him.

Natty said, "Ms. Katz. We know about Bill Peyton and Brad Gardiner. His wife is lying in the bed next to you. She almost died of a drug overdose."

Katz looked up at them one by one and her lips started to tremble. "M-Mitzi."

"Yes," said Childress. "Lots of people are dying around here, and, frankly, we need answers or others could die too."

Tears started to stream down Katz's face and she started to shake. An alarm on her monitor sounded.

The doctor immediately cranked her meds back up and Katz slowly slid back into unconsciousness as the alarm subsided.

"That's all for now."

"But we didn't get anything," protested Childress.

Natty put a hand on his boss's arm. "We'll come back. We'll get what we need. But she needs to rest now. Let her be."

Childress looked strangely at Natty, glanced at Decker with a hike of his eyebrows, and shrugged. "Fine. But we can't let this drag on."

"It won't," said Natty.

Decker looked at Natty for a long moment before glancing at Mars, who was still gripping Katz's hand and staring down at her. He used his finger to wipe the fresh tears away from her cheeks.

"It'll be okay, Melvin," he said quietly.

"You don't know that."

"No, I don't, but we can hope it will."

"Call me when she can talk again," said Childress brusquely. He turned and left.

Natty looked after him. "He's really afraid this is going to reflect badly on him. A spy ring operating right under his nose."

"I could see how that might give him some sleepless nights," remarked Decker.

Lancaster approached him. "So what now?"

He looked between Gardiner and Katz. Then his gaze went to the window and he suddenly turned thoughtful. He looked down at his feet, then back up. "The answer's out there," he said. "We just have to keep looking."

Lancaster said, "Where? We've got everything covered that we can. But you and I know that Peyton and Gardiner and their team of spies could be out of the country by now, especially if they had access to a private jet."

"Doesn't matter. I think we can still find the answers we need."

"How?" asked Natty.

Decker glanced at him. "You just never know when a helpful witness might pop up."

"What witness?" said Natty.

Decker headed to the door. "Let's see if I can show you. But first, we have to take care of something. And take care of it right now."

75

THE UNIFORMED MAN WALKED up the steps to the top floor of a building across the street from Burlington's main hospital. He carried a sniper rifle and took up a post at a window looking out onto the street. He glanced to his right and then his left. He blended in with the counter-snipers in the area.

He manipulated his scope, and drew his sightline.

He made sure to keep to the shadows as he pointed his weapon at the window opposite his position. In his mind he envisioned the space behind the closed blinds and worked some numbers into his shot calculations.

He recalibrated his scope and then took aim once more. His trajectory calculations complete, his finger slid to the trigger. He would fire three shots, in rapid succession.

He settled down his respiration and with it his heart rate. In truth, the distance was not a problem. However, he was, in some ways, firing blind. Yet he should still be able to hit his target.

His eye and grip as steady as humanly possible, he squeezed the trigger slowly three times, moving his barrel in a precise pattern as he did so.

Then he dropped his rifle and sprinted to the back of the building. From there, he quickly made his way down the stairs and out the exit. He rushed down the street to where a car was waiting for him.

He jerked open the door and climbed in.

"Hit it," he said.

When the car didn't move, he looked over.

Four guns were pointed at his head.

Special Agent Alex Jamison, who held one of those guns, said, "You're under arrest."

* * *

Decker looked at the shards of glass strewn around the hospital room—the empty hospital room, although earlier that day it had housed both Rachel Katz and Mitzi Gardiner. They had been moved to another room well away from here, at Decker's request.

He brushed the floor with his foot where the three shots had hit. They lined up with Katz's bed. The woman, had she still been in the room, would have been dead.

But there had been no shots aimed at Gardiner.

Lancaster stood in the doorway watching Decker. When he glanced over at her, she shook her head, her lips in a straight line. It was as disapproving a look as Decker had ever seen on his old partner.

"Old sins cast long shadows," murmured Decker.

Lancaster nodded as Special Agent Bogart appeared beside her. "It's still a bitter pill to swallow," she said.

"I feel the same," replied Decker. He glanced at Bogart and then returned his gaze to Lancaster. "You ready?"

"I'm ready."

They climbed into Bogart's rental and drove over to the police station. They took the elevator to the homicide detectives' office. Lancaster opened the door and poked her head in. Natty was the only one in there, reading over a file at his desk.

Lancaster said, "Blake, you got a minute?"

He glanced over at her. "Sure, what's up?"

"You'll see. But you need to come with us. Now."

Natty looked puzzled and apprehensive. He slipped on his jacket, which had been hanging on the back of his chair, and walked out into the hall, where he saw Decker and Bogart.

"What's going on?" he said, looking at Lancaster.

"Like I said, you'll see," she replied.

"One thing, Natty," said Decker.

"What?"

"I need your gun."

"What?" said Natty, drawing back and looking stunned.

Decker put out his hand. "Your gun?"

"I'm not—"

"Yes, you are," said Bogart. He had drawn his weapon and was pointing it at Natty.

"What the hell is going on?" barked Natty. "You're breaking the law pointing your weapon at me."

"The price of admission to the party is your gun, Natty," said Decker. "No exceptions."

Natty slowly pulled his Glock from his shoulder holster and handed it, butt first, over to Decker, who made sure the safety was engaged and then pocketed it.

"I don't know what the hell you guys are accusing me of," began Natty.

"Shut up, Blake," snapped Lancaster. "And follow us."

Along the way they picked up Captain Miller, who was also looking as stern as Decker had ever seen him.

"Captain?" began a worried-looking Natty.

But Miller held up his hand. "Not now, Natty."

They walked up one more flight of stairs and headed down the hallway to the end. Decker didn't knock. He just walked in.

Peter Childress looked up from his massive desk. Behind him on the wall were an array of photos of him with local politicians and at public events, together with a shelf full of citations and awards bestowed upon him over the years.

His brow furrowed as the group walked into his office. "What are you all doing here? Is there a development?"

"Yes, there is," said Decker. "Would you please stand up?"

"Excuse me?" said Childress.

"You know the drill, Pete," said Miller. "You have to stand up."

"What the hell for?"

Lancaster came forward and took out a pair of handcuffs. "Peter Childress, stand up. Now!"

"Where the fuck do you get off—"

Lancaster grabbed him by the suspenders and yanked him out of his chair.

"I'll have your badge, Lancaster!" he roared.

"I think you got that backwards," said Decker.

Lancaster roughly cuffed Childress's hands behind his back. "Peter Childress, you're under arrest for conspiracy to commit murder, conspiracy to commit espionage, conspiracy to commit money laundering, and about a hundred other charges, but those will do."

Childress froze.

Natty stood there staring at his boss, his jaw hanging open.

Childress roared, "You all are going to prison over this shit!"

Decker stood a step forward. "We've got the guy who tried to kill Rachel Katz."

"Tried!" said Childress before catching himself. "Wh-what are you talking about?"

"I had them transferred into another room, right after we met there this morning," said Decker. "They're safe."

"Transferred? Nobody asked for my approval on that."

"Well, there was obviously a good reason for that."

"Look, I don't know what you're getting—"

He stopped when Decker started pacing around the room.

Decker counted his steps as he went. "We're about the same height, you and me, Pete. Same length of stride. Six paces over from the wall to the end of Katz's bed. Then two paces more to reach her chest."

Decker glanced at Natty, who was watching him, spellbound. "You remember him pacing like that this morning, Natty?"

The detective slowly nodded.

"He was measuring the distance from the wall to the bed, so he could feed it to the shooter. Otherwise, he'd have been shooting truly blind into that room."

"Bullshit! Prove it!" roared Childress.

In answer, Decker looked at Bogart.

The FBI agent took out his phone. "We got a warrant to tap your phone." He held up his phone. "You sent this text out thirty minutes after you left the hospital. It gives out the measurements to target the woman."

"And your guy was good," said Decker. "All three shots hit where they were supposed to."

"I don't know what 'guy' you're talking about."

Bogart said, "Well, that's funny, because the *guy* we just arrested for the attempted murders had your text on his phone. He's already talked to us, Childress, and he's already fingered you. Your ass is cooked."

"I...I," stammered Childress.

"But why not target Gardiner?" asked Decker. "Why just Katz?"

Childress shook his head and said nothing.

"Okay, did you tell Eric Tyson where Sally would be, Childress?" asked Decker. "When you arranged for *her* to be shot? Or did you just have her followed?"

The blood drained from Childress's face. He stole a glance at a stunned Natty.

"Look, Natty," began Childress. "It's...it's not like that. I..."

"You fuckin' prick!" screamed Natty. His hand went to his holster, but his gun wasn't there. He launched himself at Childress and managed to land a shot to the man's gut, doubling him over, before Decker, who had been slow to respond to the man's attack for some reason, grabbed him and pulled him away.

"Why?" screamed Natty. "What the hell did Sally ever do to you?"

"He used her, Natty," said Decker. "Like I suggested to you before. He forced her to impersonate Susan Richards, probably by threatening to tell your wife about your relationship. Then he got scared when he found out Sally was helping me. When she came out of the park with me, he had her shot."

Childress slowly straightened up, still gasping for air.

Miller stepped forward. "Not in all my forty years behind a badge have I seen anything like this. You're a disgrace, Childress."

"But you can make amends," said Decker. "By helping us."

Childress slowly shook his head. "This is a lot bigger than you think, Decker."

"All the more reason to stop it."

Childress said to Lancaster, "I want protection inside. I mean it."

"What are you scared of, Childress?" asked Lancaster.

"You all should be scared," said Childress. "Every last one of you."

76

As CHILDRESS WAS LED AWAY, Bogart said, "He might be right about that."

"Why?" asked Lancaster.

"We got back a report on those fingerprints you took of Bill Peyton."

"We couldn't find anything on him in the databases we had access to," said Lancaster.

"Well, we have access to a few more. Including some international ones, actually. And not the typical ones. But it was still very difficult for us, and that's what took so long. We actually had to turn to our friends at Mossad to score this information."

"The Israelis?" said Decker. "So I take it his name isn't Bill Peyton?"

"Not even close. His real name is Yuri Egorshin. And the general physical description given by the Israelis matches what you told us about Peyton."

"Let me guess—Russian," said Decker dryly.

"He was actually born in East Germany when the Wall was still up but came to the United States for college under a special program in place at the time. He went to Ohio State, same as you, Decker."

"How does that make sense?" asked Lancaster. "That a guy from that part of the world can just come here like that and go to school?"

"Well, he didn't come in announcing himself as a spy, and maybe then he wasn't technically one. He was a student with all the proper credentials and visas. And it showed him coming in from *West* Germany, not East Germany. Don't know how they managed that, but they did. He graduated and returned home. Sometime after that is when we believe he became associated with the KGB, or at least Mossad believes that."

"No, he was probably recruited by them before he came here for school, just so he could spy on us," said Jamison.

"That may be. Anyway, after the Wall came down, he officially became part of the FSB, the KGB's successor. He apparently worked very closely with a lot of the upper-echelon players there. Then he vanished. So, for the last twenty-odd years, no one knew where he was."

Decker said, "Well, he ended up in Burlington running a restaurant, and has for the last fifteen years. That would tie in with a Russian oligarch bankrolling Rachel Katz."

Lancaster said, "He didn't sound Russian when we met with him. He seemed pretty American to me. Whatever that means," she added.

"That's the point," said Decker. "They don't all sound like villains from James Bond films. They're supposed to blend in and seem just like everyone else. And his time in the U.S. allowed him to do that. It made him very valuable."

Bogart said, "It's more than that, actually. We dug deeper and found out that Egorshin's mother, interestingly enough, was American. She was a defector after World War II. She sought asylum in Moscow and married a Russian, Anatoly Egorshin. He was an officer in the Russian army during World War II and afterward worked for the Soviet regime in East Germany."

"Like father, like son. And his mother could have taught him American ways and speech then," said Decker. "And that probably helped him adapt when he came here for college, and also when he returned to Burlington to operate the spy ring."

"I'm sure all of that made him even more valuable to the Soviets, and then the Russians," added Bogart.

"Have we made any progress on all the people they've placed over the years?" asked Lancaster.

"It's complicated. There were no records of those people at the Grill, just the ones they were still 'processing.' And they've all vanished, as have the kitchen staff. We'll interview the other wait staff who weren't part of the operation. They may be able to tell us something that will help us track them down. And we do have an opportunity, though, in that Gardiner placed a lot of these people. We're going to reach out to as many places as we can to determine if they hired any of his recruits."

"If they're still there," said Decker. "They may have all made a run for it."

"That could be. If so, at least we're rid of them, which is something. But we'll reverse engineer this thing as best we can. Even if we can't locate these folks, we can at least assess the damage they might have done at their jobs and try to turn that around."

"It's a long shot, but it's all we have right now," conceded Decker.

Natty said to Decker, "Now I know why you took my gun. I would've shot the sonofabitch."

"I know." Decker took out Natty's pistol and handed it back to him.

"Why would Childress have done this?" asked Natty.

"Why else? Money. I think when we dig into his finances, we'll find some secret accounts flush with cash."

"Do you think Childress has been working with them all this time?" asked Lancaster.

"Think back thirteen years ago, Mary."

"Okay, the four murders."

"We were newly minted homicide detectives."

"Right."

"So brand-new detectives were sent out on a four-person murder scene with no seasoned detective to head up the investigation."

She glanced at Natty. "That's right. There were more senior detectives available to investigate the case. Including you, Blake."

Decker said, "I looked back through the records from that night. You want to guess who assigned us to that case?"

Miller said disgustedly, "Childress, when he was heading up the detective division."

"That's right. He wanted inexperienced people on that case who would jump all over the forensic evidence that had been planted and never look anywhere else."

Decker glanced at Natty. "You might have seen what we didn't see back then, Natty."

"Maybe, maybe not. But I wouldn't have figured it out all these years later, I can tell you that. Not like you did."

"Well, hindsight is twenty-twenty. And I didn't figure it out in time to save Meryl Hawkins."

Bogart said, "We'll keep looking for Egorshin and Gardiner and the rest. In the meantime, you all have to be on your top guard. From everything we know so far, you blew up a substantial spy ring operating in this country. The odds are these people will hightail it out of the country to live to fight another day."

Decker said, "But there's always a chance that they're going to hang back and exact their revenge. That's sort of a very KGB thing to do."

"Exactly," said Bogart. "In fact, there's no reason for you to stay around, Decker."

"No, there's unfinished business I have to take care of."

"Like what?" asked Bogart.

"Meryl Hawkins."

"You can't bring him back to life."

"No, but I can do the next best thing."

Both men stirred when her eyes fluttered open.

Decker and Mars were sitting next to Rachel Katz's bed in a hospital room that had no windows, for obvious reasons. Mitzi Gardiner had been moved to another windowless room, which was also heavily protected by both local police and FBI agents. They were taking no chances now.

Mars stood and took her hand. "Hey, how do you feel?" he asked.

She slowly nodded and managed a weak smile. "Better." She glanced at Decker and her expression grew solemn. "How much do you know?" she asked cautiously.

"Well, Bill Peyton is really a Russian named Yuri Egorshin, and Brad Gardiner has been placing Egorshin's spies all over the country for years now from an operation initiated at the American Grill. And we also know about the secret room underneath your restaurant where they create fake identities, backgrounds, and maybe even faces for these folks. Other than that, not much."

Katz put a hand to her face and groaned. She finally withdrew her hand and looked at the lines and tubes running over her body.

"Am I going to recover?"

"Yes, you are," said Mars. "We were just waiting for you to fully wake up."

Her mouth quivered. "I don't know what to say."

"I'll take a *shade* of the truth," said Decker. "Unless you want to tell us the whole thing."

"Can you lift my head a bit?"

Mars hit the bed control to accomplish this.

After she was settled, Katz drew a long breath. "The first thing you have to understand is that when I married David, I knew about none of this. There's still a lot I don't know."

"He'd already opened the Grill before you met," said Decker.

"Yes. And our life was good. We had the restaurant and I had my business. And he was already working on other projects. Everything was aboveboard, at least as far as I knew."

"And then the meeting with Don Richards?"

"And he was dead." Katz started to weep.

Mars handed her a tissue, which she used to dab at her eyes.

"I was devastated. It hit me out of the blue. I couldn't fathom why someone would want to kill him."

"But then?" said Decker expectantly.

"But then I was thinking of selling the Grill. I was tired of Burlington and the memory of what had happened to David. I just wanted to start over fresh."

"And something happened to make you change your mind?"

"It was Bill Peyton or this Yuri person. I had told him I was thinking of selling out. He didn't tell me a lot, but what he did tell me was stunning. He said that David was a criminal. A member of an organization that had done terrible things. And that his death was a result of that membership. He had apparently done something to anger them. They had found out and made the decision to kill him."

"Why kill the Richards family?"

"I don't know. Peyton never told me."

"Why didn't you go to the police?" asked Decker.

"Because Peyton told me that the other members of this organization were still very much around. And that if I wanted to stay alive, I would do exactly as they told me to do. They even threatened to harm my parents in Wisconsin. And my sister in California. They knew where they lived and everything."

"What did they want you to do?"

"Most importantly, I was never to sell the Grill. They wanted to keep it running for some reason."

"As I said, they were operating a spy ring in a secret room under the restaurant," said Decker.

"I didn't know that," said Katz, putting her hands over her face. "After David died, I never really went there."

"What else?"

"They told me that they would fund other business ventures. They allowed me to pick the projects and they provided the money. I assumed they did something similar for David."

"They were laundering money," said Decker. "Probably dirty oligarch money."

Katz slowly nodded. "I thought it might be something like that."

"Did you meet with anyone other than Bill Peyton on these matters?"

"Yes, there were other men. Very hard-looking men. We never met in Burlington. They flew me to Chicago. We'd meet there."

Mars said, "I wonder why they just didn't buy the Grill from you and keep doing what they were doing. They wouldn't have had to explain anything to you."

"I wondered about that too," said Katz. "But from some of the things they said, they liked, well, legitimate people fronting what they were doing. If you buy a business, there are always questions and inspections and there are ways for things to go wrong. They had set up a relationship with my husband and they wanted to keep it going exactly the same. That was clear from my discussions with them. Only now it was me, not David."

"What about Mitzi Gardiner?"

Katz looked puzzled. "That was the very odd thing. They wanted me to help her. She was a drug addict. But they paid for her rehab, and when she came out of that, they paid for a complete change in her appearance, education, clothes, plastic surgery, everything. They had me become her mentor. Teach her how to conduct herself, work in business, give her contacts. Just help mold her."

Mars looked at Decker. "Why would they do that?"

"She provided the patsy for the murders, her father."

"I get that," said Mars. "But why not just kill her? We talked about this before. And I don't buy the explanation that they were worried about the police digging deeper. Hell, she was a drug addict. They could have just made her OD and no one would have thought that she was murdered."

"That's a good question that I don't have the answer to. Yet."

"I didn't know that Hawkins was innocent," said Katz. "After Peyton met with me, I thought he'd been hired to kill David and the others."

"Didn't you have a problem with helping the daughter of the man who you believed had killed your husband?" asked Decker.

"I did, at first. But she had done nothing wrong. At least that I knew. And she was so, I don't know, fragile. And lost. I guess I just ended up wanting to help her. Making something good come from something so awful." She paused and clutched the sheets with her hand. "I guess I should have gone to the police, but I was just so scared. As time went by, I just convinced myself that it was...that it was legitimate somehow. I was just building up my businesses and living a nice life." She paused again. "But that was just me lying to myself. It's another reason I never remarried. How could I ever trust someone after what happened with David?"

"Well, considering that a prominent policeman was involved with Egorshin and his gang, you were probably wise not to go to the police," noted Decker.

"What...what will happen to me?" she said fearfully.

"I don't know."

Mars said, "Hey, Decker, like she said, she was terrified. They threatened her. She didn't know that they were spies."

"I get that, Melvin. I really do. But that part is out of my hands." He turned his attention back to Katz. "But your cooperating with the FBI will only act in your favor. You might not spend any time in prison." He paused. "In fact, I think it far more likely that you end up in witness protection. These people have long memories and assets in the most unlikely places. And they have no problem killing anyone in their way. They tried to kill you again while you were in the hospital."

"Oh my God!" Katz drew a long breath and squeezed Mars's hand. "A part of me, a big part of me, is so glad that all this is finally out in the open. It's actually such a relief. It was tearing me apart."

Mars nodded. "Speaking for someone who's seen a lot of decep- · tion in his life, I can understand that. The truth is always better. Even if it really hurts."

She glanced nervously at Decker. "Witness protection?"

"It's better than prison."

"Yeah," agreed Mars. "Just about anything is."

She looked at him curiously. "You sound like you speak from experience."

"What better place is there to speak from?" replied Mars.

DECKER AND THE HOUSE.

Again.

Where he'd found the bodies of his family. He couldn't seem to stay away, even with everything else going on. It was a magnet and he was a chunk of metal.

His phone dinged. It was from the ME. As he read down the email, he learned that more sophisticated tests had been performed on the DNA found under Abigail's fingernails. The results were shocking. It was confirmed that an additional set of DNA had been found under the nails, meaning a third party *was* involved. But they conclusively ruled out that party being a blood relation to Meryl Hawkins.

So that leaves out Mitzi Gardiner. So who then? Who's left?

As he sat in his car absorbing this, he suddenly pulled his gun and pointed it at the passenger window. At the figure who had appeared there. Then he lowered his weapon and unlocked the door.

Jamison climbed in and looked at him.

"Didn't mean to startle you," she said.

"Sure you did," he groused. "But I could have shot you."

"I have faith in your judgment, at least most times," she replied, drawing a sharp glance from him.

He resettled his gaze on the house, even as his hands played nervously over the steering wheel.

"I guess you're wondering what I'm doing here?" she asked.

"No, I'm just assuming that you thought you'd find me here when you went to the Residence Inn and I wasn't there."

"Well, you'd be wrong."

He glanced at her again.

"I was here *before* you." She pointed down the street. "My car's right over there. I saw you drive in. And I'm not alone."

Another figure appeared at the driver's-side window and tapped on the glass.

An annoyed Decker unlocked the doors once more and Mars climbed into the backseat.

"So you were spying on me?" Decker said angrily.

"How could we be, when we got here first?" said Mars. "I just wanted to see your old home, Decker. It's nice."

Decker gazed out the window. "It *was* nice," he said quietly. "The first and probably only home I'll ever have."

"Don't be too sure about that," said Mars. "Life throws you curveballs, you and I both know that."

Decker glanced in the mirror at him. "And your point?"

"Never say never. You just don't know. My future was death row. You think I ever thought I'd be here, today?"

"You were an unusual case, Melvin."

Jamison snorted. "And you're not?"

Decker fell silent and shifted his gaze to the house again.

It was late, but there was a light on in the upstairs on the left. That had been Molly's bedroom. He supposed it might be the Hendersons' little girl's room now. He didn't know why her light was on at this hour; maybe she was sick and her mother was tending to her.

He closed his eyes when powerful images and lights started to bombard him, like before. Their deaths spilling over him, threatening to bury him. He began to shake.

"Decker, you okay?" said a voice.

He felt something grip his arm and his shoulder. He opened his eyes to see Jamison's hand on his arm, and Mars clenching his shoulder. Jamison was looking at him anxiously. Mars the same.

He blinked rapidly, and, thankfully, the images vanished.

"I've been having...some issues."

"What kind?" asked Jamison.

He drew a long breath. "The memories of finding my family dead have started to just empty out of my head, over and over, the colors, the images, the..." He rubbed his temples. "I don't know when it will happen, and I can't seem to make it stop."

"But it has stopped now, right?" asked Mars while Jamison looked on with a horrified expression.

Decker glanced at her but then quickly looked away after seeing her tortured features. "For now."

"When has it happened?" asked Jamison quietly.

"Once when I was in my room." He glanced at Mars. "When you fell asleep in my room. I barely made it to the toilet. Then I went outside in the rain. I thought...I thought I was really losing it. Then, other times." He thumped the side of his head painfully.

"Had it happened to you before you came back to town this time?" asked Jamison.

"I know what you're going to say, Alex. I know I can't live in the past."

"Knowing is one thing. Doing something about it is another."

Decker didn't respond.

"What makes you come back here, Amos?" asked Mars. "I mean, Burlington, I get. But why come back to the house where it happened?"

In his mind's eye, Decker saw himself climbing, bone-tired, out of his car after an exhausting shift at work. It was nearly midnight. He was supposed to have been home hours before. But he had decided a case he was working on might get a breakthrough if he put some more time into it. He had called Cassie and told her. She hadn't been happy about it, because they were supposed to go to dinner with her brother, who was in town staying with them. But she told him she understood. She told him she knew his casework was very important to him.

My damn casework.

And then she told him that they would just go out to dinner the next night. Her brother was staying over, so they'd have another opportunity.

Another opportunity that never came to be.

Those were the last words that Decker had ever spoken to his wife. He had gone into the house with the intention of slipping into bed without waking her, and then taking her, Molly, and his brother-in-law out to breakfast the next morning. As a surprise, to make up for that night.

And then he had walked into his home and entered a nightmare.

His life had never been the same. Not in any conceivable way.

And the bottom line was clear to him.

I was not there when my family really needed me. I failed them. I failed myself. And I don't know if I can live with that.

"Decker?" prompted Mars.

"I guess I keep coming back here," began Decker. "To imagine how it could have been...different."

The light in the upstairs bedroom winked out. For some reason that made Decker withdraw even further into whatever hole he had mentally dug for himself.

His head was throbbing. It was like his brain was melting.

Something tapped on the window.

"Who the hell else did you bring?" snapped Decker.

He glanced at Jamison, who sat rigid in her seat. He eyed Mars in the mirror. He was sitting exactly the same way as Jamison.

Decker slowly turned to his left.

And saw the figure there.

And the gun pointed at his head.

He looked to his right and saw a figure and a gun at the passenger window.

Two others were at the two rear doors.

The driver's-side door was wrenched open and something struck him so hard on the back of the head that it drove his face into the steering wheel.

And that was the last thing he remembered.

79

WHEN DECKER CAME TO, he had a vision of something that felt familiar. When he opened his eyes fully and looked around, he understood why.

He was in the Richardses' old home, sitting on the floor.

In the kitchen, where Don Richards and David Katz had died.

He felt the zip ties around his wrists and ankles.

He looked next to him and saw Jamison and Mars similarly bound. They were staring across at the doorway where a man was standing.

Bill Peyton, or more correctly, Yuri Egorshin, did not seem like a happy man.

There were three other men in the room. They all looked tough, hardened, chips of iron with guns in their hands. Decker didn't recognize any of them from the American Grill. To him, they all looked like muscle. Russian muscle, which was pretty damn intimidating.

Egorshin pulled up a chair and sat down opposite the three bound people.

"You have royally messed up my work, Decker," he said quietly. "I hope you realize that."

"Well, it's sort of my job."

"If the optics weren't so bad and other…conditions not so adverse to me, I could probably beat your bullshit search at the Grill. You found all that stuff without a warrant. None of it would be admissible."

"Yeah, but the whole Russian spy thing? I'm not sure the Fourth Amendment really applies to protect people like you."

"And there we have the limits of the democracy you Americans tout so fiercely."

Decker glanced out the window into the darkness. "I'm surprised that you would bring us here."

"What? You mean witnesses? Are you concerned the DeAngelos might have seen us?" Egorshin stopped and his lips set in a firm line. "You don't have to worry about them. Whatever they might have seen, they will be able to tell no one about."

"You didn't have to do that," said Decker grimly, his features turning angry.

"Do you know what Mr. DeAngelo told me right before I put a bullet in his head?"

Decker said nothing.

"He told me that all he wanted to do was retire down south. I saved him the expense. And I needed…privacy, to deal with you and your friends."

Decker felt sick to his stomach about the fate of the DeAngelos. He said, "You've wasted a lot of time hanging around here. You could be gone from the country. Now it's too late. It's death penalty time for you."

"Please don't worry about me. I'm well provided for. I have assets in places you couldn't even imagine."

"I don't know, my imagination is pretty good. And if you're thinking about Peter Childress, you better have other assets."

"This does not concern me in the least."

"Why's that?"

"For the same reasons that the DeAngelos do not concern me."

Jamison blurted out, "You had Childress killed?"

Egorshin looked at his watch. "With confirmation twenty minutes ago. No, the assets of which I speak go far higher than a police superintendent in a nothing place like this."

"What do you want with us?"

"After every intelligence operation there must be a debriefing." Egorshin spread his hands wide. "So this, this is my debriefing."

"We're not going to tell you anything," barked Jamison.

"I cannot tell *you* how many times I have heard that over the course of my career." He held out a hand. One of his men pulled something from his jacket and handed it to Egorshin. It looked like a metal billy club.

Egorshin slid a lever on the side of the club, leaned over, and tapped Mars with the end of it. Mars instantly cried out as volts of electricity shot through him. He slumped over to the side, his breathing ragged.

"Melvin!" screamed Jamison. She tried to reach out to him, but merely fell onto her side. With a nod from Egorshin, she was pulled up and slammed back against the wall.

Decker had never once taken his gaze off the Russian. "What sort of information?"

"How much you know. Your forward-looking plans. Anything at all that would be helpful to me."

"And then you'll what, just let us go?"

"No. I will not lie to you about that, because I would not want someone to make false promises to me in such a situation. What I offer you, in exchange for your information, is this." He slipped a pistol from his jacket pocket and tapped the muzzle. "One bullet to each of your brains. You will feel nothing, I promise."

"Yeah, painless, instant death. I've heard that before. It still doesn't appeal to me."

"The information?" said Egorshin. "Or shall I give your friend another zap?" He held out the electric prod.

Decker said, "We now know pretty much everything. Rachel Katz has given her statement implicating you. We have all the information from the underground room. We've raided Brad Gardiner's office."

"And found nothing since there is nothing there."

"Well, there are other avenues of pursuit. We know you've planted spies all around the country."

Egorshin ominously took out a muzzle suppressor and spun it onto the barrel of his pistol. "What else?"

"Mitzi Gardiner will fill in the rest."

"Doubtful. Where is she?"

"Still at the hospital, under heavy guard."

"You miss my point."

Decker looked at him thoughtfully. "You didn't try to kill her at the hospital. And I wonder why you even kept her alive all these years."

Egorshin looked at one of his men and pointed to the doorway leading into the kitchen. The man left and came back a few moments later with Brad Gardiner. His hands were bound behind him and he looked disheveled and exhausted.

Decker glanced up at him. "You hung around too. Pretty stupid."

"Well, it wasn't his choice," said Egorshin. "It was mine."

"Is his name even Brad Gardiner?" said Jamison. "Or is he Russian, like you?"

Egorshin rose. "No, he's American. Like David Katz. They were in it just for the money. A lot of money. Americans love their money."

Jamison said, "Katz didn't make much money before being killed. He just owned the American Grill. Hardly an empire."

Egorshin shook his head wearily. "Where do you think he got the money to start his career? This was before he even moved here. His Mercedes and his expensive clothes and his investment portfolio worth millions and the down payment for the Grill and the various lines of credit? And how they were paid off so quickly? Katz was a marginal talent who didn't want to work too hard for his fortune."

"How did you two meet up?" asked Decker.

"Doesn't matter. In much the same way I met up with this one," he said, motioning to Gardiner. "A necessary though distasteful part of my job."

Gardiner wouldn't look at any of them. His gaze remained downcast. He was visibly trembling.

Jamison eyed Gardiner. "So you sold out your country for money. That makes you a traitor."

"And traitors deserve to be executed," said Egorshin.

Before anyone could react, the Russian placed the pistol against Gardiner's temple and pulled the trigger.

The bullet blew through the man's head and the slug plowed into the far wall of the kitchen. Brad Gardiner fell where he had stood a moment before.

80

THEY ALL STARED at the body lying on the floor of the kitchen.

"Damn," exclaimed Mars, who had recovered from the cattle prod shock and had sat up, his back flat against the wall.

Decker looked up at Egorshin. "Why kill him?"

"It reduces complications for me."

"Okay. Why a restaurant, of all things?"

"What better way to become 'Americanized'? Interacting with the customers, you learn everything: slang, dialect, mannerisms, pop culture, sports. Americans love their sports. French fries! Social media etiquette. Simply becoming Americans. Back in Russia, it would have taken us years to accomplish what I was able to have my operatives do in a few months. It was simple, but most brilliant things have an underlying simplicity."

"And the underground room?"

"Well, we couldn't exactly do up in the restaurant what was required."

"We saw the operating room."

Egorshin waved his hand dismissively. "Some of my superiors still dwelled in the Cold War days. We rarely used it. Instead, we simply recruited from our assets those who already looked westernized."

"It took us a while to figure out where the entrance was."

"May I ask how you did so?"

"Space dimensions were off compared to the area outside the kitchen."

Egorshin wagged his finger at Decker. "One of my men at the

restaurant reported that you seemed overly interested in speaking with one of the wait staff. You were clearly a man to watch."

"And to attempt to kill?" said Decker. "On the way back from Mitzi's?"

"Forgive me, it is the usual way in which we deal with difficulties."

"Eric Tyson and Karl Stevens had KI tats on their arms."

"My father was privileged to work for the KI, and so we had some of our recruits get that tattoo. However, we hid it among many hate groups' symbols to throw off detection."

"Recruits?"

Egorshin held up his hand. "That goes beyond what I can say. It is a game, and you do the same to us. But let us never lose sight of the fact that it is a game with very real consequences." He glanced at Gardiner's body.

He sat back down and slipped the gun into his waistband.

Decker said, "One thing I don't get. Mitzi said her husband placed people in high-end jobs, in law, finance, high tech, government."

"And your point?"

"Even with the new identities and such, it would be difficult for your agents to survive a background check. You can create the right docs and all, paper the schools they went to, but the background check will go to where they attended school and lived, talk to old neighbors, relatives, teachers, coworkers, and all the rest."

"That is true. And that is why we approached it in a different way."

"How?"

"First of all, Mitzi had no idea what her husband really did. She only told you what she had been told. As a matter of fact, he did *not* place our people in these so-called high-end jobs. You're right, the scrutiny would have been rather intense."

"So what did you do then?"

Egorshin smiled. "'Low-end' jobs are much better sources for intelligence collection."

"What do you consider 'low-end' jobs?" asked Jamison.

"For example, chefs for wealthy people. Security guards at sensitive corporate facilities. You would be astonished how lacking they are in vetting their security forces. We would never do it that way in Russia. Americans outsource everything. And these companies cut costs. And background checks are expensive and take time. We deploy personal drivers for executives and former government officials. It is amazing how chatty they are in their cars, as though the driver is deaf. Flight attendants on private aircraft. Domestic help, cleaning crews, and nannies with your class of movers and shakers, particularly on both coasts. Personal assistants to these same people. IT personnel who gain access to passwords and clouds and the most sensitive data, and who are on-site listening to everything. Attendants of all ilk at high-end hotels, restaurants, spas, and private retreats. Again, Americans talk as though these peons do not exist. And these peons just soak it up. Indeed, I have been on your Acela train. I simply sit there and listen to people loudly talking on their phones: lawyers and corporate executives, journalists and television news presenters, and even your government officials, giving away the most critical data like it is nothing. In my country they would be shot. I turn my recorder on and sip my drink and it is so easy. That is why we have people who work there and also wherever sensitive information can be captured by seemingly insignificant people. America is one gigantic leaking balloon and it is truly wonderful."

Jamison glanced worriedly at Decker, who kept staring at Egorshin.

"The list of these types of occupations goes on and on. The opportunities for us are endless. My agents are well trained for all that they have to do. Their work credentials are authentic. Then they just have to do their jobs and the information flows nonstop. We will bury your country without firing a shot or launching one missile. We won't have to, because you are simply defeating yourself by your own stupid carelessness. And we will be there to step in as the victor."

Jamison said, "I thought all of your spying was done in the cyber world now. Hacks and bot armies to sway public opinion."

Egorshin shrugged. "Cyber warfare certainly has its place. And it has worked well for my country against the United States and others. But while bot armies and hacking and message multiplication and the spread of false stories are effective, there is, in my opinion, no substitute for boots on the ground, what you call human intelligence. People gathering information directly from the source. Humans can deceive in infinitely flexible, subtle ways that you cannot duplicate by writing lines of code."

"I guess I can see that," conceded Jamison.

"Now tell me about Mitzi," said Egorshin.

"Why?" asked Decker.

"I have an interest. What will happen to her?"

"No telling yet. Depends on her degree of guilt."

"She may have no guilt at all."

"We believe that she set up her father."

"No, she didn't."

"How can you possibly know that?" asked Jamison.

Decker was staring strangely at Egorshin but remained quiet. He closed his eyes, and in the depths of his memory he reread his most recent email from the medical examiner.

No familial ties to Meryl Hawkins.

Decker opened his eyes and refocused on Egorshin. "I'll give you a little more debriefing. I just found out that the DNA under Abigail Richards's nails was contaminated with a third party's DNA. I thought it was Mitzi Gardiner. But the test showed the third party was unrelated to Meryl Hawkins."

"So the person was not Mitzi," said Jamison.

Decker didn't seem to hear her. He kept his gaze on the Russian. "You know, I always wondered about the name."

"Peyton is a typical American surname."

"No, not your fake name. Mitzi's *real* name."

"Why wonder about that?" said Egorshin, his features tightening a bit.

"I looked it up a while back because it's unusual for an American. Mitzi is a nickname that Germans give daughters who are named Maria. *You* were born in Germany."

Egorshin shook his head. "My father was Russian. Egorshin is not German. And East Germany was far more like Russia than West Germany."

"Maybe your father was Russian, but you and your family still lived in East Germany. And your mother was American."

"I see you have done your homework. But what is your point? Mitzi Gardiner is not German. She was born here."

"Yes, she was. And you're sixty-two years old. While Mitzi is forty."

"Decker," said Mars. "What are you getting at?"

Decker kept his focus on Egorshin. "Mitzi's mom worked in the cafeteria at Ohio State while you were a student there. At age twenty-two you would have probably been in your senior year. She was a few years older than you."

Egorshin eased back in his seat.

Jamison's jaw lowered. "Wait a minute. Are you saying?"

Decker said, "It *was* Mitzi's DNA under those nails, but it wouldn't show that she was Meryl's daughter, because she wasn't. *You're* her father. You got Lisa pregnant in college. Did she have the baby when you were still there?"

"Damn," muttered Mars.

Egorshin said in a subdued tone, "The day after she was born, I was recalled to my country."

"So you just left, without a word?"

"I loved Lisa. I...wanted to be with her. Raise the child. We named her after my paternal grandmother, Maria. But I told Lisa about the name Mitzi."

"Well, it seems to have stuck around. More than you did."

"I could not stay. It was impossible."

"So, she met Meryl, they got married. He adopted Mitzi. They probably never told her about it, she just thought Meryl was her real father, and they moved eventually to Burlington." Decker paused. "And that's why you chose *this* town for your operation when the time came."

Egorshin looked at his men and then stood and paced. "I wanted...to see what had become of her. When I arrived here to do my...work, she was..."

"A drug addict."

"It was terrible to think that she was that way. And my dear Lisa."

"Had cancer."

"Yes. There was no hope."

"What did you do then?"

"I arranged to meet Mitzi through someone."

"Her dealer, Karl Stevens?"

"Yes. I told her that I had known her mother a long time ago and I wanted to help them. I got her mother medicine and gave it to Mitzi."

"But you also set her father up for murder, with her help."

Egorshin suddenly stopped pacing and roared, "He was not her father! *I* was!"

This outburst didn't faze Decker. "You left, he didn't. He raised her. You didn't. He did his best to help her. You didn't. That's what I call a father."

Egorshin started to pace again, rubbing the back of his head in his anxiety.

Decker watched him. "You needed to get rid of David Katz. Why?"

"He was like this one," said Egorshin, motioning to the dead Gardiner. "Whatever we gave him was not enough."

"But why kill the Richardses?"

"You think we didn't have Donald Richards in our pocket too?"

"He was helping you launder funds through the bank and he wanted more?"

"It became untenable. So we acted."

"How did you get Mitzi to go along?"

He shrugged. "I told her things about Meryl that...that made her side with me. I told her I wanted to help her mother. Lisa died peacefully because of me."

"No, she died with the knowledge that her husband was an accused killer. I don't think that qualifies as peaceful."

"I don't care what you think, Decker."

"So everything was great. Until Meryl came back here to prove his innocence." Decker paused again. "And you went to the Residence Inn and you murdered a dying man."

"There was no other way."

"And you set up Susan Richards for the murder and she ends up a supposed suicide apparently from guilt. But you killed her too."

"These matters *had* to be dealt with."

"And I guess we're next."

Egorshin sat back down. "I will tell you this, Decker. There is one way for you to live. And only one. I want Mitzi. I want her to come with me."

Decker shook his head. "I don't see how that's possible. She's still unconscious in the hospital, surrounded by guards."

Egorshin pulled out his gun. "Then perhaps you should think very hard on it, unless you want me to shoot one of your friends. Which one? I'll let you pick."

When Decker said nothing, he pointed at Mars. "You, stand up."

"Wait," said Decker. "I'm the one you want. Take me out."

"No, Mr. Decker, I'm counting on you to solve my dilemma." He pointed at Mars. "Stand up. Now. Or I'll shoot you where you sit."

Mars glanced over at Decker and shook his head. "Man, this has R43 wide gap seal written all over it. I mean, shit."

Egorshin barked, "Get up. Now!"

"Okay, but I need some help. I *am* tied up."

Egorshin looked over at two of his men and nodded. The men went over to Mars, bent down, and each grabbed an arm.

As they began to lift Mars up and the bottoms of his shoes touched the floor, he exploded off his feet, headbutting the man on the right, cold-cocking him. Mars whirled and caught the other man right underneath the chin with his shoulder, slamming him into the wall. His head bounced off the hard surface, his eyes rolled back in his head, and he fell to the floor.

The moment that Mars launched into action, Decker had catapulted to his feet. Even with his feet bound, he squatted down and then leapt forward, slamming into a distracted Egorshin so hard that the FSB man was knocked completely off his feet. He soared backward, hit the sink, flipped over it, and crashed right through the window, the shattered glass ripping at him as he fell out of sight outside.

The remaining man aimed his gun at Decker and was about to pull the trigger when the sound of a shot pierced the room.

The man looked down at his chest and saw the red spot dead center there.

Decker and Mars stared over at Jamison. She had managed to roll forward, swing her legs between her wrists, grab one of the fallen men's guns, take aim and fire, all within the span of about three seconds.

The last man fell to his knees and then toppled forward.

Jamison searched one of the men, found a clasp knife, and used it to free herself and then Decker and Mars.

Decker snatched up a gun and raced toward the front door, even as he heard a car start up. He got to the front door in time to fire at the taillights of the car being driven by Egorshin. Within a few seconds, though, it was gone.

Jamison grabbed her phone from her pocket. She called Bogart and filled him in on what had just happened.

She clicked off. "He's sending a team over here. And he's put out a BOLO."

Decker was still staring off into the night. "I'm not sure that will be enough."

Mars gave her a hug. "Damn, Alex, that was some fancy footwork back there. And nice shooting, girl."

"Thanks. But what the hell was that R43 stuff you were talking about?"

Decker turned and looked at her. "R43 wide gap seal. It was the University of Texas's favorite run option when Melvin played for them. The right tackle helps the right guard by chipping the DT, and then he and the tight end seal off the defensive end while the wideout drives the cornerback to the sideline. At the same time, the tight end peels off from the DE and engages the strong safety. That left Melvin to go wide through the gap straight to a one-on-one with the outside linebacker."

"And that would be Mr. Buckeye Decker," said a grinning Mars.

Decker looked chagrined. "He scored three touchdowns in the game on that one play, and all three times he ran right over my butt."

"Hey, man, you did your best. And you guys played us hard. I got stopped quite a few times early on in that game. But when life gives you lemons, you know what you do?"

Jamison made a face and said, "Yeah, you make lemonade. Everybody knows that."

Mars shook his head. "No, Alex, you score *touchdowns*."

Jamison said, "So by calling out that play, you told Decker what you were going to do? Take out two guys. And then Decker figured out what he was going to do?"

"That's right."

"Maybe I should start watching football, just in case that ever comes in handy again with you two."

"Hey, what life tells you is, you just never know," said Mars.

"You just never know," repeated Decker, as he turned back around and stared out into the night.

81

Decker handed her another tissue and then sat back.

Mitzi Gardiner dabbed at her eyes as she sat there in her hospital bed. She had finally regained consciousness and the doctors expected her to make a full recovery.

Decker had told her some, but not all, of what had happened. But he had told her about her husband's death. And also about his participation in Egorshin's spy operation.

"I always wondered why a guy like Brad would have chosen someone like me," she said, sniffling.

"Don't sell yourself short."

"And I can't believe that this Bill Peyton was a Russian spy named, what was it again?"

"Egorshin. And that's sort of the point. To make it not obvious."

He had decided not to tell her that Egorshin was her real father, because Decker considered Meryl Hawkins to have earned that distinction. And he wasn't sure the fragile Mitzi could actually handle the truth.

"I guess." She tossed the tissue into the trash can next to her bed and looked at him. "That's not all, is it?"

"No, it's not."

"You're here for other reasons?"

"Yes."

"What happened to Rachel?"

"She's been charged, but can probably work a deal. Since we still haven't located Egorshin, her life is in danger. She might end up in witness protection once she tells the Feds all she knows."

"But won't he come after me too?"

"Doubtful. He seems to have liked you."

"He *did* help us. I remember he got painkillers for my mom, though I knew him as Bill Peyton. I still can't believe he was a Russian."

"Yeah, but he wasn't so kind to your father."

"He told me things about my dad. Not good things."

"And they were lies. He told me they were. He just wanted to get you on his side, Mitzi. That was all."

"But I believed him. And I helped send my father to prison."

"Did you know that they planned to frame him for murder?"

She shook her head. "Absolutely not. I had no idea. I didn't know what was going on really. I was so strung out back then."

"They probably wanted to keep you in the dark, because they couldn't count on your not telling someone. But after he was charged? And then convicted?"

"I didn't know what to think. Part of me thought he was guilty."

"I think he figured out, at least partly, your complicity. But he wasn't going to do anything to implicate you in the deaths. So he just kept quiet and went to prison. It was only after he ran into Karl Stevens that his mind changed. He was dying, after all, and what Stevens told him about your involvement and the people behind it probably didn't sit well with him. So he came back here to clear his name."

"I can't say I blame him." She lay back and closed her eyes. "I'm so tired." Then she snapped forward. "Oh my God, my son, where is—"

"He's fine. He's with child services. He knows nothing about any of this, though."

"I...I can't believe I just thought of him."

And the woman did look truly stunned at her thoughtlessness, Decker observed.

"Well, you just came out of a drug coma. You can't be thinking too clearly."

"You're being too kind, Decker." She hesitated. "But I get the feeling that's about to change."

He stood and looked down at her. "Do you know how many people go through life without a second chance to get it right?"

"I...what do you mean exactly?"

"You messed up, Mitzi. You helped frame your father. He suffered greatly for that. He went to prison, where terrible things happened to him."

"I know all that. I was...I was out of my mind on drugs, Decker."

"And now you're not. You're clean and sober and hopefully thinking clearly."

"What do you want me to do?" she said warily.

"How about the right thing."

"And what is that precisely?"

"You go into court and you make a statement, clearing your father, returning him his good name, and accepting responsibility for what you did."

"And then I go to prison? That's what you're asking me to do, isn't it?"

"Well, I think I have the right to ask, considering you did your best to blow my head off back at your house."

"I...I can't go to prison. My son will have nobody."

"Maybe you won't have to."

"How?" she said pleadingly.

"This is not a typical case. I might be able to get the authorities to make a deal. You tell us what really happened, your father's reputation is restored, and you go on with your life."

"Do you really think that's possible?"

"Anything is possible. But aside from the obvious benefits to you, I think there might be something else positive in that scenario for you."

"What?"

"You've been living all these years with guilt, Mitzi. Whether you know it or not. And that does something to you. It changes you. It makes you become someone maybe you don't want to be but can do nothing to stop. Even with all the money in the world. It tears away at you little by little."

She clutched at her sheet and glanced up at him. "You...you sound like that might have happened to you."

"There was no *might* about it. I wasn't there for my family when they needed me. Because of that, they died. I'm never going to see my wife and my daughter again, and I guess I've always accepted that as my penance." Decker drew a long breath. "But that's no way to live, Mitzi. Trust me."

Tears were sliding down the woman's cheeks. She reached out and clutched his hand. Not too long ago, Decker would have flinched from this contact.

Yet when Melvin Mars had put his arm around him when Decker had been at one of his lowest points here, and then Mary Lancaster had gripped his hand in the car, just wanting the comforting embrace of another human when she had felt so scared, something had happened to Amos Decker.

And it was a good thing. Because despite all the unsettling things that his mind had been doing while he was here, the ability to be hugged or have your hand clenched by another without flinching, that simple act, which just about everyone else took for granted, had brought Decker a bit closer to the person he had once been. Before he had died on a football field and woken up as someone else entirely.

So, Decker reached out his other hand and closed it over Mitzi's.

"Will you do that, Mitzi? Will you take that step? Will you right the things you can? And finally free yourself of the guilt?"

An uncomfortably long moment passed until she spoke.

"Yes. I will."

Bogart said, "Apparently, in addition to meddling in our democratic process, Moscow is also trying to recruit the more marginalized among us and turn them into foot soldiers on our home turf, in the hopes of breeding even more division and unrest."

He, Mars, Jamison, and Decker were having dinner at Suds.

"So Eric Tyson and Karl Stevens were part of that pack?" asked Jamison.

"Right."

Decker finished his last French fry while sneaking a glance at a disapproving-looking Jamison. Then she suddenly brightened and said, "Okay, you earned your junk food quota for today. But tomorrow is another story."

Bogart said, "They found Childress in his cell, dead. It was his food. Some type of industrial chemical poison. The Russians are really good at that. They must have had more assets in the police department than just Childress. Captain Miller is currently looking into that."

"Any word on Egorshin?" asked Mars.

He shook his head. "We think he made it out of the country the same night he fled from the Richardses. He's probably back in Moscow by now. His two men whom we took into custody aren't saying anything. I'm surprised they didn't have cyanide pills in a tooth filling. We're going to get nothing from them. But we did find other records of the 'trainees' who worked at the Grill. We're using that, together with other information, to trace Egorshin's spies around the country."

"Well, I hope you find every last one of them," said Mars.

"And what will happen to Rachel Katz?" asked Decker.

"Witness protection, most likely. Same for Mitzi Gardiner and her son. Gardiner gave a full allocution in court absolving her father of the murders. His record was expunged. He's now a completely innocent man."

"And also dead," said Decker grimly. "So he'll never know."

Mars said, "Hey, man, you got to keep the faith. And my faith tells me that the man *does* know. He asked you to prove his innocence. And you did."

* * *

"Just give me a few minutes," said Decker.

He climbed out of a car that Jamison was driving, with Bogart and Mars riding in the backseat.

Bogart said, "But you are coming back with us, correct? No more detours along the way to investigate another case that pops up?"

Decker nodded. "No. I think I've had my fill of that, at least for now."

"Good, Decker," said Mars. "Because when we land back in D.C., dinner's on me. Harper's going to join us."

Decker nodded and headed off down the street. He looked up to see Mary Lancaster coming from the other direction. They met in front of Decker's old house.

"Thanks for meeting me here, Mary."

"I assumed you wanted to say goodbye." She glanced at the house. "But I'm not sure why here."

"It's complicated."

"I wouldn't have supposed otherwise."

"I'll be coming back to see you."

"You don't have to do that." She looked in the direction of the car where Jamison, Mars, and Bogart were waiting. "You have a new life, Amos. Away from here. And it's a good thing too." She glanced at the house where Decker had suffered so much misery. "You need to be free of this place, once and for all."

"I'm not going to do that, Mary."

"But why?"

"You're my friend."

"And you're my friend too. But—"

"And you're going to be experiencing some things in the coming years that I may be able to at least help you with, in some small way."

Lancaster looked down, drew out a cigarette from her pack, glanced at the smoke for a long moment, and then tossed it away.

"I'm still scared."

"There's nothing wrong with that. Most people would be. But you have Earl. And you have me."

She looked at him with perplexity. "You've changed, Amos. Since leaving here."

"How's that?"

"You just have. You seem to be..." Her voice trailed off, as she seemed at a loss for words.

"More aware of things?" said Decker, a small smile creasing his lips.

"One way of putting it."

Her features grew somber. "I appreciate the offer. And I look forward to seeing you again." She glanced at the house and then looked at him inquiringly. "But why here of all places?"

"You said you didn't know the Hendersons?"

"No, but they seem to be a nice family."

"I'm sure they *are* a nice family. And this is a fine place to raise a family."

"Well, you've surely made it nicer by getting rid of the Russians."

Decker took a step back and peered at his old digs.

"Full of memories," said Lancaster. "Especially for someone with a memory like yours."

"It *is* full of memories. Most wonderful. A few beyond horrible."

"So which ones do you hold on to?"

"In my case I don't have a choice. But I *do* have a choice in how I prioritize them."

"Do you think you can do that?"

"I can try."

Decker thought about the episodes in which the violent scenes of his finding his family murdered kept unspooling in his head.

"I can try harder, at least. I have to, in fact."

"I wish you every success on that. I really do."

Before he left, Decker surprised Lancaster by embracing her in a long hug.

"I didn't expect that," she said, when they each stepped back.

"Maybe neither did I. But...it felt good."

"Yes, Amos, it did."

Decker walked back to the car and climbed in. "I wonder what burgundy means," he said.

"What?" asked Jamison, while Bogart and Mars looked on with puzzled expressions.

"When Hawkins walked up to me at the cemetery that day, there was a burgundy color around him. I've never experienced that before."

They were all silent for a few moments, until Jamison said, "Maybe it's your brain's new way of signaling a good person in need of some help."

"If that's the case, I think I might see it a lot more often, then."

As they were sitting there, watching Lancaster head off, Mr. and Mrs. Henderson and their daughter came out of the house and got into the Nissan Sentra. They drove off a few moments later.

Jamison glanced at Decker anxiously as he watched this happening.

In the backseat, Mars said, "They look like a nice family."

"Yes," said Decker. "I expect they are."

Jamison's fingers played nervously over the steering wheel.

Mars said, "It's a happy house, then."

Jamison cast him a sharp glance in the mirror before looking at Decker once more.

"A happy house," said Decker quietly before nodding at Jamison.

She put the car in drive and they headed off.
Away from this place.
For now.
Yet Amos Decker would be back.
For a lot of reasons.

ACKNOWLEDGMENTS

To Michelle: Decker is back. If only I had his memory, you wouldn't have to get on me for all the things I forget to do.

To Michael Pietsch, for your excellence.

To Andy Dodds, Nidhi Pugalia, Ben Sevier, Brian McLendon, Karen Kosztolnyik, Beth deGuzman, Albert Tang, Bob Castillo, Kristen Lemire, Anthony Goff, Michele McGonigle, Cheryl Smith, Andrew Duncan, Joseph Benincase, Tiffany Sanchez, Morgan Swift, Matthew Ballast, Jordan Rubinstein, Alison Lazarus, Rachel Hairston, Karen Torres, Christopher Murphy, Ali Cutrone, Tracy Dowd, Martha Bucci, Rena Kornbluh, Jeff Shay, Lukas Fauset, Thomas Louie, Sean Ford, Laura Eisenhard, Mary Urban, Barbara Slavin, Kirsiah McNamara, and everyone at Grand Central Publishing, for always being so supportive.

To Aaron and Arleen Priest, Lucy Childs, Lisa Erbach Vance, Frances Jalet-Miller, John Richmond, and Juliana Nador, for always having my back.

To Mitch Hoffman, for seeing the forest *and* the trees.

To Anthony Forbes Watson, Jeremy Trevathan, Trisha Jackson, Katie James, Alex Saunders, Sara Lloyd, Claire Evans, Sarah Arratoon, Stuart Dwyer, Jonathan Atkins, Anna Bond, Leanne Williams, Natalie McCourt, Stacey Hamilton, Sarah McLean, Charlotte Williams, and Neil Lang at Pan Macmillan, for being all-around amazing. See you in September!

To Praveen Naidoo and the team at Pan Macmillan in Australia, for taking me to #1!

To Caspian Dennis and Sandy Violette, for being so cool. It was terrific seeing you on this side of the pond!

To Steven Maat and the entire Bruna team in Holland, for your great work.

To Bob Schule, for your wonderful comments and friendship.

To Roland Ottewell, for good copyediting.

To charity auction winners Christine Burlin (Community Coalition for Haiti), Kelly Fairweather (Soundview Preparatory School), Kenneth Finger (Project Kesher), Mitzi Gardiner (Muscular Dystrophy Association), and David Katz (Authors Guild). Whether your characters were good or evil, I hope you enjoyed them. And thanks for your support of such wonderful charities.

And to Kristen White and Michelle Butler, for helping me make the most of every day.